P9-EDK-113

Contemporary Voices:

The Short Story in Canada

CONTEMPORARY VOICES

VOICES

The Short Story in Canada

SELECTED BY
DONALD STEPHENS

Department of English
University of British Columbia

PRENTICE-HALL
p
h
OF CANADA, LTD.

SCARBOROUGH, ONTARIO

PS
8310
.S7
1972

/
25,816

CAMROSE LUTHERAN COLLEGE
Library

© 1972 by Prentice-Hall of Canada, Ltd.
Scarborough, Ontario

ALL RIGHTS RESERVED
No part of this book may be reproduced in any form without
permission in writing from the publishers.

Prentice-Hall Inc., Englewood Cliffs, New Jersey
Prentice-Hall International, Inc., London
Prentice-Hall of Australia, Pty., Ltd., Sydney
Prentice-Hall of India, Pvt., New Delhi
Prentice-Hall of Japan, Tokyo

Library of Congress Catalogue No. 72-465
ISBN 13-171306-X (paper) 13-171314-O (cloth)

1 2 3 4 5 76 75 74 73 72

PRINTED IN CANADA

For R.K.S.

Preface

These stories have been chosen because they are representative of the range and richness of material which has characterized the Canadian short story in recent years; they are also excellent stories. The writers each bring to their craft a multiplicity of talents and styles growing out of widely varying backgrounds, both academic and fiercely non-academic. They are not all Canadians nor do they all write about Canada, but they have all lived and worked in Canada, and in many of their stories there is that quality of quiet introspection which has often characterized the best of Canadian fiction. The stories they have written often convey a high sense of the artist's role in society, as well as lending form and meaning to private inner worlds they have both created and observed. The book will be of value not only to the student of Canadian literature, but also to the general reader interested in the growing body of creative writing in Canada.

D.S.

Acknowledgments

For permission to reprint copyrighted material, grateful acknowledgment is made to the following publishers and authors:

The Macmillan Company of Canada Limited for "Let Me Promise You" and "Haply The Soul Of My Grandmother".

Mavis Gallant and Random House, Inc. for "My Heart Is Broken". Copyright © 1961 by Mavis Gallant. Reprinted from *My Heart Is Broken,* by Mavis Gallant, by permission of Random House, Inc.

Hugh Garner for "Red Racer". Copyright by Hugh Garner, 1950, 1963, 1971, reprinted by permission.

Dave Godfrey and the peoples of Africa for "Kwame Bird Lady Day". Reprinted by permission. Fees will be used to further the anti-imperial struggle in Africa.

Oberon Press for "Something For Olivia's Scrapbook I Guess". Reprintd from *The Streets of Summer* by David Helwig, by permission.

McGraw-Hill Ryerson Limited for "After The Sirens". Reprinted from *Flying A Red Kite* by Hugh Hood, The Ryerson Press, by permission. First published in *Esquire Magazine.* Also for "The Time of Death". Reprinted from *Dance of the Happy Shades* by Alice Munro, The Ryerson Press, by permission.

The Canadian Publishers, McClelland and Stewart, Limited, Toronto, for "Horses of the Night". Reprinted by permission.

Norman Levine for "A True Story".

J. B. Lippincott Company for "The Forest Path to the Spring". From the book *Hear Us O Lord From Heaven Thy Dwelling Place* by Malcolm Lowry. Copyright © 1961 by Margerie Bonner Lowry. Reprinted by permission.

Alden Nowlan for "There Was An Old Woman From Wexford".

Mordecai Richler for "This Year At The Arabian Nights Hotel".

Jane Rule for "Theme For Diverse Instruments".

Audrey Thomas for "Aquarius".

Contents

Contemporary Voices:

The Short Story in Canada

MORLEY CALLAGHAN

Let Me Promise You

*Morley Callaghan was born in Toronto in 1903, and educated
at the University of Toronto and Osgoode Hall. He met Ernest
Hemingway while working part-time for the* Toronto Daily Star
*and in the 'twenties belonged to a circle in Paris that included
Hemingway and Scott Fitzgerald. He has written many novels
and short stories and worked for CBC radio and television. In
1951 his novel* The Loved and The Lost *won the Governor
General's Award for Fiction. He now lives in Toronto.*

Alice kept on returning to the window. Standing with her short straight nose
pressed against the window pane, she watched the rain falling and the sidewalk shining under the street light. In her black crêpe dress with the big
white nun-like collar and with her black hair drawn back tight from her
narrow nervous face she looked almost boldly handsome.

Earlier in the evening it had started to snow, then it had begun
to drizzle and now the rain was like a sharp sleet. As Alice stood at the
window, she began to wish that the ground had been covered with an unbroken layer of fine thin snow, a white sheet that would remain undisturbed
till Georgie came with his single line of footprints marking a path up to her
door. Though her eyes remained wide open, she began to dream of a bitterly
cold dry evening, of Georgie with a red scarf and a tingling face bursting in on
her, grinning, his arms wide open. But the wind drove the sleet steadily against
the pane. Sighing, she thought, "He won't come in such weather. But he
would if it weren't for the weather. I can't really expect him tonight." So she
walked away from the window and sat down.

Then her heart began to thump so slowly and heavily inside her
she could hardly move, for someone was knocking. Opening the door in a
rush, she cried, "Georgie, you dear boy, I'm so glad you came," and she
put out her hands to help him off with his dripping coat. In the light belted
coat he looked very tall and he had a smooth round face that would never
look old. The wind and the rain had left his face wet and glowing, but he was
pouting because he was uncomfortable in his damp clothes. As he pushed his
fair wavy hair back from his eyes, he said, "This isn't exactly a night for
visiting." He sat down, still a bit embarrassed by her enthusiasm, and he
looked around the room as if he thought now that he had made a mistake in

3

coming and didn't expect to be very comfortable. "It's rotten out on a night like this when it can't make up its mind to snow or rain. Maybe you didn't think I'd come."

"I wanted you to come, and because I wanted it, I thought you would, I guess," she said candidly. So many days seemed to have passed since she had been alone with Georgie that now she wanted to take his head in her hands and kiss him. But she felt too shy. A year ago, she knew, he would have been waiting anxiously for her to kiss him.

"Alice," he said suddenly.

"What's bothering you, Georgie, frowning like that?"

"What did you want me for? You said you wanted to speak about something in particular."

"Such curiosity. You'll just sit there unable to rest till you find out, I suppose," she said. She knew he was ill at ease, but she wanted to pretend to herself that he was just impatient and curious. So her pale handsome face was animated by a warm secret delight as she went across the room to a chest of drawers and took out a long cardboard box which she handed to him after making a low girlish curtsy. "I hope you like it . . . darling," she said shyly.

"What's this? What's the idea?" Georgie said as he undid the box and pulled out the tissue paper. When he saw that she was giving something to him, he became embarrassed and almost too upset to speak, and then, because he did not want to hurt her, he tried to be full of enthusiasm, "Lord, look at it," he said. "White, turtle-necked sweater. If I wore that I'd look like a movie actor in his spare time. Should I put it on now, Al?" Grinning at her, he took off his coat and pulled the white sweater over his shirt. "Do I look good? How about a mirror, Al?"

Alice held the mirror in front of him, watching him with the same gentle expression of devotion all the time, and feeling within her a contentment she had hardly dared to hope for. The high-necked sweater made his fair head look like a faun's head.

"It's pretty swell, Al," he said, but now that he couldn't go on pleasing her with enthusiasm, his embarrassment increased. "You shouldn't be giving me this, Al," he said. "I didn't figure on anything like this when you phoned me and said you wanted to see me."

"Today is your birthday, isn't it, Georgie?"

"Imagine you remembering that. You shouldn't be bothering with birthday presents for me now."

"I thought you'd like the sweater," she said. "I saw it this afternoon. I knew it would look good on you."

"But why give me anything, Al?" he said, feeling his awkwardness increasing.

"Supposing I want to?"

"You shouldn't waste your money on me."

"Supposing I have something else, too," she said teasing him.

"What's the idea, Al?"

"I saw something else, something you used to want an awful lot. Do you remember? Try and guess."

"I can't imagine," he said, but his face got red and he smiled awkwardly at being forced in this way to remember a time which only made him feel uncomfortable now when he recalled it.

Laughing huskily and showing her small even teeth because she was glad to be able to hold out something before him and tease him as she used to do, she moved lazily over to the chest of drawers, and this time took out a small leather watch case. "Here you are," she said.

"What is it, let me see," he said, for he couldn't help being curious. He got up. But when he held the watch in his hand, he had to shake his head to conceal his satisfaction. "It's funny the way you knew I always wanted something like that, Al," he said. All his life he had wanted an expensive wrist-watch like this one, but had never expected to be able to buy it, and he was so pleased now that he smiled serenely.

But after a moment he put the watch irresolutely on the table, and was too embarrassed to speak. Walking the length of the room he began to whistle. As she watched him halt by the window, Alice knew he was uneasy. "You're a great girl, Al," he was saying. "I don't know anybody like you." After pausing, he added, "Is it never going to stop raining? I've got to be on my way."

"You're not going now, George, are you?"

"Yes, I promised to see a fellow. He'll be waiting."

"George, don't go. Please don't," she said, and she clenched the wet sleeve of the coat he had lifted from the chair. He was really ashamed to be going, especially if he picked up the watch from the table, but he felt if he stayed it would be like beginning everything all over again. He didn't know what to do about the watch, so he put out his hand hesitantly, knowing she was watching him and picked it up.

"So you're just coming here like this and then going?" she said.

"I've got to."

"Have you got another girl?"

"No. I don't want another girl."

"Yet you won't stay a little while with me?"

"That's over, Al. I don't know what's the matter with you. You phoned and wanted me to drop in for a moment."

"It wasn't hard to see that you liked looking at the watch more than at me," she said moodily.

"Here, if you don't want me to take the watch, all right," he said, and with relief, he put it back on the table, and smiled.

For a moment she stared at the case, almost blinded by her disappointment, and hating his smile of relief, and then she cried out, "You're just trying to humiliate me. Take it out of my sight." She swung the back of her hand across the table, knocked the case to the floor and the watch against the wall where the glass broke, and trying not to cry, she clenched her fists and glared at him.

But he didn't even look at her. With his mouth drooping open, he looked longingly at the watch, for he realized how much he wanted it now that he saw it smashed on the floor. He had always wanted such a watch. As he looked up at her, his blue eyes were innocent with the sincerity of his full disappointment. "Gee, Al," was all he said.

The anger began to go out of her, and she felt how great was his disappointment. She felt helpless. "I shouldn't have done that, Georgie," she said.

"It was a crazy thing to do. It was such a beauty," he said. "Why did you do it?"

"I don't know," she said. She knelt down and started to cry. "Maybe it's not broken much," she faltered, moving around on her knees and picking up the pieces of glass carefully. In her hand she held the pieces but her eyes were blinking so that she could not see them. "It was a crazy thing to do," she was thinking. "It helps nothing. It can't help bring him back to me. Why does he stand there like that? Why doesn't he move?" At last she looked up at him and saw his round smooth chin above the white neck of the sweater, and her dark eyes were shining with tears, for it seemed, as he watched her without speaking or moving, that everything ought to have turned out differently. They both looked at the broken pieces of glass she held in her hand in such abject despair, and for that moment while they looked, they began to share a common, bitter disappointment which made Georgie gravely silent and drew him close to her. "Never mind, Al," he said with awkward tenderness. "Please get up."

"No. Go away. Leave me alone."

"You've got to get up from there. I can't stand here like this with you there."

"Oh, why don't you go. I know I'm mean and jealous. I wish someone would shake me and hurt me. I'm a little cat."

"No, you're not, Al. Who'd want to shake you? Please get up," he said, putting his hand on her shoulder.

"Say you'll stay, Georgie," she said, holding on to his hand. "It's so warm here. It's miserable outside. Just listen to the wind. Do you hear it? I'll get you something to eat. You don't want to go, do you?"

"It's no worse than when I came," he said, but his sudden tenderness for her was making him uneasy. He had known Al so well for a long time, she had been one of his girls, one he could feel sure of and leave at any time, but now he felt that he had never looked right at her and seen her before. He did not know her. The warmth of her love began to awe him. Her dark head, her pale oval face seemed so close to him that he might have put out his hand timidly and touched her and felt her whole ardent being under the cloth of her dress, but the sharp tremor inside him made him catch his breath, and destroyed all his old confidence. Faltering, he said, "Gee, Al, I never got you right. Not in this way. I don't want to go. Look how I want to stay."

"Georgie, listen to me," she said eagerly. "I'll get that watch for you. Or I'll get a new one. I'll save up for it. Or I'll get you anything else you say."

"Don't think about it," he said, shamefaced. "I feel just like a bum."

"But I want so much to do it, and you can look forward to it. We both can look forward. Please let me promise it to you."

She was still crouched on the carpet. He glanced at her handsome dark face above the white nun-like collar and at her soft pleading eyes. "You look lovely right now, Al," he said. "You look like a wild thing. Honest to God you do."

Touched by happiness, she smiled. Then with all her heart she began to yearn for something more to give him. If there were only more things she had and could give, she thought; if she could only give everything in the world and leave herself nothing.

MAVIS GALLANT

My Heart Is Broken

Born in Montreal in 1922, Mavis Gallant grew up in both Canada and the United States. She worked in Montreal for the National Film Board and as a feature writer for the Standard (*now* Weekend Magazine). *In 1950, she left for Europe and has since lived in Paris. Her fiction became known through her contributions to* The New Yorker. *She is the author of a novel,* Green Water, Green Sky *(1960), as well as two collections of short stories,* The Other Paris *(1956) and* My Heart is Broken *(1964).*

'When that Jean Harlow died,' Mrs. Thompson said to Jeannie, 'I was on the 83 streetcar with a big, heavy paper parcel in my arms. I hadn't been married for very long, and when I used to visit my mother she'd give me a lot of canned stuff and preserves. I was standing up in the streetcar because nobody'd given me a seat. All the men were unemployed in those days, and they just sat down wherever they happened to be. You wouldn't remember what Montreal was like then. *You* weren't even on earth. To resume what I was saying to you, one of these men sitting down had an American paper—the *Daily News,* I guess it was—and I was sort of leaning over him, and I saw in big print "JEAN HARLOW DEAD". You can believe me or not, just as you want to, but that was the most terrible shock I ever had in my life. I never got over it.'

Jeannie had nothing to say to that. She lay flat on her back across the bed, with her head toward Mrs. Thompson and her heels just touching the crate that did as a bedside table. Balanced on her flat stomach was an open bottle of coral-pink Cutex nail polish. She held her hands up over her head and with some difficulty applied the brush to the nails of her right hand. Her legs were brown and thin. She wore nothing but shorts and one of her husband's shirts. Her feet were bare.

Mrs. Thompson was the wife of the paymaster in a road-construction camp in northern Quebec. Jeannie's husband was an engineer working on the same project. The road was being pushed through country where nothing had existed until now except rocks and lakes and muskeg. The camp was established between a wild lake and the line of raw dirt that was the road. There were no towns between the camp and the railway spur, sixty miles distant.

Mrs. Thompson, a good deal older than Jeannie, had become her best friend. She was a nice, plain, fat, consoling sort of person, with varicosed legs, shoes unlaced and slit for comfort, blue flannel dressing-gown worn at all hours, pudding-bowl haircut, and coarse grey hair. She might have been Jeannie's own mother, or her Auntie Pearl. She rocked her fat self in the rocking-chair and went on with what she had to say: 'What I was starting off to tell you is that you remind me of her, of Jean Harlow. You've got the same teeny mouth, Jeannie, and I think your hair was a whole lot prettier before you started fooling around with it. That peroxide's no good. It splits the ends. I know you're going to tell me it isn't peroxide but something more modern, but the result is the same.'

Vern's shirt was spotted with coral-pink that had dropped off the brush. Vern wouldn't mind; at least, he wouldn't say that he minded. If he hadn't objected to anything Jeannie did until now, he wouldn't start off by complaining about a shirt. The campsite outside the uncurtained window was silent and dark. The waning moon would not appear until dawn. A passage of thought made Mrs. Thompson say, 'Winter soon.'

Jeannie moved sharply and caught the bottle of polish before it spilled. Mrs. Thompson was crazy; it wasn't even September.

'Pretty soon,' Mrs. Thompson admitted. 'Pretty soon. That's a long season up here, but I'm one person who doesn't complain. I've been up here or around here every winter of my married life, except for that one winter Pops was occupying Germany.'

'I've been up here seventy-two days,' said Jeannie, in her soft voice. 'Tomorrow makes seventy-three.'

'Is that right?' said Mrs. Thompson, jerking the rocker forward, suddenly snappish. 'Is that a fact? Well, who asked you to come up here? Who asked you to come and start counting days like you was in some kind of jail? When you got married to Vern, you must of known where he'd be taking you. He told you, didn't he, that he liked road jobs, construction jobs, and that? Did he tell you, or didn't he?'

'Oh, he told me,' said Jeannie.

'You know what, Jeannie?' said Mrs. Thompson. 'If you'd of just listened to me, none of this would have happened. I told you that first day, the day you arrived here in your high-heeled shoes, I said, "I know this cabin doesn't look like much, but all the married men have the same sort of place." You remember I said that? I said, "You just get some curtains up and some carpets down, and it'll be home." I took you over and showed you my place, and you said you'd never seen anything so lovely.'

'I meant it,' said Jeannie. 'Your cabin is just lovely. I don't know why, but I never managed to make this place look like yours.'

Mrs. Thompson said, 'That's plain enough.' She looked at the cold grease spattered behind the stove, and the rag of towel over by the sink. 'It's partly the experience,' she said kindly. She and her husband knew exactly what to take with them when they went on a job, they had been doing it for so many years. They brought boxes for artificial flowers, a brass door knocker, a portable bar decorated with sea shells, a cardboard fireplace that looked real, and an electric fire that sent waves of light rippling over the ceiling and walls. A concealed gramophone played the records they loved and cherished

—the good old tunes. They had comic records that dated back to the year 1, and sad soprano records about shipwrecks and broken promises and babies' graves. The first time Jeannie heard one of the funny records, she was scared to death. She was paying a formal call, sitting straight in her chair, with her skirt pulled around her knees. Vern and Pops Thompson were talking about the Army.

'I wish to God I was back,' said old Pops.

'Don't I?' said Vern. He was fifteen years older than Jeannie and had been through a lot.

At first there were only scratching and whispering noises, and then a mosquito orchestra started to play, and a dwarf's voice came into the room. 'Little Johnnie Green, little Sallie Brown,' squealed the dwarf, higher and faster than any human ever could. 'Spooning in the park with the grass all around.'

'Where is he?' Jeannie cried, while the Thompsons screamed with laughter and Vern smiled. The dwarf sang on: 'And each little bird in the treetop high/Sang "Oh you kid!" and winked his eye.'

It was a record that had belonged to Pops Thompson's mother. He had been laughing at it all his life. The Thompsons loved living up north and didn't miss cities or company. Their cabin smelled of cocoa and toast. Over their beds were oval photographs of each other as children, and they had some Teddy bears and about a dozen dolls.

Jeannie capped the bottle of polish, taking care not to press it against her wet nails. She sat up with a single movement and set the bottle down on the bedside crate. Then she turned to face Mrs. Thompson. She sat cross-legged, with her hands outspread before her. Her face was serene.

'Not an ounce of fat on you,' said Mrs. Thompson. 'You know something? I'm sorry you're going. I really am. Tomorrow you'll be gone. You know that, don't you? You've been counting days, but you won't have to anymore. I guess Vern'll take you back to Montreal. What do you think?'

Jeannie dropped her gaze, and began smoothing wrinkles on the bedspread. She muttered something Mrs. Thompson could not understand.

'Tomorrow you'll be gone,' Mrs. Thompson continued. 'I know it for a fact. Vern is at this moment getting his pay, and borrowing a jeep from Mr. Sherman, and a Polack driver to take you to the train. He sure is loyal to *you*. You know what I heard Mr. Sherman say? He said to Vern, "If you want to send her off, Vern, you can always stay," and Vern said, "I can't very well do that, Mr. Sherman." And Mr. Sherman said, "This is the second time you've had to leave a job on account of her, isn't it?", and then Mr. Sherman said, "In my opinion, no man by his own self can rape a girl, so there were either two men or else she's invented the whole story." Then he said, "Vern, you're either a saint or a damn fool." That was all I heard. I came straight over here, Jeannie, because I thought you might be needing me.' Mrs. Thompson waited to hear she was needed. She stopped rocking and sat with her feet flat and wide apart. She struck her knees with her open palms and cried, 'I *told* you to keep away from the men. I told you it would make trouble, all that being cute and dancing around. I said to you, I remember saying it, I said nothing makes trouble faster in a place like this than a grown woman behaving like a little girl. Don't you remember?'

'I only went out for a walk,' said Jeannie. 'Nobody'll believe me, but that's all. I went down the road for a walk.'

'In high heels?' said Mrs. Thompson. 'With a purse on your arm, and a hat on your head? You don't go taking a walk in the bush that way. There's no place to walk *to*. Where'd you think you were going? I could smell Evening in Paris a quarter mile away.'

'There's no place to go,' said Jeannie, 'but what else is there to do? I just felt like dressing up and going out.'

'You could have cleaned up your home a bit,' said Mrs. Thompson. 'There was always that to do. Just look at that sink. That basket of ironing's been under the bed since July. I know it gets boring around here, but you had the best of it. You had the summer. In winter it gets dark around three o'clock. Then the wives have a right to go crazy. I knew one used to sleep the clock around. When her Nembutal ran out, she took about a hundred aspirin. I knew another learned to distil her own liquor, just to kill time. Sometimes the men get so's they don't like the life, and that's death for the wives. But here you had a nice summer, and Vern liked the life.'

'He likes it better than anything,' said Jeannie. 'He liked the Army, but this was his favourite life after that.'

'There,' said Mrs. Thompson. 'You had every reason to be happy. What'd you do if he sent you off alone, now, like Mr. Sherman advised? You'd be alone and you'd have to work. Women don't know when they're well off. Here you've got a good, sensible husband working for you and you don't appreciate it. You have to go and do a terrible thing.'

'I only went for a walk,' said Jeannie. 'That's all I did.'

'It's possible,' said Mrs. Thompson, 'but it's a terrible thing. It's about the worst thing that's ever happened around here. I don't know why you let it happen. A woman can always defend what's precious, even if she's attacked. I hope you remembered to think about bacteria.'

'What d'you mean?'

'I mean Javel, or something.'

Jeannie looked uncomprehending and then shook her head.

'I wonder what it must be like,' said Mrs. Thompson after a time, looking at the dark window. 'I mean, think of Berlin and them Russians and all. Think of some disgusting fellow you don't know. Never said hello to, even. Some girls ask for it, though. You can't always blame the man. The man loses his job, his wife if he's got one, everything, all because of a silly girl.'

Jeannie frowned, absently. She pressed her nails together, testing the polish. She licked her lips and said, 'I was more beaten up, Mrs. Thompson. It wasn't exactly what you think. It was only afterwards I thought to myself, Why, I was raped and everything.'

Mrs. Thompson gasped, hearing the word from Jeannie. She said, 'Have you got any marks?'

'On my arms. That's why I'm wearing this shirt. The first thing I did was change my clothes.'

Mrs. Thompson thought this over, and went on to another thing: 'Do you ever think about your mother?'

'Sure.'

'Do you pray? If this goes on at nineteen—'

'I'm twenty.'

'—what'll you be by the time you're thirty? You've already got a terrible, terrible memory to haunt you all your life.'

'I already can't remember it,' said Jeannie. 'Afterwards I started walking back to camp, but I was walking the wrong way. I met Mr. Sherman. The back of his car was full of coffee, flour, all that. I guess he'd been picking up supplies. He said, "Well, get in." He didn't ask any questions at first. I couldn't talk anyway.'

'Shock,' said Mrs. Thompson wisely.

'You know, I'd have to see it happening to know what happened. All I remember is that first we were only talking . . .'

'You and Mr. Sherman?'

'No, no, before. When I was taking my walk.'

'Don't say who it was,' said Mrs. Thompson. 'We don't any of us need to know.'

'We were just talking, and he got sore all of a sudden and grabbed my arm.'

'Don't say the name!' Mrs. Thompson cried.

'Like when I was little, there was this Lana Turner movie. She had two twins. She was just there and then a nurse brought her in the two twins. I hadn't been married or anything, and I didn't know anything, and I used to think if I just kept on seeing the movie I'd know how she got the two twins, you know, and I went, oh, I must have seen it six times, the movie, but in the end I never knew any more. They just brought her the two twins.'

Mrs. Thompson sat quite still, trying to make sense of this. 'Taking advantage of a woman is a criminal offence,' she observed. 'I heard Mr. Sherman say another thing, Jeannie. He said, "If your wife wants to press a charge and talk to some lawyer, let me tell you," he said, "you'll never work again anywhere," he said. Vern said, "I know that, Mr. Sherman." And Mr. Sherman said, "Let me tell you, if any reporters or any investigators start coming around here, they'll get their . . . they'll never . . ." Oh, he was mad. And Vern said, "I came over to tell you I was quitting, Mr. Sherman." ' Mrs. Thompson had been acting this with spirit, using a quiet voice when she spoke for Vern and a blustering tone for Mr. Sherman. In her own voice, she said, 'If you're wondering how I came to hear all this, I was strolling by Mr. Sherman's office window—his bungalow, that is. I had Maureen out in her pram.' Maureen was the Thompsons' youngest doll.

Jeannie might not have been listening. She started to tell something else: 'You know, where we were before, on Vern's last job, we weren't in a camp. He was away a lot, and he left me in Amos, in a hotel. I liked it. Amos isn't all that big, but it's better than here. There was this German in the hotel. He was selling cars. He'd drive me around if I wanted to go to a movie or anything. Vern didn't like him, so we left. It wasn't anybody's fault.'

'So he's given up two jobs,' said Mrs. Thompson. 'One because he couldn't leave you alone, and now this one. Two jobs, and you haven't been married five months. Why should another man be thrown out of work? We don't need to know a thing. I'll be sorry if it was Jimmy Quinn,' she went on, slowly. 'I like that boy. Don't say the name, dear. There's Evans. Susini. Palmer. But it might have been anybody, because you had them all on the boil. So it might have been Jimmy Quinn—let's say—and it could have been anyone else, too. Well, now let's hope they can get their minds back on the job.'

'I thought they all liked me,' said Jeannie sadly. 'I get along with people. Vern never fights with me.'

'Vern never fights with anyone. But he ought to have thrashed *you*.'

'If he . . . you know. I won't say the name. If he'd liked me, I wouldn't have minded. If he'd been friendly. I really mean that. I wouldn't have gone wandering up the road, making all this fuss.'

'Jeannie,' said Mrs. Thompson, 'you don't even know what you're saying.'

'He could at least have liked me,' said Jeannie. 'He wasn't even friendly. It's the first time in my life somebody hasn't liked me. My heart is broken, Mrs. Thompson. My heart is just broken.'

She has to cry, Mrs. Thompson thought. She has to have it out. She rocked slowly, tapping her foot, trying to remember how she'd felt about things when she was twenty, wondering if her heart had ever been broken, too.

HUGH GARNER

Red Racer

Hugh Garner was born in England in 1913 and has lived in Toronto since the age of six. He left school early, and during the Depression worked at a variety of jobs. He travelled across the continent several times and later served in the Spanish Civil War and with the Royal Canadian Navy in World War II. He began writing in 1946 and has since written seven novels, five collections of short stories, and numerous articles. He was the winner of the Governor General's Award for Fiction (1963) for Hugh Garner's Best Stories.

The sun burned a hole in the sky and sent its thermal rays into the bare fields between the trees. The air was tense and still, as if every living organism was hoarding its strength for something vague but promised by the quiet day. Now and then Marcel Boudreau stopped his labours between the rows of yellowing leaves that topped the potato plants, and looked above the boundary of spruce and fir trees into the north-west sky.

Around the small cleared patch of farmland the wooded hills that skirt the Gaspé Coast had the appearance of a dirty patched fur rug laid in massive folds by some forgotten giant hand. From the ridges of the hills to the narrow valley in which the homestead lay, the thick forest growth was yellow, interspersed with the still heavy green of the coniferous trees.

The man leaned his weight upon the handle of his hoe and allowed his glance to drop from the sky to the rude clapboard house he had built against the wagon road. His wife and children moved about in the shade between the house and stable, the mumbled noises of their voices and laughter showing him their lack of apprehension. He was glad they did not share the concern he felt for the *something* that lay above the valley like the brooding anger of a god.

He went about his hoeing again with redoubled effort, letting the fatigue in his arms and the sweat under his shirt relieve him of the anxiety that he had felt since morning. When he reached the end of the row he paused and wiped his face with his handkerchief. He glanced toward the minuscule pasture in which his old horse was grazing and found corroboration for his feelings in the sight of the animal's stance: the horse stood in wary alertness, ears back, its forefeet pawing the turf in a corner near the fence.

Again he searched the washed blue of the sky, looking for signs of an approaching storm. There was nothing but a few thin wisps of cumulus against the brow of a hill, and the throbbing white disc of the sun. The August day followed almost two weeks of hot dry weather that had plagued Eastern Canada. Here, a few miles inland from the Gulf of St. Lawrence, the thick forests cut off all succouring breezes from the sea.

His throat felt parched and raw, and glad of the excuse his thirst gave him, he dropped the hoe and made his way towards the house. At his approach his wife looked up from her sewing and stared at his face. He knew by her glance that his apprehension was showing in his eyes.

"How's the potatoes looking, Marcel?" she asked in French, her tone still deferential even after twelve years of marriage.

"They're pretty dry. I pulled one a while ago though and they look all right."

"I wouldn't want them to spoil. We'd never get through the winter without potatoes."

"It seems to me we're in for a storm—there's a feeling of it in the air. We sure need some rain bad."

He finished the hoeing during the afternoon, and after supper sat down beside the radio, listening to the nasal twang of a pseudo-cowboy from a New Brunswick station singing a lament while he chorded dismally on a mail-order guitar.

In the evenings when work was finished for the day it seemed to him that the past twelve years' effort had not been in vain. It had been heart-breaking at first, the effect of a long day's work dwarfed to insignificance by the seemingly immobile forest, but bit by bit—despite cold and hunger and privation—the small clearing had grown into the semblance of a farm.

Antoinette, his wife, was busy in a corner of the single first-floor room of the house bathing the youngest of their five children in a washtub on the floor. Apart from his wife and children his possessions were meagre; a ten-year-old bay gelding of uncertain lineage, a scrub Holstein cow, a two-hundred-pound pig now fattening for the winter's meat, a few hens, a cat, and a half-wild collie bitch. He had fifty acres of paid-up land of which fifteen were cleared, a small weatherproof house, log barn, three iron beds, a wood range, radio and sewing machine. Not a very impressive total of possessions in return for twelve years of labour, but enough to make a man feel a sense of achievement on an evening like this—a sense of fulfillment and security which thousands strove for in vain.

After the children had been put to bed upstairs Antoinette pulled a chair closer to the radio and began cutting patches from a pair of his old overalls with which to mend those belonging to his eldest boy.

They sat together in the gathering darkness, talking about the little things that filled their lives, grateful for the quiet of the room now that the children were asleep. The cowboy left the air and was replaced by the music of a Toronto dance orchestra carried by the network. The tympanic beat punctuated their conversation. When it grew too dark to see what she was doing, Antoinette lit a kerosene lamp and stood it on the sewing machine.

Another half hour went by, then Marcel climbed the stairs to bed, followed a few minutes later by his wife.

He awoke in the darkness with a foreboding that something was wrong. Stealing out of bed he picked up the clock from a chair and carried it into the grey light from the window. The hands pointed to three-twenty-five. He looked up into the sky and felt a sense of relief as he saw the stars making their silver pointed patterns in the ceiling of darkness.

Hurriedly pulling on his trousers and shoes he made his way down the stairs and out into the yard. The collie crept with stiff-legged indolence from beneath the steps and followed him as he walked across the narrow space to the barn. Everything was as it should be there. He circled the small building and stood for a moment staring into the pasture. The horse and cow were huddled together in uncommon intimacy in the corner nearest the road, their heads across the top rail of the fence. He thought, there may be bears around, and let his eyes sweep the surrounding ground looking for a tell-tale black shape. There was nothing to break the familiar profile of the fields.

He stood still, trying to pin-point the presentient feeling that filled the air, and then, suddenly, he knew what it was. He sniffed the night breeze and his heart stood still for the few seconds it took him to swing around. Down the length of the valley wafted the almost imperceptible odour of burning timber; the northland's smell of destruction, the red racer, a forest fire.

Looking up at the rim of the hills he now saw what he had been unable to see before: a faint pink line to the north-west, undulating incandescently against the deeper gloom of the night. He hurried into the house and awakened his wife, telling her in a few tense sentences what she should do. As she dressed hurriedly in the darkness he ran outside again to where the horse was standing in the pasture.

In half an hour they were ready to leave. The horse was tethered in the yard, harnessed to the wagon that contained the sewing machine, radio, the trussed-up pig and a pile of jumbled clothing upon which the children sat in sleep-broken expectancy. The cow lowed forlornly from the end of a rope by which she was tied to the wagon gate.

The upper air was now a mass of smoke, and vagrant wisps were carried down across the yard. From time to time a faint gossamer spread of powdered ash floated down upon the wagon. From the hills came a noise like a giant boiling cauldron, and a south-east breeze stirred the branches of the trees as it rushed into the vacuum left by the roaring flames of the racing fire.

Marcel worked out the position of the fire roughly, gauging its distance at not more than a mile. It appeared to be working its way swiftly across the range of hills in a direction that should carry its main sweep along the ridge that lay a mile north of his small homestead. From the sight now of the shooting flames with their plumed caps of black oily smoke he estimated its probable width as a mile and a half. If his calculations were correct it meant that the fire would skirt his farm to the north, leaving his property untouched. He said a silent prayer that this should happen, but he well knew the almost casual waywardness of a forest fire, that in one minute can shift its direction ninety degrees, and skipping a half mile of forest, break out anew in another spot and with an entirely different destination. It was because of this knowledge of a fire's unpredictability that he had made the preparations to flee down the road through the hills to the coastal strip.

"I guess we'd better get going," he said to his wife, who was sitting on the wagon seat staring at the house as if reluctant to tear her eyes away.

"Not yet," she said slowly. "Maybe the fire won't come this way."

"We can't tell, and I don't want to take a chance."

"It took us so long to build it, Marcel. When I think of all the work we put into it, and the new kitchen stove we bought with the money you earned on the drive last spring . . ."

"We can replace a house and stove," he answered.

"Twelve years' work . . ." she said, unable to finish the sentence; unable to say, "Twelve years' work to be wiped out in a night."

He shrugged, pretending it was nothing. "We'll get the kids out anyway. We're young enough to start again."

She did not admit that she heard him. There was a faint overtone of hope in her voice as she said, "Even if the fire comes this way it may not cross the pasture."

He looked around him at the miles and miles of forest, among which his little farm was but the imprint of a heel in a field of grass. Then he said, "You're only wishing, 'Toinette. You know as well as me that it would jump the pasture as easy as the dog can jump the creek. It's no use hoping for a miracle—if the fire swings this way, the farm goes, and that's that."

The baby began to whimper in her blanket, and the mother shushed her, rocking back and forth on the narrow seat of the wagon. Marcel went to the horse's head to untie the rope that held the nervous animal to the clothes-line post, and as he did so he heard the truck coming along the road. He left the tethered horse and hurried round to the front of the house.

Headlights flickered through the trees and then became a bright glare as the truck rounded a bend fifty yards away. It was travelling fast, but before it came abreast of the house it slowed down and finally stopped. Ned hurried over to the cab.

"Are you Boudreau?" an old man's voice asked in English.

"Yes."

"My name's McKendrick. I'm the fire warden from Ste. Gironde. We're picking up every man we can to fight that fire on the ridge. You'd better get in back with the others."

"What about my wife and kids? They're back behind the house in the wagon. I was just about to set off to the settlement."

"There's no need for them to leave here. That fire's been going dead east since yesterday morning. We're going to build a break up along the forks of the creek and try to back-flash the fire so that it'll burn itself out in the second-growth stuff over east of the third ridge. We need every man we can get, so you'd better get in the back."

"Just a minute while I tell my wife," Marcel said, running back to the rear of the house.

He told his wife what the fire warden had said, feeling reassured now by the older man's words. He told her to keep the horse harnessed and ready to go, and to watch the fire. If it came into full view along the brow of the hill she was to set off for town as fast as she could go.

"I wish you could stay here with me," she said, although there was a note of resignation in her voice as she spoke.

"The warden says there's no danger here. We're only going up to the forks of the creek. I'll be back for breakfast," he said, hurrying away again through the faint illumination reflected by the north-west sky.

The back of the truck was already crowded with a silent mass of men, and they set off with a meshing of gears along the narrow road.

"Hello, Marcel," said a voice at his elbow.

He turned to see Omer Michaud, his nearest neighbour from five miles down the road, standing beside him.

"Hello, Omer. They got you, too, eh?"

The man nodded.

From Michaud he learned that the fire had begun the previous morning almost ten miles from its present position. It had been caused by a construction crew burning slash at the site of a new highway bridge. The small fire had crept through the grass and undergrowth beside the road, unnoticed by the construction men. Later on while they were gathered at their camp for lunch the small creeping flames had touched off a dried-out pile of cedar bark, and the fire had increased its size by immediate multiplication. When next it was seen it was advancing at a rapid pace through a stand of fir and hemlock, its feelers climbing thirty-foot trees like reversed lightning. From then on its size and speed had increased until it became the roaring killer now sweeping across the hills.

When the truck reached the end of the wide summer road the twenty-odd men aboard it jumped to the ground, and the fire warden handed out picks, shovels and axes for the job ahead of them. "There's two bulldozers on their way up from the settlement," he said, "but we'll have to make do with what we've got until they arrive."

He outlined his plan to them, tracing it on the ground with the point of a pick. In the reflected light from the dull-glowing sky the men stood around in a silent circle, their faces serious. Marcel recognized Pelletier the postmaster and three or four office workers from the mill. A pair of young men attired in light slacks and cotton jackets had the appearance of summer visitors. The others were farmers from around the settlement and a company woodsman or two.

The plan was a sound one. The fire was heading into a fork made by the junction of one creek with another. By widening the inner bank of one of the creeks several feet, it might be possible to induce the fire to take the path of least resistance across the other creek and down a long winding gully to where a burned-over valley could slow down and absorb the fire's hunger. This valley had suffered a fire several years before, and now its surface was covered with the sparse growth of small birch, poplar, wild cherry and stub maple that springs up on fire-ravaged land.

"Now, you know what to do, boys," McKendrick said. "Clear the trees and brush back at least ten feet from the south creek, and work the break as far along the stream as you can before she gets too hot to stay there. There's a crew of fifty men with pumps down in the valley and they'll check her after we send it their way. Young Bill Howlett in the tower on White Mountain is following the fire with his glasses and he'll phone out for more help if it's needed. When you can't work any longer up there, make it towards the hills. We'll be over there with the truck."

The men followed each other up the narrow winter road a short distance until they reached the south creek. Without pausing they set to work with their axes on the trees and shrubs, letting them fall, and dragging them back from the creek bank. The dull red glow by which they worked was soon dimmed by the sun which sent a pale light through the ugly smoke that now stretched to the horizon.

Marcel threw himself into the job, knowing that all he owned depended on their efforts to swing the fire to the east. After an hour's gruelling work he looked behind him and saw that they had succeeded only in advancing about twenty-five yards from the forks. He thought, it isn't enough, and he began hacking at the growth in a frenzy of desperation.

The noise of the flames, and the sound of falling trees, now almost deafened the small crew of men, and from the clouds of acrid smoke fell burning embers the size of a man's hand, which struck the ground with an explosive crack. The men extinguished these with their boots or with the frantic slappings of discarded shirts.

As the flames approached, the heat became unbearable, and the men's faces were raw with it beneath their covering of grime and sweat. Their efforts to widen a longer fire-break along the creek bank had to be given up, and instead they tried unsuccessfully to stifle the small pilot fires set up by the burning brands. It was a losing fight. No sooner would one fire be extinguished than its place would be taken by two or more new ones breaking out behind them.

Soon they were forced to retreat before the searing heat into the relative coolness of the scorched trees beyond the creek. Most of the gang hurriedly made their way east through the woods to the rendezvous with McKendrick on the farther ridge. Michaud asked Marcel to go too, but he shook his head, pointing down to the valley. Michaud shrugged and hurried after the others.

Marcel watched the blinding line of the fire's advance as it hurled itself through the trees. The dense smoke made breathing difficult, but worse still was the lack of oxygen as the gigantic combustion ate into the air supply surrounding it. He lowered himself to the ground and began inching back through the scrub, unmindful now of the shower of sparks and embers that hurtled through the tops of the trees above him, setting them alight with a crackling roar. As he crawled along the ground he saw three foxes, a vixen and two pups, racing across his path. With a new-found clarity he watched the course of the foxes' flight. He was facing away from the fire now, and the small red animals had passed, roughly, from west to east. Knowing that the intelligence of the fox would not allow her to lead her pups into the fire's path it could only mean one thing: their efforts to swing the fire to the east had been wasted, it had hurtled their shallow break almost without pause, and even now was eating down the valley towards his homestead.

For the first time he felt the hopelessness of his position—the lonely, trapped feeling of being deserted, and with no aid to look forward to. He crawled up a small knoll, hoping to put it between himself and the fire, before changing course in the direction of his home.

There was a frantic crashing of the undergrowth behind him, and he turned in time to see a lost member of the fire-fighting crew rushing along the advancing line of the fire. The man was one of the summer visitors, his once-grey slacks now black and ripped to ribbons around his bleeding legs, and his scorched and blackened face twisted with his efforts to breathe.

"Hey!" Marcel shouted, pushing himself up on his knees. "Come back! Come back!"

The man did not hear him. He made the vital mistake of trying to charge uphill before the flames instead of staying beneath them. Marcel watched with mounting horror as the man's crazed efforts to escape took him beneath a flaming arch of burning trees, which collapsed slowly, enveloping him in a fiery net. There was a piercing scream above the noise, then the flames roared on over the scene.

Sobbing with fatigue and fright Marcel crawled slowly over the height of the knoll, his handkerchief held to his face to protect it from the heat and smoke. He fell down the farther slope and lay against a tree while he batted out his smouldering overalls with blistered hands that were like the clumsy claws of a feebled bird.

When the flames began licking across the summit of the small rise he clambered to his feet and stumbled down the hill, bumping into the trees, freeing his feet from the tangle of long grass and undergrowth, unable now to see through the smoke and the matted curtains of his scorched and fused eyelashes.

His feet found the gravelled surface of a dried-up stream at the foot of the hill, and he made his way to the right along the creek bed. As his jarring steps carried him toward the valley floor the smoke thinned a little and the noise dimmed to a steady roar on the slopes above him. He knew that the fire would be slowed momentarily by its vertical path down the hill, so when his shoes splashed through the water of a spring he paused and laved his smarting eyes with the cool clear water. Then he flopped down in the wet earth and drank his fill, letting the gurgling water caress his blistered chest and back. Refreshed now, and feeling a new surge of strength, he hurried along the creek.

As he ran he watched a small fire springing up on the slope above him, caused by a vagrant spark or ember. The sight startled him, and he prayed that Antoinette and the children were already on their way down the road to the safety of the settlement. But then he noticed a peculiar thing about the blaze—it was crawling uphill in the direction of the main fire. He stared for a minute before he realized that the slope formed a natural flue from the valley, and the brisk wind that was rushing across the flatlands supplied the draft.

A crazy plan was formed in his mind at the sight. If he fired the whole length of the hill it might be possible to backflash the main fire—that is, lay waste the slope by burning its covering of trees and vegetation so that the advancing flames would stop short on the summit for lack of combustible material in their path. In this way the fire could be made to continue east towards the spot chosen by the fire-warden and his crews, and where they were preparing and widening a long fire-break.

It was worth the attempt only if he could be sure that his wife and family were safely out of the way. There was the great danger that his efforts might be in vain, and the time wasted make it impossible to flee when the fire began its race across the valley. And there was the probability that the backflash might become the forerunner of the main fire and thus advance its line the few hundred yards it needed to bridge the distance between its position on the hill and the valley floor.

He stood a moment in fearful hestitation before making up his mind, gambling his safety and the safety of his family against the possible saving of his house and land. Then, his life and future depending on the cast of a die, he ran several yards down the bank of the trickling stream and gathered an armful of spruce bark from a brown flattened pile he had left there when peeling pulpwood in the spring.

Twisting some in his hand he ran up the few feet of slope and held it in the flames until it smouldered and took fire. He inched his way through the trees, touching his rough torch to the dry crackling underbrush.

It caught fire slowly at first, but as he moved along he turned his head and watched the thin crawling pattern of flames take hold and begin to roar through the trees. He felt an exultation as he twisted new torches from the bundle of bark under his arm, lighting them from the fires he had already kindled.

As he advanced along the base of the slope he could hear the crackling destruction behind him as the fire accelerated up the hill. It had a new music in his ears, of aid and succour, as its sound supplied the counter-point to the enveloping roar of the advancing fire from above.

In a few minutes the hill became an inferno, the flames rushing through the trees with a terrible unleashing of thermal power, reducing the thirty-year growth of fir and spruce to blackened poles and smoking ash in a matter of minutes. The man stood back behind the small creek amazed at the destruction he had caused.

At times a slackening of the breeze would cause the flames to flicker almost gently beneath the wide ceiling of smoke, and he would watch with heart-stopping expectancy for the fire to change course and rush down upon him.

As the fire climbed the hill he moved along the creek bank extinguishing small blazes that had sprung up behind it, stamping them into the ground as he executed a joyful dance upon the earth. For a long time it was touch and go. The two blazes advanced against each other, each striving for mastery. Behind the one he had made was a narrow fifty-yard strip of ravished earth that might prove ineffective in stopping the fire's main advance. He watched the clash, his tongue between his teeth and his blistered hands clenching at his sides. The two fires met with a giant roar, and the flames leaped high against the pall of smoke. Then, slowly, the red leaping fires on the slope sunk to the charred and blackened ground, and the blaze swung away to the east and ate its way across the hills.

After another half hour had passed, and he had stamped out all the small borderline blazes, he left the scene of his triumph and pushed his way headlong through the valley trees toward his farm.

Antoinette met him at the gate, her face wearing a tired smile behind her smoke-smeared features. She was inarticulate with happiness as she took his arm and led him into the house. He sat on a chair and allowed her to film his face and hands with vaseline, staring through the window at the fire as it retreated east along the top of the hills. She made a pot of tea, almost caressing the shiny stove as she went about her task, her faced flushed from the heat and happiness that rose about her. When they had finished their tea Marcel went into the yard, untied the horse and cow, and liberated the trussed-up pig, driving them into the small stable. The children were once more playing around the house as Antoinette carried the bundles of clothing from the wagon.

He asked her, "Why did you stay here when you saw the fire on the slope?" trying to make his voice gruff and authoritative.

She did not answer him, but instead went quickly about her work, stopping now and then to stare at the burning hills. Once, when Marcel looked into her face he saw that there were two tear streaks down the sides of her nose, so he made himself busy carrying the radio and sewing machine into the house.

Later on he pulled on a fresh shirt and made ready to leave again for the fire-break the crews were building above the hills across the valley. His wife tried to prevent him going, but there was a light in his eyes that she had never seen before.

He said his good-byes, warning the oldest children not to go near the still-smouldering patch above the farm, and set off towards the road. The fire was now an impersonal thing that had slowed to a crawl through the bush and scrub along the hills, its terror gone with its defeat. As he passed the potato patch, from habit he pulled one of the plants, and looked into the north-west sky for a sign of rain. Behind the greying smoke several horse tails of cirrus cloud were sweeping across the sky, heralding the approach of a storm. He laughed to himself as he remembered his apprehension of the day before, and he hurried up the road towards the waiting fire-crews, afraid that the rain might cheat him of his victory.

DAVE GODFREY

Kwame Bird Lady Day

Dave Godfrey was born in Manitoba in 1938. He did graduate work at the University of Iowa, travelled in West Africa as a trumpet player, and worked in lumber camps and at other jobs in Canada. He now lives in Toronto, where he lectures at the University of Toronto. He has helped to found three Canadian publishing houses, the House of Anansi, New Press, and Press Porcépic. He has contributed stories to magazines and anthologies, and his work includes Death Goes Better With Coca-Cola *(1967),* The New Ancestors, *which won the Governor General's Award for Fiction in 1971, and* Selected Stories, *published by the House of Anansi in 1972.*

Like over-ripe mangoes.

There is no action in the world which is ever accidental; be it love or murder there are always reasons, hundreds of reasons. As witness the action of Gamaliel Kofi Harding in beating . . . Ah? *Attend! Attend!* Witness? An impossibility. Since to witness you would have to observe the agony I am observing. And I, I have already watched this madness grow. So that I cannot *witness* insanity myself. Although I can taste like choked-down bile its implications even now, in my stomach, the rot of over-ripe mangoes. Putrefaction. Goat skins. Lost hopes.

So do not witness; pretend. Pretend for a moment that you are plugged in to my cosmic lusts and hates, the little fog of my manipulations. Forget what I am: *pharmakos.* I do not know myself what I am. Michael Burdener named. *Pharmakos* and creator of victims and tormentors. Plug in to the high voltage of Africa.

There is music in the night. The calabash is passed, full of palmwine and smuggled gin. Gamaliel is host within his walled estate.

Gamaliel Kofi Harding: drummer, nightclub owner, defender of Lost Coast against invective by means of even greater scurrility in defence of Lost Coast's Redeemer, former journalist and boxer, litigant, Buddhist, lover, victim. Or vitalist heroic? Or victim pass victim? Observe him.

"Would rotten us forever," says GKH. "A thousand years of history leading up to this, fraud though he be, and you would expect us to throw him, and history, down into the dirt. Your brain is still grey, Burdener.

No matter how much love my sister gives you, your brain will remain grey. To throw into the dirt such a man. There will be no counter-coup; no coup with force. Who do you think would join in it. The Sandhurst fools? Bedaiako? Alegba? Entretou?"

He is a tall man, massive. Edgy now. Caught in a hundred frustrations. Gamaliel Harding, to put it simply, is about to decide whether to beat me or to beat once more his son, Kwame Bird Lady Day. I am directing him towards his son. Not that I have always escaped my beatings, or wanted to, but in this case, in all certainty, for Gamaliel to beat his son— in my presence—to break further thus those tenuous links between father and son, would be in full accord with the deepest levels of my plans and my plotted deception.

"Ah, but the objective conditions," Burdener says. "The state of the bank reserves. Myth and lie can keep them hidden only so long."

"A hundred years is not long. You forget that." GKH knows that he lies. The sweat is rich on his brow. His hands are limp, relaxing from the rhythm that he has created. Those at his party do not crowd near; their rhythm is still fed on his creation. But some begin to depart, sensing that there will be less music now. The two Gene Krupa sets are pushed against the far edge of the railing which surrounds the platform on which they sit. GKH's energy is not spent, but caught prophetically in that sign.

In the darkness of the low places, thousands of frogs beep their radar sounds against the night. GKH's wall is swept by searchlights that glint off the concrete-formed swimming pool. Chatter follows the gin and the palmwine which Kwame Bird Lady Day and the drummer apprentices serve without smiles. Beyond the searchlights, red warnings flash on the radio tower within Flagstaff House. And within the greater walled estate, what music entertains our Redeemer? What delights of creation have exhausted him? In his private wildlife zoo, do the three giraffes brought down from the Niger long for the lost freedom of the thornbush savannahs? No. Food is all.

"Reserves of a hundred and ninety million pounds. Wafted away. Where is your industry? Who controls it? Old Mister Kayser is your real saviour. Kofi Kayser of California and New Mexico. Redeemer Kayser. What a selling out of the people. Trade in the masses for a California eunuch and a million-pound bribe. And for what else? A handful of Indian cloth factories. And stool carvers. And state corporations that are bled dry before they even get into running gear. And two Hungarian sugar factories that have already taken six years to get into non-production. You know it. Half of the wealth of the country is in Swiss banks, financing Swiss cheese. And not a match in the whole bloody country. No tyres. And women demonstrating for milk—knocking the hats off the officers. Work and happiness. Work for us and the masses and happiness for him and his six mistresses." All this Burdener says, Burdener the economic genius. Burdener the co-inventor of the anti-neoimperialism catechism. "Your black Redeemer has brought you to the kingdom of dust and poverty."

Ah, plug in. I, Burdener have the upper hand now. As Gamaliel fumes beneath his sweat. Preparing to kick out at me or at Kwame Bird. In the latter case permitting me to observe his degradation, the rotting of his kra. But a mere three weeks ago the opposite held. Never forget that time,

Burdener. When I had no knowledge. Cynicism and craft are not enough; knowledge must be added.

In Flagstaff House proper, beneath the radio tower, behind his larger walls (more than three miles of them, all swept by machine gun fire, if necessary, as well as by floodlights), does our Redeemer, our Khakhi pass Khakhi, our Okyeame, our Oye Ade Ye, does he suspect the process building up against him? Is his sleep troubled and does he decide in dreams to add another hundred men to his Security Service. Times change, change.

Gamaliel had taken me, those three weeks ago, into the bush, to the shrine at Ntofro. It was *abisa* time at the shrine. Confessions of evil were being heard. Confessions of envy, of cannibalism of the *kra,* of imposition of accident or sterility, of night flights, of theft, adultery and magical abortions. From mind to mind flow the atomic particles of guilt and fear. The *obosomfo,* caught by the drumming and the blasts of those neutrons of fear, watches his own mind dissociate as the power enters him and the penitent supplicants unwind their tales of horror and absurdity.

But Gamaliel has come only to buy goat skins from the *sinkwafo,* from the guardians of the sacred animals. He ignores the bombardment of guilt. Spits on my awe of the prophetic *obosomfo.* Laughs his private splitlip laugh at my grandiose scheme (to move one whole shrine back to London, force the city supplicants to strip before confession, create a clockwound machine to be sacrificed, invent bizzare penances and suggest death—all the time watching the quid flow in like honey). *Bisa* means to ask or implore. *Kra* is from the Egyptian. Perhaps. *Ka*: soul.

A drawnfaced, plumpbodied woman approaches the confessional dais, an egg in either hand, her long cloth disarrayed, her eyes sweeping over the surrounding supplicants, the elbowjostling, asswagging women, but obviously her eyes caught more firmly by demons within the great time-wreaked field or force of her selfcauterizing soul. From the dais, the spokesman, the *okyeame,* calls her to deliver her statement, but her evil will not let her speak. A knifestroke across her tongue. He coaxes her as he would a child, but she cannot respond. He is unable to accept the egg proffered by her trembling right hand. Her breathing quickens from the bellows of her inner despair; her howling begins, breaks forth, as a child (shivering my own soul like dynamite thrown against old brick walls), building up almost instantly to that overload point where cries weaken painfully into blubbering, a wrist of pain around the throat, a blow of inchoked pain and then a tugblast of wailing.

"*M'agya, m'agya, m'agya.*"

Gamaliel bids four bob.

"*M'agya, m'agya, m'agya.*"

That loss of the father. Time never changes. As wailed Madame la Generale when Foma Fomitch was dragged from her; Ajaiyi accepting his inherited poverty. But she gets no further than the cry. Body refusing her; memory refusing her; soulforce refusing her. Caught at the thorn moment before the proton of matter kisses the antiproton and finds the star of annihilation.

"*M'agya, m'agya, m'agya.*"

And in behind her wailing body the other supplicants press. Peace to you, auntie. The *obrafohene* allows a different sufferer to catch his eye, to come forward to weep forth her tale; *abisa* time at the shrine of Ntofro. The woman, the plumpbodied woman in the green cloth, is dragged away by the *sinkwafo* to be given a preliminary bath of purification: forbidden according to standard ritual but obviously necessary now. There is an interruption finally to Gamaliel's bargaining.

But to me he does not speak. I either understand or I do not. The woman he does not notice. When his *sinkwafo* leaves, Gamaliel stares into the skins of the slaughtered goats, one by one, searching for flaws and weaknesses.

The priest, the *obosomfo,* shouts at a new woman, "Death is outside your door."

"Mmere dane, dane; mmere dane, dane." The thronged drum talks. Like an old washerwoman, like a retired cinema usher. Times change, change. Quietly a single drum; the rest of the chorus silent. *Mmere dane, dane.*

As the *obosomfo* quivers in the possession of his *obosom.* In front of him the women, one of whom he questions. In front of him, the *nkotoba* clubs, none of which will move until the sinful do dream that their bodies are beaten by the scourges of the *obosom.* In front of him the *dua,* sin's chopping block, glint and grease of egg yolk and egg white, fresh and dried. A cylinder of cotton wood from the rainforest. The arms of the *obosomfo* folded; tassels of *mpese-mpese* dancing as his head nods and jerks; his face a bambara mask in which eyes without hate or charity roll through seas of frenzy. The questions burst out at the new woman.

"Dawuruma, dawuruma," the new woman smiles. Her confession is made. "Grace and mercy. I will bring a fowl."

Gamaliel's *sinkwafo* returns to laugh at an offer of six bob.

The woman in the green cloth comes back up from the river. Fatter, with happiness feeding her now, with the white clay still butterfresh on her body, milky in the folds of her throat flesh. Her long green cloth she laughingly uses as a towel on her still damp, immensely fat body. O, o, Michael Burdener, watch out. Obruni Burdener. Grey Burdener. European Burdener.

"Babaso, babaso," she laughs and comes waddling towards me.

Filthy woman. Her cloth droops from her breast and reveals two teats like those of Cassandra, hanging down below her stomach. All of her jiggles. Her audience knows what to expect. Her tongue has been saved from the knife. The *abisa* turns to observe; the *okyeame* leads the *obosomfo* back into the sanctuary to recharge his forces. A *pharmakos* break from the serious business of the shrine.

Filthy woman. She swallows half of her lower lip to imitate my jaw defect. All the while approaching. Filthy hypomaniac. *"Babaso, babaso."* I give her a good swipe on the face, but she is dancing off to freedom.

"Really! Mr. 'Brunyi. Mr. Schoolteacher. Sergeant Whiteman." She laughs. "Such treatment of a woman." It infuriates me that she is literate. This is the end result of clerk-education.

"You should know from your books the sins of judgement of *babaso*. Who can escape? How many lady students have you infected? Not the mighty can escape, not even the white-white teacher."

Her face is desperate, disappearing inside her mouth. She makes an obscene gesture, as though she is a man painfully pissing. She comes nearer, snatching at my head, as though she were pulling tufts of hair from my scalp.

The other supplicants are amused out of their misery. But that is not enough to satisfy her. She struts like a major-domo, stalking them down with precision, but they flee from her. "*Babasoman, babasoman,*" they laugh and scream. Am I safe? Has she stolen this *kra* she has invented for me? She looks at me carefully, then stands very rigidly, with her hands curled backward in anger behind her thighs at the end of stickstiff arms. I can only flee. "You will never dance, *babasoman,*" she hollers.

"Before the Redeemer you were a king," she says. "King-kingking," baring teeth that are clenched like a snarling dog's. "King-kingking."

"Now he has made you a gift, a gift of England. Which is so fine, which is *soooo* heaven. You may eat it all, Mr. 'Brunyi. Eat the gold, eat the people, eat the cocoa, eat the women, eat the knowledge that you have bled from us. The Redeemer is our King. The Redeemer has brought us the electric dam. The Redeemer has brought all the children free schoolbooks. We will be the wise; you will be the *babasoman*. Ours is the work and happiness. You are the foolman."

"*Mommra, mommra, mommra.* O cum, cum, cum, cum, cum," she laughs and begs, coaxes and mocks at my stiffly departing back. "Cum, cum, cum, cum, cum. O *mommra, mommra, mommra. O mommra.*" Why hasn't Gamaliel gone and cuffed her one? Knocked the black mickey out of her? Why will he not chant our catechism against her? Why am I always seeking shelter when wisdom is in my right hand?

Again, from a safe vantage point by the gates to the shrine compound, I regard the world. This plump woman, tormentor of my weak *kra,* awaiting her turn again in the *abisa* crowd. When the moment arrives, she does not wail *m'agya* or talk *basa-basa*. Yet neither does she confess coherently. The white clay dried now on her face and cracking with her exertions, the *kra* forces within her whipcrack her toward her third act.

She is attacked from all sides by birds, by dogs, by fish, by winds, by strange noises; but she rebuffs all. She bares her teeth, flaps her long teats, dances. Her laughter is a hunter's gun, her laughter is an electric prod, her laughter is a fish net, her laughter is an electric fan of superatomic forces, her laughter is a louder drum than all those of the attacking world. She collapses in the spent pool of her laughter and once again the *sinkwafo* carry her from in front of the dais of the *obosomfo*.

Gamaliel has purchased his goat skins.

"The female African personality," Burdener says. Making his great mistake. "A mad loony bitch. I'd lock her up in a police station loo for a month and flog some manners into her. Is that your Lost Coast innate humanism? Innate idiocy. Flogging bitch. Racism, I call it. Out and out racism. Worse than an Ibo lawyer. You arguing there with that minor-minor fraud while the chief fraud pretends to dissociate, arguing over half a quid's worth of bloody rotting stinking goat skins. Why didn't that tickle her satiric fancy?"

GKH permits me to rant. Encourages me to rant. His mind already plotting my self-betrayal.

Within five minutes we are out of the shrine and out of the bush. The dark highway beneath us. The lorries slow down as we approach, for few people in Lost Coast possess Land Rovers now, except the police and the Security Service. Indentations and bogholes in the road are marked with oracular yellow lines, symbols of future repairs. GKH drives slowly, conserving his tyres, defending his fuelpump against overexertion.

"Back to civilisation," he says, as a lorry loaded with fat market women jerks to a dead halt in front of him—without signalling. "You can calm down now, Uncle," he says. "No longer no need to act like Nigerian."

"Purges are what you need," rants Burdener. "Not a counter-coup. Get rid of the goatstink of half of the women and you'd find some respect possible for the proletariat—white or black. Or yellow. That old bitch should be hung-and-quartered."

At the police barricade of this northeast entrance to Agada we are waved through without examination. GKH is a known friend of the Redeemer and Obatala and Iden. The road beyond is jammed and pummelled with honking lorries. The Obatala Roundabout only increases the chaos. A clerk on a brandnew Honda has smashed into the right door of a doctor's black Cresta. The doctor is calling the clerk a fool, while bystanders surge about and debate the legal merits of their chosen side. Once beyond that mess, we enter the fourlane section of Lumumba Avenue and the goat skins seem to stench less abominably.

But Burdener rants on.

"White. No other reason than because I'm white. Wouldn't treat me like an individual if it kept her in new clothes for the rest of her life. No reason beyond racism for her to treat me with a madwoman's cruelty. Picking on my ugliness, my deformity. Inventing worse ones. Like vultures coming down on chickens. If you weren't black she'd have been down on you even more quickly—standing there like a woman bargaining for skins that smell like rotten fish. Because your bloody Redeemer can't loosen up enough to let you buy the real thing. But you are—black—and you're safe here, and I have to submit to that indignity, that stupid insanery. Flopping her teats at me like a Jersey cow. What kind of mentality is that?"

But GKH knows what fire of hell he is preparing me for; GKH says nothing. At the gate of his walled estate, he honks without impatience. Kwame Bird Lady Day unlocks the gate, unloads the goat skins from the Land Rover, checks the pressure of the tyres. Together they carry the goat skins to the ash pit and then retire.

Building their plot; letting my own misaimed shot poison my limbs.

Mystery. Waiting. Slowly the poison. I recreate the scene of mockery. Gamaliel knocks her with a swipe of his drummer's wrist to the earth. Or, I grant her wisdom, and she, stool mother now, reincarnation of

Cleopatra and Persephone, guider to the diamonds and gold of old Mali, inescapably beautiful Ashanti princess Sister Marcella of Honeywell in white calico and brown ankles of deerivory, she grants me embraces, and I am whole, wealthy, *kra*-restored, loved, and *éminence grise* to Disraeli and King Arthur. Death is at your door, I shout, and she quivers to my feet like a stranded, starved slave on the 1823 streets of Liverpool. Sweet dog, I say, hear my will.

But out into the dark night of musicless reality stride-stalks Gamaliel Kofi Harding, *opanyim,* elder of some new, nearly memberless *ntoro;* reserved, reclusive, meditative. The wisdom and the mystery of the world revolve in his head; why has he need to speak or to observe? Purity and impurity belong to oneself. No one can purify another. He has three records out on Decca and two on London; who should not honour him? His *kra* is of the new Africa, the Redeemer's Africa; who would dare to put obstacles in the path?

"Time for the mysteries, Uncle." He stands in a pair of American boxer shorts, naked except for those, beads plummeting into his chest hair, his feet bare and braced firmly on the earth surrounding the ash pit, his dark, hairy body whitewashed with sticky talcum powder, a fresh egg in either hand.

"*Akwaba,*" he says. "Time for '*nohyira.* Purification." And as I step forward he swings out one hand and crashes the egg on top of my head. Trickles of yolk eat down behind my ears.

"It won't do," Burdener hollers, loosing his tongue, enjoying the hatred that skittles out. "Did she think I do not know the meaning of *babaso?* Does she think I don't know it's her blessed Redeemer who's driving the country into the arms of the fascist military? Work and happiness. Death and corruption is closer. He should make her his representative to Russia. Idiot socialism is what you have here. Purges are what you need. Purges. *Babaso.* It's her who's syphilitic. It's the country what's syphilitic.

"The peace of Allah on you, Uncle," says GKH. Swinging the other hand and its egg against my chest, knocking me down onto the ashy earth, jumping astride me, peeling off my shirt, rubbing the split egg into my heart.

"No one can purify another," he says, pulling the drying egg out of my hair and gouging it with the heel of his palm into my frenzied eyes.

"Do you know what *m'agya* means?" he asks, letting me up, letting me stumble to my feet.

"Of course I know," I scream. "*My father,* who was killed by the Boers, castrated and driven to suicide in their gutting prisons. Electrical shocks driven through his testicles until he confessed that he was a communist. For defending women like that. For speaking up for them in court and helping their husbands escape to Lost Coast. That was my father and look at how that woman treated me. Racism."

"Do you know, Uncle, that for a certain time, a long certain time covering all of my life, that woman who tormented you, that woman who can no longer control her laughter, that woman you scorn, she was my mother."

And saying it, watches me run from his walled estate. Saying it, he twists the knife into all my plans. Tears open my jaw. Makes me, as she could essentially not, a *babasoman*. Watches me run from his walled estate, his eyes on me as I plunge into a taxi. Fleeing from the eyes of the Flagstaff radio tower. Driving for two hours through the streets of Agada until my newfound trusted ally, Mamadu the taxi driver, with innumerable deft flourishes of deceptive driving, feints down oneway streets, scurries through backalleys, and sudden U-turns on Lumumba Avenue, frees us from the following vengeance. Sudden, swift, heartletting knifestroke of Gamaliel Kofi Harding's vengeance.

Knowledge is necessary for directed evil: that becomes my newly discovered rule at this moment of panic and despair. Knowledge is an *nkotoba* club. And having come close to destroying me, having broken my own faith in my ability to build the most profound of human relations between myself and this powerful hero of the movement for freedom from neo-colonialism, having tricked and deceived me for no real purpose other than humiliation, Gamaliel Kofi Harding at the same instant gives me the clue towards the method of his own now inevitable destruction. Knowledge is necessary. Burdener's vengeance.

I throw him off as though he were the most amateur bushman of the security forces. Safe now, confident of my own power, restored by the intensity of my own intellect, I visit the offices of Dr. Champs, discover what time he, Dr. Champs, plans to leave his office. And within an hour of that moment, with Mamadu waiting with revved engine in the back alley, I have broken into Champ's office, in my Don John's villain cape, doing my own Borachio work, but doing it with the utmost efficiency, and have uncovered the file on Gamaliel's mother, the mad woman of the green cloth, the lever with which I will destroy Gamaliel and have him help me destroy this now fraudulent revolution, this capitalistic Redeemer, this scourge of Africa.

Back to my rooms in the Ambassador. A long night of copying. And back with Mamadu to Champs' office. All restored. All complete. The file now my possession, my club.

CASE 229. HARDING, DELICACY, Of Agada, Akante. Female. Born 1904, in Silla (Abidjan).

SHRINE: Ntof at Ntofro.

REASON FOR REFERRAL: Initially amenorrhea; later fear of becoming an *obayifo*.

FAMILY HISTORY:

Parents: Mixed. Both literate. Town dwellers, no cocoa. Mother Akante of good lineage; father Canadian sailor arrived in S. [Silla] November 9, 1896, possible deserter: cap retained by daughter [Delicacy] with 'Sardinian' lettered on band: not used as *suman* but obviously of memory value. Until 1914 apparently communicated between Agada and Abidjan with a variety of girls, i.e. French and English speakers. Delicacy born 1904, on a voyage to Abidjan, but given British citizenship by consulate there and raised in Silla. Mother became a trader in Agada from 1914-1922 while father absent: matches, kerosene, kola, cloth. Father returned 1922 with Brazilian citizenship, opened "Bamboo Grog Shop." Delicacy was married 1925 (late) to Kofi Harding (form. Kwarteng), first Akante inspector of schools, at price of one thousand pounds. Shop sold 1931, father lived until 1939 off proceeds of mother's trading, lost over Atlantic in smuggled flight via American air force DC3. Mother set up Dymankoma shrine 1941, of which she became *obosomfo*. Died 1963 of cancer and complications.

    Siblings. Mother bore seven children, of which only one died, three were fathered by others than Canadian sailor, and one was shot by Japanese sniper in Burma, 1943. His death certificate was visible in mother's shrine until 1963.

    PERSONAL HISTORY:

    Childhood: The patient says she was happy. Remembers trips to Abidjan and many of the girls. Apparently a favourite of all. Disliked uncle with whom they lived after 1914, but not compound life. "This is your sister, share with her your mango," is a phrase she remembers from that time.

    DELICACY'S FIRST PRAYER

But here is no continuing society, here are false redeemers;
Not a sharing but a continual theft, of goods, and of the good.
The vultures eat through the roof to unwind the heart,
The dogs in the street chop at feet that run only to and
From the prisons of Usher Fort; the gods who might save
Us, choke us with telephone wires to a kingdom whose king
Is a Moshi hound with bellyfull of warring strangers:
Ghost-skinned, evil-lipped, impatient as a hoard of monkeys
Before us a mango orchard. Hear us, a great fear is all around
Us. Hear us. Dark naked women at night in the midwife's room.
Delivering up wombs full of children who long for the vulture's cloth.

    Schooling: Standard VII, then spent four years in a teacher-training college, finishing in 1921. Unusual at the time, but obviously reflecting maternal determination rather than the influence of any paternal mores.

    Work: Taught in primary school, although if male would have qualified for a middle school. Met Kofi Harding here in his first (and only) year of the inspectorate. Never resumed teaching after early child-bearing was finished, but worked with mother in Agada market during what she once called her "ten years of punishment and pain in the desert." Took over stand and business after mother set up shrine and seems to have become happier and more prosperous.

    Marriage: Obviously the root cause of this illness. The strength of character which sustained her during the marriage and child-rearing approaches stubbornness, and is still visible in the variety of defences she used against the *obayifo* messengers and the vitality with which she retells such battles. Husband however has never fulfilled his early promise, on which so much was obviously staked. The thousand pounds dowry was used to purchase grounds and buildings for a middle school, but this has never been a success and after the reorganization following independence was for a short time turned into a primary school. Mr. Harding seems to have been adaptable enough to make the correct friends again however, and the school is once more accepting students of an age capable of responding to his almost proverbial excesses of sexual energy. The resultant litigation and payments drain off funds which might otherwise go to repairs or expansion, so that the school is little changed physically from its 1925 state. The husband, being a methodist, has taken no other wives. Among the many children of his unions, "innumerable as the flies on a dead cow" she states, the only son he seemed to show interest in was granted a scholarship to Roumania after being displaced from school during the imprisonment of the Redeemer. Since his return, he has shown no interest in his father, which seems to please the patient. She claims to have been infertile since 1941 because of her husband's *babaso* (despite subsequent marriage).

Children: Five born, four living. Oldest: Gamaliel, drummer and entrepreneur, b. 1925. Daughter, Margaret Rose (nom d'enfance), married to Ambassador to Mexico does not stay in same compound but visits frequently, b. 1926. Son, died at birth 1927. Son, George, now professor of science at the University here, antagonistic towards father, uninterested in relations with mother, offered to pay bill for medicine but rarely visits, b. 1928. Daughter, Ama, b. 1939, married to M. Burdener (white, personal acquaintance). According to patient, later infertility was because of husband's *babaso*.

Households: A progression. On the father's return in 1922 she spent school holidays in family home behind "BGS" [Bamboo Grog Shop], returning to uncle's compound often for visits. On marriage, as expected, moved into Kwarteng compound and remained there throughout child-bearing. Closeness of children indicates some level of modernity. Apparently husband's infidelity wasn't discovered until still-birth of sixth child in 1941. Reaction abnormal. Refused to visit, clean or cook for husband, despite pressure from both mothers and families. Extremity of situation can be shown by the fact that she left Kwarteng compound to take rooms in Agada on her own. Some restriction prevented her from teaching and eventually she had to return to live with and work for mother. Father by this time was apparently alcoholic and living alone when shop was sold. Has lived from 1943 until 1950 with half-sister whose husband is a tinsmith and who works herself as a cashier at Kingsway. Helps support these children. In 1950 she married a widower with four children, Mr. Awotchwi, of Silla, apparently in the clear understanding that she could retain her state of continency. Lived with him until he became seriously involved politically with Alegba's conservative party and then returned to tinsmith's compound, 1958 to present. Her youngest daughter, Ama, continued to be supported by Awotchwi even after Delicacy left.

Katamenia: Menopause prolonged, began 1959. Travels to shrines and progressive breakdown dates from this time, five years ago.

DELICACY'S SECOND PRAYER

We do not wish to learn anything more.
Who taught of the pain of the bladder,
liquid fire burning the body
The earth curling in disgust.

Who taught of pain in the back's hard wires,
falling like grains of harmattan earth
Into the maize we prepare for supper,
That which must be pounded still
Though pain pulls us to the fire.
Who taught of the heavy rain floods,
Leaving houses mounds of sand
Leaving maize crippled as young beggars
Leaving the city foul with fever.
One year everywhere is sweet yam and fish,
One year a woman pounds her complaints,
One year tough cassava is not found.
One year all are giddy-giddy.
No, we were taught of circles and Rome,
Bishops landing on the shores
of Britain, the mining of doves,
Why the Sahara is eating land,
And when Wilberforce freed the queen.
We have found the political kingdom
and several old men have disappeared
Unaccountably, and many have fled.
Biscuits arrive but no milk from Holland.
We do not wish to learn of anything more.
No one taught of my private terrors,
My shadows, my secret fears,
The snake that eats within my womb.

PREVIOUS ILLNESSES: (1) Her first illness occurred in 1959 and many good witnesses at Ntof still remember it. She was accompanied by her son George. She complained in the usual fashion: "I am pregnant, the pregnancy will not go. Some ones are chopping within my womb." She was depressive but not *basa-basa*. Her confession included the unusual assertion that she often turned herself into a man. This was infinitely shocking to the witnesses and probably accounted for their good memory of the case. The clerk, perhaps because of the son's presence, went beyond the usual legal "coverage" listing of persons asserted harmed or killed, and recorded a full list of the fantasies confessed at the *abisa*. She appeared much calmed by this and the baths, and the *obosomfo* told her to return home, think of residual sins, and return with payment. She apparently quarrelled with George over this payment and did not return to this particular shrine for some years.

(2) The second time that the patient appeared at this shrine was in July, 1963, when I first saw her. I had not then heard her earlier history and should not have singled her out for special notice had she not come, openly and confidently to my quarters to greet me. I asked why she had come to the shrine and she complained of bad dreams. As soon as she had entered her room at night she would hear voices outside her window and door and see them bringing a light to look for her, a troop of women among whom were her mother, her half-sister and her daughter, Ama. When she made no answer they often brought something like a "lorry crank" and

wound up the outside of the door, and then they came in. She always became stiff with fear and then they carried her away. This has continued ever since. She insists that she is not asleep when she sees and hears these people. She laughs, and refers to Gamaliel who she states is a "figmeat of his own mind."

If she does go to sleep, they come in through chinks and crevices, "like refrigerated air": they take her spirit away in her sleep, and in her dreams she often finds herself in some "incorrect section of Agada" which she does not recognize, wandering lost in heavy traffic or swept into a main storm drain full of rain water and sewage which attempts to wash her towards the sea. In the daytime she is afraid to go to the market, or anywhere else, because she hears their voices and their footsteps following her. The *obayi* which they have given her take various animal forms: dogs and goats, but often transistor radios and taxicabs. She hears the taxicabs honking at her and the radios singing to her and warning her of death. Before her illness, when she went to the market she never really noticed the flocks of vultures, but now the troop has sent them to her house, roosting on her roof, urging her to come and travel with them.

She was a tall, well-nourished; comely woman, humourous, somewhat sarcastic and pleasant-voiced. She seemed of above-average intelligence, quietly competent, industrious and self-reliant. Her diction was typical of the *Agada Times* in its earlier days, unselfconsciously colourful. If she has indeed remained continent since 1943 against the powerful pressures of her society, the preponderance of calm and repose in her character is amazing.

She went home after a few days.

DELICACY'S THIRD PRAYER

The sound is inside the compound
The sound is outside the compound
The sound claws on the roof.
May nothing I have be stolen,
May nothing I am be led.
Nyame, protect my ear.
May the tree that carries
The roof be strong as steel.
The sound carries three drums.
May none be struck,
May the hammered pegs
That hold the goatskin
Be stolen by the crows.
May the owl and the python
Lose their messages,
The sound of the dark
And the sound of the morning fear
Be blown from this roof
Till the windows are filled-in,
The door made son of the wall
And the wall become an eye.

PRESENT ILLNESS: Late in February, the patient arrived again in Ntof, much distressed and in obvious decline. The dry harmattan season had become an omnipresent voice of her *obayi* and a normal catarrh was proof that they were draining her *kra* by day as well as by night.

She came to greet me, in a much more distracted fashion than before. She said that the night after going to the *obosomfo* she had dreamt that she was in an unpainted shabby lorry which was running away with her and that although the driver kept shouting at her to "drop here, drop here," she was unable to jump out and was hurtled towards the sea.

She has decided that this will be her final shrine. Her sensations often include giddiness, headache and blackness before her eyes. Sometimes bright flickering lights appear before her eyes and stay only a few minutes. (Migraine scotomata?)

At the shrine she stood anxious, agitated and weeping. She talked loudly, anxiously and protestingly, saying that although she had killed her son's (G) [Gamaliel] son, she had no desire to become an *obayifo*. When she knelt to implore that the evil might be taken from her, the other women also knelt and interceded for her. The *obosomfo* feels that she has not confessed all.

She is restless, can't sit still, but can't do any work and is very bitter towards the small girl who has accompanied her. The *obayifo* have put a spider web over her eyes so that she cannot see clearly and a phonograph in her ears. She hears an unceasing sound in her belly and head, "tim, tim, tim," and knows that this is a warning from her dead mother.

FIRST INTERVIEW: *26, 2, 64.* A difficult time; it sometimes seems easier to work in the villages with an interpreter. She is obviously very confused in her relationship to me. Her face has much thinned. She is frightened, distressed and agitated; guilty over her grandson and yet defensive. States that the troop wants her to kill her oldest son (Gamaliel), but she is determined not to. She says her own evil killed her "last child" but that this was not her fault as the evil was given to her against her will. George's explanations of the menopause have obviously had no effect on her. In telling her story she became excited and kept getting up to demonstrate how the troop would wind the lorry-crank, what it felt like when they flew with her, and what sorts of cries and calls they made to her.

19, 3, 64. Last night, while she was awake, she says, the Russian doctor whom Gamaliel arranged to have examine her entered her room and made her remove her clothing before a powerful "atomic" searchlight. He chuckled *"da, da"* when she made him listen to her mother's warning within her belly. He asked her why she was resisting the call to "hunt." In the morning, being frightened, she related this to the *obosomfo's* bath water dispenser, but he reassured her that the *obosomfo* would drive these things away. She seems to feel safer in Ntof. The dry hot wind still contains voices, but when she demonstrated the way the Russian said *"da, da,"* and how he nodded his head above her naked belly, bystanders laughed at her excellent comic performance. She herself joined in the laughter. Her laughter is warm and infectious. Her face in repose however, is worried and anxious.

6, 5, 64. Intravenous amytal and methedrine. A good reaction.

13, 5, 64. Says she is better in that the *obayifo* now stand outside the city and daren't pass the police barricades on the outskirts of town, but they send vultures and goats who come and shine lights through the chinks in her room and call her to go and join the troop. They took her spirit away to Abidjan where she hasn't been since her childhood.

20, 5, 64. She came to tell me very happily that she is much better and sleeps quietly. No one can annoy her now for she is being gradually strengthened by Ntofro's protective baths. Confessions methodical.

23, 6, 64. Slight relapse after a month commuting back to her stand in the market. "Special" baths have been ordered. At night she hears the vultures on the tin roof calling to her.

28, 6, 64. Returned to tinsmith's compound.

15, 7, 64. Brought in early in the morning trembling with fear, in heavy rainstorm. The wet season certainly has arrived. She has been exceedingly anxious and unhappy all day. She dreamt that an entirely new troop took her to a new meeting tree. They were armed (?). She dreamt they asked her to make palm nut soup, but found that some of the meat was steak (her father's favourite meat) so she refused to eat. She woke and lay sleepless and frightened but did not waken the compound until morning. She intends to remain until the rains cease.

14, 9, 64. She has had several minor relapses, but now says that though the messengers still call her to join the troop she is strong in the power of the *obosomfo,* defies them and says that she will never go. She is unmistakably hypomanic in her delight in her own defiance. She does a music hall shuffle as she demonstrates how she shoos them away like pesky chickens.

18, 10, 64. Still up and down. When depressed, the vultures take over. When elated, she hears them but drives them off like thieving monkeys. She has similar triumphs in her dreams. Turned the Russian's searchlight on himself one evening. The bystanders laugh with joy in her triumphs and she claps her hands afterwards, coyly as Beatrice Lilly.

24, 10, 64. After some fluctuation she has decided to return to the tinsmith's compound. I have my doubts. The prognosis must definitely include the danger of an increase in the manic-depressive swings of the disposition, in which the schizophrenia is superimposed. Thus far no sign of the use of *sumans.* Do not close file.

Ah, but do not use it either, my good Dr. Champs. My personal acquaintance in parenthesis. Except to win yourself honour and a chair in some glassfront university, of Leeds or Sussex or Uganda. Ah, Dr. Champs, what file is ever closed. We but peep with cancerspattered eyes at our closest known ancestors. So this is the grandmother of the children I have, the woman Ama has always kept hidden from me. As you have hidden her in your careful records. Which of your own fantasies are recorded in this process, which of your own needs and fears? My rational man. My good doctor. This bringer of knowledge with which to trip up Gamaliel, bringer of knowledge of my own wife's mother, the one unspoken of now by my assimilated beauty, my Ama. Ama, what does Dr. Champs know of you?

"A century is not a long time."

Gamaliel, are you still present? Hands clenched, ready to strike out at me, at the uncle of your children. To destroy me in the unwritten second volume of your autobiography.

More people are leaving the walled estate. Music is sure-sure not coming again.

"You said that, Gamaliel. But it's long enough for five generations to come to strength; one of which—not yours and not mine—may break us all out of this foulness."

Dark men, I see them. With hair unkempt; ironic and bitter smiles on their lips. Entering a church of the Atomic Apostolic Regeneration and Recognition, where white-frocked deacons pray to God for their deliverance while the women sway in search of the older, earlier, mindthrusting and mindcalming religions. Nine silver chalices of fertility on the altar decked with frangipani blossoms. Entering to rape before destroying, to taste forced mysteries before mutilation. The deacons hung in their white frocks from the wildmorningglory hung rafters. Their madeinamerica priest, chantless now as before, chopped up thin as wafers and fed in pieces through the great New York religion counterproducer to foul it up forever.

"Gamaliel, you will never break away from this. You fail yourself as you failed your mother. Your son fails you; the Americans devour his *kra* and you do nothing. You will not beat out the evil."

"No."

"Test him."

"The school has tested him."

"The school knows nothing. You have said that yourself, a thousand times. Test him."

"He has drummed for the old man. He will do well."

"Fifteen, and he smokes hashish like a Hausa petty-petty man."

"Kwame."

"Yes, father."

"Show to your uncle by marriage your back."

Ribbed. With scars. Upon scars. *Carte d'identité abstraite.* Like an antelope blinded in thorn country and flayed alive by its own torture-tossings.

"Who is a young man's duty to hate?"

"The enemies."

"Who are the enemies?"

"All those who hate the blacks."

"What are their weapons?"

"Innumerable."

"What are examples?"

"There are many levels."

"How would you divide them?"

"Military. Economic. Inventive. Personal."

"How will we defeat them?"

"Through Unity."

"Who will bring us Unity?"

"Ode Ye Ado. The Redeemer."

Gamaliel smiles at this display of memory, as though Delicacy has been made whole again, recreated in the image of her grandson, her long years of deprivation and struggle rewarded with gold and flesh rather than with madness. For a moment, brief, hearing the night about me like a child's cloak of velvet and seeing this smile of ancestry, I want only to give Gamaliel this moment of atonement accomplished. Most of the guests have left out into the night, the music being all completed, but yet a few drift about as though reluctant to leave. Or, they are spies of the Security Forces. It is as though, from within my chest my heart has grown arms and wishes to reach out and embrace all of those who still long to live by these rhythms in gentleness. Something dances in my heart. But all that is of short duration. There are no accidents.

Facing his father, his back still to me, Kwame Bird Lady Day shivers into a mock stupidity, hearing my voice at his back.

"That is merely the first of the catechism. What any small boy should know. When it comes to the breakdown of the economic, few are more foolish than you. You will never reach the point at which the wise can question the Redeemer."

All the marks of manhood approached shimmer in his body as he turns to me. A gangling thinness. A fear of lacking sufficient pride.

"What is the primary purpose of neocolonialists in Africa?"

"Division."

Then he stumbles. The ball of learning hits a corner and bounces off erratically, and, as the mind spins to catch it, he trips, the ball speeds up again, strikes him, disappears into the sky, strikes him again from behind and dribbles into inaction before he can catch it. "Multiplication," he smiles out weakly.

Gamaliel's fist, holding the short whip of antelope hide thongs, crashes into his son's shoulder blades.

"Softly yet," says Burdener. "How many offices of U.S.I.A. in Africa?"

"Forty."

"Fifty-two. Was Ghedema its spy in Lost Coast?"

"Yes."

"Does it have other spies and informers?"

"Hundreds."

"When will they be rooted out?"

"Only when Unity is come."

"What will be their punishment?"

"The punishment of castration."

But I get to lead him no more, for at that moment Gamaleil knocks him to the ground remembering Delicacy dancing into death unjustified, and in the fury of futility begins to beat him with the thongs, the blows of the *nkotoba* club that he will, soon, or eventually, use upon himself, the blows of recognition of vast deception. Screaming out the inversion of the catechism which Kwame Bird Lady Day still incoherently repeats in snatches and fragments.

"Our kingkingking Redeemer. Why has he betrayed our freedom?

Who is the *kramu* man who leads him to bleed the people? Are we to be slaves again, child? Is this the fruit of our revolution? Strange fruit. The money-money man who can only steal from us. Answer me, child."

The five thongs come down on the quivering back of the child, raising now the old scars, opening them to the night. Small dog bones on the tips of the thongs. Knifestrokes opening his son's *kra* to the spirits of a long night, denying vainly his participation in all in which he participates.

"Who owns NADECO and uses it to keep us in poverty? Who takes the bribes of the BOAC while his people starve to death? How will such a man be tortured? What will come after castration? Making us fools in all of Africa. Biting us with the sleeping sickness of his madness. Buying up the houses of the poor. Selling licenses to import only to his friends. Suspicion and madness everywhere. All who speak truth burned into the jails. Answer me child. For this we have raised you."

The thongs come down with each question and at a certain point the child no longer scoops out his shallow answers of trust, but simply lies there quivering in the pool of his agony dreams.

"M'agya, m'agya," he murmurs. "M'agya, m'agya."

In twenty minutes all will be calm. Gamaliel will retire to his room and weep for hours. I will bathe the wounds of Kwame Bird Lady Day and dress him in a gown of white calico and tell him sad tales of the hatred of fathers, inform of the variety of small arms available in the world, question him on his sexual life, point out the flaws of his father and create fantasies of his own life with the fall of the Redeemer and the redistribution of all his mistresses and their red Thunderbirds and MGs amidst the population. Soothe his twitching mouth with fresh limeade, he whose back now jerks like a blown lorrytyre as the thongs and thorns of his despising father dig into his flesh, releasing his *kra* to the dark night.

"*M'agya,*" he murmurs. "*M'agya, m'agya, m'agya.*"

DAVID HELWIG

Something For Olivia's Scrapbook I Guess

David Helwig was born in Toronto in 1938. He was educated at the University of Toronto and the University of Liverpool, and now lives in Kingston, Ontario, where he teaches English at Queen's University. He has contributed poems and short stories to many literary magazines, and is the author of The Streets of Summer *(1969), a collection of short stories, and a novel entitled* The Day Before Tomorrow *(1971).*

I was alone in the shop as I watched the two of them coming up the street. Olivia was on television being interviewed with a discovery, Harold Bettmann, 'one of the most exciting young sculptors working in Canada today' (Toronto *Star*). I felt a bit sorry for Olivia over the Harold thing. He is not a nice young man, and to a bystander he seems too obviously to be trying to reach the top of the mountain of success by a route beginning with a tunnel into my wife's private parts. Still, I knew better than to say anything to her. Anyway, they were on television together, and I certainly wasn't going to watch. So I stood in the front window and watched Barrow Man and the girl.

I wasn't really suprised to see her tagging along after Barrow Man as he came up the street. Women can smell it on him, I've often observed that. My wife, for example: when Barrow Man walks into a room she shuts her mouth and sits very still licking her lips now and then. And that's about the only time she stops talking. You wouldn't think there'd be any mystery about him; at least a couple of times I've heard him going out the back door as I came in the front, but still, when he comes into a room, Olivia shuts her gob and sits with that funny look on her face. No one else does that to her, and there are lots better looking than Barrow Man, more charming, more intelligent. But women like him. They look at that bony face, and that thick hair, and they smell whatever it is he has and bingo. So I wasn't surprised to see this young girl following him along the street as he pushed his barrow of tatty flowers.

Our place is just north of Yorkville, where Yorkville is going to expand next, that's what the real estate man says. Anyway Olivia and I have a shop there, full of handicrafts and imported odds and ends that nobody buys. Barrow Man lives next door with a gang of others, upstairs from something that's trying to be a coffee house.

Barrow Man is unscrupulous, have I established that? Suppose not. Well he is, but just about women, just about sex really. I've seen him fill a fifteen-year-old with wine and take her upstairs without even paying much attention to who she is. He thinks it's good for them, that's the secret, and otherwise he's kind and generous. Only for him it's not an otherwise. He thinks that sex is good for any woman at any time and place whether she thinks so or not. Maybe that's what women see in him.

So as I say, I wasn't surprised that afternoon when I saw the girl following Barrow Man up the street. He'd been down at his usual spot on Cumberland selling flowers that he'd picked from parks and gardens the night before or got from florists who were ready to throw them out. Flowers have been getting a lot of publicity this year, and he sold them cheap and made enough to stay alive.

The girl who was following him up the street was dressed in clothes that were worn almost to tatters and were too big for her. Every few feet she would stop. It seemed as though Barrow Man could hear when her feet stopped moving, for he would turn around almost immediately and motion to her with his hand. Gradually she would get up her courage and move forward a few feet. It took them five or ten minutes to cross the distance between the point where I first saw them and the house. Barrow Man's missionary zeal amazed me. To go to all this trouble when he could have half a dozen women in the neighbourhood for the asking. Old Jane, whose room was next to his, was an attractive and universally accommodating girl.

When they reached the front of the house, Barrow Man made an elaborate gesture indicating that he lived there and inviting the girl to sit down at one of the outside tables. It was then I caught on that she must be a deaf mute. From the way she was dressed, you'd think he'd picked her up at the Salvation Army or an orphanage somewhere. She sat down at a table and Barrow Man disappeared inside.

The girl had a strange flat frightened face that looked straight ahead and gave the impression that she was waiting for some kind of blow to fall on her from behind. Call me sentimental, but I didn't much like the idea of Barrow Man seducing this pathetic little deaf mute.

He came out of the house with a lemonade for her and put it on her table. She didn't want to touch it in a way, but she was probably hot and thirsty and needed it. Barrow Man kept after her and she finally took a drink. While she was drinking, Barrow Man went over to the barrow of flowers that he had left at the curb and took out a handful of zinnias that he must have got from somebody's garden. He carried them over to the girl and gave them to her. I had to admire his technique.

I walked out of our shop and along the pavement toward the two of them. Just as I got to the barrow of flowers, I thought of a way to neutralize what he'd done. I took a bunch of chrysanthemums, a little wilted and obviously second-hand, and carried them over to the girl. She was holding the gaudy zinnias in her hand, and she didn't move or object when I began to put the chrysanthemums in her hair. The hair was full of tats so it was easy to find places to stick the flowers. It was soft, too, and reminded me of the days when Olivia's hair was brown.

Two kids about sixteen, a boy and girl who had the room across from Jane but hardly ever came out, had seen us from the window and appeared from the house. They'd lived there for weeks, but this was only the second time I'd seen them. They joined in the game, running to get flowers and carrying them to the table. They put them on the girl or placed them around her. Jane was looking out the upstairs window and threw me a couple of paper flowers from her room. I wound the wire stems around the girl's wrists. Within a few minutes, the barrow was stripped of all its flowers which now covered the girl, the chair she sat in and the table in front of her. She made a lovely funeral. The four of us and Jane, who had come downstairs, and even Walter, who had come out of the shop, stood and admired her. Barrow Man tried to get her to smile and finally she did. She seemed to relax a little and looked at the flowers, for the first time really.

'Who is she?' It was one of the young kids that asked.

'I don't know who she is,' Barrow Man said. 'She was hanging around near my stand all afternoon.'

'What are you going to do with her?' I said.

'Well, right now,' he said, 'she looks so gorgeous I wouldn't dare touch her.'

'Maybe you should take it easy.'

'What do you think I am? I'm full of loving kindness. I sell flowers and make people happy. I let you crazy people steal every one of my flowers to give her. I just want to make her happy.'

'But not everyone has the same idea of what will make her happy,' Jane said.

'You mean sex,' Barrow Man said. 'You're all against sex. What a lot of nervous people you must be.' He walked over to the girl, picked up her hand, and kissed the back of it.

'I'm hungry,' he said, 'and I suppose she is too. Some of you nervous people who stole my flowers should buy us something to eat.'

'Get them some food, Walter,' I said. 'I'll pay.'

It was after six, so I went home, closed the shop, and made myself a sandwich. I planned to go back next door, but I can't afford to eat at Walter's prices. With my sandwich I had a couple of stiff drinks of rye and water which didn't do anything very metaphysical to me. I went back over to see what was happening next door, taking the bottle with me in a paper bag. What Barrow Man calls the fuzz is very active around our streets.

The girl was still sitting at her table with Barrow Man and was still covered with flowers. She had drawn a bit of a crowd from the houses nearby, and Walter was doing some business for a change. I paid him for what Barrow Man and the girl had eaten and sat down at the table with them. I poured out of my bag into a coffee cup and gave Barrow Man some, too.

I looked at the girl. She seemed pretty puzzled but not too unhappy about the whole thing. The boy from upstairs had obviously decided to rejoin society and brought out a guitar. People started singing. That worried Walter who was sure it would cost him his licence and invited everybody inside. When we got in, the place was so crowded that Barrow Man locked the front door and put up a CLOSED sign. Walter pulled the curtains shut, and

I took my bottle out of its paper bag. The deaf mute sat in the middle of the room in her flowers, apparently puzzled by what was going on, but everyone smiled and gestured at her, and she got used to it. I offered her a drink, but she smelled it and made a face. Walter put some music on his record player and several people formed a circle and danced around the girl. I didn't feel like dancing and concentrated on my whisky.

I finally drank enough to lose track of time, and from that point on, the party was a series of moments in a sea of noise.

First moment: someone gave her a pencil and paper, and she wrote one word. JESUS. In large scrawled capitals.

Second moment: at Jane's urging, Barrow Man publicly announced that he would not seduce the deaf mute. He called it a sentimental gesture.

Third moment: the unknown girl from upstairs began a beautifully graceful and sinuous dance.

I watched her for about twenty seconds before I decided that I couldn't take it. I went out the back door, climbed over the fence and into my yard. I stood among the few blades of brown grass that flourish there. The house was dark and I didn't want to go in. Did go in. The memory of that girl covered with flowers got to me and made me want to do something for her, not that there was anything to do.

I was making my breakfast the next morning when I heard Olivia come in. It was quarter after eight. I couldn't really figure out why she'd got up so early. Didn't occur to me until she walked into the bedroom and started to undress that she hadn't been to bed. We've only got a couple of small rooms at the back of the shop, and from where I was standing, I could see her undressing. I watched. I think of it as one of my conjugal rights, although it's not really much of a sight. Olivia is a skinny little thing with no breasts to speak of and pathetic little hips. She looked so pale and dragged out as she took off her clothes that I fought off the temptation to say something witty about the long interview.

'Do you want some food?' I said.

She shook her head and climbed into bed. One way or another Harold must have given her a rough time. When I walked into the bedroom, she turned her face away.

'You missed a new arrival last night,' I said. 'Barrow Man found a strange little deaf mute somewhere. I don't know why, but everyone got excited when she turned up and gave her a big party. Even Barrow Man got into the act; he promised to refrain from debauching her. At least for the time being. It was all very strange.'

She turned over and looked at me. That's not really the right way to describe it; she stared at my face as though something distasteful was wiggling its way out of the eyeballs.

'Don't you ever read the newspapers?' she said.

In the circumstances, that struck me as a strange question, and I didn't answer. After all we've been married nine years and she knows my reading habits. Pretty clearly it was a smart crack, but its relevance escaped me.

'She's a deaf mute about seventeen wearing old clothes that don't fit properly,' Olivia said.

I nodded.

'The police are looking for her. She stabbed her mother to death with an ice pick in some little town in Muskoka and then hitch-hiked to Toronto before anyone found the body. The story was in the paper this morning and on television last night.'

I thought for a few seconds and started out of the room.

'Are you going to phone the police?' she said.

'No. I'm going to warn Barrow Man that they're after her so he can hide her somewhere.'

'Are you out of your mind?' As she said this, she sat up in bed, the sheet falling off her and exposing her scrawny chest. For some crazy reason, I wanted her right at that moment, but I have developed a strong resistance to such impulses and I conquered this one. At least temporarily. She went on shouting at me.

'Why in the name of all that's wonderful are you going to try to keep her away from the police? Apparently her mother drank and beat her. They'll just send her to some place where she can be looked after.'

'Some nice place like the bughouse.'

'I don't know, but I know you have no business interfering. Just phone the police and tell them where she is, and they'll look after her all right. You're getting as crazy as those kids next door. Have they been giving you marijuana or something?'

'You know, Olivia,' I said in my best Cary Grant manner, 'I find your shrill grating soprano very sexy.'

She got the message and covered herself with the sheet.

'You're not really going to keep her away from the police are you?'

'Unless you distract me with your subtle feminine wiles and mysterious allure, I'm going to see Barrow Man right now.'

She flopped down in bed.

'I should have you committed,' she muttered.

'And a very Merry Christmas to you, too,' I said and walked down the hall and out. As I walked up to the door of the place next to us, Walter was putting out the tables and chairs. He said Barrow Man was still in bed, and that the girl was in Jane's room.

I went upstairs and walked into Barrow Man's room. Jane sat up bleary-eyed in the bed and said hello.

I apologized.

'All right,' Jane said. 'Nothing going on. You want Barrow Man.'

'Yeah.'

She reached out and shook him.

'Do you have a cigarette?' she said.

I shook my head, and she gave Barrow Man another poke. Jane, like Olivia, was sitting in bed naked down to where the sheet covered her. She is an ample girl, and as I stood there, I drew certain comparisons between her and my wife. Jane poked Barrow Man twice more, and he began to make noises. Another hard poke in the ribs and he turned over.

'What's the matter?' he said.

'Olivia tells me our little friend is wanted by the police. She did in her mother with an ice pick.'

'The old lady probably deserved it. Anyway, Olivia's a liar isn't she?'

'Don't really know. She says it's in the paper.'

'Everything in the paper is a lie.'

'What will they do to her if they find her?' Jane said.

'Put her on trial. Send her to some kind of institution.'

'Nasty,' Barrow Man said.

'Poor thing,' Jane said. For some reason that prompted her to cover herself with the sheet. I refrained from asking why.

'What shall we do with her?' Barrow Man said.

'Turn her in or hide her,' I said.

Barrow Man scratched his head.

'Don't suppose you have a cigarette.'

I shook my head.

'We can't just turn her in,' Jane said. 'I'd feel like a Judas if we did. After last night.'

'Of course we didn't know last night,' I said.

'Doesn't make any difference,' Barrow Man said.

'No,' I said, 'it doesn't.'

'Let's hide her somewhere,' Jane said.

'Where?' Barrow Man said. 'The fuzz will be watching the streets pretty carefully.'

'We could put her in our back shed until tonight,' I said.

'Maybe no need,' Barrow Man said. 'Just keep her in the house and if the fuzz shows up slip her out to your back shed.'

'I wonder if she knows they're after her?' Jane said.

'She can probably guess,' I said, 'if she really did go at her old lady with an ice pick.'

'Let's go and see her,' Jane said. She climbed out of bed, stood there naked without embarrassment, stretched and put on a short cotton dress that she found on the floor beside the bed. Barrow Man pulled on a pair of pants and we went down the hall to the next door. Jane lifted her hand to knock, realized there wasn't much point, and stuck her head in. She opened the door and walked in. We followed her.

The girl was sitting on the floor at the far side of the room. She looked terrified as we walked in, and I wondered why. There was an unpleasant smell in the room, but it didn't much surprise me. Jane always looks a bit dirty. The girl was staring straight ahead.

'Oh my god,' Jane said. 'She's not housebroken.'

She pointed to the other corner of the room, at a brown lump that was unmistakably the source of the smell. I looked back at the girl who was hiding her face in her skirt.

'Look,' I said. 'She's worried about it. I guess she didn't know where to go.'

Barrow Man went over to her and lifted her face. He tried to indicate to her that it was all right, that we didn't care about the mess in the corner and that Jane would clean it up right away. Jane got a little cardboard box and did. She took it away to dispose of. Meanwhile Barrow Man started another little pantomime, asking her if she had been hitch-hiking. She nodded.

'How in hell can I ask her if she knows the cops are after her?'

'Try a traffic cop,' I said, 'or a motorcycle.'

Barrow Man had a go at it, but the girl looked confused. Barrow Man patted her on the head and sat down. Jane walked into the room. I jumped from my chair and attacked her with an imaginary ice pick. She didn't look very surprised, for she has believed for some time that I am a man full of suppressed vices. She believes this because I have never tried to make her, in spite of numerous opportunities and substantial provocation. After I had finished with Jane I turned to the girl. She looked sick. I pointed to her and nodded my head. She buried her face in her skirt again.

'Oh well,' I said, 'I thought we might find out something.'

'Looks to me as though she did it,' Jane said.

'Maybe,' I said.

'I'll take her down to get some breakfast,' Jane said.

Barrow Man stood up.

'Keep her in your room today. I'm going to try and find some flowers to sell. If the cops show up, put her in that back shed.'

Jane took the girl by the arm and led her downstairs. I followed them to the bottom of the stairs, then turned down the hall toward the front door. On my way, I ran into Walter, who was looking worried as usual.

'You getting much business these days?' he said.

'The usual.'

'I don't know how long I can hold out. I've got to eat.'

'Belly god,' I said and walked back to my own house of sorrows.

It was almost nine and I left the door of the shop unlocked and walked back to the kitchen. Olivia was asleep in the bedroom, but something made me think she'd been up after I left. My sense of smell is sometimes very acute. She'd probably phoned the police.

I put on the kettle to make some coffee and stood in the doorway, looking in at her. She dyes her hair a colour they call champagne and it was all wild and fluffy around the little face that looked weak and pinched like that of an undernourished child.

When I had made my coffee, I took it into the shop, closed the door to the kitchen behind me and sat down at my work table near the front door. To amuse myself, I did the week's disastrous arithmetic.

It was less than half an hour after I sat down at my work table that I looked out the window and saw a police car pull up next door. I got up and ran to the back door, climbed over the low fence that separates the yards, nipped in the kitchen door and up the back stairs. As I crossed the kitchen, I could see down the hall to where the cops were coming in the front door. There were two of them, big uniformed public servants with thick necks, and at that moment, it seemed to me that I was even crazier than Olivia gave me credit for being. But my mother had died in a particularly nasty government institution (a fact I have never told Olivia) and I didn't want to see this little girl put away under the thumb of some dykey matron or frustrated social worker. I grew up with social workers.

When I got to the upstairs hall, I ran as quickly as I could to Jane's room and opened the door. The girl started at me, frightened as a bird. I gestured to her to come with me, but she didn't move. She probably didn't trust me since I had ice-picked Jane. I tried to take her arm. No dice. I ran next door to Barrow Man's room to see if Jane was there, but the room was empty. Downstairs I could hear the voices of Walter and the cops, and I knew that Walter would give her up as soon as sneeze if that was the way to avoid trouble. He had given a hostage to Fortune when he opened the coffee house, and Fortune was getting pretty good mileage out of it.

I went back into the room, spent three seconds trying to calm the girl, then picked her up and carried her along the hall and down the back stairs.

My physical condition is not outstanding. By the time we got to the kitchen, I was dizzy and thought I'd faint before I could get the girl out of there. She wasn't quite fighting me off, but she wasn't making it easy either. But for a change I got a lucky break. Jane came into the hall and into the kitchen.

'The cops are out there,' she whispered.

'I know. I'm trying to get her out into our back shed, but she's afraid of me.'

Jane reached out to the girl and took her hand. The girl looked a little relieved. We all slipped out the back door and over the fence. When I finally got the lock on the back shed undone, the girl refused to go in until Jane went with her. Jane took her hand and led her in among the cartons and snow shovels. She turned around and looked at me.

'Do I have to stay here?'

'She'll feel a lot better.'

'Well,' Jane said, 'I just want you to know that I wouldn't do it for anybody else but you.'

'I like you, too,' I said. Then I locked the door of the shed and went back into our shop. I sat down at the front table looking innocent. A few minutes later, I saw the cops leave and drive away. From the kitchen, I got our transistor radio and put it on in the shop to listen to the news bulletins. Within a couple of hours, they were saying that the girl had been reported seen in the Yorkville area and that the police were checking this.

I was pretty sure that they would be back soon. They knew she had been in the house last night, Walter must have told them that, and they would probably have someone watching the house in case she came back. In a couple of hours when they turned up no trace of her, they would come back and try to put more pressure on everyone in the house, threaten arrests for drugs or contributing to juvenile delinquency. Luckily no one there saw me leave with the girl, so that no amount of pressure could tip them off where she was. Which suited me fine.

At quarter to twelve I started making lunch, and made extra of everything for the girls in the shed. I took it out on tinfoil plates, feeling like part of one of Tom Sawyer's games. Jane complained of the discomfort of the shed, so I passed in a couple of folding cots so they could lie down. All this, I tried to do in such a way that it would not look suspicious from any of the upstairs windows nearby. Good old Tom Sawyer, where would I have been without him?

It was about two o'clock when Olivia got up and wandered into the front of the shop with a towel wrapped around her.

'There's nobody here but me,' I said. 'You might as well get dressed.'

'Spare me your wit until I wake up a bit. Where's that girl you were telling me about?'

'In our back shed.'

'Not really.'

'The cops came looking for her next door, so I slipped her out the back and put her in the shed.'

'They're going to put you in jail, do you know that? Or they're going to send the men in white coats for you. Either way, there's going to be nothing left of you around here except your clothes. Unless I keep a scrapbook of your newspaper clippings.' She shook her head. 'It should make quite a trial. Tell me that's why you're doing it, that it's just a publicity gimmick so the store will get mentioned in the paper. That must be it.'

'I'm doing it because I don't want her put in an institution.'

'Well, you're going to end up in one, the way you're going. I really find it all just a little bit hard to understand. Are you going to leave her in the shed forever? You could drill a hole in the wall and charge a dime to peek in. God, when the police find her, I'll be able to charge admission to see you. The man with a hole in his head.' She turned away.

'Don't phone the cops again, Olivia,' I said. 'Or I'll break your neck.'

'You're developing a taste for cheap melodrama,' she said as she disappeared.

I could hear her in the shower and moving around in the bedroom getting dressed. Half an hour later, she was headed out the front door. She'd just raised the hem on her shortest skirt another four or five inches. I hoped whatever she had on underneath looked good.

'I have to see some people downtown,' she said.

'Just don't phone the cops,' I said.

She left. I watched out the window as she walked down the street, her skinny legs very white in the sun. When she disappeared round a corner, I didn't have the energy to move away from the window, and I was still standing there when Barrow Man appeared and began pushing his empty cart along the street toward me. As he passed the window, I tapped on it and motioned him in. He left his barrow by the side of the road and came in.

'The cops were here,' I said, as soon as he was inside the door.

'Did you get her out?'

'Just in time. She and Jane are in the back shed.'

'What's Jane doing there?'

'It was the only way I could get the girl to go in.'

Barrow Man giggled.

'I got hold of a friend of mine,' he said, 'who's got a place out in the country. It's just a beaten-up old farmhouse but she'll probably be all right there. He says he can use a housekeeper if she wants to work.'

'That sounds fine, but how are we going to get her out of here.'

'I said we'd meet him at nine-thirty tonight.'

'But they'll have cops all over.'

'Suppose so.'

'We might just sneak her past in the dark.'

'What we really need is something to attract their attention, start a riot or something.'

'We could burn a house down.'

'Wait a minute, wait a minute.'

He was thinking. I could tell by the look on his face.

'Look,' he said. 'I'll light a fire on my barrow and lead the cops away with that. It will draw a crowd for sure. Then you grab the girl and take off.'

'It'll ruin your barrow.'

'I'll get a new one. You got any old paint and turpentine?'

'In the back shed.'

I gave him the key.

'Watch for the girl,' I said. 'Don't let her out.'

It was at that moment that a customer came into the shop. I knew it must be a mistake and went to clear it up, but I ended up by selling something. I thought it must be some kind of omen. When I looked out the back I saw that Barrow Man had his little cart covered with cardboard boxes that held half the old paint from our shed. If he wasn't careful he'd burn down the whole neighbourhood. He stuck his head in the back door.

'Nine-thirty tonight, okay?'

I said it was okay.

'You meet my friend two blocks up Avenue Road. A brown station-wagon.'

I nodded and he closed the door. I went back to work in the shop. For hours I sat and waited.

Finally, at suppertime, I brought Jane and the girl into the house. I couldn't see taking another meal out to the shed, and I figured they might as well be inside. After supper, I turned on the television set for them, and the three of us watched it until it started to get dark. A little bit after nine, we all went into the shop and sat by the front window waiting for Barrow Man to light his fire.

At nine-fifteen he did it. It was a dandy. He must have had about ten gallons of paint and solvents on his barrow, and when they went up, one whole area of the street was lit. We could see him grab the handles of his barrow and start down a side street with it.

'He's going to burn himself,' Jane said.

'Or get arrested for arson,' I said. 'Let's go.'

We led the girl out the front door and along the street away from the fire. All evening, she had been looking more and more withdrawn, and now she seemed completely out of touch. We led her along dark streets and she followed, but apparently with no idea of where she was going or why. I wanted badly to talk to her, just two or three words. Anything. Jane had tried to explain to her during the day what was going on, had even printed notes for her, but we didn't know if she could read, and nothing seemed to reach her.

We approached Avenue Road a block below the meeting-place we had arranged. The traffic was very heavy, and as we stood on the corner I saw something beside me move. It was the girl who suddenly ran into the road, miraculously made her way past half a dozen speeding cars and ran down the street on the other side. Jane and I stood and watched her, helpless until the traffic slowed a bit.

By the time we got across the road, she had disappeared. For perhaps half an hour, we walked along the streets, down alleys and lanes, but there was no sign of her. We went to tell the driver that she wasn't coming, but he was gone. He must have got tired of waiting. There was nothing more we could do. We walked down Avenue Road toward home.

'Well,' I said. 'That's it.'

'She must have been pretty frightened.'

'Poor little idiot. The police will find her eventually and put her in a box.'

'Maybe that's best.'

'No,' I said. 'That's not ever best for anybody.'

Jane reached out and took my hand.

'I suppose we were crazy to even try it,' I said .

'Maybe.'

'Tell Barrow Man I'll give him some money for a new cart.'

'If I'm talking to him, I'll tell him.'

We walked on down the dark streets. Jane was still holding my hand. She has big hands and feet. We didn't look at each other until we got home. Down the street where Barrow Man had lit his fire, there were still a few people hanging around.

'I wonder if the cops got Barrow Man,' I said.

'I doubt it,' she said.

I knew that now I had to look at her as we stood there in the street. Looked, knowing what I would see. She wanted to come in with me. And why not? Olivia wouldn't be home until morning, and if she was, she wasn't likely to say a hell of a lot, not in the circumstances. I looked down at Jane's face again. It was a wide face, not pretty, but warm and gentle. I wondered where Olivia was and what she was doing. Or having done to her. I kissed Jane on the forehead and turned away.

'I'll see you tomorrow,' I said.

I walked into the house. And don't start asking me why.

HUGH HOOD

After The Sirens

Born in Toronto in 1928, Hugh Hood was educated at the University of Toronto, from which he received a Ph.D. degree in 1955. He now lives in Montreal, where he teaches English at the University of Montreal. He is the author of a collection of stories, Flying A Red Kite *(1963), and two novels,* White Figure, White Ground *(1964), and* A Game of Touch *(1971).*

They heard the sirens first about four forty-five in the morning. It was still dark and cold outside and they were sound asleep. They heard the noise first in their dreams and, waking, understood it to be real.

"What is it?" she asked him sleepily, rolling over in their warm bed. "Is there a fire?"

"I don't know," he said. The sirens were very loud. "I've never heard anything like that before."

"It's some kind of siren," she said, "downtown. It woke me up."

"Go back to sleep!" he said. "It can't be anything."

"No," she said, "I'm frightened. I wonder what it is. I wonder if the baby has enough covers." The wailing was still going on. "It couldn't be an air-raid warning, could it?"

"Of course not," he said reassuringly, but she could hear the indecision in his voice.

"Why don't you turn on the radio," she said, "just to see? Just to make sure. I'll go and see if the baby's covered up." They walked down the hall in their pajamas. He went into the kitchen, turned on the radio and waited for it to warm up. There was nothing but static and hum.

"What's that station?" he called to her. "Conrad, or something like that."

"That's 640 on the dial," she said, from the baby's room. He twisted the dial and suddenly the radio screamed at him, frightening him badly.

"This is not an exercise. This is not an exercise. This is not an exercise," the radio blared. *"This is an air-raid warning. This is an air-raid warning. We will be attacked in fifteen minutes. We will be attacked in fifteen minutes. This is not an exercise."* He recognized the voice of a local announcer who did an hour of breakfast music daily. He had never heard the

51

man talk like that before. He ran into the baby's room while the radio shrieked behind him: *"We will be attacked in fifteen minutes. Correction. Correction. In fourteen minutes. In fourteen minutes. We will be attacked in fourteen minutes. This is not an exercise."*

"Look," he said, "don't ask me any questions, please, just do exactly what I tell you and don't waste any time." She stared at him with her mouth open. "Listen," he said, "and do exactly as I say. They say this is an air-raid and we'd better believe them." She looked frightened nearly out of her wits. "I'll look after you," he said; "just get dressed as fast as you can. Put on as many layers of wool as you can. Got that?"

She nodded speechlessly.

"Put on your woollen topcoat and your fur coat over that. Get as many scarves as you can find. We'll wrap our faces and hands. When you're dressed, dress the baby the same way. We have a chance, if you do as I say without wasting time." She ran off up the hall to the coat closet and he could hear her pulling things about.

"This will be an attack with nuclear weapons. You have thirteen minutes to take cover," screamed the radio. He looked at his watch and hurried to the kitchen and pulled a cardboard carton from under the sink. He threw two can openers into it and all the canned goods he could see. There were three loaves of bread in the breadbox and he crammed them into the carton. He took everything that was wrapped and solid in the refrigerator and crushed it in. When the carton was full he took a bucket which usually held a garbage bag, rinsed it hastily, and filled it with water. There was a plastic bottle in the refrigerator. He poured the tomato juice out of it and rinsed it and filled it with water.

"This will be a nuclear attack." The disc jockey's voice was cracking with hysteria. *"You have nine minutes, nine minutes, to take cover. Nine minutes."* He ran into the dark hall and bumped into his wife who was swaddled like a bear.

"Go and dress the baby," he said. "We're going to make it, we've just got time. I'll go and get dressed." She was crying, but there was no time for comfort. In the bedroom he forced himself into his trousers, a second pair of trousers, two shirts and two sweaters. He put on the heaviest, loosest jacket he owned, a topcoat, and finally his overcoat. This took him just under five minutes. When he rejoined his wife in the living room, she had the baby swaddled in her arms, still asleep.

"Go to the back room in the cellar, where your steamer trunk is," he said, "and take this." He gave her a flashlight which they kept in their bedroom. When she hesitated he said roughly, "Go on, get going."

"Aren't you coming?"

"Of course I'm coming," he said. He turned the radio up as far as it would go and noted carefully what the man said. *"This will be a nuclear attack. The target will probably be the aircraft company. You have three minutes to take cover."* He picked up the carton and balanced the bottle of water on it. With the other hand he carried the bucket. Leaving the kitchen door wide open, he went to the cellar, passed through the dark furnace room, and joined his wife.

"Put out the flashlight," he said. "We'll have to save it. We have a minute or two, so listen to me." They could hear the radio upstairs. *"Two minutes,"* it screamed.

"Lie down in the corner of the west and north walls," he said quickly. "The blast should come from the north if they hit the target, and the house will blow down and fall to the south. Lie on top of the baby and I'll lie on top of you!"

She cuddled the sleeping infant in her arms. "We're going to die right now," she said, as she held the baby closer to her.

"No, we aren't," he said, "we have a chance. Wrap the scarves around your face and the baby's, and lie down." She handed him a plaid woollen scarf and he tied it around his face so that only his eyes showed. He placed the water and food in a corner and then lay down on top of his wife, spreading his arms and legs as much as possible, to cover and protect her.

"Twenty seconds," shrieked the radio. *"Eighteen seconds. Fifteen."*

He looked at his watch as he fell. "Ten seconds," he said aloud. "It's five o'clock. They won't waste a megaton bomb on us. They'll save it for New York." They heard the radio crackle into silence and they hung onto each other, keeping their eyes closed tightly.

Instantaneously the cellar room lit up with a kind of glow they had never seen before, the earthen floor began to rock and heave, and the absolutely unearthly sound began. There was no way of telling how far off it was, the explosion. The sound seemed to be inside them, in their bowels; the very air itself was shattered and blown away in the dreadful sound that went on and on and on.

They held their heads down, hers pushed into the dirt, shielding the baby's scalp, his face crushed into her hair, nothing of their skin exposed to the glow, and the sound went on and on, pulsing curiously, louder than anything they had ever imagined, louder than deafening, quaking in their eardrums, louder and louder until it seemed that what had exploded was there in the room on top of them in a blend of smashed, torn air, cries of the instantly dead, fall of steel, timber, and brick, crash of masonry and glass—they couldn't sort any of it out—all were there, all imaginable noises of destruction synthesized. It was like absolutely nothing they had ever heard before and it so filled their skulls, pushing outward from the brainpan, that they could not divide it into its parts. All that they could understand, if they understood anything, was that this was the ultimate catastrophe, and that they were still recording it, expecting any second to be crushed into blackness, but as long as they were recording it they were still living. They felt, but did not think, this. They only understood it instinctively and held on tighter to each other, waiting for the smash, the crush, the black.

But it became lighter and lighter, the glow in the cellar room, waxing and intensifying itself. It had no color that they recognized through their tightly-shut eyelids. It might have been called green, but it was not green, nor any neighbor of green. Like the noise, it was a dreadful compound of ultimately destructive fire, blast, terrible energy released from a bursting sun, like the birth of the solar system. Incandescence beyond an infinite number of lights swirled around them.

The worst was the nauseous rocking to and fro of the very earth beneath them, worse than an earthquake, which might have seemed reducible to human dimensions, those of some disaster witnessed in the movies or on television. But this was no gaping, opening seam in the earth, but a threatened total destruction of the earth itself, right to its core, a pulverization of the world. They tried like animals to scrabble closer and closer in under the north cellar wall even as they expected it to fall on them. They kept their heads down, waiting for death to take them as it had taken their friends, neighbors, fellow workers, policemen, firemen, soldiers; and the dreadful time passed and still they did not die in the catastrophe. And they began to sense obscurely that the longer they were left uncrushed, the better grew their chances of survival. And pitifully slowly their feelings began to resume their customary segmented play amongst themselves, while the event was still unfolding. They could not help doing the characteristic, the human thing, the beginning to think and struggle to live.

Through their shut eyelids the light began to seem less incandescent, more recognizably a color familiar to human beings and less terrifying because it might be called a hue of green instead of no-color-at-all. It became green, still glowing and illuminating the cellar like daylight, but anyway green, nameable as such and therefore familiar and less dreadful. The light grew more and more darkly green in an insane harmony with the rocking and the sound.

As the rocking slowed, as they huddled closer and closer in under the north foundation, a split in the cellar wall showed itself almost in front of their hidden faces, and yet the wall stood and did not come in on top of them. It held and, holding, gave them more chance for survival although they didn't know it. The earth's upheaval slowed and sank back and no gaps appeared in the earth under them, no crevasse to swallow them up under the alteration of the earth's crust. And in time the rocking stopped and the floor of their world was still, but they would not move, afraid to move a limb for fear of being caught in the earth's mouth.

The noise continued, but began to distinguish itself in parts, and the worst basic element attenuated itself; that terrible crash apart of the atmosphere under the bomb had stopped by now, the atmosphere had parted to admit the ball of radioactivity, had been blown hundreds of miles in every direction and had rushed back to regain its place, disputing that place with the ball of radioactivity, so that there grew up a thousand-mile vortex of cyclonic winds around the hub of the displacement. The cyclone was almost comforting, sounding, whistling, in whatever stood upright, not trees certainly, but tangled steel beams and odd bits of masonry. The sound of these winds came to them in the cellar. Soon they were able to name sounds, and distinguish them from others which they heard, mainly sounds of fire—no sounds of the dying, no human cries at all, no sounds of life. Only the fires and cyclonic winds.

Now they could feel, and hear enough to shout to each other over the fire and wind.

The man tried to stir, to ease his wife's position. He could move his torso so far as the waist or perhaps the hips. Below that, although he was in no pain and not paralyzed, he was immobilized by a heavy weight. He

AFTER THE SIRENS ~ 55

could feel his legs and feet; they were sound and unhurt, but he could not move them. He waited, lying there trying to sort things out, until some sort of ordered thought and some communication was possible, when the noise should lessen sufficiently. He could hear his wife shouting something into the dirt in front of her face and he tried to make it out.

"She slept through it," he heard, "she slept through it," and he couldn't believe it, although it was true. The baby lived and recollected none of the horror.

"She slept through it," screamed the wife idiotically, "she's still asleep." It couldn't be true, he thought, it was impossible, but there was no way to check her statement until they could move about. The baby must have been three feet below the blast and the glow, shielded by a two-and-a-half-foot wall of flesh, his and his wife's, and the additional thickness of layers of woollen clothing. She should certainly have survived, if they had, but how could she have slept through the noise, the awful light, and the rocking? He listened and waited, keeping his head down and his face covered.

Supposing that they had survived the initial blast, as seemed to be the case; there was still the fallout to consider. The likelihood, he thought (he was beginning to be able to think) was that they were already being eaten up by radiation and would soon die of monstrous cancers, or plain, simple leukemia, or rottenness of the cortex. It was miraculous that they had lived through the first shock; they could hardly hope that their luck would hold through the later dangers. He thought that the baby might not have been infected so far, shielded as she was, as he began to wonder how she might be helped to evade death from radiation in the next few days. Let her live a week, he thought, and she may go on living into the next generation, if there is one.

Nothing would be the same in the next generation; there would be few people and fewer laws, the national boundaries would have perished—there would be a new world to invent. Somehow the child must be preserved for that, even if their own lives were to be forfeited immediately. He felt perfectly healthy so far, untouched by any creeping sickness as he lay there, forcing himself and the lives beneath him deeper into their burrow. He began to make plans; there was nothing else for him to do just then.

The noise of the winds had become regular now and the green glow had subsided; the earth was still and they were still together and in the same place, in their cellar, in their home. He thought of his books, his checkbook, his phonograph records, his wife's household appliances. They were gone, of course, which didn't matter. What mattered was that the way they had lived was gone, the whole texture of their habits. The city would be totally uninhabitable. If they were to survive longer, they must get out of the city at once. They would have to decide immediately when they should try to leave the city, and they must keep themselves alive until that time.

"What time is it?" gasped his wife from below him in a tone pitched in almost her normal voice. He was relieved to hear her speak in the commonplace, familiar tone; he had been afraid that hysteria and shock would destroy their personalities all at once. So far they had held together. Later on, when the loss of their whole world sank in, when they appreciated the full extent of their losses, they would run the risk of insanity or, at least, extreme neurotic disturbance. But right now they could converse, calculate, and wait for the threat of madness to appear days, or years, later.

He looked at his watch. "Eight-thirty," he said. Everything had ended in three-and-a-half hours. "Are you all right?" he asked.

"I think so," she said, "I don't feel any pain and the baby's fine. She's warm and she doesn't seem frightened."

He tried to move his legs and was relieved to see that they answered the nervous impulse. He lifted his head fearfully and twisted it around to see behind him. His legs were buried under a pile of loose brick and rubble which grew smaller toward his thighs; his torso was quite uncovered. "I'm all right," he said, beginning to work his legs free; they were undoubtedly badly bruised, but they didn't seem to be crushed or broken; at the worst he might have torn muscles or a bad sprain. He had to be very careful, he reasoned, as he worked at his legs. He might dislodge something and bring the remnant of the house down around them. Very, very slowly he lifted his torso by doing a push-up with his arms. His wife slid out from underneath, pushing the baby in front of her. When she was free she laid the child gently to one side, whispering to her and promising her food. She crawled around to her husband's side and began to push the bricks off his legs.

"Be careful," he whispered. "Take them as they come. Don't be in too much of a hurry."

She nodded, picking out the bricks gingerly, but as fast as she could. Soon he was able to roll over on his back and sit up. By a quarter to ten he was free and they took time to eat and drink. The three of them sat together in a cramped, narrow space under the cellar beams, perhaps six feet high and six or seven feet square. They were getting air from somewhere although it might be deadly air, and there was no smell of gas. He had been afraid that they might be suffocated in their shelter.

"Do you suppose the food's contaminated?" she asked.

"What if it is?" he said. "So are we, just as much as the food. There's nothing to do but risk it. Only be careful what you give the baby."

"How can I tell?"

"I don't know," he said. "Say a prayer and trust in God." He found the flashlight, which had rolled into a corner, and tried it. It worked very well.

"What are we going to do? We can't stay here."

"I don't even know for sure that we can get out," he said, "but we'll try. There should be a window just above us that leads to a crawl-space under the patio. That's one of the reasons why I told you to come here. In any case we'd be wise to stay here for a few hours until the very worst of the fallout is down."

"What'll we do when we get out?"

"Try to get out of town. Get our outer clothes off, get them all off for that matter, and scrub ourselves with water. Maybe we can get to the river."

"Why don't you try the window right now so we can tell whether we can get out?"

"I will as soon as I've finished eating and had a rest. My legs are very sore."

He could hear her voice soften. "Take your time," she said.

When he felt rested, he stood up. He could almost stand erect and with the flashlight was able to find the window quickly. It was level with his face. He piled loose bricks against the wall below it and climbed up on them until the window was level with his chest. Knocking out the screen with the butt of the flashlight, he put his head through and then flashed the light around; there were no obstructions that he could see, and he couldn't smell anything noxious. The patio, being a flat, level space, had evidently been swept clean by the blast without being flattened. They could crawl out of the cellar under the patio, he realized, and then kick a hole in the lath and stucco which skirted it.

He stepped down from the pile of brick and told his wife that they would be able to get out whenever they wished, that the crawl space was clear.

"What time is it?"

"Half-past twelve."

"Should we try it now?"

"I think so," he said. "At first I thought we ought to stay here for a day or two, but now I think we ought to try and get out from under the fallout. We may have to walk a couple of hundred miles."

"We can do it," she said and he felt glad. She had always been able to look unpleasant issues in the face.

He helped her through the cellar window and handed up the baby, who clucked and chuckled when he spoke to her. He pushed the carton of food and the bucket of water after them. Then he climbed up and they inched forward under the patio.

"I hear a motor," said his wife suddenly.

He listened and heard it too.

"Looking for survivors," he said eagerly. "Probably the Army or Civil Defense. Come on."

He swung himself around on his hips and back and kicked out with both feet at the lath and stucco. Three or four kicks did it. His wife went first, inching the baby through the hole. He crawled after her into the daylight; it looked like any other day except that the city was leveled. The sky and the light were the same; everything else was gone. They sat up, muddy, scratched, nervously exhausted, in a ruined flower bed. Not fifty feet away stood an olive-drab truck, the motor running loudly. Men shouted to them.

"Come on, you!" shouted the men in the truck. "Get going!" They stood and ran raggedly to the cab, she holding the child and he their remaining food and water. In the cab was a canvas-sheeted, goggled driver, peering at them through huge eyes. "Get in the back," he ordered. "We've got to get out right away. Too hot." They climbed into the truck and it began to move instantly.

"Army Survival Unit," said a goggled and hooded man in the back of the truck. "Throw away that food and water; it's dangerous. Get your outer clothing off quick. Throw it out!" They obeyed him without thinking, stripping off their loose outer clothes and dropping them out of the truck.

"You're the only ones we've found in a hundred city blocks," said the soldier. "Did you know the war's over? There's a truce."

"Who won?"

"Over in half an hour," he said, "and nobody won."

"What are you going to do with us?"

"Drop you at a check-out point forty miles from here. Give you the scrub-down treatment, wash off the fallout. Medical check for radiation sickness. Clean clothes. Then we send you on your way to a refugee station."

"How many died?"

"Everybody in the area. Almost no exceptions. You're a statistic, that's what you are. Must have been a fluke of the blast."

"Will we live?"

"Sure you will. You're living now, aren't you?"

"I guess so," he said.

"Sure you'll live! Maybe not too long. But everybody else is dead! And you'll be taken care of." He fell silent.

They looked at each other, determined to live as long as they could. The wife cuddled the child close against her thin silk blouse. For a long time they jolted along over rocks and broken pavement without speaking. When the pavement smoothed out the husband knew that they must be out of the disaster area. In a few more minutes they were out of immediate danger; they had reached the check-out point. It was a quarter to three in the afternoon.

"Out you get," said the soldier. "We've got to go back." They climbed out of the truck and he handed down the baby. "You're all right now," he said. "Good luck."

"Good-bye," they said.

The truck turned about and drove away and they turned silently, hand in hand, and walked toward the medical tents. They were the seventh, eighth, and ninth living persons to be brought there after the sirens.

CAMROSE LUTHERAN COLLEGE
Library

MARGARET LAURENCE

Horses of the Night

Margaret Laurence was born in Neepawa, Manitoba, in 1926, and attended the University of Manitoba. In 1950 she went to Africa and lived in Somaliland and Ghana. She has since lived in British Columbia and England. In 1969-70 she spent the academic year as writer-in-residence at the University of Toronto. She has written both short stories and novels, one of which, A Jest of God, *won the Governor General's Award for Fiction in 1966.*

I never knew I had distant cousins who lived up north, until Chris came down to Manawaka to go to high school. My mother said he belonged to a large family, relatives of ours, who lived at Shallow Creek, up north. I was six, and Shallow Creek seemed immeasurably far, part of a legendary winter country where no leaves grow and where the breath of seals and polar bears snuffled out steamily and turned to ice.

"Could plain people live there?" I asked my mother, meaning people who were not Eskimos. "Could there be a farm?"

"How do you mean?" she said, puzzled. "I told you. That's where they live. On the farm. Uncle Wilf—that was Chris's father, who died a few years back—he got the place as a homestead, donkey's years ago."

"But how could they grow anything? I thought you said it was up north."

"Mercy," my mother said, laughing, "it's not *that* far north, Vanessa. It's about a hundred miles beyond Galloping Mountain. You be nice to Chris, now, won't you? And don't go asking him a whole lot of questions the minute he steps inside the door."

How little my mother knew of me, I thought. Chris had been fifteen. He could be expected to feel only scorn towards me. I detested the fact that I was so young. I did not think I would be able to say anything at all to him.

"What if I don't like him?"

"What if you don't?" my mother responded sharply. "You're to watch your manners, and no acting up, understand? It's going to be quite difficult enough without that."

"Why does he have to come here, anyway?" I demanded crossly. "Why can't he go to school where he lives?"

"Because there isn't any high school up there," my mother said. "I hope he gets on well here, and isn't too homesick. Three years is a long time. It's very good of your grandfather to let him stay at the Brick House."

She said this last accusingly, as though she suspected I might be thinking differently. But I had not thought of it one way or another. We were all having dinner at the Brick House because of Chris's arrival. It was the end of August, and sweltering. My grandfather's house looked huge and cool from the outside, the high low-sweeping spruce trees shutting out the sun with their dusky out-fanned branches. But inside it wasn't cool at all. The woodstove in the kitchen was going full blast, and the whole place smelled of roasting meat.

Grandmother Connor was wearing a large mauve apron. I thought it was a nicer colour than the dark bottle-green of her dress, but she believed in wearing sombre shades lest the spirit give way to vanity, which in her case was certainly not much of a risk. The apron came up over her shapeless bosom and obscured part of her cameo brooch, the only jewellery she ever wore, with its portrait of a fiercely bearded man whom I imagined to be either Moses or God.

"Isn't it nearly time for them to be getting here, Beth?" Grandmother Connor asked.

"Train's not due until six," my mother said. "It's barely five-thirty, now. Has Father gone to the station already?"

"He went an hour ago," my grandmother said.

"He would," my mother commented.

"Now, now, Beth," my grandmother cautioned and soothed.

At last the front screen door was hurled open and Grandfather Connor strode into the house, followed by a tall lanky boy. Chris was wearing a white shirt, a tie, grey trousers. I thought, unwillingly, that he looked handsome. His face was angular, the bones showing through the brown skin. His grey eyes were slightly slanted, and his hair was the colour of couchgrass at the end of summer when it has been bleached to a light yellow by the sun. I had not planned to like him, not even a little, but somehow I wanted to defend him when I heard what my mother whispered to my grandmother before they went into the front hall.

"Heavens, look at the shirt and trousers—must've been his father's, the poor kid."

I shot out into the hall ahead of my mother, and then stopped and stood there.

"Hi, Vanessa," Chris said.

"How come you knew who I was?" I asked.

"Well, I knew your mother and dad only had one of a family, so I figured you must be her," he replied, grinning.

The way he spoke did not make me feel I had blundered. My mother greeted him warmly but shyly. Not knowing if she were expected to kiss him or to shake hands, she finally did neither. Grandmother Connor, however, had no doubts. She kissed him on both cheeks and then held him at arm's length to have a proper look at him.

"Bless the child," she said.

Coming from anyone else, this remark would have sounded ridiculous, especially as Chris was at least a head taller. My grandmother was the only person I have every known who could say such things without appearing false.

"I'll show you your room, Chris," my mother offered.

Grandfather Connor, who had been standing in the living room doorway in absolute silence, looking as granite as a statue in the cemetery, now followed Grandmother out to the kitchen.

"Train was forty minutes late," he said weightily.

"What a shame," my grandmother said. "But I thought it wasn't due until six, Timothy."

"Six!" my grandfather cried. "That's the mainline train. The local's due at five-twenty."

This was not correct, as both my grandmother and I knew. But neither of us contradicted him.

"What on earth are you cooking a roast for, on a night like this?" my grandfather went on. "A person could fry an egg on the sidewalk, it's that hot. Potato salad would've gone down well."

Privately I agreed with this opinion, but I could never permit myself to acknowledge agreement with him on anything. I automatically and emotionally sided with Grandmother in all issues, not because she was inevitably right but because I loved her.

"It's not a roast," my grandmother said mildly. "It's mock-duck. The stove's only been going for an hour. I thought the boy would be hungry after the trip."

My mother and Chris had come downstairs and were now in the living room. I could hear them there, talking awkwardly, with pauses.

"Potato salad," my grandfather declaimed, "would've been plenty good enough. He'd have been lucky to get it, if you ask me anything. Wilf's family hasn't got two cents to rub together. It's me that's paying for the boy's keep."

The thought of Chris in the living room, and my mother unable to explain, was too much for me. I sidled over to the kitchen door, intending to close it. But my grandmother stopped me.

"No," she said, with unexpected firmness. "Leave it open, Vanessa."

I could hardly believe it. Surely she couldn't want Chris to hear? She herself was always able to move with equanimity through a hurricane because she believed that a mighty fortress was her God. But the rest of us were not like that, and usually she did her best to protect us. At the time I felt only bewilderment. I think now that she must have realised Chris would have to learn the Brick House sooner or later, and he might as well start right away.

I had to go into the living room. I had to know how Chris would take my grandfather. Would he, as I hoped, be angry and perhaps even speak out? Or would he, meekly, only be embarrassed?

"Wilf wasn't much good, even as a young man," Grandfather Connor was trumpeting. "Nobody but a simpleton would've taken up a homestead in a place like that. Anybody could've told him that land's no use for a thing except hay."

Was he going to remind us again how well he had done in the

hardware business? Nobody had ever given him a hand, he used to tell me. I am sure he believed that this was true. Perhaps it even was true.

"If the boy takes after his father, it's a poor lookout for him," my grandfather continued.

I felt the old rage of helplessness. But as for Chris—he gave no sign of feeling anything. He was sitting on the big wing-backed sofa that curled into the bay window like a black and giant seashell. He began to talk to me, quite easily, just as though he had not heard a word my grandfather was saying.

This method proved to be the one Chris always used in any dealings with my grandfather. When the bludgeoning words came, which was often, Chris never seemed, like myself, to be holding back with a terrible strained force for fear of letting go and speaking out and having the known world unimaginably fall to pieces. He would not argue or defend himself, but he did not apologise, either. He simply appeared to be absent, elsewhere. Fortunately there was very little need for response, for when Grandfather Connor pointed out your shortcomings, you were not expected to reply.

But this aspect of Chris was one which I noticed only vaguely at the time. What won me was that he would talk to me and wisecrack as though I were his same age. He was—although I didn't know the phrase then—a respecter of persons.

On the rare evenings when my parents went out, Chris would come over to mind me. These were the best times, for often when he was supposed to be doing his homework, he would make fantastic objects for my amusement, or his own—pipecleaners twisted into the shape of wildly prancing midget men, or an old set of Christmas-tree lights fixed onto a puppet theatre with a red velvet curtain that really pulled. He had skill in making miniature things of all kinds. Once for my birthday he gave me a leather saddle no bigger than a matchbox, which he had sewn himself, complete in every detail, stirrups and horn, with the criss-cross lines that were the brand name of his ranch, he said, explaining it was a reference to his own name.

"Can I go to Shallow Creek sometime?" I asked one evening.

"Sure. Some summer holidays, maybe. I've got a sister about your age. The others are all grownup."

I did not want to hear. His sisters—for Chris was the only boy —did not exist for me, not even as photographs, because I did not want them to exist. I wanted him to belong only here. Shallow Creek existed, though, no longer filled with ice mountains in my mind but as some beckoning country beyond all ordinary considerations.

"Tell me what it's like there, Chris."

"My gosh, Vanessa, I've told you before, about a thousand times."

"You never told me what your house is like."

"Didn't I? Oh well—it's made out of trees grown right there beside the lake."

"Made out of trees? Gee. Really?"

I could see it. The trees were still growing, and the leaves were firmly and greenly on them. The branches had been coaxed into formations of towers and high-up nests where you could look out and see for a hundred miles or more.

"That lake, you know," Chris said. "It's more like an inland sea. It goes on for ever and ever amen, that's how it looks. And you know what? Millions of years ago, before there were any human beings at all, that lake was full of water monsters. All different kinds of dinosaurs. Then they all died off. Nobody knows for sure why. Imagine them—all those huge creatures, with necks like snakes, and some of them had hackles on their heads, like a rooster's comb only very tough, like hard leather. Some guys from Winnipeg came up a few years back, there, and dug up dinosaur bones, and they found footprints in the rocks."

"Footprints in the *rocks*?"

"The rocks were mud, see, when the dinosaurs went trampling through, but after trillions of years the mud turned into stone and there were these mighty footprints with the claws still showing. Amazing, eh?"

I could only nod, fascinated and horrified. Imagine going swimming in those waters. What if one of the creatures had lived on?

"Tell me about the horses," I said.

"Oh, them. Well, we've got these two riding horses. Duchess and Firefly. I raised them, and you should see them. Really sleek, know what I mean? I bet I could make racers out of them."

He missed the horses, I thought with selfish satisfaction, more than he missed his family. I could visualise the pair, one sorrel and one black, swifting through all the meadows of summer.

"When can I go, Chris?"

"Well, we'll have to see. After I get through high school, I won't be at Shallow Creek much."

"Why not?"

"Because," Chris said, "what I am going to be is an engineer, civil engineer. You ever seen a really big bridge, Vanessa? Well, I haven't either, but I've seen pictures. You take the Golden Gate Bridge in San Francisco, now. Terrifically high—all those thin ribs of steel, joined together to go across this very wide stretch of water. It doesn't seem possible, but it's there. That's what engineers do. Imagine doing something like that, eh?"

I could not imagine it. It was beyond me.

"Where will you go?" I asked. I did not want to think of his going anywhere.

"Winnipeg, to college," he said with assurance.

The Depression did not get better, as everyone had been saying it would. It got worse, and so did the drought. That part of the prairies where we lived was never dustbowl country. The farms around Manawaka never had a total crop failure, and afterwards, when the drought was over, people used to remark on this fact proudly, as though it had been due to some virtue or special status, like the Children of Israel being afflicted by Jehovah but never in real danger of annihilation. But although Manawaka never knew the worst, what it knew was bad enough. Or so I learned later. At the time I saw none of it. For me, the Depression and drought were external and abstract, malevolent gods whose names I secretly learned although they were concealed from me, and whose evil I sensed only superstitiously, knowing they threatened us but not how or why. What I really saw was only what went on in our family.

"He's done quite well all through, despite everything," my mother said. She sighed, and I knew she was talking about Chris.

"I know," my father said. "We've been over all this before, Beth. But quite good just isn't good enough. Even supposing he managed to get a scholarship, which isn't likely, it's only tuition and books. What about room and board? Who's going to pay for that? Your father?"

"I see I shouldn't have brought up the subject at all," my mother said in an aloof voice.

"I'm sorry," my father said impatiently. "But you know, yourself, he's the only one who might possibly—"

"I can't bring myself to ask Father about it, Ewen. I simply cannot do it."

"There wouldn't be much point in asking," my father said, "when the answer is a foregone conclusion. He feels he's done his share, and actually, you know, Beth, he has, too. Three years, after all. He may not have done it gracefully, but he's done it."

We were sitting in the living room, and it was evening. My father was slouched in the grey armchair that was always his. My mother was slenderly straight-backed in the blue chair in which nobody else ever sat. I was sitting on the footstool, beige needlepoint with mathematical roses, to which I had staked my own claim. This seating arrangement was obscurely satisfactory to me, perhaps because predictable, like the three bears. I was pretending to be colouring into a scribbler on my knee, and from time to time my lethargic purple crayon added a feather to an outlandish swan. To speak would be to invite dismissal. But their words forced questions in my head.

"Chris isn't going away, is he?"

My mother swooped, shocked at her own neglect.

"My heavens—are you still up, Vanessa? What am I thinking of?"

"Where is Chris going?"

"We're not sure yet," my mother evaded, chivvying me up the stairs. "We'll see."

He would not go, I thought. Something would happen, miraculously, to prevent him. He would remain, with his long loping walk and his half-slanted grey eyes and his talk that never excluded me. He would stay right here. And soon, because I desperately wanted to, and because every day mercifully made me older, quite soon I would be able to reply with such a lightning burst of knowingness that it would astound him, when he spoke of the space or was it some black sky that never ended anywhere beyond this earth. Then I would not be innerly belittled for being unable to figure out what he would best like to hear. At that good and imagined time, I would not any longer be limited. I would not any longer be young.

I was nine when Chris left Manawaka. The day before he was due to go, I knocked on the door of his room in the Brick House.

"Come in," Chris said. "I'm packing. Do you know how to fold socks, Vanessa?"

"Sure. Of course."

"Well, get folding on that bunch there, then."

I had come to say goodbye, but I did not want to say it yet. I got to work on the socks. I did not intend to speak about the matter of college, but the knowledge that I must not speak about it made me uneasy. I was afraid I would blurt out a reference to it in my anxiety not to. My mother had said, "He's taken it amazingly well—he doesn't even mention it, so we mustn't either."

"Tomorrow night you'll be in Shallow Creek," I ventured.

"Yeh." He did not look up. He went on stuffing clothes and books into his suitcase.

"I bet you'll be glad to see the horses, eh?" I wanted him to say he didn't care about the horses any more and that he would rather stay here.

"It'll be good to see them again," Chris said. "Mind handing over those socks now, Vanessa? I think I can just squash them in at the side here. Thanks. Hey, look at that, will you? Everything's in. Am I an expert packer or am I an expert packer?"

I sat on his suitcase for him so it would close, and then he tied a piece of rope around it because the lock wouldn't lock.

"Ever thought what it would be like to be a traveller, Vanessa?" he asked.

I thought of Richard Halliburton, taking an elephant over the Alps and swimming illicitly in the Taj Mahal lily pool by moonlight.

"It would be keen," I said, because this was the word Chris used to describe the best possible. "That's what I'm going to do someday."

He did not say, as for a moment I feared he might, that girls could not be travellers.

"Why not?" he said. "Sure you will, if you really want to. I got this theory, see, that anybody can do anything at all, anything, if they really set their minds to it. But you have to have this total concentration. You have to focus on it with your whole mental powers, and not let it slip away by forgetting to hold it in your mind. If you hold it in your mind, like, then it's real, see? You take most people, now. They can't concentrate worth a darn."

"Do you think I can?" I enquired eagerly, believing that this was what he was talking about.

"What?" he said. "Oh—sure. Sure I think you can. Naturally."

Chris did not write after he left Manawaka. About a month later we had a letter from his mother. He was not at Shallow Creek. He had not gone back. He had got off the northbound train at the first stop after Manawaka, cashed in his ticket, and thumbed a lift with a truck to Winnipeg. He had written to his mother from there, but had given no address. She had not heard from him since. My mother read Aunt Tess's letter aloud to my father. She was too upset to care whether I was listening or not.

"I can't think what possessed him, Ewen. He never seemed irresponsible. What if something should happen to him? What if he's broke? What do you think we should do?"

"What can we do? He's nearly eighteen. What he does is his business. Simmer down, Beth, and let's decide what we're going to tell your father."

"Oh Lord," my mother said. "There's that to consider, of course."

I went out without either of them noticing. I walked to the hill at the edge of the town, and down into the valley where the scrub oak and poplar grew almost to the banks of the Wachakwa River. I found the oak where we had gone last autumn, in a gang, to smoke cigarettes made of dried leaves and pieces of newspaper. I climbed to the lowest branch and stayed there for a while.

I was not consciously thinking about Chris. I was not thinking of anything. But when at last I cried, I felt relieved afterwards and could go home again.

Chris departed from my mind, after that, with a quickness that was due to the other things that happened. My Aunt Edna, who was a secretary in Winnipeg, returned to Manawaka to live because the insurance company cut down on staff and she could not find another job. I was intensely excited and jubilant about her return, and could not see why my mother seemed the opposite, even though she was as fond of Aunt Edna as I was. Then my brother Roderick was born, and that same year Grandmother Connor died. The strangeness, the unbelievability, of both these events took up all of me.

When I was eleven, almost two years after Chris had left, he came back without warning. I came home from school and found him sitting in our living room. I could not accept that I had nearly forgotten him until this instant. Now that he was present, and real again, I felt I had betrayed him by not thinking of him more.

He was wearing a navy-blue serge suit. I was old enough now to notice that it was a cheap one and had been worn a considerable time. Otherwise, he looked the same, the same smile, the same knife-boned face with no flesh to speak of, the same unresting eyes.

"How come you're here?" I cried. "Where have you been, Chris?"

"I'm a traveller," he said. "Remember?"

He was a traveller all right. One meaning of the word *traveller* in our part of the world, was a travelling salesman. Chris was selling vacuum cleaners. That evening he brought out his line and showed us. He went through his spiel for our benefit, so we could hear how it sounded.

"Now look, Beth," he said, turning the appliance on and speaking loudly above its moaning roar, "see how it brightens up this old rug of yours? Keen, eh?

"Wonderful," my mother laughed. "Only we can't afford one."

"Oh well—" Chris said quickly, "I'm not trying to sell one to you. I'm only showing you. Listen, I've only been in this job a month, but I figure this is really a going thing. I mean, it's obvious, isn't it? You take all those old wire carpet-beaters of yours, Beth. You could kill yourself over them and your carpet isn't going to look one-tenth as good as it does with this."

"Look, I don't want to seem—" my father put in, "but, hell, they're not exactly a new invention, and we're not the only ones who can't afford—"

"This is a pretty big outfit, you know?" Chris insisted. "Listen, I don't plan to stay, Ewen. But a guy could work at it for a year or so, and save —right? Lots of guys work their way through university like that."

I needed to say something really penetrating, something that would show him I knew the passionate truth of his conviction.

"I bet—" I said, "I bet you'll sell a thousand, Chris."

Two years ago, this statement would have seemed self-evident, unquestionable. Yet now, when I had spoken, I knew that I did not believe it.

The next time Chris visited Manawaka, he was selling magazines. He had the statistics worked out. If every sixth person in town would get a subscription to *Country Guide*, he could make a hundred dollars in a month. We didn't learn how he got on. He didn't stay in Manawaka a full month. When he turned up again, it was winter. Aunt Edna phoned.

"Nessa? Listen, kiddo, tell your mother she's to come down if it's humanly possible. Chris is here, and Father's having fits."

So in five minutes we were scurrying through the snow, my mother and I, with our overshoes not even properly done up and our feet getting wet. We need not have worried. By the time we reached the Brick House, Grandfather Connor had retired to the basement, where he sat in the rocking chair beside the furnace, making occasional black pronouncements like a subterranean oracle. These loud utterances made my mother and aunt wince, but Chris didn't seem to notice any more than he ever had. He was engrossed in telling us about the mechanism he was holding. It had a cranker handle like an old-fashioned sewing machine.

"You attach the ball of wool here, see? Then you set this little switch here, and adjust this lever, and you're away to the races. Neat, eh?"

It was a knitting machine. Chris showed us the finished products. The men's socks he had made were coarse wool, one pair in grey heather and another in maroon. I was impressed.

"Gee—can I do it, Chris?"

"Sure. Look, you just grab hold of the handle right here."

"Where did you get it?" my mother asked.

"I've rented it. The way I figure it, Beth, I can sell these things at about half the price you'd pay in a store, and they're better quality."

"Who are you going to sell them to?" Aunt Edna enquired.

"You take all these guys who do outside work—they need heavy socks all year round, not just in winter. I think this thing could be quite a gold mine."

"Before I forget," my mother said, "how's your mother and the family keeping?"

"They're okay," Chris said in a restrained voice. "They're not short of hands, if that's what you mean, Beth. My sisters have their husbands there."

Then he grinned, casting away the previous moment, and dug into his suitcase.

"Hey, I haven't shown you—these are for you, Vanessa, and this pair is for Roddie."

My socks were cherry-coloured. The very small ones for my brother were turquoise.

Chris only stayed until after dinner, and then he went away again.

After my father died, the whole order of life was torn. Nothing was known or predictable any longer. For months I lived almost entirely within myself, so when my mother told me one day that Chris couldn't find any work at all because there were no jobs and so he had gone back to Shallow Creek to stay, it made scarcely any impression on me. But that summer, my mother decided I ought to go away for a holiday. She hoped it might take my mind off my father's death. What, if anything, was going to take her mind off his death, she did not say.

"Would you like to go to Shallow Creek for a week or so?" she asked me. "I could write to Chris's mother."

Then I remembered, all in a torrent, the way I had imagined it once, when he used to tell me about it—the house fashioned of living trees, the lake like a sea where monsters had dwelt, the grass that shone like green wavering light while the horses flew in the splendour of their pride.

"Yes," I said. "Write to her."

The railway did not go through Shallow Creek, but Chris met me at Challoner's Crossing. He looked different, not only thinner, but—what was it? Then I saw that it was the fact that his face and neck were tanned red-brown, and he was wearing denims, farm pants, and a blue plaid shirt open at the neck. I liked him like this. Perhaps the change was not so much in him as in myself, now that I was thirteen. He looked masculine in a way I had not been aware of, before.

"C'mon, kid," he said. "The limousine's over here."

It was a wagon and two horses, which was what I had expected, but the nature of each was not what I had expected. The wagon was a long and clumsy one, made of heavy planking, and the horses were both plough horses, thick in the legs, and badly matched as a team. The mare was short and stout, matronly. The gelding was very tall and gaunt, and he limped.

"Allow me to introduce you," Chris said. "Floss—Trooper—this is Vanessa."

He did not mention the other horses, Duchess and Firefly, and neither did I, not all the fortnight I was there. I guess I had known for some years now, without realising it, that the pair had only ever existed in some other dimension.

Shallow Creek wasn't a town. It was merely a name on a map. There was a grade school a few miles away, but that was all. They had to go to Challoner's Crossing for their groceries. We reached the farm, and Chris steered me through the crowd of aimless cows and wolfish dogs in the yard, while I flinched with panic.

It was perfectly true that the house was made out of trees. It was a fair-sized but elderly shack, made out of poplar poles and chinked with mud. There was an upstairs, which was not so usual around here, with three bedrooms, one of which I was to share with Chris's sister, Jeannie, who was slightly younger than I, a pallid-eyed girl who was either too shy to talk or who had nothing to say. I never discovered which, because I was so reticent with her myself, wanting to push her away, not to recognise her, and at the same time experiencing a shocked remorse at my own unacceptable feelings.

Aunt Tess, Chris's mother, was severe in manner and yet wanting to be kind, worrying over it, making tentative overtures which were either ignored or repelled by her older daughters and their monosyllabic husbands. Youngsters swam in and out of the house like shoals of nameless fishes. I could not see how so many people could live here, under the one roof, but then I learned they didn't. The married daughters had their own dwelling places, nearby, but some kind of communal life was maintained. They wrangled endlessly but they never left one another alone, not even for a day.

Chris took no part at all, none. When he spoke, it was usually to the children, and they would often follow him around the yard or to the barn, not pestering but just trailing along in clusters of three or four. He never told them to go away. I liked him for this, but it bothered me, too. I wished he would return his sisters' bickering for once, or tell them to clear out, or even yell at one of the kids. But he never did. He closed himself off from squabbling voices just as he used to do with Grandfather Connor's spearing words.

The house had no screens on the doors or windows, and at meal times the flies were so numerous you could hardly see the food for the iridescent-winged blue-black bodies squirming all over it. Nobody noticed my squeamishness except Chris, and he was the only one from whom I really wanted to conceal it.

"Fan with your hand," he murmured.

"It's okay," I said quickly.

For the first time in all the years we had known each other, we could not look the other in the eye. Around the table, the children stabbed and snivelled, until Chris's oldest sister, driven frantic, shrieked, *Shut up shut up shut up.* Chris began asking me about Manawaka then, as though nothing were going on around him.

They were due to begin haying, and Chris announced that he was going to camp out in the bluff near the hayfields. To save himself the long drive in the wagon each morning, he explained, but I felt this wasn't the real reason.

"Can I go, too?" I begged. I could not bear the thought of living in the house with all the others who were not known to me, and Chris not here.

"Well, I don't know—"

"Please. Please, Chris. I won't be any trouble. I promise."

Finally he agreed. We drove out in the big hayrack, its slatted sides rattling, its old wheels jolting metallically. The road was narrow and dirt, and around it the low bushes grew, wild rose and blueberry and wolf willow with silver leaves. Sometimes we would come to a bluff of pale-leaved poplar trees, and once a red-winged blackbird flew up out of the branches and into the hot dusty blue of the sky.

Then we were there. The hayfields lay beside the lake. It was my first view of the water which had spawned saurian giants so long ago. Chris drove the hayrack through the fields of high coarse grass and on down almost to the lake's edge, where there was no shore but only the green rushes like floating meadows in which the water birds nested. Beyond the undulating reeds the open lake stretched, deep, green-grey, out and out, beyond sight.

No human word could be applied. The lake was not lonely or untamed. These words relate to people, and there was nothing of people here. There was no feeling about the place. It existed in some world in which man was not yet born. I looked at the grey reaches of it and felt threatened. It was like the view of God which I had held since my father's death. Distant, indestructible, totally indifferent.

Chris had jumped down off the hayrack.

"We're not going to camp *here*, are we?" I asked and pleaded.

"No. I just want to let the horses drink. We'll camp up there in the bluff."

I looked. "It's still pretty close to the lake, isn't it?"

"Don't worry," Chris said, laughing. "You won't get your feet wet."

"I didn't mean that."

Chris looked at me.

"I know you didn't," he said. "But let's learn to be a little tougher, and not let on, eh? It's necessary."

Chris worked through the hours of sun, while I lay on the half-formed stack of hay and looked up at the sky. The blue air trembled and spun with the heat haze, and the hay on which I was lying held the scents of grass and dust and wild mint.

In the evening, Chris took the horses to the lake again, and then he drove the hayrack to the edge of the bluff and we spread out our blankets underneath it. He made a fire and we had coffee and a tin of stew, and then we went to bed. We did not wash, and we slept in our clothes. It was only when I was curled up uncomfortably with the itching blanket around me that I felt a sense of unfamiliarity at being here, with Chris only three feet away, a self-consciousness I would not have felt even the year before. I do not think he felt this sexual strangeness. If he wanted me not to be a child—and he did —it was not with the wish that I would be a woman. It was something else.

"Are you asleep, Vanessa?" he asked.

"No. I think I'm lying on a tree root."

"Well, shift yourself, then," he said. "Listen, kid, I never said anything before, because I didn't really know what to say, but—you know how I felt about your dad dying, and that, don't you?"

"Yes," I said chokingly. "It's okay. I know."

"I used to talk with Ewen sometimes. He didn't see what I was driving at, mostly, but he'd always listen, you know? You don't find many guys like that."

We were both silent for a while.

"Look," Chris said finally. "Ever noticed how much brighter the stars are when you're completely away from any houses? Even the lamps up at the farm, there, make enough of a glow to keep you from seeing properly like you can out here. What do they make you think about, Vanessa?"

"Well—"

"I guess most people don't give them much thought at all, except maybe to say—*very pretty*—or like that. But the point is, they aren't like that. The stars and planets, in themselves, are just not like that, not *pretty*, for heaven's sake. They're gigantic—some of them burning—imagine those worlds tearing through space and made of pure fire. Or the ones that are absolutely dead—just rock or ice and no warmth in them. There must be some, though, that have living creatures. You wonder what *they* could look like, and what they feel. We won't ever get to know. But somebody will know, someday. I really believe that. Do you ever think about this kind of thing at all?"

He was twenty-one. The distance between us was still too great. For years I had wanted to be older so I might talk with him, but now I felt unready.

"Sometimes," I said, hesitantly, making it sound like *Never*.

"People usually say there must be a God," Chris went on, "because otherwise how did the universe get here? But that's ridiculous. If the stars and planets go on to infinity, they could have existed forever, for no reason at all. Maybe they weren't ever created. Look—what's the alternative? To believe in a God who is brutal. What else could He be? You've only got to look anywhere around you. It would be an insult to Him to believe in a God like that. Most people don't like talking about this kind of thing—it embarrasses them, you know? Or else they're not interested. I don't mind. I can always think about things myself. You don't actually need anyone to talk to. But about God, though—if there's a war, like it looks there will be, would people claim that was planned? What kind of a God would pull a trick like that? And yet, you know, plenty of guys would think it was a godsend, and who's to say they're wrong? It would be a job, and you'd get around and see places."

He paused, as though waiting for me to say something. When I did not, he resumed.

"Ewen told me about the last war, once. He hardly ever talked about it, but this once he told me about seeing the horses into the mud, actually going under, you know? And the way their eyes looked when they realised they weren't going to get out. Ever seen horses' eyes when they're afraid, I mean really berserk with fear, like in a bush-fire? Ewen said a guy tended to concentrate on the horses because he didn't dare think what was happening to the men. Including himself. Do you ever listen to the news at all, Vanessa?"

"I—"

I could only feel how foolish I must sound, still unable to reply as I would have wanted, comprehendingly. I felt I had failed myself utterly. I could not speak even the things I knew. As for the other things, the things I did not know, I resented Chris's facing me with them. I took refuge in pretending to be asleep, and after a while Chris stopped talking.

Chris left Shallow Creek some months after the war began, and joined the Army. After his basic training he was sent to England. We did not hear from him until about a year later, when a letter arrived for me.

"Vanessa—what's wrong?" my mother asked.

"Nothing."

"Don't fib," she said firmly. "What did Chris say in his letter, honey?"

"Oh—not much."

She gave me a curious look and then she went away. She would never have demanded to see the letter. I did not show it to her and she did not ask about it again.

Six months later my mother heard from Aunt Tess. Chris had been sent home from England and discharged from the Army because of a mental breakdown. He was now in the provincial mental hospital and they did not know how long he would have to remain there. He had been violent, before, but now he was not violent. He was, the doctors had told his mother, passive.

Violent. I could not associate the word with Chris, who had been so much the reverse. I could not bear to consider what anguish must have catapulted him into that even greater anguish. But the way he was now seemed almost worse. How might he be? Sitting quite still, wearing the hospital's grey dressing-gown, the animation gone from his face?

My mother cared about him a great deal, but her immediate thought was not for him.

"When I think of you, going up to Shallow Creek that time," she said, "and going out camping with him, and what might have happened—"

I, also, was thinking of what might have happened. But we were not thinking of the same thing. For the first time I recognised, at least a little, the dimensions of his need to talk that night. He must have understood perfectly well how impossible it would be, with a thirteen-year-old. But there was no one else. All his life's choices had grown narrower and narrower. He had been forced to return to the alien lake of home, and when finally he saw a means of getting away, it could only be into a turmoil which appalled him and which he dreaded even more than he knew. I had listened to his words, but I had not really heard them, not until now. It would not have made much difference to what happened, but I wished it were not too late to let him know.

Once when I was on holiday from college, my mother got me to help her clean out the attic. We sifted through boxes full of junk, old clothes, schoolbooks, bric-a-brac that once had been treasures. In one of the boxes I found the miniature saddle that Chris had made for me a long time ago.

"Have you heard anything recently?" I asked, ashamed that I had not asked sooner.

She glanced up at me. "Just the same. It's always the same. They don't think there will be much improvement."

Then she turned away.

"He always used to seem so—hopeful. Even when there was really nothing to be hopeful about. That's what I find so strange. He *seemed* hopeful, didn't you think?"

"Maybe it wasn't hope," I said.

"How do you mean?"

I wasn't certain myself. I was thinking of all the schemes he'd had, the ones that couldn't possibly have worked, the unreal solutions to which he'd clung because there were no others, the brave and useless strokes of fantasy against a depression that was both the world's and his own.

"I don't know," I said. "I just think things were always more difficult for him than he let on, that's all. Remember that letter?"

"Yes."

"Well—what it said was that they could force his body to march and even to kill, but what they didn't know was that he'd fooled them. He didn't live inside it any more."

"Oh Vanessa—" my mother said. "You must have suspected right then."

"Yes, but—"

I could not go on, could not say that the letter seemed only the final heartbreaking extension of that way he'd always had of distancing himself from the absolute unbearability of battle.

I picked up the tiny saddle and turned it over in my hand.

"Look. His brand, the name of his ranch. The Criss-Cross."

"What ranch?" my mother said, bewildered.

"The one where he kept his racing horses. Duchess and Firefly."

Some words came into my head, a single line from a poem I had once heard. I knew it referred to a lover who did not want the morning to come, but to me it had another meaning, a different relevance.

Slowly, slowly, horses of the night—

The night must move like this for him, slowly, all through the days and nights. I could not know whether the land he journeyed through was inhabited by terrors, the old monster-kings of the lake, or whether he had discovered at last a way for himself to make the necessary dream perpetual.

I put the saddle away once more, gently and ruthlessly, back into the cardboard box.

NORMAN LEVINE

A True Story

Born in Ottawa in 1924, Norman Levine was educated at McGill University. He served with the R.C.A.F. in the Second World War and since 1949 has spent most of his time in England. He has written a novel entitled From A Seaside Town, *and two collections of short stories,* One Way Ticket *(1961), and* I Don't Want To Know Anyone Too Well *(1971). In 1965-66 he was writer-in-residence at the University of New Brunswick.*

I got into Riverside as the first grey light of the dawn came. It was too early to go to the address I had. So I walked around the place trying to find somewhere open for a cup of coffee. There was nothing. Just this river that went through the place with sloping muddy banks. You could smell the mud. And empty streets with lovely names like Gay and Joy.

Shortly after eight a small café opened in the town square and I went in. A woman was on her hands and knees washing the floor. She went behind the counter and from a steaming urn gave me some weak coffee in a glass. I sat by the wall radiator with my hands around the glass of coffee and tried to get some warmth in me.

At nine I took a taxi across the bridge and up a hill to what looked like a suburb. But it was deceptive. For the suburb extended only to the depth of one street. Behind it lay fields, as far as the horizon. The taxi driver found the address and I went down a country road to a detached house that had its top overhanging the bottom.

Within minutes of meeting my landlady—a small woman but bright, like a bird—she told me she was a widow ("not bad for fifty-four") that her relations were in Australia and she was thinking of going there herself. I had a small kitchen, a bedroom, and a sitting-room above her. It all looked new, especially the floors which were highly polished. Outside the window there was a nice looking tree with yellow green leaves, a field with apple trees. And on the road that I had come on I saw a girl in a light raincoat, a whippet was beside her. I watched until the road turned and the girl and the dog disappeared. Then I began to unpack.

The widow said she was pleased that I was a schoolmaster. They thought a great deal of the man I was replacing. She began to tell me useful tips about Riverside: how to get to the post-office, the school, the Palace Hotel.

I went out hoping to see the girl with the whippet.

I didn't see her until the weekend when I was out walking on the country road. We both had a good look at each other. She was tall, around five foot eight, with short blonde hair, a broad face, but it looked very white. I thought she had anaemia.

On Monday, I got up early and walked into Riverside. I hadn't realized how wealthy it was. Street after street of large wooden houses, painted mostly white. Squirrels on the lawns, the sidewalks, the trees. I came to one of the two main streets. The stores were still closed. Only by the drugstore was a neon sign working, telling the time and the temperature. I went through an empty park with flower beds and children's swings. And past the park was the school. A brick building with white windows. It stood on high ground and on its side were fields that went down to the river.

In the staff room I was introduced to the other masters. All were wearing black academic gowns except myself and the new biology master, a New Zealander, who was also starting this term. He was soft-spoken, wore glasses, and kept to himself. But once when we had a free period and we were alone in the staff room he told me that he believed in reincarnation. He was sure he was going to come back in some other form.

I had the first and the last years in English. The older ones were already set in their ways. I don't think it mattered who was there in front of them. But the young ones were different. I set them an essay to write. When I got their books back, I was surprised to see how old fashioned was their use of language. They spoke like boys of their age. But they wrote in such an archaic way that anyone would think they were brought up on bad Victorian novels. I decided to try and break this. For their next essay I told them to walk outside where they lived, with a watch, and write down what they saw and when they saw it.

The change in their writing was dramatic. Even if all it had at the start was: "5.10 p.m. A herd of Jersey cows come down the road. The farmer is at the back. There are sixteen cows. A crow flew over them." Another had: "I went fishing after school by the river. The river is at the bottom of our farm. I got a bite at 4.42. It was a large pike."

School stopped at four but I never got back to the widow's house until after five when it was too late to see the girl walking on the road. Only on weekends when I went out in the afternoon would I meet her. We now said Hello and a few words about the weather. But she gave me no further encouragement.

My stay with the widow was temporary—the headmaster had sent me her address as a place to stay until I could find something for myself —and at the beginning of November I moved to a farm in the country. It was owned by the Browns. They let a small wing of their farmhouse in the summer to tourists. I took it until June. The place was six miles from Riverside but as Mrs. Brown drove in every morning to bring her son to the school she would take me as well. And I would take the bus back.

The farm was in a valley in the richest farming country I had ever seen. Low hills all around, cows and horses on the slopes and in the lush grass at the bottom. There were also apple orchards and countless rabbits. And at dusk I would watch a pair of buzzards working their territory. The Browns were Anglo-Irish. And what they were doing out here seemed ridiculous. You expected them to live somewhere like Surrey, Sussex, or Bucks. To go to Henley and Wimbledon, read *The Tatler*. But I have since come across others, like the Browns, who have come from sophisticated societies in Europe, and have chosen to live out their lives in obscure provincial Canadian towns. Mrs. Brown looked like an Amazon Girl Guide with a ruddy complexion and short curly brown hair. Although she was in her forties she thought she was still a girl and I would sometimes see her skipping with a rope and breathlessly calling out children's rhymes. She named all their cows after flowers. And every morning as I had breakfast I would watch Daisy, Rose, Lily, Buttercup, going by the door. Mr. Brown was an ex-Colonel. A tall thin man with a moustache and a pork-pie hat that he wore with the brim down. He spoke of *gels* for girls. And looked more at home with horses than anything else. They had been farming here a few years. And I heard that none of the local farmers gave them more than another three. But they were wrong. They didn't know how tough this breed was. Although going by appearances their farm looked hopeless. Everything inside their house was in a continual state of untidiness. Mrs. Brown had her mother down for three weeks. And the old woman took a broom and began to go after the cobwebs while all around her was disorder.

Then things seemed to go wrong for the Browns. They had their own water supply, but it often froze in winter. They had their own electricity, but the generator or pump went wrong and Brown couldn't fix it. He tried kicking the machinery and sometimes that helped. Though often I made my meals by candlelight using a primus. But the oddest sight was to see the Browns deliver milk. They would load up the small Ford with milk bottles that he had filled up. And then the ex-Colonel and the ex-Girl Guide Leader, both well over six feet, drove into Riverside and began to deliver small bottles of milk, from door to door.

~ ~ ~

Late one Friday afternoon I was waiting for the bus in the square to take me back to the farm when I saw the girl but without the whippet.

"I thought you had gone," she said. "I haven't seen you. Have you been sick?"

I told her that I moved and suggested that we meet for a drink tomorrow in the Palace Hotel.

Next evening I came into the hotel a few minutes early, but she was already there sitting in the darkened lounge.

"Could we," she said, "have coffee instead of a drink?"

"Of course," I said.

We went into the coffee bar. And while we had coffee she told me her name was Marie Youneau. I told her mine.

"The new teacher?"

"Yes," I said.

She told me that she had not long come out of a sanatorium and was living with her married sister.

I told her I came from Ottawa but I had never seen such rich farming country until I arrived here.

She said her sister's husband was out of work.

"It must be depressing," I said.

"I had a lovely dress," she said. "Blue and white. It was very gay. I liked it very much. Then I had to wear it every day and watch it get worn out and shabby."

I don't know what it was. Whether being in a sanatorium for so long or living in this backwater. But there was an awkwardness about her, something incomplete.

"I break things easily," she said. "I leave jam jars undone . . . toothpaste tubes off . . . my sister gets angry and follows me . . . just doing up things I leave undone."

"Why do you do it?"

"I don't know," she said.

We left the Palace Hotel and walked towards the other main street for a Chinese meal. There are five restaurants in Riverside, all run by Chinamen. I led her through a narrow connecting sidestreet. It was very dark. I didn't want to bump into anyone from the school. I put my hand around her waist and drew her closer.

"I know what you want," she said.

Over the meal she said that she believed there was a one and only. And you knew when he came along. And that it wasn't right to go to bed until you were married.

I didn't say anything to that. She had guessed my intentions. But I expected even a refusal to be a bit more sophisticated than this.

Outside, after the meal, we walked towards the river. It was cold and clear. I watched the neon signs from the other side reflect in the water as long bands of red, green, and the moving white of car lights. Neither of us had spoken for some time. Then she said.

"I'm sorry."

"For what?" I said.

"I don't know . . . I don't seem to know how to behave with other people . . .They see me once . . . but they don't see me again . . . I don't have friends . . . I don't seem able to give enough . . ."

I took her hand. We stopped walking. I saw she was crying. I kissed her. But she was moving her head, it felt awkward, as if I was off-balance. I tried again.

"I must go home," she said immediately we had separated. "I'll miss the last bus."

"I'll get you a taxi."

"I'd better come back by bus or else my sister will think something was wrong."

"Can't you tell her you were out having a drink?"

She became evasive. "She wouldn't like it."

We walked to the bus station. She put her arm through mine. And there was a small green bus by the side of the building.

"Will I see you again?" she asked.

"Of course," I said.

I watched her get on the bus. Then went and got a taxi that brought me back to the farm.

Next day the first snow fell, then frost. And getting into Riverside became difficult. I came in on Friday night—when all the stores were open and the farmers came in for their shopping—looking for her. I tried again next week.

Then I had to leave to spend Christmas and New Year's with my parents in Ottawa. And it was after I was back and school had restarted, that I read the notice of her death in the local paper.

I went in to see the headmaster.

"I'd like to take the rest of the morning off."

"Yes," he said. "Is it a relative?"

"No, a friend."

~ ~ ~

The crematorium was some distance away from Riverside and the taxi took twenty minutes to get there. I had never seen a funeral before. When I arrived there were only empty cars and trucks outside in the snow.

As I entered the chapel I saw, on the right-hand side of the aisle, four people dressed in black with heads slightly bowed, sitting together. I instinctively joined them. On the other side of the aisle there were about twenty to thirty people—entire families with children—all with bibles, dressed in their everyday clothes. There was nothing sad about them at all. They looked lively and curious at the few of us in black. The two sides seemed so incongruous. A cheerful man in a light grey suit took the service. And it was obvious that he belonged to the other side of the aisle. He quoted a lot from the bible. And gave references to look up. And those on the other side did. They seemed to know the bible well. I guess she belonged to them. And I wondered what it was that made her lose the certainty that they had. Sometimes the man in the light grey suit referred to "Sister Youneau . . . this was not the end, it was only the first step." And there was an occasional sob from one of the women from our little group in black.

Half an hour later I was walking up to the entrance of the school. The New Zealander joined me.

"Isn't it a glorious day," he said.

"It is," I said.

The sun was shining. The snow on the ground and the trees glistened. We could see our breath in the cold still air.

MALCOLM LOWRY

The Forest Path to the Spring

Malcolm Lowry was born in England in 1909. At the age of seventeen he became a deckhand on a tramp steamer, and sailed to the Far East. He returned to England to study at Cambridge, where he received a B.A. degree in English and Classics in 1932. He travelled extensively in Spain, the United States and Mexico. He came to Canada in 1939, where he lived in a beach shack at Dollarton, near Vancouver. In 1954 he returned to England, where he died suddenly in 1957. Among his novels, Under The Volcano (1947) *is the best known. A collection of short stories,* Hear Us Oh Lord From Heaven Thy Dwelling Place *received the Governor General's Award for Fiction in 1961.*

To Margerie, my wife

At dusk, every evening, I used to go through the forest to the spring for water.

The way that led to the spring from our cabin was a path wandering along the bank of the inlet through snowberry and thimbleberry and shallon bushes, with the sea below you on the right, and the shingled roofs of the houses, all built down on the beach beneath round the little crescent of the bay.

Far aloft gently swayed the mastheads of the trees: pines, maples, cedars, hemlocks, alders. Much of this was second growth but some of the pines were gigantic. The forest had been logged from time to time, though the slash the loggers left was soon obliterated by the young birch and vines growing up quickly.

Beyond, going toward the spring, through the trees, range beyond celestial range, crowded the mountains, snow-peaked for most of the year. At dusk they were violet, and frequently they looked on fire, the white fire of the mist. Sometimes in the early mornings this mist looked like a huge family wash, the property of Titans, hanging out to dry between the folds of their lower hills. At other times all was chaos, and Valkyries of storm-drift drove across them out of the ever reclouding heavens.

Often all you could see in the whole world of the dawn was a huge sun with two pines silhouetted in it, like a great blaze behind a Gothic cathedral. And at night the same pines would write a Chinese poem on the moon. Wolves howled from the mountains. On the path to the spring the mountains appeared and disappeared through the trees.

And at dusk, too, came the seagulls, returning homeward down the inlet from their daily excursion to the city shores—when the wind was wailing through the trees, as if shot out of a catapult.

Ceaselessly they would come flying out of the west with their angelic wings, some making straight down the inlet, others gliding over the trees, others slower, detached, staggering, or at a dreadfully vast height, a straggling marathon of gulls.

On the left, half hidden among the trees in monolithic attitudes of privacy, like monastic cells of anchorites or saints, were the wooden backhouses of the little shacks.

This was what you could see from the path, which was not only the way to the spring but a fraction of the only footpath through the forest between the different houses of Eridanus, and when the tide was high, unless you went by boat, the only way round to your neighbors.

Not that we had any neighbors to speak of. For the greater part of the year we were often almost alone in Eridanus. My wife and myself, a Manx boatbuilder named Quaggan and occasionally some of Quaggan's sons, a Dane, Nicolai Kristbjorg, and a Channel Islander called Mauger, who had a fishing boat, *Sunrise*, were usually the sole inhabitants, and once we were quite alone the whole winter.

Yet for all their air of abandonment most of the little shacks were prettily and neatly painted and some had names too. Next to ours was Dunwoiken, and by the spring, on the right, the steps went down to Hi-Doubt, which, as if indeed in doubt, was not built upon piles sunk in the hardpan of the beach, but on log rollers, so that the whole could be floated away the easier if necessary to another place, and in this country it was not an uncommon sight to see a house, mounted on such rollers, its chimney smoking, drawn by a tug, sailing downstream.

The very last and northernmost shack of all, the one nearest the mountains, was called Four Bells, and was owned by a kindly engine driver, whose real home was in the Prairies.

On the opposite side, the right of the path, across the mile of water, ran the railway track along the other bank of the inlet, in the same way that the path ran along our bank, with more little shacks mysteriously under the embankment.

We always thought we could tell when the engine driver was bringing his train back with the prospect of a sojourn at Four Bells, where perhaps he could just make out over the water from his cab his sailing craft tugging at anchor like a little white goat, by the way he would sound his whistle gloriously in welcome. It was his fireman no doubt did so but Mr. Bell whom one felt to be the artist. The sound after hallooing across the inlet to us would echo for fully a minute down the gorges and back and forth across the mountains and always the day after this happened, or that evening, smoke would be seen coming out of the chimney of Four Bells.

And on other days during the storms in the same manner thunderclaps would go crashing and echoing down the inlet and the gorges.

Four Bells was not called Four Bells because its owner was an old seafarer, as I had been, but because his name was Bell, his family was three, so they were indeed Four Bells. Mr. Bell was a tall rawboned man with a red weather-beaten face and the quizzical poetical longing and responsible look appropriate to his profession, but no sooner was the smoke going, and himself tacking up and down in his catboat, than he was once more happy as the child who had dreamed of being an engine driver.

Deep-sea freighters came down the inlet silently to the timber port invisible round the point beyond Four Bells or with a great list, tilted like wheelbarrows, sailed outward bound, their engines saying:

> *Frère* Jacques
> *Frère* Jacques
> *Dor*mez-vous?
> *Dor*mez-vous?

Sometimes too, on the seaboard of the night, a ship would stand drawn, like a jeweled dagger, from the dark scabbard of the town.

Since we were in a bay *within* the inlet, the city, like the town— by which latter I mean Eridanus Port at the sawmill—the city was invisible to us, *behind* us on the path, was our feeling; almost opposite us was Port Boden, seen only as power lines ruled across the dawn or gentian and white smoke of shingle mills, and on the opposite bank too, though nearer the city, was the oil refinery. But the point southward blocked for us what would have been, beyond wide tide flats, a distant view of the cantilever bridges, skyscrapers and gantries of the city, with more great mountains that way too, and on this southerly point stood a lighthouse.

It was a whitewashed concrete structure, thin as a match, like a magic lighthouse, without a keeper, but oddly like a human being itself, standing lonely on its cairn with its ruby lamp for a head and its generator strapped to its back like a pack; wild roses in early summer blew on the bank beside it, and when the evening star came out, sure enough, it began its beneficent signaling too.

If you can imagine yourself taking a pleasure steamer down the inlet from the city some afternoon, going toward the northern mountains, first you would have left the city harbor with its great freighters from all over the world with names like *Grimanger* and ΟΙΑΙΠΟΥΣ ΤΥΡΑΝΝΟΣ and its shipyards, and then to starboard would be the railway tracks, running away from the city along the bank, through the oil-refinery station, along the foot of steep cliffs that rose to a high wooded hill, into Port Boden, and then, curving out of sight, beginning their long climb into the mountains; on the port side beneath the white peaks and the huge forestation of the mountain slopes would be tide-flats, a gravel pit, the Indian reserve, a barge company, and then the point where the wild roses were blowing and the mergansers nested, with the lighthouse itself; it was here, once around the point with the lighthouse dropping astern, that you would be cutting across our bay with our little cabins under the trees on the beach where we lived at Eridanus, and that was our path going along the bank; but you would be able to see from your steamer what we could not, right around the next point at Four Bells, into Eridanus Port—or, if this happens to be today, what was Eridanus Port and is now a real estate subsection; perhaps you would still see people waving at you before that though, and the man with the megaphone on your steamer who points out the sights would say contemptuously, "Squatters; the government's been trying to get them off for years," and that would be ourselves, my wife and me, waving to you gaily; and then you would have passed our bay and be sailing directly northwards into the snow-covered mountain peaks, past numerous enchanting uninhabited islands of tall pines, down gradually into the narrowing gorge and to the uttermost end of that marvelous region of wilderness known to the Indians as Paradise, and where you may even today, among the advertisements for dyspeptic soft poisons nailed to trees, have, for the equivalent of what used to be an English crown, a cup of chill weak tea with a little bag in it at a place called Ye Olde Totemlande Inne.

This side of Four Bells were two nameless shacks, then Hangover, Wywurk, Doo-Drop-Inn and Trickle-In, but no one lived in these houses save in summer and they were all deserted for the rest of the year.

At first, rowing past it—for the names appeared on the side of the houses facing the water—the majestic name Dunwoiken had struck my imagination and I thought it must have been built by some exiled Scotsman, remembering his former estate, fallen on evil days, yet living amidst scenery that reminded him of the mountains and lochs of home. But that was before I understood its name was cousin-german to Wywurk and that both words were, in a manner of speaking, jokes. Dunwoiken had been built by four firemen—that is to say city firemen, not ship's firemen, as I had been—but immediately they built it they lost interest and never came back to the beach, though they must have rented or sold it, for over the course of years people came and went there.

Having once seen the joke about some of these names—and intended timbre of pronunciation, more sinister than at first met the eye— they began to irritate me, especially Wywurk. But apart from the fact that Lawrence wrote *Kangaroo* in a house called Wyewurk in Australia (and he was more amused than irritated), though I did not know this at the time, the irritation itself really springs I now think from ignorance, or snobbery. And in these days when streets and houses are mere soulless numbers is it not a survival of some instinct of unique identity in regard to one's home, some striving with ironic humor and self-criticism of this very estate of uniformity, for identity itself, in however bad taste? And even were it not, were they any more pretentious or unimaginative than the lordly sources they parodied? Is Inglewood a more imaginative name than Dunwoiken? Is Chequers? Or The White House? Is Maximilian's Miramar to be preferred to Maple View? And is Wuthering Heights not merely weathered out of its cuteness? But irritate me they did then, and most especially Wywurk. The holophrastic brilliance of this particular name, and more obvious sympathetic content, never failed to elicit comment from the richer passersby in motorboats, who, having to shout in order to make themselves heard on board above the engine, could be very well overheard on shore. But in later years, when we lived nearer to it, I soon learned to be grateful for the distraction this name provided.

For the sea-borne comments, carrying to our ears and which were invariably hurtful or cruel and cut us to the heart before the motorboats reached Wywurk, never failed to be appreciative on their passing Wywurk itself. First there was the brilliance of the pun to be discussed as it dawned upon them, then its philosophic content to be disputed among the boat's occupants, as a consequence of which they would disappear round the northward point in that mood of easy tolerance that comes only to the superior reader who has suddenly understood the content of an obscure poem.

Hangover—no doubt simply a statement of fact commemorating some cherished and even forgotten or perhaps permanently catastrophic state of mind, for we never saw anyone enter or leave this house and have not till this day—rarely inspired more than a passing chuckle. While Four Bells, whose name had been chosen with love, rarely excited comment either.

Eventually I realized that the hamlet was really two hamlets, that it was divided almost precisely into the houses with names, and the houses without names, though these two hamlets, like interpenetrating dimensions, were in the same place, and there was yet another town, or sort of town, by the sawmill round the northward point sharing our name Eridanus, as did the inlet itself.

The houses with names—with the exception of Four Bells, for Mr. Bell's sojourns were any season—Hangover, Wywurk, Hi-Doubt and so on, belonged to people who just came to Eridanus for the week end in summer, or for a summer holiday of a week or two. They were electricians, loggers, blacksmiths, mostly town-dwellers earning good salaries but not sufficient to afford summer houses at one of the settlements further up the inlet where land could be bought if, which was a point indeed, they would have cared to buy it; they built their little shacks here because it was government land and the Harbor Board, upon whom I often felt must have sat God Himself, did not object. Most of these summer people had children, most of them liked to fish for sport, and to do what they felt they were supposed to do on a summer holiday. When they came most of them had a wonderful time doing these things and then they went away again—I regret to say much to the relief of ourselves and the sea-birds—in some few cases no doubt to turn into the very sort of people who later would make cruel remarks, as from the superior vantage of their motorboats they observed the lowly homes of the squatters who still actually lived in such places.

The others, who lived for the most part in the houses without names, were all, with one exception, deep-sea fishermen who had been here many many years before the summer people came, and who had their houses here by some kind of "foreshore rights" allowed to fishermen. The exception was the Manx boatbuilder whose boat shed was large as a small church and built of hand-split cedar shakes, and whose floating pier bisected the bay and constituted its own general landing, the only thing perhaps that made the little impromptu port an entity, and he seemed to be the father or grandfather of most of the other fishermen, so that, in the way of Celts, it was a little like a big family the entrance to which, for an outsider, I was to find by no means easy.

Sometimes when it was stormy, in the later days, we used to sit in his shack strewn with a litter-like neatness, with bradawls and hacksaws, frows and nailsets and driftbolts, and drink tea, or when we had any, whisky, and sing the old Manx fishermen's hymn while the tempest howled across the inlet and the water, scarcely less loud, rushed with a mighty enthusiasm down his hemlock flume.

Because we were drinking tea or whisky inside while his sons, the fishermen, were outside—and moreover the strange life we were leading had made my wife and me by this time have an aversion even to fishing—now and then we sang it a bit ironically. Nonetheless in our way we must have meant what we sang. I had a guitar salved, not from my days as a jazz musician, but an older one from my days as a ship's fireman, my wife had a beautiful voice, and both the old man and I had not bad bass voices.

There is no hymn like this great hymn sung to the tune of Peel Castle with its booming minor chords in which sounds all the savagery of the sea yet whose words of supplication make less an appeal to, than a poem of God's mercy:

> *Hear us, O Lord, from heaven Thy dwelling place,*
> *Like them of old in vain we toil all night,*
> *Unless with us Thou go who art the Light,*
> *Come then, O Lord, that we may see Thy face.*
>
> *Thou, Lord, dost rule the raging of the sea*
> *When loud the storm and furious is the gale,*
> *Strong is Thine arm, our little barks are frail,*
> *Send us Thy help, remember Galilee . . .*

When the wild roses began to blow on the point by the light-house in June, and the mergansers swam in and out of the rocks with their little ducklings perched on their backs, these fishermen went away, sometimes singly, sometimes in pairs, sometimes three or four boats joined together, like proud white giraffes their newly painted fishing boats with their tall gear would be seen going round the point.

They went to sea, and some of them never returned, and as they went to sea, so Eridanus was taken over by the summer people.

Then on Labor Day, as if swept away by the great wash of the returning fishermen's craft wheeling across the bay and breaking all along the length of the beach, reaching within the bay at last with the successive thunder of rollers, the summer people would depart, back to the city, and the fishermen, their boats singly or in pairs, would have come home again.

They were only a bare half-dozen fishermen all told who lived in Eridanus so that one stormy equinox, when Kristbjorg, who had been sailing alone up to Alaska, in his sturdy stub-nosed old tub painted green, to differentiate it from the others, had still not returned, he left a gap.

Quaggan, my wife, and myself, were repairing Quaggan's iron stove with a mixture of wood ashes, asbestos and salt, and at the same time singing the fishermen's hymn, when Kristbjorg, a bald strong wide but child-ish-faced Dane, who lived as he fished absolutely alone too, walked right in. Soon we were all singing something very different—a Danish song of his, his translation of which may be written as follows:

> *It blew a storm in the red-light district*
> *It was blowing so hard that not a sailor*
> *Was blown off the sea but a pimp was blown*
> *Off the street. It blew through the windows,*
> *And it rained through the roof—*
> *But the gang chipped in and bought a pint.*
> *And what is better*
> *When a bunch of soaks are together—*
> *Even when the roof is leaking?*

Kristbjorg always came round to say good-by with solemnity before he sailed for the summer, as if for the last time. But we found that he sometimes liked to delay his return beyond the period necessary so that he would be missed by us, and missed indeed he was.

"We were anxious about you, Nicolai, we thought you were never going to get back in this weather."

But it would turn out that he had been back and had been lurking in the city for a week.

". . . In the city got a little exercise. Been sitting humped up in the old boat so long. I never saw a street flusher. They just letting the old grime go. The streetcars are getting so humpy and dumpy!—I ran into a couple of bottles of rye. . . . I thought a little walking would speed the old ticker. . . ."

Quaggan loved all kinds of wood and did not care much to fish (save locally, off the end of his pier, just before he went visiting his grand-children). "Hemlock is very sweet that way," he would say tenderly of his doughty flume that had survived a quarter of a century without decay.

There was another lonely man from the Yorkshire moors, who lived quite alone down beyond the lighthouse, and though he seldom came up to our little bay we saw him, from time to time, when we walked down to the point. It was his joy to make sure that the automatic lighthouse was working, he told us, and in fact he would start to talk, as if half to himself, as soon as he saw us approaching.

"The heagles, how they fly in great circles! Nature is one of the most beautiful things I ever saw in my life. Have you seen the heagle yesterday?"

"Yes, we did, Sam—"

"Why the heagle went round to get his bearings, to look over the country. Two miles wide, hin great circles . . . Pretty soon you'll see crabs under these stones, and then it will be spring. They're some crabs in spring no bigger than a fly. Now have you ever seen how an elephant was constroocted? And where did those old Romans get them shields but from the rooster's wings?"

"Roosters, Sam?"

"Aye. And take in the desert now—the Sahara—where camels stamp with hooves like great spittoons upside down. One day they built a railroad—" he would lean against his lighthouse, nodding his head, "—but *hin*sects heat up all the wooden ties. Aye. So now they make the ties out of metal shaped like camels' hooves. . . . Nature is one of the most beautiful . . . And soon the birds, and pretty soon the crabs will bring the spring, my dearies, and the deer swimming right across the bay with their hantlers, beautiful, sticking up like branches on a floating tree, swimming, swimming across to this here lighthouse, right here, in spring. . . . Then you'll see dragonflies like flying machines back-pedaling. . . ."

The summer people rarely saw the fearful depredations their houses had to suffer in the winter, nor knew, during those hard months, what it was like to live in them. Perhaps they wondered why their summer homes had not been swept away by the storms they had heard shrieking and whipping against their city windows, the timbers they could imagine striking the piles and foundations of their shacks, the tempest, always the worst since 1866, that they read about in the city paper called the *Sun,* bought at a time of day when the real sun had gone down without, for that matter, sometimes ever having come up: the day after that they might motor out, leaving their cars—for unlike us they had cars—up on the road, and shake their heads to find their houses still there. How well we built, they would say. It was true. But the real reason was that there was that about Eridanus, existing by grace of God and without police or fire or other civic protection, that made its few inhabitants thoughtful. And a spirit would have seen that the fishermen during the winter had protected those summer homes as their own, but by the time summer arrived the fishermen had gone, not asking or expecting thanks. And while the fishermen were away it is also true that the summer people would not readily see damage happen to a fisherman's house, if they had lived long enough on the beach to think about it, that was, or happened to have been fishermen themselves, as was sometimes the case, or were old people.

This was Eridanus, and the wrecked steamer of the defunct Astra line that gave it its name lay round the point beyond the lighthouse, where, its engines failing, it had been driven ashore in a wild faen wind decades ago, carrying a cargo of cherries-in-brine, wine, and old marble from Portugal.

Gulls slept like doves on its samson posts where grasses were blowing abaft the dead galley, and in early spring pecked their old feathers off to make room for their new shiny plumage like fresh white paint. Swallows and goldfinches swept in and out of the dead fiddley. A spare propeller blade upright against the break of the poop had never been removed. Down below lever weight and fulcrum slept in an eternity of stillness. Grass grew too from the downfallen crosstrees and in the dead winches wildflowers had taken root —wildflowers, spring beauties and death camass with its creamy blooms. And on the stern, seeming to comment on my own source, for I too had been born in that terrible city whose main street is the ocean, could still be almost made out the ghost of the words: *Eridanus*, Liverpool—

We poor folk were also Eridanus, a condemned community, perpetually under the shadow of eviction. And like Eridanus itself, in its eternal flux and flow, was the inlet. For in the heavens at night, as my wife first taught me, dark and wandering beneath blazing Orion, flowed the starry constellation Eridanus, known both as the River of Death and the River of Life, and placed there by Jupiter in remembrance of Phaethon, who once had the splendid illusion that he could guide the fiery steeds of the sun as well as his father Phoebus.

Legend merely states that Jupiter, sensing the danger to the world, shot a thunderbolt which, striking Phaethon, hurled him, his hair on fire, into the River Po, then that, in addition to creating the constellation in Phaethon's honor, in pity he changed Phaethon's sisters into poplar trees that they might always be near and protect their brother. But that he went to all this trouble suggests that he, even as Phoebus, was impressed by the attempt, and must have given the whole matter some thought. Recently our local paper, showing a surprisingly sudden interest in classical mythology, has claimed to see something insulting in the name of our town of a political, even an international nature, or as denoting foreign influences, as a result of which there has been some agitation, on the part of some distant ratepayers, with I know not what motives, to change its name to Shellvue. And undoubtedly the view in that specified direction is very fine, with the red votive candle of the burning oil wastes flickering ceaselessly all night before the gleaming open cathedral of the oil refinery—

II

It was on Labor Day, years ago at the beginning of the war, just after we had been married, and thinking it would be both our honeymoon and our first and last summer holiday together, that my wife and I, strangers from the cities, myself almost from the underworld, came to live in Eridanus. But we did not see it at all then as I have described it now.

The beach was crowded, and when we first came down to it from the road, after having taken the bus from the city, and emerged on it from the cool green benison of the forest, it was as if we had suddenly stumbled upon a hidden, but noisy popular resort. Yet it must have been the garishness and strangeness of daylight and the sun itself which gave it to me, long used to the night and sleeping fitfully during these daylight hours, the quality of a nightmare.

It was a scorching hot afternoon and seven Scots were sitting inside the tiny cabin we'd been told we might rent for a small sum by the week, with the woodstove going full blast, and the windows shut, cackling, and finishing, as their last holiday meal, some sort of steaming mutton broth.

Outside the mountains were covered with heat haze. The tide was out—so far out it did not occur to me it would ever come in—the foreshore, along the whole length of which people were digging for clams, was stony, or covered with huge barnacled rocks, that made me fear for my young wife's feet, for which, since they were so small and delicate, I had a special feeling of protection. Further down by the water's edge the beach was strewn with seaweed and detritus and didn't even look like a possible place to swim.

Nor was anybody in swimming, though children shouted and

squealed, paddling in the mud, among the tide-flats, from which arose the most impressive and unusual stink I ever smelt in my life. This archetypical malodor on investigation proved partly to emanate from the inlet itself, which was sleeked as far as the eye could reach with an oil slick I quickly deduced to be the work of an oil tanker lying benignly at the wharf of the refinery I have mentioned opposite the lighthouse, so that now it looked as though one certainly could never swim at all; we might as well have come to the Persian Gulf. And to add to the heat, which further suggested the Persian Gulf, as we crunched thoughtfully over the barnacles and exoskeletons of crabs, or avoiding the deposits of tar or creosote, sank up to our ankles instead in slippery reeking slime, or splashed into pools themselves preened with peacock feathers of oil, came, from high up the beach, a blast of hot breath and ashes from a dozen clambakes, round the fires of which, it seemed to us, hundreds of people were howling and singing in a dozen languages.

As human beings we loved no doubt to see people enjoying themselves, but as a honeymoon couple seeking privacy we felt increasingly we had come to the wrong place, all the more so since it began to remind me of arriving in some fifth-rate seaside resort for a one-night stand.

That is how selfish lovers are, without an idea in their heads for anyone save themselves. As against this the worthy Scot from whom we rented the cabin, though poor himself and clearly struggling with that thrift in his own nature which so long supposed to be traditional had now become a fact, was extremely generous. He saw at once that we had come because it was all we could afford and before he and his fellow Scots had departed the shack was ours for the month at a rental of twelve dollars, he having lowered this from fifteen himself.

"But do ye ken boots, young man," he asked sharply.

"Boots?"

"Aye, lad, I'm fussy about me boot."

So the Scotsman's boat was generously thrown in. I had once been a ship's engineer, I explained, not caring to say ship's fireman.

But could you rent Paradise at twelve dollars a month? was our thought, the next morning, as from the porch of the shack, gazing on the scene of absolute emptiness and solitude, we watched the sunrise bringing the distant power lines across the inlet at Port Boden into relief, the sun sliding up behind the mountain pines, like that blaze behind the pinnacles of a Gothic cathedral, hearing too, from somewhere, the thrilling diatonic notes of a foghorn in the mist, as if some great symphony had just begun its opening chords.

From the oil company's wharf just visible down the inlet the oil tanker had vanished, and with it the oil slick; the tide was high and cold and deep and we swam, diving straight off the porch, scattering into dividing echelons a school of minnows. And when we came up, turning round, we saw the pines and alders of our forest high above us. To us lovers the beach emptied of its cheery crowd seemed the opposite of melancholy. We turned again and there were the mountains. After that we swam sometimes three and four times a day.

We rowed the Scotsman's boat down the inlet and picnicked on an island, uninhabited, with a deep cove where we drew up in the boat, among wild asters and goldenrod and pearly everlasting. The further reaches of the inlet, under the soaring snowcapped mountains, were now in September a deserted heaven for ourselves alone. We could row all day and once beyond Eridanus Port scarcely see another boat. One day later we even rowed to the other side of the inlet, across to the railway. This was partly because right under the railway embankment on the opposite side were dimly to be discerned, as I said, some more little shacks, scattered and smoke-blackened, but above which sometimes a strip of the metals themselves at noontide would seem to be rippling in motion with the inlet sparkling just below; still, we used to wonder how ever people could live so close to the noise of trains. Now our curiosity would be satisfied. The row over toward the railway, that had promised to be anything but picturesque, grew more beautiful by the minute as we drew out of our own bay. For these people—a few old pioneers and retired prospectors, maybe a handful of railroadmen and their wives who didn't mind the noise—poor like ourselves but whom we had patronized in our minds for being yet poorer, were richer in that they could see round the point of the inlet and right down it, could see beyond the timber port of Eridanus, the very highest mountains of all, the Rocky Mountains themselves, that were for us hidden by the trees of our forest, though both of us saw range beyond range of the Cascades—the great Cordilleras that ribbed the continent from Alaska to Cape Horn—and of which Mount Hood was no less a part than Popocatepetl. Yes, fine though our view was, they had a finer, for they saw the mountains to the south and west too, the peaks beneath which we lived, yet could not see at all. As we rowed along the shore in the warm late afternoon light these great peaks were reflected in and shadowed the flowing water, and seemed to move along with us, so that my wife spoke of Wordsworth's famous peak, that strode after him; this was something similar, she said, though very different, because there was nothing threatening about this apparent movement; these peaks that followed us were, rather, guardians. Many times were we to see this phenomenon, as of a whole mountainside or ridge of pines detaching themselves and moving as we rowed, but never did it, or they, seem "after" us: it seemed a reminder of duality, of opposing motions born of the motion of the earth, a symbol even while an illusion, of nature's intolerance of inertia. When we finally rowed back the sunset light was falling on the tiered aluminum retorts of the oil refinery, so that it looked to us, so infatuated were we (though this was before the time I would have thought it looked like an open cathedral at night, for the flickering candle of oil waste wasn't there), like a strange and beautiful musical instrument.

But still we did not see Eridanus as a place to live. The war was on, many of the ships that passed and sent the commotion of their washes over the beach were cargoed with obscenities toward death and once I had found myself saying to my wife:

"It's a hell of a time to live. There can't be any of this nonsense about love in a cottage."

I was sorry I'd spoken like that for I seemed to see a trembling hope die out of her face, and I took her in my arms. But I had not intended to be cruel; nor was she a sentimentalist, and anyhow we hadn't got a cottage, nor much hope of having one in the foreseeable future. The shadow of the war was over everything. And while people were dying in it, it was hard to be really happy within oneself. It was hard to know what was happy, what was good. Were we happy, good? Or, being happy at such a time, what could one do with one's happiness?

One day when we were out rowing we came across a sunken canoe, a derelict, floating just beneath the surface in deep water so clear we made out its name: *Intermezzo.*

We thought it might have been sunk on purpose, perhaps by two other lovers, and it was this that kept us from salving it. And we reflected, yes, that was perhaps all our lives here would be, an intermezzo. Indeed we had not asked for, or expected, more than a honeymoon. And we wondered where those other lovers were now.

The war? Had the war separated them? And would the war separate us? Guilt and fear came over me and anxiety for my wife, and I began to row back gloomily and in silence, the calm sunlit peace of the inlet turned for me into the banks of some river of the dead, for was not Eridanus also the Styx?

Before I had married, and after I left the sea, I had been a jazz musician, but my health had been ruined by late hours and one-night stands all over the hemisphere. Now I had given up this life for the sake of our marriage and was making a new one—a hard thing for a jazz musician when he loves jazz as much as I.

At the beginning of the war I had volunteered. I had been rejected, but now, with my new life, my health was beginning vastly to improve.

Even now, as I rowed, sluggishly and unhappily though I was pulling, I could feel the improvement. Little by little self-discipline, a sense of humor and our happy life together were wreaking a miracle. Was this effort toward life and health merely to be a probationship for death? Nonetheless it was a matter of simple honor to attempt to fit myself for the slaughter if humanly possible, and it was as much this as for my marriage that I had given up my old life of night clubs, and incidentally nearly my only means of making a reasonable living, though I had saved enough for us to live on for a year and possessed a small income from royalties on records, for a few of which I was part composer.

What if we should continue to live here? The idea did not strike me seriously, or from any considered depths of my mind, merely flickered across my horizon like one of those sourceless evanescent searchlight beams that used occasionally to flash over the mountains from the vague direction of the city, "where they were probably opening a grocery store," as my wife laconically used to observe. Cheap it would certainly be. But then honeymoons were surely not events that by their nature were supposed to continue. And far worse than the notion of "intermezzo" was that, on one plane, it would be like living on the very windrow of the world, as that world had not hesitated to remind us.

And while a summer holiday, even a protracted summer holiday, was one thing, how hard it would be to actually live here, for my wife to cope with the old cookstove, lack of plumbing, oil lamps, no ordinary comforts of any kind in cold weather. Ah yes, it would be too hard for her, even with my help (for though I had a sort of slow-witted strength, I did not have the co-ordinated handiness and practicality usually native to the sailor). It might be fun for a week, even a month, but to live here meant accepting the terms of the most abject poverty, would be almost tantamount, I thought, to renouncing the world altogether, and when I reflected in what dead earnest we would be playing the game in winter, I simply laughed: of course it was out of the question.

I backed water with my oars, turning the boat round. High up the alders and the pines swayed against the sky. The house stood prettily on its simple lines. But below the house, underneath it, on the beach, were its foundations of piles and wooden stringers and its interlaced tracery of cross-braces, like the frozen still machinery between the two paddleboxes of a paddlesteamer.

Or it was like a cage, as I rowed nearer, where one-by-twos, through which I saw the machinery, were nailed vertically to the stringers of the front porch, acting, one might explain, remotely like a train's cowcatcher, to prevent timbers at flood tide from drifting beneath the house and undermining the foundations.

Or beneath, it was like a strange huge cage where some amphibious animal might have lived, there on the beach, when often at low tide, resetting a cross-brace, amidst the seaweed smells, I felt as if I were down in the first slime, but in which work I delighted as I delighted in the simplicity of the stresses of the foundations I was looking at, that unlike most foundations were of course above ground, as in the most primitive of all houses.

It was simple and primitive. But what complexity must there have been in the thing itself, to withstand the elemental forces it had to withstand? A ton of driftwood, launched with all the force of an incoming high tide with an equinoctial gale behind it, the house would thus withstand, and turn aside harmlessly.

And suddenly, as I helped my wife out and tied up the boat, I was overwhelmed with a kind of love. Standing there, in defiance of eternity, and yet as if in humble answer to it, with their weathered sidings as much a part of the natural surroundings as a Shinto temple is of the Japanese landscape, why had these shacks come to represent something to me of an indefinable goodness, even a kind of greatness? And some shadow of the truth that was later to come to me, seemed to steal over my soul, the feeling of something that man had lost, of which these shacks and cabins, brave against the elements, but at the mercy of the destroyer, were the helpless yet stalwart symbol, of man's hunger and need for beauty, for the stars and the sunrise.

First we had decided to stay only till the end of September. But the summer seemed just beginning and by the middle of October we were still there, and still swimming every day. By the end of October the glorious Indian summer was still golden and by the middle of November we had decided to stay the winter. Ah, what a life of happiness had now opened before us! The first frosts came, and there was silver driftwood on the beach, and when it grew too cold to swim we took walks through the forest where the ice crystals crackled like rock candy under our feet. And then came the season of fogs, and sometimes the fog froze on the trees and the forest became a crystal forest. And at night, when we opened the window, from the lamps within our shadows were projected out to sea, on the fog, against the night, and sometimes they were huge, menacing. One night, coming across the porch from the woodshed with a lantern in one hand and a load of wood under the other arm, I saw my shadow, gigantic, the logs of wood as big as a coffin, and this shadow seemed for a moment the glowering embodiment of all that threatened us; yes, even a projection of that dark chaotic side of myself, my ferocious destructive ignorance.

And about this time we began to reflect with wonder: this is our first home.

"Moonrise of the dying moon."

"Sunrise of the dying moon, in a green sky."

"White frost on the porch and all the roof . . . I wonder if it's killed poor Mr. McNab's nasturtiums. It's the first heavy frost of the year. And the first clear sunrise in a month."

"There's a little flotilla of golden eyes under the window."

"The tide is high."

"My poor seagulls, they're hungry. How cold your feet must be down there, in that icy water. The cat ate all your bones—I found them on the floor—the wretch. The bones I saved from the stew last night."

"There's a raven sitting on the top of the big cedar, and a fine, foul, fearsome creature he is too!"

"Look—now! The sunrise."

"Like a bonfire."

"Like a burning cathedral."

"I must wash the windows."

"Part of what makes this sunrise so wonderful isn't just pure nature. It's the smoke from those wretched factories at Port Boden."

"The sunrise does things to these mists."

"I must put out some breakfast for the cat. He'll come in very hungry from his dawn prowl."

"There goes a cormorant."

"There goes a great loon."

"The frost sparkles like diamond dust."

"In a few minutes now it will melt."

So each morning, before the really cold days when I got up myself, I would be wakened by my wife's comments while lighting the fire and making the coffee, as if now upon a continual sunrise of our life, a continual awakening. And it seemed to me that until I knew her I had lived my whole life in darkness.

III

Now the great tides and currents in their flux and flow fascinated us. It was not merely because of the exigencies of our boat, which was not our property, which we could not anchor, and which it was not always possible to keep on a float, that it was necessary to watch them. In the great high tides of winter, with the Pacific almost level with our floor, the house itself could be in jeopardy, as I have said, from the huge timbers or uprooted trees racing downstream.

And I learned too that a tide which to all appearances is coming in may be doing so only on the surface, that beneath it is already going out.

Quaggan, the Manx boatbuilder whom we had now met, told us, rocking under our windows in his boat one warmer evening when the settlement was like a minuscule Genoa or Venice in a dream, of the Manx belief that at the new moon the birds on the ninth wave out from the shore are the souls of the dead.

Nothing is more irritating and sorrowful to a man who has followed the sea than the sound of the ocean pounding mercilessly and stupidly on a beach. But here in the inlet there was neither sea nor river, but something compounded of both, in eternal movement, and external flux and change, as mysterious and multiform in its motion and being, and in the mind as the mind flowed with it, as was that other Eridanus, the constellation in the heavens, the starry river in the sky, whose source only was visible to us, and visible reflected in the inlet too on still nights with a high brimming tide, before it curved away behind the beautiful oil refinery round the Scepter of Brandenburg and into the Southern Hemisphere. Or, at such a time of stillness, at the brief period of high tide before the ebb, it was like what I have learned the Chinese call the Tao, that, they say, came into existence before Heaven and Earth, something so still, so changeless, and yet reaching everywhere, and in no danger of being exhausted: like "that which is so still and yet passes on in constant flow, and in passing on, becomes remote, and having become remote, returns."

Never was the unfortunate aspect of the beach on that first day exactly to repeat itself. If oil sometimes appeared on the waters it was soon gone, and the oil itself was oddly pretty, but in fact the discharge of oil by tankers into the harbor reaches was about that time put a stop to by law. But when the law was broken and the oil slicks appeared it was miraculous with what swiftness the flowing inlet cleansed itself. It was the cleanest, the coldest, freshest, most invigoratingly beautiful water I have ever swum in, and when they spoke of damming the inlet, when a British brewery interest later talked of turning the whole place into a stagnant fresh water basin, perverting even those pure sources and cutting it off from the cleansing sea altogether, it was as if for a moment the sources of my own life trembled and agonized and dried up within me. Tides as low as those on that first day, also, were of course exceptional. And at low tide the mud flats themselves were interesting, seething with every imaginable kind of strange life. Tiny slender pale turquoise starfish, fat violet ones, and vermilion sunstars with twenty pointed arms like children's paintings of the sun; barnacles kicking food into their mouths, polyps and sea-anemones, sea-cucumbers two feet long like orange dragons with spikes and horns and antennae, lone strange wasps hunting among the cockles, devilfish whose amours sound like crackling machine-gun fire, and kelp, with long brown satin streamers, "when they put their heads up and shake them, that means the tide is slackening," Quaggan told us. Round the point northwards beyond the seaport were indeed miles of muddy flats at the lowest tides with old pilings like drunken giants bracing each other up, as if staggering homeward evermore from some titanic tavern in the mountains.

At night, sometimes all seemed still, at rest on the beach and the flats, wrapped in a quietude of reflection. Even the barnacles slept, we felt. But we found we had never made a greater mistake. It is only at night that this great world of the windrow and tide-flats really wakes up. We discovered that there were little shellfish called Chinese Hats that only walked at night, so that now when night fell, we had a standing joke, and would turn to one another laughing to say in sepulchral tones:

"It is night, and the Chinese Hats are on the move!"

And equally the rocks on the beach that at first had seemed only to threaten my wife's tiny feet became a factor of delight. The difficulty of walking over them at half tide down to swim was simply overcome by wearing old tennis shoes. And in the morning when one got up to make the coffee, with the sun blazing through the windows so that it was like standing in the middle of a diamond—or looking out through the windows into the inlet where in the distance the struggling sunlight turned a patch of black water into boiling diamonds—I began to see these intermediate rocks as with Quaggan's eyes, the eyes of a Celt, as presences themselves, standing round like Renan's immutable witnesses that have no death, each bearing the name of a divinity.

And of course we got much of our wood from the beach, both for making repairs round about the place and for firewood. It was on the beach we found one day the ladder that was later to be so useful to us and that we had seen floating half awash. And it was also on the beach that I found the old cannister that we cleaned and that in the end I used to take each evening to the spring for water.

The Scot had left us two small rain barrels for rain water, but long before I found the cannister drinking water had begun to constitute one of our most serious problems. On the highway beyond the forest was a general store and garage with a water tap next to the petrol pump and it was in every way possible, though tiresome, to take a bucket and obtain water from this source and bring it down through the forest, and most of the summer people would do just this. But we discovered that where possible the real beach dwellers avoided doing so, though this was largely a point of honor, for the storekeeper, a good man, did not mind, and the beach people provided him a major source of revenue. But he paid taxes and we did not, and also the ratepayers in the district were in the habit of using the slightest excuse to make a public issue of the existence of the "wretched squatters" at all upon the beach, whose houses, "like malignant sea-growths should be put to the torch"—as one city newspaper malignantly phrased it. What use saying to such as they: "Love had he found in huts where poor men lie." For these reasons the permanent residents, or even the summer people who had been there for some time, preferred to obtain their water from a natural spring or source. Some had sunk wells, others, like Quaggan, had flumes which conducted water down from the mountain streams flowing through the forest, but we did not find that out until afterwards, for at this time we had scarcely met those who were to become our neighbors and friends, and a good quarter of a mile separated us from each of our two nearest ones, from Quaggan to the north, and Mauger to the south. The Scotsman had left us a small barrel filled with fresh water and told us that he always replenished this by rowing to a spring about half a mile away, round the point with the lighthouse, and beyond the wharf of the barge company. So every few days I would load the barrel and a bucket into the boat and my wife and I rowed there with them. This stream ran all the year round but was so shallow you couldn't scoop your bucket into it. You had to fill it where a waterfall, about a foot high, poured through rocks, where you could put your bucket under.

The beach here, in a no man's land between the barge company and the Indian reserve, was very flat and low, not sandy, but covered with a deep slimy ooze and growths of seaweed: when the tide was low the boat was grounded about a hundred feet from the waterfall on the shore, and you had to wrestle the barrel back from the creek over the ooze and through shallow water, sinking in the muck. On the other hand at high tide the sea came right up over the waterfall covering it completely, though afterwards it was pure again. So that you had to time it exactly at half tide when you could come in fairly close with your boat or it was an all but impossible task. Even at best it is difficult for me now to see how we got so much fun out of that particular chore. But perhaps it just seems like fun now because of the memory of our despair on the day when we found we couldn't go there any more; for the moment it seemed that on this account we would really have to leave Eridanus altogether.

It was by now late in November, and less than a month to the winter solstice, and we were still lingering on; the sparkling morning frosts, the blue and gold noons and evening fogs of October, had turned suddenly into dark or stormy sunrises, with sullen clouds driving through the mountains before the north wind. One morning, in order to take advantage of the half tide, I, having taken over from my wife, rose well before sunrise to make the coffee. Jupiter had been burning fiercely and when I rose, though it was eight-fifteen, the waning moon was still bright. By the time I'd brought my wife her coffee there was a dawn like china, or porcelain. Earlier there had been a black mackerel sky with corrugated rose. Always my wife loved me to describe these things to her, even if inaccurately, as was more often the case, as she would describe them to me when she got up first in warmer days.

But apparently I was wrong about the sunrise, as I had been wrong about the tide's incoming, because later, toward ten o'clock, we were still drinking coffee and still waiting for the sun to come up and the tide to come in. It had become a calm, rather mild day with the water like a dark mirror and the sky like a wet dish clout. A heron standing motionless on a stone by the point looked unnaturally tall, and for a moment we remembered we had seen men working out there with lanterns the other night: perhaps the heron was some kind of new buoy. But then this tall buoy moved slightly, mantling itself in condor wings, then stood motionless as before.

All this time, though, the sun actually had been rising, had, for other people beyond the hill across the water, already risen. I say the hill, for no longer as in September did the sun rise in the east, over the sea, over Port Boden, with the power lines ruled across it, or in the northeast where the mountains were, but ever more toward the south, behind this wooded hill above the railroad tracks.

But now suddenly an extraordinary thing happened. Far south of the power lines, directly above the invisible railway, above where the blackened shacks under the embankment were, the sun struggled up, the only live thing in a gray waste, or rather it had abruptly appeared, the sun, as a tiny circle with five trees in it, grouped round its lower rim like church spires in a teacup. There was, if you shut your eyes and opened them wide again hard, no glare, only this platinum circle of sun with the trees in it, and no other trees to be seen for fog, and then clouds minutely drawn over the top, the sun taking in more trees along the hilltop as it slanted up. Then for a moment the sun became suffused, then it looked like a skull, the back of a skull. We shut our eyes and opened them again and there was the sun, a tiny little sun, framed in one of the window panes, like a miniature, unreal, with these trees in it, though no other trees were to be seen.

We took the boat and rowed to the creek and found a new notice:

PRIVATE PROPERTY   KEEP OFF

But we decided to fill the barrel anyhow this last time. Someone came running down the slope gesticulating angrily and in my haste to get the boat away, which was hard aground with the increased weight of the barrel, one of its hoops became loosened, and by the time we'd got home not only was the barrel nearly empty but we had nearly sunk the Scotsman's boat too. My wife was crying and it was now raining and I was angry; it was wartime and we could scarcely buy another barrel, and in the quarrel—one of our very first—which ensued, we had almost decided to leave for good when I caught sight of the cannister on the beach left by the receding tide. As I examined it the sun came half out, casting a pale silver light while the rain was still falling in the inlet and my wife was so entranced by the beauty of this that she forgot all the harsh things that had been said and began to explain about the raindrops to me, exactly as if I were a child, while I listened, moved, and innocently as if I had never seen such a thing before, and indeed it seemed I never had.

"You see, my true love, each is interlocked with other circles falling about it," she said. "Some are larger circles, expanding widely and engulfing others, some are weaker smaller circles that only seem to last a short while. . . . The rain itself is water from the sea, raised to heaven by the sun, transformed into clouds and falling again into the sea."

Did I know this? I suppose so, something like it. But that the sea itself in turn was born of rain I hadn't known. Yet what she said was uttered with such inexpressible wonder I repeat that, watching, and listening to her, it was like the first time I'd witnessed the common occurrence of rain falling into the sea.

So terrible and foreign to the earth has this world become that a child may be born into its Liverpools and never find a single person any longer who will think it worth pointing out to him the simple beauty of a thing like that. Who can be surprised that the very elements, harnessed only for the earth's ruination and man's greed, should turn against man himself?

Meantime the sun was trying to burst forth again and we knew that its showing itself as a skull had been a pose. As if it were the beam from that lighthouse at Cape Kao that they say can be seen seventy-six miles away, so we saw spring. And that I think was when we really decided to stay.

As for the cannister it was of a kind that I had seen on shipboard used in the bosun's or engineer's mess as a filter in those days when I had been a fireman and I surmised that it had been thrown overboard from an English ship. Whether it was my imagination or not, it smelled of lime juice. Such filters are intended for water but it used to be common practice to put lime juice in them. Now the lime juice that is standard for the crew on English ships is so strong undiluted that they used to use it for scrubbing the mess tables white—a few drops in a bucket of water would do the trick—but on metal it can have a corrosive as well as a cleansing effect and it struck me that some green mess boy had possibly put too much lime juice in this filter by mistake, or with insufficient dilution, the bosun had come off duty thirsty, drawn himself a draught of nice quenching rust, torn the filter off the wall, threatened to crown the unfortunate mess boy with it, and then thrown it overboard. Such was the little sea story I made up for my wife about it as I set about converting it into a good clean water container for ourselves.

Now we had a cannister but still no honorable place to get water. The same day we met Kristbjorg on the path.

"—and there's your wand," he said.

"What?"

"Water, Missus."

It was the spring. Wand, or a word like it, though not pronounced the way it looks, was apparently either the Danish or Norwegian for water, or if not the word Kristbjorg sometimes used. It had been there all the time, not a hundred yards from the house, though we hadn't seen it. No doubt because it had been an extremely dry and protracted Indian summer, it had not started running till late, by which time we had got used to its not being there, so we hadn't seen it. But for a moment it had been as if Kristbjorg had waved a magic wand and suddenly, there was the water. And the kind soul went and brought a bit of iron piping to make it easier to fill our cannister from it.

IV

Nor shall I ever forget the first time I went down that path to the spring for water. The evening was highly peculiar. In the northeast a full moon like a burning thistle had risen over the mountains. Mars hovered over the moon, the sole star. On the other side of the water a bank of fog stretched along the coastline the length of the inlet, luminous in the east opposite the house, but becoming black toward the south and west to the far right beyond the trees on the headland—that was, from our porch, from the path, the headland with the lighthouse was behind me, but it was such a strange evening I kept turning round—through which the fog showed like spirals and puffs of smoke, as though the woods were on fire. The sky was blue in the west, shading down to a pastel-like chalky sunset against which the trees were etched. A spindly water tower stood out above the fog over there. It had been dark inside the house but now I was outside on the path it was light. This was six o'clock and in spite of the blue sky to the west a patch of moonlight was reflected in the water by a diving float. The tide was high below the trees. In one instant, however, when I reached the spring, the moon went behind a cloud and it was dark: the reflection disappeared. And when I got back there was a blue fog.

"Welcome home," my wife smiled, greeting me.

"Ah yes, my darling, it really *is* home now. I love those curtains you made."

"It's good to sit by the window and look when it's beautiful outside, but when it's a gloomy twilight I like to pull the curtains, and feel from the dark night withdrawn, and full of lamplight inside."

"None of this nonsense about love in a cottage?"

I was lighting the oil lamps as I said this, smiling as I reflected how this unprophetic and loveless remark had become a loving catchphrase, and enchanted now by the golden color of the flame of the lighted oil lamps against their pretty blue holders backed with fluted tin brackets like haloes, or a monstrance.

"But now it's night, and the Chinese Hats are on the move!" We laughed, as I turned down the flame of a wick that was smoking the chimney.

And outside the tide was sweeping in still further from the Pacific until we could hear it washing and purling under the house itself. And later we lay in bed listening to a freighter's engines as they shook the house:

> *Frère* Jacques
> *Frère* Jacques
> *Dormez*-vous?
> *Dormez*-vous?

But the next morning when the gulls sailed outward bound to the city shores the clear cold sun streamed right into the two rooms of our house filling it with brilliant incessant water reflections and incandescence of light as if it knew that soon the world would start rolling through the mountainous seas of winter toward inevitable spring. And that evening after the last gulls had come to rest, when the moonlight came in there was time for it to embroider the waving windows of our house with their curtains on the unresting tide of Eridanus that was both sea and river.

Thereafter at dusk, when the gulls came floating home over the trees, I used to take this cannister to the spring. First I climbed the wooden ladder set into the bank made into steps that had replaced the Scotsman's old broken steps, that led up from our porch to the path. Then I turned right so that now I was facing north toward the mountains, white plumaged as gulls themselves with a fresh paint of snow; or rose and indigo.

Often I would linger on the way and dream of our life. Was it possible to be so happy? Here we were living on the very windrow of existence, under conditions so poverty stricken and abject in the eyes of the world they were actually condemned in the newspapers, or by the Board of Health, and yet it seemed that we were in heaven, and that the world outside—so portentous in its prescriptions for man of imaginary needs that were in reality his damnation—was hell. And for these illusory needs, in that hell of ugliness outside Eridanus, and for the sake of making it a worse hell, men were killing each other.

But a few evenings later, returning homeward along the path, I found myself possessed by the most violent emotion I had ever experienced in my life. It was so violent it took me some time to recognize what it was, and so all-embracingly powerful it made me stop in my tracks and put my burden down. A moment before I had been thinking how much I loved my wife, how thankful I was for our happiness, then I had passed to thinking about mankind, and now this once innocent emotion had become, for this is indeed what it was, hatred. It was not just ordinary hatred either, it was a virulent and murderous thing that throbbed through all my veins like a passion and even seemed to make my hair stand on end and my mouth water, and it took in everyone in its sweep, everyone except my wife. And now, again and again I would stop on the path as I came back with water, putting down my burden as I became possessed by this feeling. It was a hatred so all-consuming and so absolutely implacable that I was astounded at myself. What was all this hatred? Were these really my feelings? The world, surely, one could hate the world for its ugliness, but this was like hatred of mankind. One day, after I had been turned down again for the army, it occurred to me that in some mysterious way I had access to the fearful wrath that was sweeping the world, or that I stood at the mercy of the wild forces of nature that I had read man had been sent into the world to redeem, or something that was like the dreadful Wendigo, the avenging, man-hating spirit of the wilderness, the fire-tortured forest, that the Indians feared and believed in still.

And in my agonized confusion of mind, my hatred and suffering *were* the forest fire itself, the destroyer, which is here, there, all about; it breathes, it moves, and sometimes suddenly turns back on its tracks and even commits suicide, behaving as though it had an idiot mind of its own; so my hatred became a thing in itself, the pattern of destruction. But the movement of the forest fire is almost like a perversion of the movement of the inlet: flames run into a stand of dry inflammable cedar, yellow flames slice them down, and watching, one thinks these flames will roll over the crest of the hill like a tidal wave. Instead, perhaps an hour later, the wind has changed, or the fire has grown too big for itself, and is now sucking in a draft that opposes its advance. So the fire doesn't sweep up the hill, but instead settles back to eat the morsels of the trees it felled during its first rush. So it seemed was this hatred behaving, turning inward and back upon myself, to devour my very self in its flames.

What was wrong with me? For nearly all was unselfishness in our little settlement. Like benevolent mountain lions, I had discovered, our neighbors would wait all day, only to perform an unselfish act, to help us in some way, or bring a gift. A smile, a wave of the hand, a cheery greeting was a matter of great importance here too. Perhaps they thought us a bit shiftless but they never let us know it. I remembered how Mauger, the Channel

Islander, would reconnoiter in his boat, looking at our house, trying to pick the best time to bring us some crabs, or salmon, without inconvenience to us, for which he would accept no payment. To the contrary, he would pay us for the privilege of giving us the crabs by enriching us with stories and songs.

Once he told us of a salmon he saw drown an eagle. The eagle had flown away with a salmon in its claws that he had not wanted to share with a flock of crows, and rather than give up any part of its booty it had allowed itself finally to be dragged under the waves.

He told us that in the northern regions where he fished there were two kinds of ice, blue and white: live and dead. The white was dead so could not climb. But the blue ice would come and calmly ravish an island of all her beauty of trees and moss, bleed her lichen to the rock, and leave her bare as the Scotsman's door he had come to help us mend.

Or he would tell us of Arctic visions, of winds so strong they blew in the outgoing tide in which were found strange fish with green bones—
When he came back in September he loved to sing:

> *Oh you've got a long way to go*
> *You've got a long way to go*
> *Whether you travel by day or night*
> *And you haven't a port or a starboard light*
> *If it's west or eastward ho—*
> *The judge will tell you so—*

Or he would sing, in his curious jerky voice with its accents of the old English music hall, and which was more like talking:

> *Farewell, farewell, my sailor boy*
> *This parting gives me pain . . .*

And we too had grown unselfish, or at least different, away from the tenets of the selfish world. Eternally we watched Quaggan's float to see that it was safe and if it broke away without his knowledge, or when he was in the city, we brought it back, no matter how bad the weather, honestly hoping he would not know it was us, yet proud that it had been ourselves, for had it not been, it would have been someone else.

No one ever locked their doors, nobody ever discussed anyone else meanly. Canonical virtues must not be assumed for the inhabitants of Eridanus however. Though one point should be made in regard to the womenfolk of the fishermen. With the exception of those who were married, there never were any women. The unmarried fishermen often lent their shacks to their friends in the summer, but they were sacrosanct when they returned. What they did in the city was their own business, yet they never brought whores, for example, to their shacks. The attitude of the solitary fisherman toward his shack, and his boat, was not dissimilar. In effect his love for the one was like his love for the other. Perhaps his shack was less a part of him than his boat and his love for his shack was more disinterested; I think one reason for this is that their little cabins were shrines of their own integrity and independence, something that this type of human being, who seems almost to have disappeared, realizes can only be preserved without the evil of gossip.

And actually each man's life was in essence a mystery (even if it looked like an open book) to his neighbor. The inhabitants varied in political and religious beliefs and unbeliefs and were certainly not sentimental. There was at one time, in later years, a family with three children living in Eridanus by necessity and not by choice and they were indeed convinced that it was "beneath them," and that the true values were to be found in "keeping up with the Joneses." They let themselves sink into degradation, as seeming to be the conventional counterpart of poverty, without ever having looked at a sunrise. I recall that their dishevelment and general incapacity caused some rather sharp comment among the fishermen and everyone was relieved when they left, to move into a slum in the city, where they certainly did not have to carry their water from a spring and where their only sight of a sunrise was behind warehouses. And even ourselves were not entirely absolved from identifying such a life with "failure," something we certainly should have outgrown. And I remember very well how we used to drift along in our little boat in the sun, or sit by the fire in the gentle lamplight if it was night and cold weather, and murmur together our daydreams of "success," travel, a fine house, and so on.

And everything in Eridanus, as the saying is, seemed made out of everything else, without the necessity of making anyone else suffer for its possession: the roofs were of hand-split cedar shakes, the piles of pine, the boats of cedar and vine-leaved maple. Cypress and fir went up our chimneys and the smoke went back to heaven.

There was no room for hatred, and resuming my load of the cannister, I resolved to banish it—after all it was not human beings I hated but the ugliness they made in the image of their own ignorant contempt for the earth—and I went back to my wife.

But I forgot all my hatred and torment the moment I saw my wife. How much I owed to her! I had been a creature of the night, who yet had never seen the beauty of the night.

My wife taught me to know the stars in their courses and seasons, and to know their names, and how she always laughed like a peal of merry little bells telling me again about the first time she made me really look at them. It was early in our stay at Eridanus while I, used to being up all night and sleeping during the day, could not accustom myself to the change of rhythm, and the silence, and darkness all around us. Because I found it hard to sleep, in the small dark hours of one moonless night she took me walking deep into the forest; she told me to put out my electric torch and then, in a moment, she said, look up at the sky. The stars were blazing and shooting through the black trees and I had said, "My God, I never saw anything like that in my life!" But I never could see the patterns she pointed out and she always had to teach me afresh each time, until one late autumn night there was a brilliant full moon. That night there was frosted driftwood and a slow silver line of surf on the beach. Above the night itself flashed with swords and diamonds. Standing on the porch she pointed out Orion—"See, the three stars of his belt, Mintaka, Alnilam, Alnitak, there's Betelgeuse above in his right shoulder, and Rigel below in his left knee—" and when I saw it at last she said, "It's easier tonight because the moonlight drowns all but the brightest stars."

I reflected how little I had known of the depths and tides of a woman until now, her tenderness, her compassion, her capacity for delight, her wistfulness, her joy and strength, and her beauty, that happened through my wild luck to be the beauty of my wife.

She had lived in the country as a child and now returning after her years in the cities it was as if she had never left it. Walking through the forest to meet her returning from the store I would sometimes come upon her standing as still and alert as the wild creature she had seen and was watching, a doe with her fawn, a mink, or a tiny kinglet on a bough over her head. Or I would find her on her knees, smelling the earth, she loved it so much. Often I had the feeling that she had some mysterious correspondence with all nature around her unknown to me, and I thought that perhaps she was herself the eidolon of everything we loved in Eridanus, of all its shifting moods and tides and darks and suns and stars. Nor could the forest itself have longed for spring more than she. She longed for it like a Christian for heaven, and through her I myself became susceptible to these moods and changes and currents of nature, as to its ceaseless rotting into humus of its fallen leaves and buds—nothing in nature suggested you died yourself more than that, I began to think—and burgeoning toward life.

My wife was also an accomplished cook, and though the wood-burning cookstove we had reminded us of Charlie Chaplin's in *The Gold Rush*, she somehow turned our limited and humble fare into works of art.

Sometimes, when we were most troubled in heart because of the war, or fear we would be separated, or run out of money, she would lie in bed laughing in the dark and telling me stories to make me laugh too, and then we would even make up dirty limericks together.

We found we could rarely do any outside work together, like splitting wood, or making repairs, or especially when we built the pier, without singing; the jobs begat the songs, so that it was as if we had discovered the primitive beginnings of music again for ourselves; we began to make up our own songs, and I began to write them down.

But it was the accompaniment of her speech, of her *consciousness* of everything that impressed me then, half absurd, wholly perceptive, it intensified our whole life.

"See the frost on the fallen leaves, it's like a sumptuous brocade." "The chickadees are chiming like a windbell." "Look at that bit of moss, it's a miniature tropical forest of palm trees." "How do I know the cascara from the alder trees? Because the alders have eyes." "Eyes?" "Just like the eyes on potatoes. It's where the young shoots and branches drop off." "We shall have snow tonight, I can smell it on the wind." Such was our small talk, our common gossip of the forest.

My old life of the night, how far away that seemed now, my life in which my only stars were neon lights! I must have stumbled into a thousand alcoholic dawns, but drunk in the rumble seat I passed them by. How different were the few drinks we drank now, with Quaggan or Kristbjorg, when we could afford it or when there was any. Never had I really looked at a sunrise till now.

Once or twice on Sundays some of the boys who'd played with

me came out to see us, when they happened to be filling a week's engagement in the city at the Palomar Dance Hall, or on the stage at the Orpheum cinema. Many combinations had been broken up during the war and my old band was not the same now, but whatever the world may think jazz musicians not merely possess unusual integrity but are among the most understanding and spiritual men and they did not tempt me back to my old life, knowing that would kill me. It was not that I imagined that I was transcending jazz: I could never do that or wish to, and they wouldn't have let me get away with that illusion either. But there are some who can stand the racket and some who cannot. No one can be fool enough to think that Venuti or Satchmo or the Duke or Louis Armstrong have "ruined their lives" by living what I have pretentiously called "a life of the night." For one thing it is their lives and it has for me the aspects of a very real glory, of the realest kind of true acceptance of a real vocation. On one plane I can see them laughing their heads off at this kind of language. But they would know that what I say is true.

I belonged, somehow, way in the past, to the days of prohibition —as a matter of fact I have still not quite lost my taste for bootleg booze— and Beiderbecke, who was my hero, and Eddie Lang who taught me to play. Jazz had advanced since those days and Mr. Robert Hackett is capable of flights that would have been difficult even for Bix. But I was attached romantically to those days as I was to the obsolete days of stokeholds. I had never been able to play sweet music, and I had rarely been able to play very sober either, and I was in danger of worse when I quit, and all this my colleagues, filled with grave polite wonder at this extraordinary life I was leading, and on whose hangover-concealing faces the pieces of plaster betrayed the heroism and decency of their visit at all, thoroughly appreciated. They had brought me an old gramophone which could be wound by hand, since of course we had no electricity, and a collection of our old recordings, and I understood too, through the familiar jargon into which we all would familiarly fall, that their serious impression was that I would have to do something creative with my life if I did not want somehow to go to pieces, for all my happiness.

One bitter gray day with the north wind shrilling through bare iron trees and the path through the forest almost unnegotiable with ice and frozen snowdrifts, there was a sudden commotion outside. It was some of the boys from my old band and they had brought me a small, second-hand cottage piano. Can you conceive of the self-sacrifice, the planning, the sheer *effort* inherent in this act? They had taken up a collection, had somehow found the instrument, and since it was only on Sunday they could visit me, and being Sunday they could not hire anyone to help them, they had hired a truck and driven out, and finally brought this piano to me through the frozen forest, over that all but impassable path.

After this my friends sent me from time to time many hot arrangements to work on for them. And they also made it possible for me to supplement my income in a manner that gave me great pleasure and is besides, so far as I know, unique. That is, I was able to provide on many occasions the titles for certain hot numbers, when it came to recording them, that had grown out of improvisation. In the old days such titles would seem to grow out of the number itself, and in this category are the titles for such numbers as For No Reason at All in C, and the piano solos In a Mist, In the Dark, of Beiderbecke. Walking the Dog is the title of an unknown masterpiece of Eddie Lang's, Black Maria is another. Little Buttercup—the tune so far as I know having nothing to do with the air in *H.M.S. Pinafore*—and Apple Blossom are two of Venuti's in a poetical vein, and Negroes have always been particularly good at titling such numbers. But latterly despite some brilliant titlings in bebop, and some superlative efforts such as Heavy Traffic on Canal Street (a swing version of Paganini's Carnival in Venice) and the Bach Bay Blues by the New Friends of Rhythm, even the genius of our brother race has begun to fail in this respect. One day my friends got stuck for a title in San Francisco and half joking, half serious, asked my advice on a Christmas card for a number they were recording with a small combination shortly after the New Year. We wired them: Suggest Swinging the Maelstrom though cannot be as good as Mahogany Hall Stomp God bless you happy new year love.

Thereafter I received many inquiries of this nature and most of my suggestions being used, half joking but wholly considerate, I would receive a sum of money out of all proportion to what I would ordinarily have earned from any royalties on the sale of the record in question. Some titles which I supplied and you may recognize are, besides Swinging the Maelstrom— Chinook, Wild Cherry, Wild Water, Little Path to the Spring, and Playing the Pleiades—and I did a variation on Bix that I worked out on the piano, calling it Love in a Mist.

Little Path to the Spring! In this extraordinary manner I had earned enough, the way we were living, to keep us for the next two or three years, and to provide some reassurance for my wife were I eventually to be called up. And all these things I used to think of on the path itself while I was getting water, like some poverty-stricken priest pacing in the aisles of a great cathedral at dusk, who counting his beads and reciting his paternoster is yet continually possessed by the uprush of his extraneous thoughts. Ah, little path to the spring! It struck me that I must be at bottom a very humble man to take such creative pleasure from such an innocent source, and that I must be careful not to let my pride in this humbleness spoil everything.

That first winter in Eridanus was a difficult one for us, in many ways; used as we were to city life our primitive existence here on the beach —simple enough in summer and warm weather—propounded problems every day for which we had no answer, and yet always we solved them somehow, and it forced upon us feats of strength or endurance which we often performed without knowing how or why; and yet looking back on it now I remember much profound happiness.

V

In our part of the world the days are very short in winter, and often so dark and gray it is impossible to believe the sun will ever shine again; weeks of icy drenching rain, interspersed by the savage storms that sweep down the inlet from the mountains when the sea roared around and under us and battered our shack until it seemed sometimes January would never end, though once in a long while would come a day of blinding sunlight and clarity, so cold the inlet fumed and the mist rose from the water like steam from a boiling caldron, and at night my wife said of the stars, "Like splinters of ice in a sky of jet."

The wintry landscape could be beautiful on these rare short days of sunlight and frostflowers, with crystal casing on the slender branches of birches and vine-leaved maples, diamond drops on the tassels of the spruces, and the bright frosted foliage of the evergreens. The frost melted on our porch in stripes, leaving a pattern against the wet black wood like a richly beaded cape flung out, on which our little cat tripped about with cold dainty paws and then sat hunched outside on the windowsill with his tail curled round his feet.

One dark windy day deep in January, when there seemed no life or color left in a sodden world and the inlet looked like the Styx itself, black water, black mountains, low black clouds shuddering and snarling overhead, we walked down to the lighthouse.

"—And soon the crabs will bring the spring—" Sam called to us. "But crabs . . . I had a friend, a diver—thief he was in private life, never come home without somethink, even if it was only a nail. Aye. Basement like a junkyard . . . Well, this time he goes down, down, down, you know, deep. Then he gets scairt.—Why? Migrations of billions of crabs, climbing all around him, migrating in the spring, aclambering around him, aswallering and stretching their muscles."

"!"

"Aye. Perhaps they see something *else* down there—who knows? Because he was so crazy scairt he wouldn't speak to no one for two weeks. But after that, he sings like nightingales, and he'd talk the head off any wooden duck. . . . And soon the crabs, my dearies, and soon the birds will bring the spring. . . ."

It was about this time we began to read more. I went to the city library and took out a "country card" which entitled me to take away a shopping bag full of books at once. The city, that already, in a few hours, had begun to render our existence an almost impossible fable, so that I seemed to know with sad foresight how even its richest comforts that one day we might in cowardice yearn for, and finally have, would almost suffocate all memory of the reality and wealth of such a life as ours, the city, with its steam heat, its prison bars of Venetian blinds, its frozen static views of roofs and a few small dingy gardens with clipped shrubs that looked, in the winter dusk, like chicken croquettes covered with powdered sugar. And ah, after being away from my wife for all these hours, to return from the city to discover the house still in place and the inlet sleeked and still, the alders and the cedars high, the pier there—for we had built a little pier—the sky wide and the stars blazing! Or, making my way down the sodden slippery path with the trees tossing and groaning about me in the tempest and the darkness, to make again the port, the haven of lamplight and warmth.

But then at night sometimes the elemental despair would begin again and we would lose all hope for terror at the noise, the rending branches, the tumult of the sea, the sound of ruination under the house, so that we clung to one another like two little arboreal animals in some midnight jungle—and we were two such animals in such a jungle—until we could laugh again at the very commotion, the very extremity of duty to a house filled with an anxiety of love like that of officers for a sailing ship in a gale. Though it was in the early mornings of high tide when getting breakfast that this wild elemental menace often proved the most unnerving, with the gray sea and white caps almost level with the windows, and the rain dashing against them, the sea crashing and hissing inshore under the house, causing horrible commotions of logs jarring thunders dithering the whole little shack so that the lamp brackets rattled with the windows, past which a drifting timber sailed threatening the pier, and beyond the smoke of the factories in Port Boden was just a rainy gray, while leaves were falling into the sea; then our boat hurling itself about down below would seem in jeopardy, at the same time there would be the sound of breaking branches in the forest, the great maple tree would seethe and roar, while the tossing floats squealed piteously, and the loops of Mauger's fishing nets hung on the porch would flap like mad ghosts; and then be motionless; and all the anxiety that had been stretched to its utmost tension repeating, would the poor boat be hurt, the pier against which a thud was like a blow at the heart, relaxed too: though only an instant, the next moment it had all started again, so that what with the wind, the thunderous boomings, the delight in the swiftness outside, the anxiety within and without, the pride that one had survived, the sense of life, the fear of death, the appetite for breakfast as the bacon and coffee smells went singing down the gale every time one opened the door—I was seized sometimes with an exuberance so great that I wanted to dive swiftly into that brimming sea to acquire a greater appetite still, either that or because the sea seemed safer than the house.

But then we went out to a morning of wild ducks doing sixty downwind and golden-crowned kinglets feeding in swift jingling multitudinous flight through the leafless bushes, and another day of winter companionship would draw down to an evening of wind, clouds, and seagulls blowing four ways at once, and a black sky above the trembling desolate alders, the heart clothed already in their delicate green jewelry I had never really seen, and the gulls whitely soaring against that darkness, where suddenly now appeared the moon behind clouds, as the wind dropped, transillumining its own soaring moonshot depths in the water, the moon reflected in the half-moonlit clouds in the water down there, and behind, in the same translunar depths, the reflection of the struts and cross-braces of our simple-minded pier, safe for another day, disposed subaqueously in some ancient complex harmony of architectural beauty, an inverse moonlight geometry, beyond our conscious knowledge.

With February the days were noticeably longer and brighter and warmer, the sunrise and sunset were sometimes bright and beautiful again, there would be a sudden warm bright noon, or even a whole day that melted the ice in the brooks and set them running, or a day of sunlight when one could look through the trees at heaven, where luminous Aconcaguas sailed God's blue afternoon.

In the evening when I went for water, which I always liked to time to coincide with the seagulls' evening return over the trees and down the inlet, the twilight was growing longer, and chickadees and kinglets and varied thrushes flitted in the bushes. How I loved their little lives, now I knew their names and something of their habits, for my wife and I had fed them all winter and some were even quite tame, regarding me fearlessly near at hand. Just past Dunwoiken the path took a sharp dip down toward the beach, at a steep gradient, then it turned to the left, up a small slope, and there was the spring that came down from the mountains, where I filled my cannister. Ah, the pathos and beauty and mystery of little springs and places where there is fresh water near the ocean.

We called it the spring though in one way it was not. It was a lively little brook but it was called the spring because it was only a little further up that it emerged from underground. It was a source of water, a source of supply; that is why it was called the spring; it is a nuisance, but not insignificant, that I have to use the same word for this as for the season.

One evening on the way back from the spring for some reason I suddenly thought of a break by Bix in Frankie Trumbauer's record of Singing the Blues that had always seemed to me to express a moment of the most pure spontaneous happiness. I could never hear this break without feeling happy myself and wanting to do something good. Could one translate this kind of happiness into one's life? Since this was only a moment of happiness I seemed involved with irreconcilable impulses. One could not make a moment permanent and perhaps the attempt to try was some form of evil. But was there not some means of suggesting at least the existence of such happiness, that was like what is really meant by freedom, which was like the spring, which was like our love, which was like the desire to be truly good.

One cold rainy day I met Quaggan, a wiry homunculus, in a Cowichan sweater knitted by Indians in a series of friezes; he was in the path, cutting cascara bark.

"Proteus path," he said musingly.

"Proteus?"

"Aye. The man who cut this trail. Blacksmith, lives in the city now. We used to call it the Bell-Proteus path, for 'twas Bell helped him," said the old man, scuttling off into the dusk with his bright purgative load.

When I returned home I looked up Proteus in the dictionary which had been left behind by the Scotsman (who with uncanny insight had not returned it for twenty years to the Moose Jaw Public Library) together with some essays of Renan and a Bible, the loan of one Gideon, which was in the woodshed, and discovered—though I can't say I didn't more or less know it before—that he was a prophetic sea-god in the service of Poseidon. When seized, he would assume different shapes.

But how strange this was, I thought. Here Proteus was a man, who had given his name to this path. But he was also a god. How mysterious! And Eridanus too, that was a ship and the name of our hamlet and seaport, and inlet, and also a constellation. Were we living a life that was half real, half fable? Bell's name had no meaning I knew of. Neither had Quaggan's. Kristbjorg might have Christ-like virtues but he was anything but Christ-like. And yet I could not help remembering Hank Gleason, the bull fiddle's, pronouncement on Eridanus that Sunday. "Out of this world, brother," he had said. It gave me an uneasy feeling for a moment, like seeing one of those grotesque films in which they use animated cartoons with real figures, a mixture of two forms; it was also the feeling, though I couldn't put my finger on it, such as I had about Wywurk or Hi-Doubt. And yet did the confusion come from pinning the labels of one dimension on another? Or were they inextricable? As when, just about this time, the oil refinery decided to put a great sign over the wharfs, as an advertisement: SHELL. But for weeks they never got around to the S, so that it was left HELL. And yet, my own imagination could not have dreamt anything fairer than the heaven from which we perceived this. (In fact I was even fond of the evil oil refinery itself that at night now, as the war demanded more and more lubrication, was often a blaze of lights like a battleship in harbor on the Admiral's birthday.) But these problems I could never solve: if I could even state them in my "music"—for I had taken to bouts of composition on the cottage piano—I would be doing well.

And then, before I had time to think, I would seem to be getting water again, walking as if eternally through a series of dissolving dusks down the path. And at last the night would come like a great Catherine wheel.

It was a very still evening, and I had gone later than usual. There were quiet lamps already gleaming in Quaggan's shack, in Kristbjorg's, and on the point in Four Bells, though I knew none of their owners were at home for I had just seen all three of them through the trees going to the store. I think it was the stillness, the quietude, with the tide in, and the fact of the lamps burning in the empty houses by the sea that must have reminded me of it. Where had I read of the Isle of Delight—in Renan of course—where the birds sing matins and lauds at the canonical hours? The Isle of Delight, where the lamps light of themselves for the offices of religion, and never burn out for they shine with a spiritual light, and where an absolute stillness reigns, and everyone knows precisely the hour of his death, and one feels neither cold nor heat nor sadness nor sickness of body or soul. And I thought to myself, these lights are like those lights. That stillness is like this stillness. This itself is like the Isle of Delight. And then I thought to myself, stopping in the path: what if we should lose it? And with this thought of all-consuming anxiety I would always pause with a sigh. And then came the season spring and I forgot this anxiety too.

VI

Ah, not till that year had I observed a spring!

We went out on the porch and looked at the spring stars: Arcturus, Hercules the giant, the Lion and the Sea Serpent, the Cup, the Crown, and Vega in the Lyre.

One morning we saw our two great loons in their black and white high plumage, diving and calling softly to each other with low clear whistles, and that day the first bright leaves of the green dragons came thrusting through the earth on the path near the spring.

We were speaking together of these things that evening when suddenly we stopped talking at an apparition of terrifying beauty: in the darkness, in the northeast sky, within a circular frame, appeared the crosstrees of a windjammer on fire: the blazing crosstrees of a windjammer in port, no sails, just the masts, the blazing yards: a whole blazing Birkenhead Brocklebank dockside of fiery Herzogin Ceciles: or as if some ancient waterfront scene of conflagration in neighboring old windjammered Port Boden had been transported out of the past, in miniature, into the sky: now, to the right within the miniature frame, turned blackened crumbling yards: and now one lone silvery mast, ash-gray, with its naked canted yards, a multiple tilted cross, chording it perpendicularly, sinking below the circular frame, ascending, of blazing gold; we laughed out of sheer joy, for it was just the full moon rising clear of the pines behind the mountains, and often it must do this, but who looked at it? Who could see it? Could anyone else see it? I had never seen it. Why had God given this to us?

—And often I was to ask this: My God, why have You given this to us? But when the moon waned, rising further and further south, the sun would rise further and further north. And the truth of this simple fact, learned also from my wife, for the first time the following morning, confronted in the sky, not by a blazing windjammer, but by a spectacle such as might have been beheld by a shipwrecked seaman on a spar, seeing, at sunrise, the becalmed ship of the Ancient Mariner. Through the window the sea was so calm in the mist it rose up steep as a wall. Mr. Bell's float seemed above us, halfway up the window, with far below that—a little later—divided not by sea or reflected mountains but by what seemed space itself, the orange sun rising still, barred with angry clouds. But the windjammer stood broadside in the sun; three masts, sad in the doldrums, tilted yards. And then the next moment had turned so that there was just this one gigantically tall mast, cross-boomed, coming toward us, changing into the tallest pine on the hill, as the rising sun left it behind. And I thought of my grandfather, becalmed in the Indian Ocean, the crew dying of cholera, my grandfather giving orders finally, at the beginning of wireless, to the oncoming gunboat, to be blown up himself with the ship.

That night there were two evening herons in the moon at high tide, the herons projected large and primeval before it, the one flapping high, blocking a moment the moon itself, the other, engines switched off, gliding low an inch above the moonstruck swelling water to land noiselessly on the float: a *squark* when they met, the one waiting for the other, and then flying off together: the bat turned into a firefly before the moon, and the cat's magical rites: and the tide full and high beneath the window: the swim at high tide, and love at high tide, with the windows liquescent on the floor: and waking again the next moment to the full tide again in the dawn, and the lights of the oil tanker still on alongside the oil-refinery port: and waking to the sudden O'Neillian blast of a ship's siren taking your soul to Palembang in spite of yourself, and again, the swim, the swim at dawn! And the shell-pink chiffon, my wife probably said, of factory smoke far in the northeast at Port Boden, and the four aluminum gas tanks, that later would come out in all their ugliness, like four golden pillars (because each was left half in shadow) to a Greek temple, and behind the old chemical factory like a ghost of a Grecian ruin and behind the four golden pillars a silent climbing train like a chain of golden squares: and the wash of a passing motorboat under the window like carved turquoise in onrushing movement toward you: and then the oil tanker lying under the pillars and retorts at the refinery like Troy, the pillars reflected in the water: the wonderful cold clean fresh salt smell of the dawn air, and then the pure gold blare of light from behind the mountain pines, and the two morning herons, then the two blazing eyes of the sun over the Cascade foothills, and the five gaunt growing pines caught tall in the circular frame, and then with such a blast of light it seemed to cut a piece out of the hill, the herons flying, the oiltanker sailing with the morning tide—

Oh, what light and love can do to four gas tanks at sunrise over the water!

And how different the forest path was now, in spring, from the other seasons we had known it: summer, autumn and winter. The very quality of the light was different, the pale green, green and gold dappled light that comes when the leaves are very small, for later, in summer with the leaves full out, the green is darker and the path darker and deeply shady. But now there was this delicate light and greenness everywhere, the beauty of light on the feminine leaves of vine-leaved maples and the young leaves of the alders shining in sunlight like stars of dogwood blossoms, green overhead and underfoot where plants were rushing up and there were the little beginnings of wildflowers that would be, my wife said, spring beauties, starflowers, wild bleeding hearts, saxifrage and bronze bells. Or on some cool still mornings came the mysterious fogs: "Anything can happen in a fog," she said, "and just around the next corner something wonderful will happen!"

And now it was spring and we had not lost our way of living; in fact, with the money I'd earned we had bought a little house further up the beach between Kristbjorg's and Four Bells under a wild cherry tree for a hundred dollars. No one had lived in this house for years and it was badly in need of repairs and of cleaning so that we did not move into it until May and we worked very hard to make it clean and sound and beautiful.

In early spring we had not yet moved into our second house and this is the time I am really thinking of when I say that each evening at dusk I used to go down the path for water. Carrying my cannister I would pass along the back of Dunwoiken, descend the sharp gradient toward the beach, then turn left again, up a little slope, to the spring. Then I set the cannister under the iron piping Kristbjorg had put there and waited for it to fill. While it filled I watched the gulls coming up the inlet or gazed up the trunks of the trees to the highest pinnacles of the smallest branches trembling like a moonsail, and breathed the scents of evening: the rich damp earth, myrtle and the first wild crabapple and wild cherry blossoms, all the wild scents of spring, mingled with the smell of the sea and from the beach the salt smells, and the rasping iodine smell of seaweed.

But one evening I forgot to do this and found myself to my surprise not looking at anything nor smelling anything. And now, all of a sudden, very different seemed the journey back. Though the cannister only held four gallons, and since I had become stronger, the task ought to have seemed much lighter than before, yet on this evening it began to weigh a ton and it was just slip and slide, one foot after another. I found myself stopping for breath every moment. The worst part was the dip down which on the way to the spring I had run so gaily, but which had become a veritable hill of difficulty on the return journey, so that I had to drag rather than carry my cannister up it. And now I stopped and cursed my lot. What had happened now? Now that the spring we had so longed for had come, now that our life on the beach seemed doubly secure with our new house—what was I bothering about now? It seemed to me as though all our prayers having been answered and myself for once having nothing in the world to worry about, for the moment, I had to find something to irk me in this chore. It was as though man would not be contented with anything God gave him and I could only think that when God evicted him from Paradise it served him right.

And now no matter how happy I had been all day the awe-inspiring thoughts were as if waiting for me here at the spring. Somehow I always made it back, but somehow too, for the first time, I came to dread this simple little chore. It wasn't as if this were a mere malaise of self-centeredness. Each of us thought more of the other than of himself. Nor was it a matter of mutual self-absorption. Sincerely we considered our neighbors. Quaggan had indeed grown so fond of us he made a red mark on his calendar every time we went to see him. . . . One day I saw an old frayed but strong rope on his path, cast away on a tree stump, and I thought: yes, that is the awful end of such thoughts. Had I actually been tempted to kill myself? Aghast at the thought I took the rope back and reaved it up for use.

But at the same time that I dreaded it I was also aware that I looked forward to it, looked forward to the walk to the spring, which was like going toward the future, toward our new little house. It was a sweet time of the day when the sun sank and the only part of the day in which I was really apart from my wife, unless I counted my "work." I did not look forward to it because I would be separated from her but precisely because I was then able to enjoy the pleasure of returning to her, as if after a long journey. The journey might be, or had become, a sort of anguish, but we always met again with cries of joy and relief after this interminable separation of not more than twenty minutes.

But again, I thought, was the chore even anguish? In the surroundings there was everywhere an intimation of Paradise, in the little job, so far from mechanical, a sense of simple human accomplishment. I thought of the old ladder we had salved from the beach. This too was an accomplishment. At first we had pushed it away, but it had drifted back again and this seemed like a sign to use it. And I reflected: yes, and like this vermiculated old ladder, stinking with teredos and sea-worms, washed down from the sawmill, this sodden snag, half awash when I first saw it, is the past, up and down which one's mind every night meaninglessly climbs!

But I had salved this ladder last autumn, in the days when I used to lie awake brooding in the night, which now I never did. And the ladder no longer stank, or smelled of teredos. Much of it was good, and hacking out the rotten wood, I had put its frame to use, and indeed converted it into these very steps I was even now climbing down to greet my wife on the porch, with joy after my gloomy thoughts, carrying my burden, the same steps up which I had set forth twenty minutes ago on my path to the spring.

Yet a ladder was a ladder, however transmuted, and the past remained. It was in this way I came to the conclusion that it was not the chore itself, because it was heavy, but something to do with my thoughts, something that was always elicited on my return journey, especially when I came to the hill, that I really dreaded. Though I did not understand this until after I had met the mountain lion, and shortly after I had met the mountain lion something else happened that put it right out of my mind for many years, until, in fact, the other day.

The cougar was waiting for me part way up a maple tree in which it was uncomfortably balanced, to one side of the hill section of the path, and what is strange is that I should have met it on the return journey without having noticed it, just as I hadn't noticed the rope, if it was there, on my way to the spring.

A logger had once told me that if you set fire to your mittens and throw them at a mountain lion that would take effect, and I know that bears are often very susceptible to human laughter. But this folklore—and there is a great deal about mountain lions in these parts—did not help. All I immediately knew was that I had no sort of weapon, and that it was impractical as well as useless to make any movement of running away. So I stood traditionally and absolutely still. Then we simply waited, both of us, to see what the other would do, gazing straight into each other's eyes at short range; in fact it was only his gleaming topaz eyes and the tip of his tail twitching almost imperceptibly that showed me he was alive at all.

Finally I heard myself saying something like this to the mountain lion, something extraordinary and absurd, commanding yet calm, my voice as unreal to myself as if I'd just picked myself up from a lonely road after falling off a motorcycle and in shock were adjuring the wilderness itself to aid, a fact one half recalls under chloroform afterwards. "Brother, it's true. I like you in a way, but just the same, between you and me, get going!" Something like that. The lion, crouched on a branch really too small for him, caught off guard or off balance, and having perhaps already missed his spring, jumped down clumsily, and then, overwhelmed, catlike, with the indignity of this ungraceful launching, and sobered and humiliated by my calm voice—as I liked to think afterwards—slunk away guiltily into the bushes, disappeared so silently and swiftly that an instant later it was impossible to believe he'd ever been there at all.

At the time I completely forgot the rest of my return journey, though ludicrously it turned out I had not failed to bring the cannister with me, nor do I have any recollection at all of coming down the steps. I had to warn my wife not to go out, then row round to warn the neighbors and see that the alarm was given to the forest warden; I rowed, close inshore, straining my eyes through the gloom to warn anyone else I might see on the forest path. But night was coming on and I saw no one.

I didn't even see the lion again, which, when he ran off, according to later reports, did not stop until ten miles away when he jumped right through the glass window of a trapper, who offered him his elbow to eat while with the other hand, I truly regret to say, the man reached for a carving knife to cut the beast's throat, after which the trapper was obliged to row for several hours, as penance, to get aid in his underdrawers; when we heard this we mourned the animal a bit, in our way.

But that night as we lay in bed, and the moon shone through the window, with my arms around my wife and our cat purring between us, I saw that the only reason I had not been afraid of the mountain lion—otherwise I must have been a fool and I do not for this reason escape the charge—was that I was more afraid of something else. It was true, although this was less due to courage than a naïve ignorance, that I was not very afraid of mountain lions even when there was a report of them. But then I did not really believe in them. I must have been afraid—I mean I must have been afraid in some way of the lion—but at the hill on the spring path have been already gripped by the anticipation of a so much greater fear that the concrete fact even of a lion had been unable to displace it. What was it I feared? Lying in bed with my arms around my wife, listening to the roar of the surf we couldn't see, for it was a fierce low tide—I felt so happy that all of a sudden I could not for the life of me give it a name. It seemed something past, and that was what it was, though not in the sense in which I was thinking. Even when one is happiest it is possible to entertain, with one section of one's mind, the most ghoulish reflections, and so I did now, before I went to sleep, but now as at a distance, as if in retrospect. It was as though I had entered the soul of a past self, not that of the self that merely brooded by night, but an earlier self to whom sleep meant delirium, my thoughts chasing each other down a gulf. Half conscious I told myself that it was as though I had actually been on the lookout for something on the path that had seemed ready, on every side, to spring out of our paradise at us, that was nothing so much as the embodiment in some frightful animal form of those nameless somnambulisms, guilts, ghouls of past delirium, wounds to other souls and lives, ghosts of actions approximating to murder, even if not my own actions in this life, betrayals of self and I know not what, ready to leap out and destroy me, to destroy us, and our happiness, so that when, as if in answer to all this, I saw a mere lion, how could I be afraid? And yet mysteriously the lion was all that too.

But the next night, and upon nights after, something even more curious happened, as I say, that caused me to forget this till now.

The next evening when I went for water all I can remember is that on my way there, or on setting out, I was certainly prepared for another encounter with the mountain lion, of whose sad demise we had not yet heard, and prepared to be conventionally afraid of him, I suppose, though I went unarmed (it was because I didn't have a gun) and my wife, who had no fear of anything on earth save spiders, was curiously unapprehensive about it and had implicit faith in me. Actually, at the bottom of her mind, so great was her love of wild animals and her understanding of them, a love and understanding I came to share, I felt sometimes she may have wished I had charmed the animal home for a companion instead of scaring him away.

Something about the aspect of the mountains that evening distracted me from the lion. Though it was a warm evening, it was windy, and the mountains were wild with chaos, like an arctic island seen through snow.

And indeed it had snowed far down on the mountains in the last three nights, though I was not reminded by this snow that it was this changeable weather that had driven the cougar down to the warmer regions in search of food. The wind roared and howled through the rolling treetops like an express train. It was a chinook—the kind of faen wind that years before at night had driven the S.S. *Eridanus*—Liverpool—ashore with her cargo of old marble, wine, and cherries-in-brine from Portugal. The further mountains grew nearer and nearer until they looked like the precipitous rocky cliff-face of an island gashed with guano. The nearer hills were very light but their inner folds grew ever darker and darker. In the chaos high up there appeared a church of blue sky by mistake, as if put in by Ruysdael. A gull whose wings seemed almost a maniacal white suddenly was drawn up, driven straight up perpendicularly into the tempest. One of Quaggan's sons passed me running on the path:

"It's blowing real hard. I'm just dashing madly to see how things were."

I remember this Celtic way of expressing it delighted me: maybe his boat, or more likely Kristbjorg's, who was in the city, was dragging its anchor, and I said to give me a shout if he wanted any help. I remember filling the cannister with the cold mountain water pouring down. Gulls were blowing backwards above the trees and one came to rest on the roof of Hi-Doubt. How touching the gull, dovelike there, with his white blowing feathers! But the next thing I remembered was that I was singing and had passed the hill without remembering a single step I had taken or with any recollection of its difficulty; and the next thing I was down the steps, cannister and all, with no clear vision once more of how this had been managed, and my wife was greeting me as usual, as if I'd come back from a long journey. To the mountain lion I had given no thought at all. It was like a dream, with the difference that it was reality.

The next time I set off with the cannister I recall almost a precisely similar thing happened, though this was just a quiet spring evening, the mountains remote and still, muffled at their base by a great scarf of mist that rose without division from the calm reflecting sea. The journey to the spring seemed much the same, though even this seemed more dreamy, mysterious, and accomplished in a shorter time. But once more, on the way back, I was only conscious of the hill when I realized that I had traversed it without effort.

At the same time I became conscious of my gloomy thoughts again, but in a quite different way: how can I say it? It is as if I saw those thoughts at a distance, as if below me. In one sense I did not see them but heard them, they flowed, they were like a river, an inlet, they comprised a whole project impossible to recapture or pin down. Nonetheless those thoughts, and they were abysmal, not happy as I would have wished, made me happy in that, though they were in motion they were in order too: an inlet does not overflow its banks, however high the tide, nor does it dry up, the tide goes out, but it comes in again, in fact as Quaggan had observed, it can do both at once; I was aware that some horrendous extremity of self-observation was going to be necessary to fulfill my project. Perhaps I have not mentioned my project, or rather what I conceived my project to be.

VII

Though this may at first seem inconsistent with my dismissal of this project as "my music," "my bouts of composition," or "my work," I had been haunted for months by the idea of writing a symphony in which I would incorporate among other things, for the first time in serious music (or so I thought), the true feeling and rhythm of jazz. I did not share, among other perplexities of my vocation, the vocation that I had not yet discovered, the common romantic conception of the superiority of music over words. Sometimes I even thought poetry could go further, or at least as far, in its own medium; whereas music, destined to develop in terms of ever more complex invention (I knew this because I had mastered, almost accidentally, the whole-tone scale), seemed to me then to have its unconscious end in silence, whereas the Word is the beginning of creation itself. Despite this I always felt, as a practicing jazz musician, that the human voice managed to spoil a given instrumental record. To contradict this again, my wife and I loved to sing, and sometimes I felt our life together to be a kind of singing.

How well I recall struggling through all these, and many more, contradictions and perplexities. I finally even prayed, and the other day, looking through some scraps of early work saved from our fire, I encountered, half burnt, the edges scorched and crumbling, the following, written as it were over a score: *Dear Lord God, I earnestly pray you to help me order this work, ugly chaotic and sinful though it may be, in a manner that is acceptable in Thy sight; thus, so it seems to my imperfect and disordered brain, at the same time fulfilling the highest canons of art, yet breaking new ground and, where necessary, old rules. It must be tumultuous, stormy, full of thunder, the exhilarating Word of God must sound through it, pronouncing hope for man, yet it also must be balanced, grave, full of tenderness and compassion, and humor. I, being full of sin, cannot escape false concepts, but let me be truly Thy servant in making this a great and beautiful thing, and if my motives are obscure, and the notes scattered and often meaningless, please help me to order it, or I am lost . . . .*

But despite my prayers my symphony refused to order itself or resolve itself in musical terms. Yet I saw what I had to do clearly. I heard these thoughts ordering themselves as if pushed off from me: they were agonizing, but they were clear, and they were my own, and when I returned home I tried again to put them down. But here I was beset by further difficulties, for when I tried to write the music, I had to put it down first in words. Now this was peculiar because I knew nothing about writing, or words, at that time. I had read very little and my whole life had been music. My father—who would have been the first to laugh at this way of putting it—had played French horn in the first performance in 1913 of Stravinsky's Sacre du Printemps. My father was with Soutine too, and knew and respected Cocteau, though he was a very proper kind of Englishman in some respects. Stravinsky he worshiped, but he died at about the age I am now, before the Symphony of Psalms at all events, so I had many lessons in composition and was even brought up, though I had no formal musical education, on Stravinsky's children's pieces. I grew to share my father's wild enthusiasm for the Sacre but to this day I believe it to be in one important respect rhythmically deficient —in a way I won't go into—and that Stravinsky knew nothing at all about jazz, which also goes for most other modern composers. I reflected briefly that though my unconscious, and even conscious, approach to serious music had been almost entirely through jazz, nonetheless my rhythmical touchstone had proved an uncanny method of separating the first-rate from the not quite first-rate, or of differentiating the apparently similar or related in merit and ambition: on this view, of modern composers, both Schönberg and Berg are equally first-rate: but as between Poulenc and Milhaud, say, Poulenc is somewhere, but Milhaud, to my ear, nowhere at all. What I am really getting at is probably that in some composers I seem to hear the very underlying beat and rhythm of the universe itself, but to say the least I am, it is admitted, naïve in expressing myself. However, I felt that no matter how grotesque the manner in which my inspiration proposed to work through me, I had something original to express. Here was the beginning of an honesty, a sort of truthfulness to truth, where there had been nothing before but truthfulness to dishonesty and self-evasion and to thoughts and phrases and even melodies that were not my own. Yet it is queer that I had to try and put all this into *words*, to see it, to try and see the thoughts even as I heard the music. But there is a sense in which everybody on this earth is a writer, the sense in which Ortega—the Spanish philosopher whom I have recently read thanks to one of the summer people, a schoolmaster, and now one of my best friends, and who lent me his books—means it. Ortega has it that a man's life is like a fiction that he makes up as he goes along. He becomes an engineer and converts it into reality— becomes an engineer for the sake of doing that.

I am bound to say that even in the worst of my struggles I did not feel like Jean Christophe; my soul did not boil "like wine in a vat," nor did my "brain hum feverishly," at least not very loudly: though my wife could always judge the degree of my inspiration by the increasing tempo of my sniffs, which, if I was really working, would follow a period of deep sighs and abstracted silence. Nor did I feel "This force is myself. When it ceases to be I shall kill myself." As a matter of fact I never doubted that it was the force itself that was killing me, even though it possessed none of the above dramatic characteristics, and I was in every way delighted that it should, for my whole intention seemed to be to die through it, without dying of course, that I might become reborn.

The next time I went for water, despite the fact that I had forearmed myself consciously against any illusion, almost exactly the same thing happened; this time indeed the feeling came more strongly than ever, so that it seemed in fact, to me, as if the path were shrinking at both ends. Not only was I unconscious of the hill, and the weight of the cannister, but I had the decided impression that the path *back* from the spring was growing shorter than the path *to* it, though the way there had seemed shorter too than on the previous day. When I returned home it was as if I had flown into my wife's arms, and I tried to tell her about it. But no matter how hard I tried I could not express what the feeling was like—beyond saying that it was almost as if a "great burden had been lifted off my soul." Some such cliché as that. It was as if something that used to take a long and painful time now took so little time I couldn't remember it at all; but simultaneously I had a consciousness of a far greater duration of time having passed during which something of vast importance to me had taken place, without my knowledge and outside time altogether.

No wonder mystics have a hard task describing their illuminations, even though this was not exactly that; yet the experience seemed to be associated with light, even a blinding light, as when years afterwards recalling it I dreamed that my being had been transformed into the inlet itself, not at dusk, by the moon, but at sunrise, as we had so often also seen it, suddenly transilluminated by the sun's light, so that I seemed to contain the reflected sun deeply within my very soul, yet a sun which as I awoke was in turn transformed, Swedenborgwise, with its light and warmth into something perfectly simple, like a desire to be a better man, to be capable of more gentleness, understanding, love—

There has always been something preternatural about paths, and especially in forests—I know now for I have read more—for not only folklore but poetry abounds with symbolic stories about them: paths that divide and become two paths, paths that lead to a golden kingdom, paths that lead to death, or life, paths where one meets wolves, and who knows? even mountain lions, paths where one loses one's way, paths that not merely divide but become the twenty-one paths that lead back to Eden.

But I did not then need the books to be deeply conscious of this mysterious feeling about paths. I had never heard of a path that shrank before, but we had heard of people who disappeared altogether, people who are seen walking along one moment, and then the next have vanished: and so, overlooking the fact that the experience might have some deeper significance, and solely with the purpose of deliciously making our flesh creep, we made up a story along those lines that night in bed. What if the path became shorter and shorter until I should disappear altogether one evening, when coming back with the water? Or perhaps this story was a means of propitiating fate for the miraculous fact that we had not been separated by not assuming it to be a smug certitude, a form of inoculation, since we still might be separated by the war (I had been rejected a second time by then, probably for being half-witted), against such a separation, and at the same time a kind of parable of the "happy ending" of our lives come what might—for no matter what we might make up about the character on the path, I myself was certainly going to come back from the spring and that journey to end in, for us, a glorious lover's meeting.

But in fact the path did seem in effect to get shorter and shorter, if the impression was never again to be accompanied by quite the same sense of incommunicable experience. No matter how consciously I determined to remember on the outward journey, it always turned out that I had climbed the hill coming back without giving it a thought. And so realistic had our little story become that not many evenings after when I came back with water at dusk my wife came running to meet me, crying:

"Oh my God! I'm so glad to see you!"

"My darling. Well, here I am."

So genuine was the relief on my wife's face, and so genuine was my own feeling at meeting her again, that I was sorry we'd ever made up such a story. But it was a wonderful and profound moment. And just for an instant I felt that had she not come down the path to meet me, I might indeed have disappeared, to spend the rest of my extraterritorial existence searching for her in some limbo.

Up above the topmasts of the trees swayed against the April sky. Suddenly the gulls appeared, as if shot out of a catapult, hurtling downwind above the trees. And over my wife's shoulder, coming across the inlet toward the lighthouse, I saw a deer swimming.

This reminded me that despite the wind it was warm enough for me to start swimming again—I had virtually given up in December—so I went straight in, and it was as though I had been baptized afresh.

It was soon after this that we moved into our little house under the wild cherry tree that we'd bought from the blacksmith.

This house burned down three years later and all the music I had written burned with it, but we built another house ourselves, with the help of Quaggan, Kristbjorg and Mauger, out of driftwood and wood from the sawmill at Eridanus Port, which was now being torn down to make way for a real estate subdivision.

We built it on the same spot as the old house, using the burned posts for part of our foundations that now, being charred, were not susceptible to rot. And the music got itself rewritten too somehow, in a way that was more satisfactory, for I had only to come back to the path to remember parts of it. It was as if the music had even been written during some of these moments. The rest, as any creative artist will understand, was only work.

But I never could recapture my symphony after losing it by fire. And so, still struggling with words as well as music, I wrote an opera. Haunted by a line I had read somewhere: "And from the whole world, as it revolved through space, came a sound of singing," and by the passionate desire to express my own happiness with my wife in Eridanus, I composed this opera, built, like our new house, on the charred foundations and fragments of the old work and our old life. The theme was suggested probably by my thoughts of cleansing and purgation and renewal and the symbols of the cannister, the ladder and so on, and certainly by the inlet itself, and the spring. It was partly in the whole-tone scale, like *Wozzeck*, partly jazz, partly folksongs or songs my wife sang, even old hymns, such as Hear Us O Lord from Heaven Thy Dwelling Place. I even used canons like Frère Jacques to express the ships' engines or the rhythms of eternity; Kristbjorg, Quaggan, my wife and myself, the other inhabitants of Eridanus, my jazz friends, were all characters, or exuberant instruments on the stage or in the pit. The fire was a dramatic incident and our own life, with its withdrawals and returns, what I had learned of nature, and the tides and the sunrises I tried to express. And I tried to write of human happiness in terms of enthusiasm and high seriousness usually reserved for catastrophe and tragedy. The opera was called *The Forest Path to the Spring*.

VIII

Our first little house we had rented from the good Scotsman passed into other hands on his death, though sometimes we used to go down the path by the spring and look at it, and it was only the other day that we did this again. Many years have passed.

Mauger was dead: Bell had gone, and old Sam by the light-house; but Kristbjorg and Quaggan, now seventy-five and a great-grandfather, were still very much alive, and living in the same place. As usual people were threatening to throw us off the beach but somehow we were still there. Mauger's shack toward the lighthouse with its newly shingled roof stood desolate, but we did not feel sad to look at it. His life had been too well accomplished and he died saying, "I never felt better in my life."

We happened to be completely broke when he died but someone had sent some laurels in the shape of an anchor to his funeral where, in the funeral parlor, a woman sang Nearer My God to Thee through a grille and the minister read the Twenty-third Psalm in an improved version. Our suggestion that this be followed by Hear Us O Lord from Heaven Thy Dwelling Place having been abandoned, since no one save ourselves and Quaggan could sing it, our suggestion was likewise neglected. That almost anything be substituted for Nearer My God to Thee, a hymn he hated since his father had been a stoker on the *Titanic*.

There were huge pretentious faked marble Corinthian pillars in the undertaker's parlor on either side of the minister as he read and I kept seeing these change before my eyes into the stanchly beautiful lousy old wooden piles covered with blue mussels on which Mauger's house (and I doubt not more likely, in heaven, should it stand, St. Peter's too) stood. Another fisherman, his brother, was taking the house with its green reticulated nets hanging out to dry. And I thought how selflessly, taking time from their own work, and accepting no money for it, Quaggan and Kristbjorg and Mauger had helped us build our new house, helped us, though all old men, with the cruel work of putting in our foundations, in fact supplied half the foundations themselves. Mauger must have been grateful there were so many who loved him and I was surprised how many at his funeral were summer people we didn't know. Kristbjorg, one of his best friends, had his own ideas about death and had not come at all. Still, he seemed to be there too. When we stopped on the way out to look at Mauger in his coffin he seemed to be smiling, with a twinkling look beneath his heavy mustaches, even mysteriously to be singing to us under his breath:

> *Still you've got a long way to go*
> *You've got a long way to go*
> *Whether you travel by day or night . . .*
> *The judge will tell you so . . .*

Our hamlet on the beach had scarcely changed. On the front of our first house where we had been so happy was a large wooden plaque bearing a name that perhaps had no merit even according to the special categories of waggery through which one was obliged to perceive it: Wuzz-it-2-U? But otherwise it had been improved. The porch had been widened, it had a wireless aerial—maybe someone even listened to our opera upon it, but we hoped not. For the local authorities on hearing rumors of an opera by a local composer had seen an excellent instrument with which to belabor our position on the beach again, so that for a while such embarrassing headlines as OPERATIC SQUATTERS ENDANGER DIGNITY OF CITY—WE NEED SEWERS NOT SYMPHONIES—RICH COMPOSER PREFERS RATSNEST OF PERVERSION were not uncommon, until another fourteen-year-old taxpayer's son committed a sex crime, and the next mayor committed a murder; so that fortunately we did not have long to wait. The house now had a roof ladder, though my old ladder still did duty as steps. There was a new roof-jack and a new chimney. Feeling like thieves we peeked in the window. But where else could all nature look in too, and the house still have privacy? For it did. It was not merely that the sunlight came in, but the very movement and rhythm of the sea, in which the reflections of trees and mountains and sun were counter-reflected and multi-reflected in shimmering movement within. As if part of nature, the very living and moving and breathing reflection of nature itself had been captured. Yet it was built in such a cunningly hidden manner that no one could see into it from a neighboring house. One had to peek in like a thief to do that. A tree we had planted in the back was now the height of the shack, a dogwood clustered like white stars, another wild cherry that had failed to blossom for us was a snow of blooms, while our own primroses we had left for the Scotsman were in flower: fireweed too had sown itself from the seeds of that beautiful willow herb, our unbidden guest, blown downwind from our second house. Once during a winter, when we were in Europe, a child had been born there in a snowstorm. There was a new stove, but the old table and two chairs where we ate in front of the window were still there. There was the bunk where we had spent our honeymoon—and what a long honeymoon it had turned out to be—and desired each other and anguished at the fear of losing each other and our hearts had been troubled, and we had seen the stars and the moon rise, and listened to the roar of the surf on the wild stormy nights of our first winter, and the grandmother of the cat that accompanied us now had slept with us and pulled our hair in the morning to wake us up— Valetta, long since gathered to the rest of her strange moonkind. Yet who would think, to look at the place idly, with its ramshackle air, its sense of impermanence, of improvisation, that such a beauty of existence, such happiness could be possible there, such dramas have taken place? Look at that old hut, the passerby shouts in his motor launch above the engine, laughing contemptuously: oh well, we'll be pulling down all those eyesores now. Start here, and keep going! Autocamps for the better class, hotels, cut down all those trees, open it up for the public, put it on the map. Nothing but receivers of stolen goods and a few old pirates live in the ratsnests anyway. Squatters! The government's been trying to get them off for years!

It was there that our own life had come into being and for all its strangeness and conflict, a pang of sadness struck us now. Longing and hope fulfilled, loss and rediscovery, failure and accomplishment, sorrow and joy

seemed annealed into one profound emotion. From the porch where we stood
we could see dimly—for there was suddenly a spring fog billowing in across
the water—right across the arc of the bay to where our next house had
burned down and there was no tragedy about that either. Our new house
stood clearly visible in its place, though as we watched it began to be
swallowed up by the fog.

As the mist rolled up toward us, beginning to envelop us, the
sun still trying to maintain itself like a platinum disc, it was as if the essence
of a kind of music that had forever receded there, that seemed evoked from
the comments of my wife as she looked through this window, out on to this
porch in the first days when we'd just meant to spend a week, or in the autumn when we still stayed on, while she was making the coffee, talking to herself partly for my benefit, describing the day to me, as if I had been like a
blind man recovering his sight to whom she had to teach again the beauties
and oddities of the world, as if it became unlocked, began to play, to our
inner ear, not music but having the effect of music, not sentimental at all, but
fresh and innocent, and only moving because it was so happy, or because
happiness is moving; or it was like a whispering of the ghosts of ourselves.
"Sunrise of the dying moon, in a green sky ... White frost on the porch and
all the roofs, the first heavy frost of the year ... There's a little flotilla of
golden eyes under the window, and the raccoons have been here during the
night, I can see their tracks ... The tide is high. My poor seagulls, they're
hungry. How cold your feet must be down there, in that icy water ... Look—
now! like a bonfire! Like a burning cathedral. I must wash the windows.
There's a wash from a fishing boat like a strand of silver Christmas tinsel. The
sunrise does things to these mists. ... I must put out some breakfast for the
cat. He'll come in very hungry from his dawn prowl. There goes a cormorant. There goes a great loon. The frost sparkles like diamond dust. I used
to think it was fairy diamonds as a child. In a few minutes it will melt and the
porch will be wet and black, with a sprinkling of harlequin leaves. The mountains look very hazy and far away this morning, that's a sign it will be a good
day. ..."

Strange magnificent honeymoon that had become one's whole
life.

We climbed the steps—they were the same steps made from my
ladder and they still held—and began to walk into the mist and down the path
to the spring. The fog was thick in the forest, like smoke pouring toward us as
from a funnel beneath the bushes, in which it was curious to hear the inter-
mittent insulated twitterings of birds gradually hushing. Talking of those first
days, my wife remembered how once for nearly a month there had been a fog
so thick we couldn't see across the inlet, and what boats went by unseen, only
known by a mournful continued hooting of foghorns and lonely bells. Sometimes Kristbjorg's boat had appeared dimly as it did now and the point ahead
would fade in and out and sometimes we could scarcely see beyond the
porch, so that it had been like living at the edge of eternity. And we remembered too the days when it had been dark and freezing with a film of ice on
the blackened porch and the steps, and the lamp going until ten o'clock in the

morning. And the ships that would steer by dead reckoning listening for the echo of their hooters from the bank, though we could hear their engines, as we heard a ship's engine now, going very softly:

Frère Jacques
Frère Jacques
Dormez-vous?
Dormez-vous?

And the snowstorms in which there was no echo. And the sense of the snow driving on the night in the world outside too, and such a storm as would yield no echo. And ourselves seemed the only lamp of love within it.

Or there would seem something about these little shacks, as there did now, as mysterious and hidden as the never-found nest of the marbled murrelet, that also haunted these shores.

The path had scarcely changed; nor, here, had the forest. Civilization, creator of deathscapes, like a dull-witted fire of ugliness and ferocious stupidity—so unimaginative it had even almost managed to spoil the architectural beauty of our oil refinery—had spread all down the opposite bank, blown over the water and crept up upon us from the south along it, murdering the trees and taking down the shacks as it went, but it had become baffled by the Indian reserve, and a law that had not been repealed that forbade building too near a lighthouse, so to the south we were miraculously saved by civilization itself (of which a lighthouse is perhaps always the highest symbol) as if it too had become conscious of the futility of pretending that it was advancing by creating the moribund. And it was the same way to the north, where battles between real estate sharks over the living and dead body of Eridanus Port had resulted in the return, little by little, of the jungle itself, and vines and thimbleberry already covered the ill-surveyed lots of the subsection among the few trees that had been left. But some people lived happily there after all, who could afford it. And even beautifully. For man—whose depredations, where they did not threaten the entire country with drought and desolation, sometimes by accident provided a better view—had not succeeded yet in hacking down the mountains and the stars.

The bells of a train, slowly moving northward along the coast tracks began to sound through the fog across the water. I could remember a time when these bells had seemed to me exactly like the thudding of school bells, summoning one to some unwelcome task. Then they had seemed like somber church bells, tolling for a funeral. But now, at this moment, they struck clear as gay chimes, Christmas bells, birthday bells, harbor bells, pealing through the unraveling mist as for a city liberated, or some great spiritual victory of mankind. And they seemed to mingle with the song of the ship now distant, round the point—but so great a conductor of sound is water that its engines thudded as if at a fathom's distance:

Dormez-vous?
Dormez-vous?
Sonnez les matines!
Sonnez les matines!

And ourselves? How had we changed? We were many years older. We had traveled, been to the Orient, and Europe, grown rich and poor again, and always returned here. But were we older? My wife seemed young and beautiful and wild as ever, far more so. She still had the figure of a young girl and she had the wonder of a young girl. Her wide frank long-lashed eyes still changed color from green to yellow like a tiger cub's. Her brow could become chaotic with frowns and it is true that despair had once carved lines of suffering on her face, though I thought these signs vanished or came at will with her moods; they vanished when she was alive and interested, and she was uniquely alive, vivid and exciting.

"He no longer loves the person whom he loved ten years ago," said gloomy old Pascal. I quite believe it. "She is no longer the same, nor is he. He was young, and she also: she is quite different. He would perhaps love her yet, if she were what she was then." So gloomy profound old Pascal, the unselfish helper of my youth in other ways, had once seemed to threaten our future age. And yet not so. Surely I loved her now much more, I had more years to love with. Why should I expect her to be the same? Though she was the same in a way, just as this spring was the same, and not the same, as the springs of years ago. And I wondered if what really we should see in age is merely the principle of the seasons themselves wearing out, only to renew themselves through another kind of death. And indeed the seasons themselves in their duration and character had changed, or seemed to have changed, much more than she. Our winters came more forthrightly down from the arctic now, in the East they were getting our old Western winters, and this winter had been the longest and gloomiest we had ever known, and one had almost seemed to feel the onset of another ice age, another search for Eden. So much more welcome and sweeter the spring, now it had come. I myself however had aged in appearance. I had even quite a few white hairs, on one side, and our latest joke was that I was "graying at the temple." On the other hand I did not feel older, and bodily I was twice as strong, and I was in every way full of health. The port of fifty now seemed to me quite blithe, and as for old Pascal, he had died younger than I was now. The poor old chap would not have said such things if he'd only lived a bit longer, I thought.

"I wonder where Kristbjorg is, these days."

"There he is."

And here he had just appeared, stepping out of the mist. He had been fishing up the Fraser River, because he was "in death" as he said, his more than explicit phrase for "in debt." But the cold for the first time had caused him to move into the city for a while last winter, though he had left his boat for Quaggan and ourselves to look after. He was getting on for seventy, and was much thinner, but hale and hearty, and many lines seemed to have been smoothed from his face. He no longer sang the song about the storm in the red-light district but he still wore the same lumberjacket and good Irish tweed trousers he had worn in his fifties when not ten years older than I was now and I had thought him an old man, though now I thought him nearer my own age.

"Why there you are, Nicolai, we missed you."

"Ah well, this weather's changing, Missus. . . . Been in town . . . The streetcars are getting so humpy and dumpy, I never saw a street flusher. They just letting the old grime go. . . . I ran into a couple of bottles of rye. . . ."

He passed into the mist and we continued along our path, the Bell-Proteus path, that on the reverse journey had once long since seemed to get so much longer, and then so much shorter. The fog was lifting and I thought:

How wrongly we interpreted that whole strange experience. Or rather how was it that it had never occurred to us, seriously, to interpret it at all, let alone to see it as a warning, a form of message, even as a message that shadowed forth a kind of strange command, a command that, it seemed to me, I had obeyed! And yet, all my heeding of any warning it contained would not have averted the suffering immediately ahead. Only dimly, even now, did I understand it. Sometimes I felt that the path had only seemed to grow shorter because the burden, the cannister, had grown lighter as I grew physically stronger. Then again I could become convinced that the significance of the experience lay not in the path at all, but in the possibility that in converting the very cannister I carried, the ladder down which I climbed every time I went to the spring—in converting both these derelicts to use I had prefigured something I should have done with my soul. Then of course, and pre-eminently there was the lion. But I lacked spiritual equipment to follow such thoughts through. This much I understood, and had understood that as a man I had become tyrannized by the past, and that it was my duty to transcend it in the present. Yet my new vocation was involved with using that past—for this was the underlying meaning of my symphony, even my opera, the second opera I was now writing, the second symphony I would one day write—with turning it into use for others. And to do this, even before writing a note, it was necessary to face that past as far as possible without fear. Ah yes, and it was that, that I had begun to do here. And if I had not done so, how could we have been happy, as we now were happy?

How could I have helped you, I seemed to be saying to my wife, in the deepest sense even have loved you? However would we have found strength to endure the more furious past that was then ahead of us, to endure the fire, the destruction of our hopes, our house, to be rich and poor, known and unknown again, to endure the fear, the onset and the defeat of disease— even of madness, for to be deprived of one's house may, in a sense, be said to be like being deprived of one's rational faculty. How else have survived the shrieks of a dying piano, even, as a matter of fact, have come, somehow, to see something actually funny about all that? And how, above all, have found strength to rebuild on the same spot, right in the teeth of the terror of fire that had grown up between us and that had also been defeated? And I remembered the time when, homeless, having lost everything we had in the world, we had been drawn, not many weeks after the fire, to the still malodorous ruin of that house, before dawn, and watching the sun rise, had seemed to draw strength out of the sunrise itself for the decision once more to stay, to rebuild that haunted ruin we loved so much that we created our most jubilant memory that very day, when careless of its charred and tragic smell we wonderfully picnicked within it, diving off the blackened posts into the natural swimming pool of our old living room and frightening away I have no doubt the devil himself, who, the enemy of all humor in the face of disaster, as of all human delight, and often disguised as a social worker for the common good —for that we had saved the forest was not so important as that we had seemed to threaten some valuable potential real estate—wants nothing so much as that man shall believe himself unfriended by any higher power than he.

And yet, on the other side, else life would be composed of mere heroics that were all vain gestures to oneself, it had been necessary to go beyond remorse, beyond even contrition. I have often wondered whether it is not man's ordeal to make his contrition active. Sometimes I had the feeling I was attacking the past rationally as with a clawbar and hammer, while trying to make it into something else for a supernatural end. In a manner I changed it by changing myself and having changed it found it necessary to pass beyond the pride I felt in my accomplishment, and to accept myself as a fool again. I'm sure that even old Hank Gleason, though he would put this into better English, or different English, would see my point. Nothing is more humbling than the wreckage of a burned house, the fragments of consumed work. But it is necessary not to take pride in such masterly pieces of damnation either, especially when they have become so nearly universal. If we had progressed, I thought, it was as if to a region where such words as spring, water, houses, trees, vines, laurels, mountains, wolves, bay, roses, beach, islands, forest, tides and deer and snow and fire, had realized their true being, or had their source: and as these words on a page once stood merely to what they symbolized, so did the reality we knew now stand to something else beyond that that symbolized or reflected: it was as if we were clothed in the kind of reality which before we saw only at a distance, or to translate it into terms of my own vocation, it was as if we lived in a medium to which that in which our old lives moved, happy though they were, was like simply the bald verbal inspiration to the music we had achieved. I speak in terms of our lives only: my own compositions have always fallen far short of the great, indeed they will never perhaps be anything more than second-rate, but at least as it seemed to me there was room for them in the world, and I—and we—had happiness in their execution.

We were still on earth, still in the same place, but if someone had charged us with the notion that we had gone to heaven and that this was the after life we would not have said him nay for long. Moreover if we had been charged with formerly having been in hell for a while we could probably have had to say yes too, though adding that on the whole we liked that fine, as long as we were together, and were sometimes even homesick for it, though this life had many advantages over the other.

Still, indeed, we had the hellish fear of losing our third little house but now the joy and happiness of what we had known would go with us wherever we went or God sent us and would not die. I cannot really well express what I mean but merely set this down in the Montaigne-like belief— or as someone said, speaking about Montaigne—that the experience of one happy man might be useful.

The fog began to lift and we saw the train, it was drawn by a diesel engine of sinister appearance (the first one I ever saw in my life but I recognized it from the photogravure pictures in the *Sun*) departing quite silently now into the future to become obsolete and romantic in turn. Men could not do altogether without the nostalgic mountain-borne wailing of the old steam engines it seemed, so it had been equipped with a device, a touching compromise, that mooed like a cow intermittently as it slid along into the mountain pines.

But even in that moo, of nautical timbre, as it slid into the great Cordilleras, among these northern cousins of Popocatepetl, so that those working on the lines must think that a freighter approached, it was possible to detect I thought, that note of artistry which denoted Mr. Bell, a signal to his old home, and the good people, English immigrants, an electrician and his family, who now inhabited it.

The wash from the invisible freighter, the wash still invisible itself from where we were on the path, could be heard breaking all along the curve of the beach as it approached us, and simultaneously it began, slowly at first, and gently, to rain, and as the wash of undulating silver rippling into sight transversely spent itself against the rocks we stopped to watch the rain like a bead curtain falling behind a gap in the trees, into the inlet below.

Each drop falling into the sea is like a life, I thought, each producing a circle in the ocean, or the medium of life itself, and widening into infinity, though it seems to melt into the sea, and become invisible, or disappear entirely, and be lost. Each is interlocked with other circles falling about it, some are larger circles expanding widely and engulfing others, some are weaker, smaller circles that only seem to last a short while. And smiling as I remembered my lesson I thought of that first time when we had seen the rain falling into a calm sea like a dark mirror, and we had found the cannister and decided to stay.

But last night I had seen something new; my wife had called me out of bed to the open window to see what she first thought was a school of little fishes breaking the still water just beneath, where the tide was high under the house. Then we saw that the whole dark water was covered with bright expanding phosphorescent circles. Only when my wife felt the warm mild rain on her naked shoulder did she realize it was raining. They were perfect expanding circles of light, first tiny circles bright as a coin, then becoming expanding rings growing fainter and fainter, while as the rain fell into the phosphorescent water each raindrop expanded into a ripple that was translated into light. And the rain itself was water from the sea, as my wife first taught me, raised to heaven by the sun, transformed into clouds, and falling again into the sea. While within the inlet itself the tides and currents in that sea returned, became remote, and becoming remote, like that which is called the Tao, returned again as we ourselves had done.

Now, somewhere in the unseen west where it was setting, the sun broke through the clouds, sending a flare of light across the water turning the rain into a sudden shower of pearls and touching the mountains, where the mist rising now almost perpendicularly from the black abysses fumed heavenward in pure white fire.

Three rainbows went up like rockets across the bay: one for the cat. They faded and there, in the east, a widening rift of clouds had become a patch of clear rain-washed sky. Arcturus. Spica. Procyon overhead, and Regulus in the Lion over the oil refinery. But Orion must have already set behind the sun so that, though we were Eridanus, Eridanus was nowhere to be found. And on the point the lighthouse began its beneficent signaling into the twilight.

And the spring? Here it was. It still ran, down through the jack-in-the-pulpits, down toward Hi-Doubt. It purified itself a bit as it came down from the mountains, but it always carried with it a faint tang of mushrooms, earth, dead leaves, pine needles, mud and snow, on its way down to the inlet and out to the Pacific. In the deeper reaches of the forest, in the somber damp caves, where the dead branches hang bowed down with moss, and death camass and the destroying angel grow, it was haggard and chill and tragic, unsure measurer of its path. Feeling its way underground it must have had its dark moments. But here, in springtime, on its last lap to the sea, it was as at its source a happy joyous little stream.

High above the pine trees swayed against the sky, out of the west came the seagulls with their angelic wings, coming home to rest. And I remembered how every evening I used to go down this path through the forest to get water from the spring at dusk. . . . Looking over my wife's shoulder I could see a deer swimming toward the lighthouse.

Laughing we stooped down to the stream and drank.

ALICE MUNRO

The Time of Death

Born in Wingham, Ontario in 1931, Alice Munro attended the University of Western Ontario. She moved to British Columbia in 1951, where she now lives in Victoria. Her stories have appeared in many Canadian literary magazines, and were collected in Dance of the Happy Shades, *which won the Governor General's Award for Fiction in 1968. In 1971 she published* Lives of Girls and Women, *a novel which has received wide critical acclaim.*

Afterwards the mother, Leona Parry, lay on the couch, with a quilt around her, and the women kept putting more wood on the fire although the kitchen was very hot, and no one turned the light on. Leona drank some tea and refused to eat, and talked, beginning like this, in a voice that was ragged and insistent but not yet hysterical: I wasn't hardly out of the house, I wasn't out of the house twenty minutes—

(Three-quarters of an hour at the least, Allie McGee thought, but she did not say so, not at the time. But she remembered, because there were three serials on the radio she was trying to listen to, she listened to every day, and she couldn't get half of them; Leona was there in her kitchen going on about Patricia. Leona was sewing this cowgirl outfit for Patricia on Allie's machine; she raced the machine and she pulled the thread straight out to break it instead of pulling it back though Allie had told her don't do that please it's liable to break the needle. Patricia was supposed to have the outfit for that night when she sang at a concert up the valley; she was singing Western pieces. Patricia sang with the Maitland Valley Entertainers, who went all over the country playing at concerts and dances. Patricia was introduced as the Little Sweetheart of Maitland Valley, the Baby Blonde, the Pint-Size Kiddie with the Great Big Voice. She did have a big voice, almost alarming in so frail a child. Leona had started her singing in public when she was three years old.

Never was ascared once, Leona said, leaning forward with a jerky pressure on the pedal, it just comes natural to her to perform. Her kimona fallen open revealed her lean chest, her wilted breasts with their large blue veins sloping into the grey-pink nightgown. She don't care, it could be the King of England watching her, she'd get up and sing, and when she was through singing she'd sit down, that's just the way she is. She's even got a good name for a singer, Patricia Parry, doesn't that sound like you just heard it announced over the air? Another thing is natural blonde hair. I have to do it up in rags every night of her life, but that real natural blonde is a lot scarcer than natural curly. It don't get dark, either, there's that strain of natural blondes in my family that don't get dark. My cousin I told you about, that won the Miss St. Catharines of 1936, she was one, and my aunt that died—)

Allie McGee did not say, and Leona caught her breath and plunged on: Twenty minutes. And that last thing I said to her as I went out the door was, you keep an eye on the kids! She's nine years old, isn't she? I'm just going to run acrost the road to sew up this outfit, you keep an eye on the kids. And I went out the door and down the steps and down to the end of the garden and just as I took the hook off the gate something stopped me, I thought, *something's wrong!* What's wrong, I said to myself. I stood there and I looked back at the garden and all I could see was the cornstalks standing and the cabbages there frozen, we never got them in this year, and I looked up and down the road and all I could see was Mundy's old hound laying out in front of their place, no cars comin' one way or the other and the yards all empty, it was cold I guess and no kids playin' out—And I thought, My Lord, maybe I got my days mixed up and this isn't Saturday morning, it's some special day I forgot about— Then I thought all it was was the snow coming I could feel in the air, and you know how cold it was, the puddles in the road was all turned to ice and splintered up—but it didn't snow, did it, it hasn't snowed yet—And I run acrost the road then over to McGee's and up the front steps and Allie says, Leona, what's the matter with you, you look so white, she says—

Allie McGee heard this too and said nothing, because it was not a time for any sort of accuracy. Leona's voice had gone higher and higher as she talked and any time now she might break off and begin to scream: Don't let that kid come near me, don't let me see her, just don't let her come near me.

And the women in the kitchen would crowd around the couch, their big bodies indistinct in the half-light, their faces looming pale and heavy, hung with the ritual masks of mourning and compassion. Now lay down, they would say, in the stately tones of ritual soothing. Lay down, Leona, she ain't here, it's all right.

And the girl from the Salvation Army would say, in her gentle unchanging voice, You must forgive her, Mrs. Parry, she is only a child. Sometimes the Salvation Army girl would say: It is God's will, we do not understand. The other woman from the Salvation Army, who was older, with an oily, sallow face and an almost masculine voice, said: In the garden of heaven the children bloom like flowers. God needed another flower and he took your child. Sister, you should thank him and be glad.

The other women listened uneasily while these spoke; their faces at such words took on a look of embarrassed childish solemnity. They made tea and set out on the table the pies and fruitcake and scones that people had sent, and they themselves had made. Nobody ate anything because Leona would not eat. Many of the women cried, but not the two from the Army.

Allie McGee cried. She was stout, placid-faced, big-breasted; she had no children. Leona drew up her knees under the quilt and rocked herself back and forth as she wept, and threw her head down and then back (showing, as some of them noticed with a feeling of shame, the dirty lines on her neck). Then she grew quiet and said with something like surprise: I nursed him till he was ten months old. He was so good, too, you never would of known you had him in the house. I always said, that's the best one I ever had.

In the dark overheated kitchen the women felt the dignity of this sorrow in their maternal flesh, they were humble before this unwashed, unliked and desolate Leona. When the men came in—the father, a cousin, a neighbour, bringing a load of wood or asking shamefacedly for something to eat—they were at once aware of something that shut them out, that reproved them. They went out and said to the other men, Yeah, they're still at it. And the father who was getting a little drunk, and belligerent, because he felt that something was expected of him and he was not equal to it, it was not fair, said, Yeah, that won't do Benny any good, they can bawl their eyes out.

George and Irene had been playing their cut-out game, cutting things out of the catalogue. They had this family they had cut out of the catalogue, the mother and father and the kids, and they cut out clothes for them. Patricia watched them cutting and she said, Look at the way you kids cut out! Lookit all the white around the edges! How are you going to make those clothes stay on, she said, you didn't even cut any fold-over things. She took the scissors and she cut very neatly, not leaving any white around the edges; her pale shrewd little face was bent to one side; her lips bitten together. She did things the way a grown-up does; she did not pretend things. She did not play at being a singer, though she was going to be a singer when she grew up, maybe in the movies or maybe on the radio. She liked to look at movie magazines and magazines with pictures of clothes and rooms in them; she liked to look in the windows of some of the houses uptown.

Benny was trying to climb up on the couch. He grabbed at the catalogue and Irene hit his hand. He began to whimper. Patricia picked him up competently and carried him to the window. She stood him on a chair looking out, saying to him, Bow-wow, Benny, see bow-wow— It was Mundy's dog, getting up and shaking himself and going off down the road.

Bow-wow, said Benny interrogatively, putting his hands flat and leaning against the window to see where the dog went. Benny was eighteen months old and the only words he knew how to say were Bow-wow and Bram. Bram was for the scissors-man who came along the road sometimes; Brandon was his name. Benny remembered him, and ran out to meet him when he came. Other little kids only thirteen, fourteen months old knew more words than Benny, and could do more things, like waving bye-bye and clapping hands, and most of them were cuter to look at. Benny was long and thin and bony and his face was like his father's—pale, mute, unexpectant; all it needed was a soiled peaked cap. But he was good; he would stand for hours just looking out a window saying Bow-wow, bow-wow, now in a low questioning tone, now crooningly, stroking his hands down the window-pane. He liked you to pick him up and hold him, long as he was, just like a little baby;

he would lie looking up and smiling, with a little timidity or misgiving. Patricia knew he was stupid; she hated stupid things. He was the only stupid thing she did not hate. She would go and wipe his nose, expertly and impersonally, she would try to get him to talk, repeating words after her, she would put her face down to his, saying anxiously, Hi, Benny, *Hi*, and he would look at her and smile in his slow dubious way. That gave her this feeling, a kind of sad tired feeling, and she would go away and leave him, she would go and look at a movie magazine.

She had had a cup of tea and part of a sugar-bun for breakfast; now she was hungry. She rummaged around among the dirty dishes and puddles of milk and porridge on the kitchen table; she picked up a bun, but it was sopping with milk and she threw it down again.

This place stinks, she said. Irene and George paid no attention. She kicked at a crust of porridge that had dried on the linoleum. Lookit that, she said. Lookit *that!* What's it always a mess around here for? She walked around kicking at things perfunctorily. Then she got the scrub-pail from under the sink and a dipper, and she began to dip water from the reservoir of the stove.

I'm going to clean this place up, she said. It never gets cleaned up like other places. The first thing I'm going to do I'm going to scrub the floor and you kids have to help me—

She put the pail on the stove.

That water is hot to start with, Irene said.

It's not hot enough. It's got to be good and boiling hot. I seen Mrs. McGee scrub *her* floor.

They stayed at Mrs. McGee's all night. They had been over there since the ambulance came. They saw Leona and Mrs. McGee and the other neighbours start to pull off Benny's clothes and it looked like parts of his skin were coming away too, and Benny was making a noise not like crying, but more a noise like they had heard a dog making after its hind parts were run over, but worse, and louder— But Mrs. McGee saw them; she cried, Go away, go away from here! Go over to my place, she cried. After that the ambulance had come and taken Benny away to the hospital, and Mrs. McGee came over and told them that Benny was going to the hospital for a while and they were going to stay at her place. She gave them bread and peanut butter and bread and strawberry jam.

The bed they slept in had a feather tick and smooth ironed sheets; the blankets were pale and fluffy and smelled faintly of mothballs. On top of everything else was a Star-of-Bethlehem quilt; they knew it was called that because when they were getting ready for bed Patricia said, My, what a beautiful quilt! and Mrs. McGee looking surprised and rather distracted said, Oh, yes, that's a Star-of-Bethlehem.

Patricia was very polite in Mrs. McGee's house. It was not as nice as some of the houses uptown but it was covered on the outside with imitation brick and inside it had an imitation fireplace, as well as a fern in a basket; it was not like the other houses along the highway. Mr. McGee did not work in the mill like the other men, but in a store.

George and Irene were so shy and alarmed in this house that they could not answer when they were spoken to.

They all woke up very early; they lay on their backs, uneasy between the fresh sheets, and they watched the room getting light. This room had mauve silk curtains and Venetian blinds and mauve and yellow roses on the wallpaper; it was the guest room. Patricia said, We slept in the guest room.

I have to go, George said.

I'll show you where the bathroom is, Patricia said. It's down the hall.

But George wouldn't go down there to the bathroom. He didn't like it. Patricia tried to make him but he wouldn't.

See if there is a pot under the bed, Irene said.

They got a bathroom here they haven't got any pots, Patricia said angrily. What would they have a stinking old pot for?

George said stolidly that he wouldn't go down there.

Patricia got up and tip-toed to the dresser and got a big vase. When George had gone she opened the window very carefully with hardly any noise and emptied the vase and dried it out with Irene's underpants.

Now, she said, you kids shut up and lay still. Don't talk out loud just whisper.

George whispered, Is Benny still in the hospital?

Yes he is, said Patricia shortly.

Is he going to die?

I told you a hundred times, no.

Is he?

No! Just his skin got burnt, he didn't get burnt inside. He isn't going to die of a little bit of burnt skin is he? Don't talk so loud.

Irene began to twist her head into the pillow.

What's the matter with you? Patricia said.

He cried awful, Irene said, her face in the pillow.

Well it hurt, that's why he cried. When they got him to the hospital they gave him some stuff that made it stop hurting.

How do you know? George said.

I know.

They were quiet for a while and then Patricia said, I never in my life heard of anybody that died of a burnt skin. Your whole skin could be burnt off it wouldn't matter you could just grow another. Irene stop crying or I'll hit you.

Patricia lay still, looking up at the ceiling, her sharp profile white against the mauve silk curtains of Mrs. McGee's guest room.

For breakfast they had grapefruit, which they did not remember having tasted before, and cornflakes and toast and jam. Patricia watched George and Irene and snapped at them, Say please! Say thank-you! She said to Mr. and Mrs. McGee, What a cold day, I wouldn't be surprised if it snowed today would you?

But they did not answer. Mrs. McGee's face was swollen. After breakfast she said, Don't get up, children, listen to me. Your little brother—

Irene began to cry and that started George crying too; he said sobbingly, triumphantly to Patricia. He did so die, he did so! Patricia did not answer. *It's her fault*, George sobbed, and Mrs. McGee said, Oh, no, oh, no! But Patricia sat still, with her face wary and polite. She did not say anything until the crying had died down a bit and Mrs. McGee got up sighing and began to clear the table. Then Patricia offered to help with the dishes.

Mrs. McGee took them downtown to buy them all new shoes for the funeral. Patricia was not going to the funeral because Leona said she never wanted to see her again as long as she lived, but she was to get new shoes too; it would have been unkind to leave her out. Mrs. McGee took them into the store and sat them down and explained the situation to the man who owned it; they stood together nodding and whispering gravely. The man told them to take off their shoes and socks. George and Irene took theirs off and stuck out their feet, with the black dirt-caked toenails. Patricia whispered to Mrs. McGee that she had to go to the bathroom and Mrs. McGee told her where it was, at the back of the store, and she went out there and took off her shoes and her socks. She got her feet as clean as she could with cold water and paper towels. When she came back she heard Mrs. McGee was saying softly to the store-man, You should of seen the bedsheets I had them on. Patricia walked past them not letting on she heard.

Irene and George got oxfords and Patricia got a pair she chose herself, with a strap across. She looked at them in the low mirror. She walked back and forth looking at them until Mrs. McGee said, Patricia never mind about shoes now! Would you believe it? she said in that same soft voice to the store-man as they walked out of the store.

After the funeral was over they went home. The women had cleaned up the house and put Benny's things away. Their father had got sick from so much beer in the back shed after the funeral and he stayed away from the house. Their mother had been put to bed. She stayed there for three days and their father's sister looked after the house.

Leona said they were not to let Patricia come near her room. Don't let her come up here, she cried, I don't want to see her, I haven't forgot my baby boy. But Patricia did not try to go upstairs. She paid no attention to any of this; she looked at movie magazines and did her hair up in rags. If someone cried she did not notice; with her it was as if nothing had happened.

The man who was the manager of the Maitland Valley Entertainers came to see Leona. He told her they were doing the program for a big concert and barn-dance over at Rockland, and he wanted Patricia to sing in it, if it wasn't too soon after what happened and all. Leona said she would have to think about it. She got out of bed and went downstairs. Patricia was sitting on the couch with one of her magazines. She kept her head down.

That's a fine head of hair you got there, Leona said. I see you been doing it up your ownself. Get me the brush and comb!

To her sister-in-law she said, What's life? You gotta go on.

She went downtown and bought some sheet music, two songs: May the Circle Be Unbroken, and It Is No Secret, What God Can Do. She had Patricia learn them, and Patricia sang these two songs at the concert in Rockland. People in the audience started whispering, because they had heard about Benny, it had been in the paper. They pointed out Leona, who was dressed up and sitting on the platform, and she had her head down, she was crying. Some people in the audience cried too. Patricia did not cry.

In the first week of November (and the snow had not come, the snow had not come yet) the scissors-man with his cart came walking along beside the highway. The children were playing out in the yards and they heard him coming; when he was still far down the road they heard his unintelligible chant, mournful and shrill, and so strange that you would think, if you did not know it was the scissors-man, that there was a madman loose in the world. He wore the same stained brown overcoat, with the hem hanging ragged, and the same crownless felt hat; he came up the road, calling like this and the children ran into the houses to get knives and scissors, or they ran out in the road calling excitedly, Old Brandon, old Brandon (for that was his name).

Then in the Parry's yard Patricia began to scream: I hate that old scissors-man! I hate him! she screamed. I hate that old scissors-man, I hate him! She screamed, standing stock-still in the yard with her face looking so wizened and white. The shrill shaking cries brought Leona running out, and the neighbours; they pulled her into the house, still screaming. They could not get her to say what was the matter; they thought she must be having some kind of fit. Her eyes were screwed up tight and her mouth wide open; her tiny pointed teeth were almost transparent, and faintly rotten at the edges; they made her look like a ferret, a wretched little animal insane with rage or fear. They tried shaking her, slapping her, throwing cold water on her face; at last they got her to swallow a big dose of soothing-syrup with a lot of whisky in it, and they put her to bed.

That is a prize kid of Leona's, the neighbours said to each other as they went home. That *singer,* they said, because now things were back to normal and they disliked Leona as much as before. They laughed gloomily and said, Yeah, that future movie-star. Out in the yard yelling, you'd think she'd gone off her head.

There was this house, and the other wooden houses that had never been painted, with their steep patched roofs and their narrow, slanting porches, the wood-smoke coming out of their chimneys and dim children's faces pressed against their windows. Behind them there was the strip of earth, plowed in some places, run to grass in others, full of stones, and behind this the pine trees, not very tall. In front were the yards, the dead gardens, the grey highway running out from town. The snow came, falling slowly, evenly, between the highway and the houses and the pine trees, falling in big flakes at first and then in smaller and smaller flakes that did not melt on the hard furrows, the rock of the earth.

ALDEN NOWLAN

There Was An Old Woman From Wexford

*Alden Nowlan was born near Windsor, Nova Scotia, in 1933.
He left school early, and worked at a variety of jobs before be-
coming a newspaper reporter and later night news editor of*
The Telegraph-Journal *in Saint John, New Brunswick. He has
published several collections of poetry, including* The Mysterious
Naked Man, *and one collection of short stories,* Miracle At
Indian River. *In 1968 he won the Governor General's Award
for Poetry.*

There was the absolute darkness that is possible only in places where human
beings are few and live far apart, a darkness in which the only solids are those
close enough to touch. So nothing was substantial except his own body and
the bed on which he lay listening to the sound of his grandmother singing.

It was hot, and the nightjars were whistling outside his window.
It was strange and a little disquieting to hear the birds whistling in the darkness. He had kicked away the quilts and wiggled, more than half asleep, out
of his clammy underwear, so that now he lay curled up in the salty smell of
his naked body, the moist pubescent odour of himself.

Her singing had awakened him many times during the past
month. Sometimes he almost wept, sometimes, although he tried not to admit
it to himself, he wished that something, anything, even death would shut her
up, and sometimes he went back to sleep without thinking about it at all.

She had sung *I Come to the Garden Alone.* He had heard her
sing it often before her illness. That's a Billy Sunday hymn, she always explained. Proudly. Her brother—one of her brothers, David, who was killed
with the Sixth Mounted Rifles, or Joseph, who could drink a forty ouncer of
navy rum and shoulder a hogshead of flour without batting an eye, her
brother had heard Billy Sunday preach in Boston or Bangor or Portland and
afterwards they took up the collection in baskets and every basket was filled
to overflowing with five, ten, twenty, fifty and one hundred dollar bills. She
described the baskets of money as Mary or Martha might have described the
miraculous loaves and fishes.

And she had sung *There is a Fountain Filled with Blood.* Seated
in her rocking chair, a hot brick wrapped in an old sweater or stuffed into an
old wool sock pressed hard against her belly to ease the pain, other bricks

warming on the back of the wood stove (Enterprise Foundry, Sackville, New Brunswick) the teapot brewing, as it always was: she added leaves (Red Rose Orange Pekoe) whenever it became too weak for her taste, emptied them only when there was no room left for water, simply opened the kitchen door and dashed them out into the yard. And what she smelled of was burning wool and ginger and cloves and a liniment called Oil of Wintergreen.

> *There is a fountain filled with blood*
> *Drawn from Emmanuel's veins*
> *And sinners plunged beneath that flood*
> *Lose all their guilty stains.*

The window blinds shrugged like the wings of some enormous mystic bird, like the wings of the blue heron that fed in the swamp between the river and the railroad. He was afraid of the blue heron, had always been afraid of it, yet he would stand sometimes for as long as thirty minutes, spying on it. From the hill overlooking the swamp the bird looked bigger and vastly stronger than he; certainly its legs were longer than his, or so it seemed to him, and he could imagine it running after him—in his imagination it ran rather than flew—and beating him down with its great beak, legs and wings. The wonder that he felt, watching it, was close to worship.

"Mother," a voice said. "Please, Mother." That would be his Aunt Lorna, who would be hugging together the flaps of a faded red wrapper, and who would not have put on her glasses. Her eyes looked naked without glasses: it was the stark white adult nakedness that made him shifty-eyed with embarrassment; and there were faint purplish indentations on her temples. *Keep The Lower Lights A'-Burning* his grandmother sang now, her voice louder, much louder, childishly derisive and defiant.

In Aunt Lorna's voice a deep-throated adult sorrow gave way reluctantly to a whine almost like that of a small girl screwing down the lid on a sob. He rolled over in bed and raised his head slightly, listening, but he could not distinguish sentences: only words jutting out like rocks from a river of murmurs. It was as if between the words *mother* and *bed* and *late* and *please*, each of them repeated many times, his aunt were droning wordlessly through her nose with the tip of her tongue pushing hard against her lower teeth.

The old woman wore a black wig shaped like an inverted soup bowl and boasted about her jet-black hair. She rouged herself with bits of crepe paper moistened with saliva and bragged about the youthful redness of her cheeks. As a young woman, after her husband went to Saskatchewan to harvest wheat and did not return, she had gone into the woods alone, with a horse, an axe and a bucksaw, and come out with wood enough to keep her five small children from freezing although, despite the fire, it got so cold at night that water froze in the kitchen pails.

> *She's only a bird in a gilded cage,*
> *A wonderful sight to see.*
> *Some think that she's happy and free from care*
> *But she's not what she seems to be.*

Once, so his grandmother had told him, a cobbler had lived in Hastings Mills, a man who made shoes and repaired them. He, Kevin, had never seen a cobbler but could remember visiting a clockmaker with his father. The clockmaker wore either a beard or a great drooping mustache, Kevin could not recall which; his skin was the colour of a plucked chicken, and his hair and suit were the same pepper and salt shade of gray. What he called his shop was only a corner of his living room, a rolltop desk and a board covered with purple velvet from which hung a great many pocket watches, some without hands, a few without faces, their inner workings exposed. The house in which he lived, unlike the other houses in the village was lighted with gas rather than kerosene. Kevin had never seen such white artificial light and the wicks, shaped like the thumbs of mittens but made from transparent gauze, almost mesmerized him. Whenever his grandmother spoke of the cobbler, Kevin gave him the clockmaker's face and hair.

The cobbler's name was Tulley Greenough. Just as it seemed important to Kevin that the man had been a cobbler and not, say, a millhand like his father, so it seemed important that his name had been Tulley Greenough and John Smith or William Jones. Tulley Greenough was a name to savour, like the names of Caleb, the son of Jephunneh the Kenizzite, and Joshua, the son of Nun, who wholly followed the Lord.

One day the cobbler learned there was a cancer in his body, a cancer being an enormous spider that fed on its victim's flesh. (They had taken a tapeworm three yards long from the stomach of her brother Joseph, the old woman said. She had seen it, preserved in a jar of alcohol. And there was the scarlet woman in Wolfville who gave birth to five gray puppies.) Knowing the cancer would eat away his vitals if he did not destroy it, Tulley Greenough cut himself open with a cobbler's knife, cut himself open, snatched out the great hairy black spider and hurled it into the open fire where, clacking and hissing, it died. Its body was as big as a man's two doubled fists.

Kevin got out of bed and groped his way to the window, knelt there with his arms and chin on the ledge, night insects twanging the screen like an out of tune mandolin, a warm breeze that smelled of fresh-cut grass causing his hair to tickle his ears and forehead.

> *There goes that Boston burglar*
> *In strong chains he'll be bound*
> *For some crime or another*
> *He's being sent to Charlestown.*

She had bought an autoharp from a salesman who wore a white linen suit and a straw hat and told her, as she never tired of repeating, that she was a contralto. A contralto. She could interpret dreams and pronounce curses. As a child she had known a witch who made tables dance. She had ridden on a street car in Boston. She could dance a clog, a jig or a hornpipe. She had seen the face of Jesus in the sky. She could make up rhymes. She could live on two dollars a week. And she was a contralto. With jet-black hair and cheeks as red as a sixteen-year-old girl's.

Allister, Kevin's cousin, had despoiled the harp in attempting, with a spike and a pair of pliers, to turn it into a guitar. She entombed the mutilated instrument in a cedar chest, taking it out occasionally before her illness to sing with it cradled, forlorn and silent, in her arms.

> *As I was leaving old Ireland*
> *All in that month of June*
> *The birds were singing merrily,*
> *All nature seemd in tune.*

Sing me a song, Granner. I like songs that tell stories best. Tell me a story, Granner. But as he had grown older he become increasingly ashamed of her. Walking beside her on the street in Windsor. Her with her shopping bag and the little frilly pink hat she'd bought at a Pythian Sisters rummage sale. The sight of that hat made him want to die and be buried and lie in his grave for a thousand years before being restored to life. Sometimes he shut his eyes tight and clenched his teeth as though preparing for a merciful bullet through the head.

> *My name is Peter Wheeler,*
> *I'm from a foreign shore.*
> *I left my native country,*
> *Never to see it more.*

And when she insisted on taking him into Livingston's Restaurant for a treat! Maple walnut ice cream with maple syrup sauce. And a root beer. For herself, a pot of tea. The coins knotted up in a handkerchief inside a change purse, the change purse at the very bottom of a handbag, the clasp of the handbag reinforced with a safety pin. Because money was immeasurably valuable, almost sacred. She would never accept the copper-coloured five-cent pieces that were being issued because of the war. And she believed threads of gold were woven into the paper notes—because if they were paper and nothing more what good would they be? When he was much younger she had shown him the threads, holding up a dollar bill to the light. And he had seen them.

Two nickels for the ice cream. One of them bearing a likeness of King George V. Another nickel for the sauce. A dime for the root beer bearing a very faint likeness of King Edward VII. A nickel and one, two, three, four, five pennies for the tea. Each coin the centre of a separate solemn transaction. And the waitress so reassured by such weakness, so strengthened by it that her eyes shone with power, like Hitler's.

> *Poor Mary she lay at the door*
> *As the wind it blew 'cross the wild moor.*

But the worst came when she brought out her lunch. A handful of crackers and a scrap of cheese wrapped in greasy brown paper. To be eaten there while the three billion other people in the world looked on and grinned.

Thinking now of the shame he'd felt, Kevin almost blubbbered, not so much out of pity for her or guilt at his secret treason, although these were part of it, as from a sudden desolate awareness of how powerless he was, of how little effect his real wishes had on himself, let alone the world that surrounded him.

He went back to bed and covered himself with the quilts. It was still uncomfortably hot but perhaps if he covered himself he would be more likely to fall asleep.

Tell me a story, Granner. There wasn't a man in the 18 counties could hold a candle to Joe Casey. That's how one such story began. Joe Casey, her father and his great grandfather, had lived in the time when a man produced everything his family used except sugar, tea, rum and tobacco. To obtain the money for sugar and tea (Joe neither smoked nor drank) he sold stovewood in Wolfville and always just before entering the town he reined in his horses, climbed down from his wagon and adjusted his load, propping it up here and there with crooked sticks, so that it would appear larger than it was. Joe Casey could fool a townsman into believing a cord was two cords and a half. His daughter was so impressed with this skill that she was still celebrating it more than forty years after his death.

It was in celebration of Joe Casey as much as from poverty or frugality that she carried a stick of chalk to the rummage sales, with which to alter prices—spitting on her fingers and rubbing out one number, using the chalk to substitute another, so that she bought a pair of shoes for fifteen cents rather than a quarter of a dollar. She could as readily have slipped the shoes into her shopping bag and paid nothing. But that would have been theft, and theft was a sin. Thou shalt not steal. But thou shalt be cunning as a serpent. Blessed are they who survive, saith the Lord.

> *Tell him since he went away*
> *How sad has been our lot:*
> *The landlord came one winter's day*
> *And turned us from our cot.*

And a candle was lit to the memory of Joe Casey when she scavenged at the Windsor dump, gathering pumpkins that had grown there and selling them from door to door. Grown right in the country, Missus, the way the good Lord intended with no fertilizer except manure. Nothin like that hothouse stuff they sell in the stores. Fresh country-grown pumpkins. Thou shalt not lie for thou art a Baptist, who was put under the water in December after a hole had been chopped in the river ice. But thou shalt outwit the townsmen for thereby cometh glory, and it is good in mine eyes. And thou shalt strive always to survive.

"Mother." This time it was the voice of Kevin's father and Kevin could see him as clearly as with eyes. Shoeless, gray wool socks darned with yarn of another colour, Levis pulled on over long-sleeved flannel underwear, the underwear partially unbuttoned because of the heat, thick curly gray hair on his chest. A belt, and suspenders that bore the word "Police" on their clasps as though designed for boys playing cops and robbers. Saying, "You can't sit here like this all night, Mother," although he knew well enough that she could, and would.

Oh, saddle up my blackest horse
  My gray is not so speedy,
And I'll ride all night and I'll ride all day
  Till I overtake my lady.

Tum-a-link-tum-tum-me-ah-lie,
  Tum-a-link-tum-ty-tee,
I'll ride all night and I'll ride all day
  Till I overtake my lady.

"Mother, Mother, Mother," said Judd O'Brien, who had said the same thing in almost exactly the same tone a year earlier when he had discovered that, by swearing that her adult children were unable to support her, she had persuaded the parish overseer of the poor to pay her two dollars a week.

The two dollars came with Perry Sandford the mailman who drove a Ford except when there was so much snow or mud that he had to harness his roan mare to a buggy or sleigh, and on the day it arrived the old woman enacted several rituals to render herself invisible, putting on a coat and hat she did not wear at any other time, a short black cloth coat with a collar, cuffs and hem of artificial fur, and a sky-blue cloche (she could dance the foxtrot and Charleston and never dreamed there were changing fashions in either clothes or dances). She went out the front door that was otherwise used only by radio licence inspectors, Jehovah's Witnesses, Mormons, peddlers and strangers asking the way to Truro or Halifax. She walked down the road, no matter how deep the snow was, or the mud, head down, limping a little, and met Perry out of sight of her son's house. He drove her to a store in a neighbouring village where she cashed the cheque and bought a little treat, a bag of peppermints or maple buds, a loaf of raisin bread that for some unknown reason she always called plum loaf, a bottle of ginger beer, a half-dozen hot cross buns or a jelly roll. (And, oh God, what a sacramental interchange it was, the offering and acceptance of a tumbler half-full of soft drink, a small slice of pastry spread with jellied strawberries. Kevin quailed at the memory of it like one who is suddenly aware that he had been paid an honour he neither earned nor desired yet is too cowardly to refuse.) What was left of the money went into the cedar chest. I've got the money to bury me, she boasted a little defiantly.

Oh western wind when wilt thou blow
  That the small rain down may rain?
Christ that my love were in my arms
  And I in my bed again.

And before he died there was such a hole in Joe Casey's throat that the tea he drank ran out through it and down his collar. He went to the barn and back on all fours and his last words, spoken to his wife who had offered to fetch him water, were, "Nobody has to wait on Joe Casey. Joe Casey can look after himself."

Now Kevin's father and aunt were talking together on the stairs. That look in her eyes, Judd, when I talked to her, I don't think she even knew who I was, I swear I don't, she'll be dead by mornin if she keeps this up, you mark my words, she'll be dead by mornin. There's nothin on God's green earth we can do for her, Lorna, you know that as well as I do, you heard what the doctor said. But he could give her somethin maybe, somethin to make her sleep. I'll be damned if he could, not if she didn't want him to. I don't know how she's hung on as long as she has, so help me God I don't.

Well, there's somethin to be thankful for: the kids are asleep.

> *There was a wild colonial boy,*
> *Jack Dugan was his name.*
> *He was born and bred in Ireland*
> *At a place called Castlemaine.*

Kevin did not know how long he had been awake. Perhaps he had slept and reawakened. He had heard her sing many songs, that was certain. But perhaps there had been times when he had only dreamt that he heard her singing. He was almost as unsure of the duration and sequence of events as he had been years before when he was delirious with pneumonia.

Should he go to the kitchen and talk with her? He had considered doing so, but was held back by fear: he was always afraid of the sick and unlike many of his fears this one was not coupled with an irresistible fascination. He was terrified of high places yet climbed the tallest trees, almost choking with a kind of suppressed phallic hysteria. But the fear inspired by the sick only made him shrink back into himself like a rabbit.

He found himself sitting on the couch in the kitchen. He was wearing his brown suit, a white shirt and a necktie, but his feet were bare. As always the wool pants made his legs itch, and he wondered why he had put them on, together with the jacket, especially when it was so hot.

A gas lamp hung from the ceiling, replacing the kerosene lamp that normally stood on the table by the window. His grandmother sat where she always sat, with her autoharp in her arms, but all of its strings had been restored.

And there was a third person in the room.

He was a man whose picture Kevin had seen in a book.

It was a very old book and had long ago disappeared. His mother had read to him from it before he could read. He remembered a poem with the refrain *curfew shall not ring tonight* and another that contained the lines:

> *Morgan, Morgan the raider*
> *And Morgan's terrible men,*
> *With Bowie knives and pistols*
> *Come galloping down the glen.*

Those poems were among the visions he had experienced in the dream time of infancy. They were one with the orchid he had brought home from a forbidden visit to the swamp and the falling star he had seen explode like a Roman candle when, in broad daylight, it crashed into the backyard.

There were pictures with the poems. In fact, the pictures were part of the poems. There was a girl in a long white dress swinging from the tongue of a bell that hung in a tower so tall the top of it must have pricked the sky. There was a boy who wore a sword and spurs, one hand grasping his horse's saddle, the other reaching out to a woman: she, too, wore a long white dress.

And there was a picture that, as far as he could recall, did not connect with anything else.

A man sat at a desk surrounded by books and manuscripts and test tubes. He wore a costume that Kevin had later seen again in pictures of Keats, Byron and Shelley. And he was staring at a skull. It was the skull that had fascinated Kevin. Often, while looking at it, he had pressed his fingers against his face so as to feel his own skull under its thin jacket of flesh. He had never looked so closely at the man, yet the picture might not have excited him so much if the man had not been there. And now the man was sitting not eight feet away from him.

Neither the man nor the old woman seemed to be aware that Kevin was there. She was performing for this man, Kevin realized, as she had performed for that other man in the white suit and the straw hat.

> *As I was going to Darby town*
> *All on a market day,*
> *I met the biggest ram, Sir,*
> *That ever fed on hay.*

She laughed, and awakening again in his own bed Kevin heard her laughing. Her laughter was so joyous that it tickled the nerves in Kevin's throat until he also laughed.

> *And didn't he ramble!*
> *He rambled up and down,*
> *And all around the town,*
> *He rambled till the butcher cut him down.*

"And what do you say to that, you old bugger? Tell me straight out now, you old fart: what do you say to that?"

"Mother, please," Lorna said.

"Mother, for God's sake," Judd said.

"Here's another one for you then, you old shitarse."

And she sang:

> *There was an old woman from Wexford,*
> *In Wexford she did dwell,*
> *Who loved her husband dearly*
> *But another man twice as well.*

Next morning when Kevin got up she was lying down in her room upstairs but by then it no longer mattered; the doctor had been there and gone and that didn't matter either. But it mattered very much, not only then but ever afterwards, that his grandmother, an old peasant woman, had sat up all through the last night of her life, singing songs to entertain herself and Death.

MORDECAI RICHLER

This Year At The Arabian Nights Hotel

Mordecai Richler was born in Montreal in 1931 and grew up in the St. Urbain Street district of the city. He attended Sir George Williams University and worked for a time as a night news editor at the CBC. He has written several novels, including The Apprenticeship of Duddy Kravitz *(1959), and* St. Urbain's Horseman *(1971). He has also written short stories, and film scripts for such films as* Life at the Top. *Since the mid-fifties he has lived in London, England; he returned, however, to become writer-in-residence at Sir George Williams University in 1968-69, and visiting professor at Carleton University in 1972. He won the* Paris Review *humour prize in 1968, and the Governor General's Award for Fiction in 1969 and 1971.*

Jake was sitting in a projection room at Pinewood, idly probing his scalp for bumps and nascent tumours, then placing a hand over his heart to listen for palpitations. He was waiting for the others to arrive so they could run through the second reel together, when Sid whacked the door open to say he had just heard, on his car radio, that the fighting had started. An Israeli spokesman had declared that, in response to an Egyptian attack, Israeli armour had gone into action. A fierce tank battle was in progress in Sinai.

Soon there were ten of them in the projection room, chain-smoking and drinking coffee round a transistor radio. This time, Jake thought, the bloody Egyptians would suck Israeli armour deeper and deeper into Sinai, then Jordan would throw everything into an assault on the Sharon Plain, cutting Israel in two where it was only twelve miles wide. Jake would have to volunteer. He would be obliged to fight.

—Golly, Dad, where'd you get those hooks?

—Had a little disagreement with a land mine, son. The mine won. But look at it this way: I won't have to worry about dirty fingernails any more.

Cairo claimed forty-four planes shot down. There was dancing in the streets. The headline in the first edition of the *Evening Standard* proclaimed that Germany was to send Israel 20,000 gas masks. 'About twenty-five years too late,' Jake hollered at the others, crushing the *Standard* into a ball.

As a high school boy in Montreal, during the forties, Jake had joined Habonim, the Labour-Zionist youth movement. On Friday nights he listened to impassioned speeches about soil redemption and saw movies glorifying life on the kibbutz, girls dancing round orange trees, their breasts jiggling. Early Sunday mornings he was out ringing doorbells for the Jewish National Fund, righteously demanding quarters, dimes, and nickels to help reclaim the desert in Eretz Yisroal. In the summertime he went to a camp in a mosquito-ridden Laurentian valley, heard more speakers, studied Hebrew, and, in the absence of Arabs, watched out for fishy-looking French Canadians. But Jake did not actually get to Israel until the spring of 1963. On arrival, he remembered, it was balmy, marvellously bright and blue; and what with London's wet gummy skies only six hours behind him, he began to feel elated. Jake stopped the first taxi he saw. 'How much do you want to take me to Tel Aviv?' he asked.

'Are we getting married? Do we need a rabbi? We'll settle the fare when we get there. So, how do you like it in Israel?'

'There's only one thing that worries me. Will it be all right to tip you? Another Jew.'

'Next to Japan,' the driver said, wheeling onto the highway, 'we have the highest accident rate in the world.'

Jake whistled, impressed.

'And that,' the driver added, 'is without benefit of drunken drivers.'

Checking in at the Garden Hotel, in Ramat Aviv, Jake, his mood altogether frivolous, toyed with the notion of announcing himself as Mr. O'Brien, just to see what sort of room, if any, they would offer a goy; but he let it go. He stopped by a poolside table for a gin-and-tonic. Lots of foot-weary, middle-aged tourists were sunning themselves.

'Have you heard their English yet, Sadie?'

'What?'

'So help me, they speak better than us. They speak like the British.'

Among the tourists was Mr. Cooper. Shooing flies away with a rolled newspaper, pondering his toes as he curled and uncurled them, the portly, bronzed Mr. Cooper, his eyes shaded by a peak cap, basked in a deck chair, his manner proprietorial. 'And where are you from?' he asked Jake.

'London,' Jake said, hastily adding that he was in fact a Canadian.

'Ah ha. And how long are you here for?'

'A week. Ten days maybe.'

'Longer you couldn't stay? This is Israel. Don't be a cheapskate.'

Jake laughed.

'And tell me, Mr. Hersh, you came over on one of our planes, you were impressed?'

'They're Boeing 707s, you know. A Gentile product.'

'And what about the pilots? Eh? This country it's a miracle. I been here seven years ago and what we done since it's remarkable. I'm not a millionaire, Mr. Hersh, and I'm not poor. I'm in sporting goods. I sell guns, sleeping bags, tents. You'd never catch me spending a night in a sleeping bag. Goys are crazy. I should complain. So, Mr. Hersh, what line of business you in?'

'The junk business,' Jake said, and he retired to his bungalow to consider the script Leopold had given him in London. One cursory glance was sufficient to depress him. Jake poured himself a brandy and rehearsed his Academy Award non-acceptance speech once more. 'As long,' it began, 'as there are no Negro directors in our industry and a Protestant can rise no higher than a grip, I must, in all honesty . . .'

Traditionally, producers were the butt of most film jokes, but Jake had found Leopold surprisingly engaging. The most uncomplicated of con men. 'On her deathbed,' Leopold had said, contemplating the ceiling with wet eyes, 'my mother, may she rest in peace, made me promise that one day I would make a picture in Israel.'

'Did she specify a sexy thriller?' Jake asked.

'I need your fresh, exciting talent. You're the only man who can direct this picture for me.'

He was also the fifth choice, Jake knew, and could not afford to be choosy.

Early the next morning a bellboy rapped on Jake's bungalow door: a Colonel Elan was waiting on the terrace for him. Elan, who was Leopold's Israeli partner, the money man, was to drive Jake to Jerusalem. Elan was squat and sinewy, his solemn face hardened by the wind. He was casually dressed. 'Shalom,' he said.

'Shalom.'

Mr. Cooper passed arm-in-arm with his wife. Mrs. Cooper wore a floppy straw hat, winged sunglasses, and flower-print pedal pushers. 'So, Mr. Hersh, have you decided to settle here yet?'

'What about you?'

'Me, I'm too old to dance the hora. So I come here and spend. It's the children's money. Do I want to be the richest man in the cemetery? The less I leave, the less the children will have to fight over, God bless them.'

Elan smiled and shook his head, his grey eyes scornful. No sooner had Jake climbed into his Ford station-wagon than Elan said, 'I wonder what that man's name was before it was Cooper.'

'And what,' Jake asked indignantly, 'was yours before it was Elan?'

'You'll find that we're a new kind of Jew here. We have restored Jewish pride.'

'By taking German reparation money?'

'It's easy to criticize.'

'I'm an old-fashioned Jew. I criticize.'

The other side of Ramle, the car began the slow winding rise and fall, rise and fall, through the bony, densely cultivated mountains. Arab villages jutted natural and ravaged as rock out of the hills. The gutted shells of armoured trucks lay overturned round bends in the narrow steepening road. Here a dried wreath hung on a charred chassis; elsewhere mounds of stone marked where a driver, trapped in the cab of his burning truck, had died an excruciating death. These ruins, spilled along the roadside, were a memorial to those who had died running the blockade into Jerusalem during the first Arab-Israeli War, at a time when the Arab Legion had held the vital heights of Bab el Wad and Kastel, an ancient Roman encampment and crusaders' castle which dominate the closest approaches to the city. 'Look here, Elan,' Jake said suddenly, 'have you read the script yet?'

'Yes.'

'It's cheap, sentimental stuff. Sex on the kibbutz. Murder. Why don't you tell Leopold to go get stuffed?'

'Because we need the foreign currency.'

In the afternoon Jake assembled with some two hundred others for the tour through Mea Shearim, the fiercely orthodox old quarter. The group, predominantly American, was composed of gaudily made-up matrons and their cigar-biting husbands, harnessed with cameras, light metres, filters and binoculars. 'Look who's here,' Mr. Cooper said, nudging his wife.

Jake waved. It was a stifling afternoon. A spritely boy hurried through the narrow, squalid streets, blowing a horn to announce the coming of the sabbath. Poor men with glazed eyes watched as the chattering tourists shuffled past, others slammed their doors as they wound towards them. Once Mrs. Cooper poked the guide with her dimpled elbow and pointed out a forlorn, olive-skinned little girl skipping rope on a square. 'Is *that one* Jewish?' she asked.

'Oh, yes,' the guide said. 'She's from Persia.'

'*Shabbat shalom*,' Mr. Cooper sang out; and he pressed a five-dollar bill into the child's hand.

Later Mr. Cooper stopped, pushed open the door to a sinking corner house, and beckoned to his wife. 'Look, Sylvia, it's not so bad inside.'

As they twisted up yet another cramped alley, Mr. Cooper turned to Jake and said, 'Take a deep breath. Stinky, isn't it? But this is holy ground, you know. I'll bet you couldn't buy a lot here for any price.'

'Possibly,' Jake said, irritated, 'you should not push open doors to peer into strangers' homes—'

'What are you talking *strangers*? We're all Jews in Israel. The soldiers are Jewish. The trees are Jewish. Even the flowers have the wrong accent. Shouldn't I feel at home here?'

Mr. Cooper was not only determined to feel at ease in Zion, he appointed himself goodwill ambassador by the poolside of the Garden Hotel, dealing severely with the least grumble.

'Tell me, Cooper, is it right I have donated so much to build this country . . . it costs a man thousands to come here . . . is it right they should charge me extra I want a cup of tea in the afternoon, I'm parched?'

'Is it right? They should squeeze every penny out of you, what they're doing here, it's a miracle. Isn't that so, Mr. Hersh?'

'Absolutely.'

'We Jews don't have to die to go to heaven. We're already here. What do you say, Mr. Hersh, you're an educated man?'

'You took the words out of my mouth.'

On Tuesday Jake drove to Ako with Elan, to look at possible locations. Old sacks had been stretched across the narrow stinking streets of the Arab marketplace, offering shade to venders and buyers alike. Donkeys, chickens, and goats wandered somnolently through the maze of stalls. The wares the venders had on display were pathetic. Rusty keys for ancient locks, faded cotton dresses, and split boots reclaimed from junk piles. Barefoot boys scampered through the muck. Flies were everywhere. 'They don't have to live like that,' Elan said. 'A lot of them own property. They bury their money in jars.'

'I've even heard,' Jake said, 'they have a secret plan for world domination. It's all outlined in something called the Protocols of the Elders of Islam.'

'Actually,' Elan said solemnly, 'there is no such thing as an "Arab". What, for instance, has an Arab in Cairo in common with a Bedouin from Iraq?'

'What,' Jake asked, 'have I got in common with a Yemenite Jew?'

'Jerusalem. All the Arabs have in common is the fact that they're Moslem. We must teach them that it's not such a bad thing to be an Arab in Israel.'

'Possibly,' Jake said, 'the trouble is they have loyalties outside their own country. Like my friend Mr. Cooper.'

The next morning Jake drove to Beersheba with Elan to look at the Arabian Nights Hotel, then still under construction. About a half hour out of Tel Aviv, the station-wagon wheeled into a lush cultivated belt. 'When I used to fly over this area in forty-eight,' Elan said, 'it was almost impossible to navigate. It was all desert. Look how green it is now.'

It was, Jake agreed, truly impressive. Then, quite suddenly, they were streaking across desert. 'We are seventy miles wide here,' Elan said. 'One day this will be our bread basket.'

Finally, the station-wagon rocked to a stop on the outskirts of Beersheba. Squinting against windblown sand, Jake saw an enormous road-house rising abruptly out of the desert. The proprietor, a Mr. Hod, hurried towards them. 'I'm putting up the finest hotel in Israel,' he said. 'We're going to have a golf course, hot springs—the works. Soon we'll have the biggest neon sign in the country: THE ARABIAN NIGHTS HOTEL. I'm even organizing a society to be called Sons of the Arabian Nights.'

'Dreamy,' Jake said.

A chauffeured limousine pulled in down the road. 'More stock-holders,' Hod said, somewhat exasperated. But he was ready with a smile as the middle-aged couple alighted from the car.

'Say,' Mr. Cooper said, 'you've got quite a baby here.'

'Have you ever seen anything like it anywhere in Israel? On the execution and investment side this is the most modern hotel in the country. The best.'

Mr. Cooper beamed. 'Quite a country, eh, Mr. Hersh?'

'In more ways than one.'

'You know how they say "Next Year in Jerusalem", Mr. Hod?

Well, we'll be saying "Next Year at the Arabian Night Hotel", won't we, Sylvia?'

Sidestepping wet cement, Hod led them inside an unfinished suite. Mrs. Cooper stopped, her brow wrinkled, before some nudes a worker had drawn in pencil on the framework of the bathroom door. 'I suppose,' she said, 'this *does* come off—'

'Sure, sure,' Hod said, with a wink for Elan. He led the Coopers over planks and puddles to the second wing of the hotel. 'We were not going to build this wing for another two years, then the demand for reservations was so high—'

'You hear, Lou?'

'—that we decided to build big before another hotel opened across the road.'

Hod led the Coopers to the unfinished Sheik's Suite. 'Ooh,' Mrs. Cooper said, holding a hand to her cheek.

'You know what it says there,' Mr. Cooper said, pointing at the archway. 'It says reserved for Lou and Sylvia Cooper.'

'Want to make reservations, speak to Mrs. Ginsburg.'

'Oh, good,' Mrs. Cooper said. 'Em, what will stockholders have to pay when you open up?'

'Stockholders will be allowed to sign for a month's credit. Like to see our kitchens?'

'We want to see everything. But . . . Em, what will stockholders have to pay?'

'Never mind, Sylvia. Who cares? This is Israel, not Miami.'

'In the United States, you know,' Mrs. Cooper persisted, 'if you bring a guest and you're a stockholder, well, once a month the guest is free . . .'

Hod scratched his head. Elan raised his eyebrows as if to say, these people, these people.

'It's very smart, you know. *It makes for goodwill.*'

'The waitresses will wear veils,' Hod said, as they emerged from the hotel again. 'I'm going to have a doorman with a long sword standing here.'

'That's for me,' Mr. Cooper said. 'I'll take the job.'

Hod didn't even smile. Jake, trailing behind, turned on Elan. 'Hod might show a little more kindness, don't you think? Mr. Cooper and his kind happen to pour a lot of money into this country.'

'It's ill-begotten.'

'I don't see anybody turning it down.'

'It's blood money. We risk our lives here. They're paying off their guilt for not settling here.'

Hod was escorting the Coopers firmly to their limousine. Mr. Cooper looked back longingly at the garden table lavishly set for a buffet lunch. 'Wait,' Jake called after them. 'Won't you join us for lunch? I'm sure Mr. Elan would be delighted.'

It was a mistake. A stupid mistake. Hod grudgingly offered everybody drinks.

'Only H$_2$O for me,' Mrs. Cooper pleaded with a weak laugh.

'Is it kosher?' Mr. Cooper asked, grinning.

'Don't worry,' Hod said impatiently. 'It's kosher, it's kosher.'

'He was only joking,' Jake said, accepting a large whisky.

Elan, Jake saw, was smiling icily. He was watching Mrs. Cooper wipe her knife and fork on the edge of the tablecloth.

'Let me drink to the Israelis at our table,' Mr. Cooper said, standing up. 'As I said to Mr. Hersh here when we first met, this country it's a miracle. I been here seven years ago and what we done since, it's remarkable. *L'chaym.*'

'*L'chaym.*'

We, Jake thought, utterly miserable, did he have to say *we?* And he hastily poured himself another large whisky.

As things turned out, Jake wasn't the only compulsive drinker. Come coffee time, Hod was knocking back large snifters of brandy. 'One day,' he said, 'I met a Spaniard in Beersheba. A rich man. He told me that in Madrid he was an anti-semite.'

'So what else is new?' Mr. Cooper said.

'He said he didn't believe these Jews could ever build a country, so he thought he'd go and see for himself. "Well, I've seen the country," he said, "and it's marvellous!" '

'Second the motion.'

' "It wouldn't surprise me," he said, "if you people had the atom bomb in five years and took over the Middle East in ten. But you're not Jews; you're different. The Jews in Spain would only fight for their families and their businesses. You're different here," he said.'

'A new kind of Jew,' Jake said, looking directly at Elan.

'Stinking Jews,' Hod exploded, 'that's us. *But we happen to like our smell here.*'

'Well, next time you run into your rich Spanish friend you tell him that the Jews in Canada have not only fought for their country—some of them even fought for Spain.'

Elan rose gravely from the table. 'Come with me one moment, Hersh. And you too, Mr. Cooper.' He led them to his station-wagon, where he flicked open the glove compartment, revealing a service revolver. 'I always carry this with me, because the *fedayin* used to be very active on this road. I tell you this, Hersh, because it seems your lousy Jewish heart bleeds for the poor Arabs. Well, the feeling is not reciprocated. The Arabs hate us. They sit by the radios in their villages and listen to venomous broadcasts from Cairo. They are waiting to slit our throats. But we do not cringe here, we are not the type. If war comes again we will fight hard and they must know it. Either we live in Israel or we drown in the sea.'

'God forbid,' Mr. Cooper said feelingly.

But Elan was not to be placated. 'And you, Mr. Cooper, do you eat kosher in America?'

'Not always.'

'But when you come to the holy land, you expect us to be good little boys, you want us to keep kosher for you. You come here to delight in

Jewish cops and Jewish soldiers, well then you pay for it, you can pay through the nose for it.'

'That's a hell of an attitude,' Jake began, 'that's—'

'Oh, you're fastidious, aren't you, Hersh? You wonder why we have vulgar hotels like this and would finance cheap exploitation films. It's because we need the currency. And that's why we also take German reparation money. So if you mean that we have compromised our lousy Jewish souls here, then you're right. This state lies and cheats and deals, just like any other. If we didn't, we couldn't survive. There are only two possibilities for the Jew,' Elan said. 'Assimilate. Or settle here.'

On the long drive back to Tel Aviv, Jake feigned sleep, anxious to avoid a further exchange with Elan. Finally, Elan dropped him outside the Garden Hotel. 'See you tomorrow,' Jake said lamely.

Elan said nothing. He nodded curtly, but he did not turn up the next morning. Late in the afternoon there was a cable from Leopold: PIC-TURE POSTPONED STOP EXPLAIN LONDON STOP RETURN IMMEDIATELY.

Mr. Cooper was taking his afternoon tea by the pool-side.

'So, Mr. Hersh, I can see that you've been drinking again.'

'We're surrounded by anti-semites here, Mr. Cooper.'

'It's the whisky talking, Mr. Hersh, not you.'

'Maybe. But we're surrounded by anti-semites all the same. Ever read Koestler?'

'Who?'

'*Darkness at Noon.* When Rubashov is in prison, as they march him up and down the yard for afternoon exercise, the crazed man behind him, another old bolshevik, repeats over and over again, "This could never happen in a socialist country." Rubashov hasn't the heart to tell him they're actually in Russia.'

'Very interesting. But this . . . Koestler; he's a communist?'

'He used to sell lemonade right here in Tel Aviv.'

'Mr. Hersh, I'm an older man, a grandfather. You live in London, is that correct?'

'Yes.'

'I been to London. Over there, everything's happened. There's only the past. Here it's a new country. Here we got to give them a chance. We got to wait and see.'

As long as the six-day war lasted, well-meaning acquaintances bought Jake drinks in the pub at Pinewood Studios.

'You've got to hand it to the Israelis,' a grip said.

'Bloody good show,' somebody else said, slapping him on the back.

'That Dayan is quite the lad, isn't he?'

Yes. The truth was Jake felt immensely relieved by the Israeli victory, even somewhat jubilant. He was also astonished. Elan, he thought, would not be the least bit astonished. Jubilant, yes; astonished, no.

Before Jake had finished editing the second reel, the six-day war was over. A blintzkrieg, *Time* called it. Israelis swam in the Suez Canal and camped on the banks of the Jordan. Jerusalem was theirs. Jerusalem, Jake thought, surprised to discover himself deeply thrilled. Somebody passed Jake the issue of *Life* magazine with the lead picture story on the Israeli war. And there, among the group of officers conferring with Dayan at the Wailing Wall, stood Elan, Colonel Elan, looking uncommonly handsome and capable.

Jake had never seen Elan again after the day at Beersheba. Neither had he ever run into the Coopers elsewhere. Elan, Jake assumed, had fought bravely, leading his men, not following after. And Mr. Cooper wherever he was today had, Jake felt sure, given generously to support the Israeli war effort. So had all the Coopers everywhere. A man came round to collect from Jake too. And much to his own embarrassment, Jake hesitated. Dayan, melodramatic eyepatch and all, was a hero. Our hero, Jake thought, with a certain pride. And yet—and yet—put this arrogant general, this Dayan, in an American uniform, call him MacArthur, call him Westmoreland, and Jake would have despised him. Jake wrote out a cheque, but unhappily. Being the old kind of Jew, a Diaspora Jew, he was bound to feel guilty either way.

JANE RULE

Theme For Diverse Instruments

Born in Plainfield, New Jersey, in 1931, Jane Rule now lives in Vancouver. She has travelled and lived in England, Southern Europe and Greece. She is the author of three novels, The Desert of the Heart *(1964),* This Is Not For You *(1970) and* Against The Season *(1971), and has written short stories for a variety of contemporary magazines.*

Although she has cared about sources, traced herself back to the Daughters of the American Revolution, the Colonial Dames, back to admirals, generals and presidents, back farther still across an ocean to a valley of giants, of free men greater than kings, importantly she herself is the source, the Amazonian mother of us all, whose personal history is the text of our inheritance and of our faith. And, if we were born to outlive and even to outgrow her, we can still never be certain that the shadows we cast are not her own. Her delusions of grandeur become our reality.

A picture of her, postcard to the world, standing in the vaulted hollow of a redwood tree, arms outstretched commanding attention. Halt! I am the measure of creation! by which we shall know the tree and the blade of grass. That's a pretty big tree. And she's ridiculous, isn't she, standing there in her Queen Mary clothes, a piece of jewelry hung around her neck like a royal honor or a trophy? Hands in white gloves, like Jim Crow in a minstrel show, but white faced, too, in the dark womb of that tree, her real, her androgynous parent. It is a very big tree, if you'll remember that she's six feet tall with a wing spread that hasn't been measured. And whichever one of us—there are a number of generations now—took that picture is taller than she, taking her as a measure, and we all do, and we all are taller than she, having her to thank for it. But we didn't begin that way.

She does not speak of the births of all her children, only the birth of the twins, two pains, one for each, and she could have had them alone in the woods, only it would have taken a little longer. Perhaps that's what she's really doing in this picture, standing between her own miraculous thighs with a fisherman's gesture, and they *were* big, too, one seven-and-a-half and one nine-and-a-half pounds. She herself weighed two hundred and eighty pounds before they were born. It took two strong men, the colored butler and the cook's boy friend, to get her up the stairs, but then she was on her own, and it was easy. Her youngest child, a girl, claimed to have miscarried twins. "Women in this family don't miscarry!" Take her, for example, and we all do. Mother of Amazons, a tribe in herself, her womb housing an army. Even the offspring of her daughters and her daughters-in-law became her children, and so have their children, generations of siblings to a common mother.

She has wanted us all to live, and we have, through childhood diseases, depressions, wars, and even her own tyranny. There have been a number of accidents but few perversions. People in this family don't . . . often. One of us stammered until she forbade it. Another held her breath until a hose knocked the wind back into her. One of us shat behind her chair, but only once. And two of us rode a pregnant sow to death, but that didn't do any good either. We have stolen and set fire to things and tried to kill each other. We have won prizes and awards and even medals. We have written poems for each other, operated on each other, given each other commissions in the army, forty percent discounts, used clothes, and some sympathy. She has wanted us all to live, and we have.

So has she: too mean to die before she can contest her brother-in-law's will, before she can legally give away all her money, before she can certify her oldest daughter for psychotic kindness; too curious to die before one son-in-law generals the whole country into action with his atomic pornography, before another defeats integration single-handed by taking a nigger to lunch, before still another wipes out an entire nation by refusing to learn Japanese; too proud to die before her youngest granddaughter marries a corporation to silence rumors of virgin birth, before her eldest great-grandson buys out Rockefeller's liberal interest with his paper route money, before at least one of her own is dead; too alive to die even after she's dead, in that backward action of second birth, in which the funeral cake becomes the communion, and we swallow her, hook, line, and sinker, to burst full grown again, some sort of transvirgin Athena, out of a redwood tree, which we call virgin timber, for all its phallic surprise.

Who in hell does she think she is, anyway? Our source, our Freudian mistake, our absolute female patriarch. Well, if you can't be human, there's only one other energetic choice, and she made it: she became an idea.

And to the next question—whose idea is she, anyway?—there is no simple answer, not even her own, though we'll have to settle down to that, too, eventually, if we're going to get anywhere. The problem is that our own point of view isn't simply reliable. This 'quarrelsome we' have already been involved in a number of discrepancies, irritations, and open arguments in just a few hundred words. We can't even always reach an agreement of subject and verb, for just there we falter between our common source and our singularities. Not even the twins are identical, the delivered or the miscarried. Some among us are convinced that 'we' is a front for only one of our number, young Arachne, a fouled up, paranoiac spider, ready to hang herself, if she's got to, for revenge. Others of us are inclined to believe that young Orestes is being pursued through these pages to some final sanctuary of forgiveness and the rule of law, the recovery of the true patriarch. But he, our literary critic, denies responsibility and claims the mild disturbance of syntax, the single entry of a four letter word (in the past tense), and the reference to myth are all group pretensions toward a middle class stream of consciousness, pretensions which one of our amateur sociologists would rather relate to the nouveau riche who advance from storing newspapers in bathtubs to planting vines in thunder mugs and lavabos. The only lawyer in the family assures us, that, whatever the case is, we'll all sue.

But not until she's gone, and we're very reluctant to let her go, for all our angry theories about her own will power. This last illness is only one example, but it will do for now. The doctors were not sure whether it was the fall that made her break her hip or the broken hip that made her fall, a common confusion of cause and effect in the circular time of the aged, where nights are measured by slow, very slow, round trips to the toilet. Anyway, she lay there on the tile floor, as all of us fear we will sooner or later, frightened and enraged and embarrassed, a foot tangled in the laundry basket, a shoulder on the scales, cheek by jowl with the toilet bowl, the nearest thing she'd had to a bedfellow for years, back against the cold side of the tub, which failed by a foot and a half to measure her length, a child's coffin. Nobody, at first, wants to be found, not like that. But pain and cold and helplessness gradually limit dignity as well as a sense of humor. She called, and one of us heard, in the dream we have all had more than once, the imperious voice which is child and mate and mother to which there is no answer but yes. And, though she couldn't be moved until the ambulance men arrived, her oldest daughter had already tugged fiercely to pull the nightdress down over the old buttocks, had covered her more completely with a blanket, had sat there on the toilet bowl to hold her mother's hand and stroke her mother's hair.

The operation took place the next day, a pin set in that joint worn out by the eighty-three years of weight, her own and ours. And there she lay, pinned together again (it wasn't the first time) like a grotesque and beloved old doll, resurrected for yet another generation. But this time, for the first time, her heart was uncertain. It would not let her simply rest and recover. It galloped, bucked, stopped against the pain, started, stopped, started, in an endless and various tantrum which bladder, bowel, stomach, lungs, and finally brain must all contend with, until the organs of her body were all her enemies, pain her one, gentle, obscene familiar. And outside the cage of her body were the needles and voices of life, opening, sewing up, deadening, quickening, scolding, scoffing, scheming, screaming. She was screaming, God, screaming. We could hear her in the parking lot, in the waiting room, in the corridors, for hours and hours until a shot of morphine that could kill a horse would quiet the world to the chronic cough, uncertain moan, fretful cry of simple mortality.

The nurses were not resigned; they quit, unwilling but also unable to command or appease such a rage. We could have allowed them to kill it, the rage, the pain, and the heart, but we are not ordinary children of an ordinary mother. What she has never allowed us to forget, we could not allow her to forget now.

Every one of her immediate children came, and other generations sent representatives. Then we organized ourselves. Sister and brother coupled for each shift at the hospital, and behind those front lines were numbers of others to cook, to drive, to answer telephones and letters. One young historian spent a month making a rather curious scrap book of the campaign in which she could later find get-well cards, pressed flowers, birth announcements, photographs, newspaper clippings, kindergarten drawings, and other small manifestos of need for which she has been so long the recipient, the marvelous garbage can to which all our triumphs are destined.

She was not what you would call co-operative even then. She spat in the face of a son, bit a daughter, tried to strangle herself with the ribbons of her bedjacket, tried to get out of bed, and emptied her bowels against her restrainers. She screamed and screamed, accusing us all of inadequacies, infidelities, brutalities, plots against her death. We were, of course, guilty. Without us she could have died, but we have wanted her to live, and she has.

One morning at dawn, after several hours of struggling sleep, she opened her eyes and spoke in her natural voice to one of her twin sons and her youngest daughter.

"How long have you been here, children?"

All our life, mama, all our life. No one begrudged these two that particular moment, for they are the handsomest among us, the first son by twenty minutes, the last daughter by ten years. And they are the tallest, too, of the first generation. He is not the most successful, and she has threatened the family honor with mythical miscarriages and premature births, but, if our mother was to be lucid again, surely the morning light should rise on beauty to make her glad of her creation.

Arrogant, brutal, bloody nonsense! (the voice of that British in-law? or Orestes back from a year at Oxford?) A circus side show, a family of pituitary freaks, suffering a glandular psychosis: we are the gentle giants to be literally looked up to, not at. Matricide is not one of our parlor tricks. Over mercy killing we choose unmerciful living, race of martyrs, race of sad clowns, Oedipal, anal, anxious, and proud.

She lives, reduced somewhat. About a hundred and fifty pounds actually. She doesn't walk at all any more, but even before the accident she didn't walk much, her spine ankylosed from severe arthritis thirty-five years ago. We have bought her a hospital bed, and the younger twin has built a derrick with a canvas swing by which she can be hoisted out of bed and lowered into her Danish invalid's chair, still hooked by a tube to her bottle of urine and to her television set by the remote control cord. She reads a little still, against the slowly growing cataracts, and she sews, making bedjackets, layettes, and padded coat hangers for us and for charity, the needle held by the flat pressure of thumb and straight first finger. She has not been able to make a fist of either hand for thirty-five years.

For company she has us and her nurses. We hang by families on all four walls, the only segregated generation the latest where the count is still important, a little population explosion all by itself between the bathroom door and the corner.

She can pay for the nurses herself now that she's mortally certain of winning her case against her dead brother-in-law. An agreement is an agreement, and he signed away his right to his estate, some ten thousand dollars, when she agreed to pay him fifty dollars a month while he lived. He didn't live long, four sick years while another widowed sister-in-law nursed him. He tried to leave his money to her out of some senile sentimentality, simply forgetting his legal debt, which was moral, too, for our father had supported that brother most of his life, poor farmer, lay preacher, childless widower whose simple pleasure it was to take a lady friend flying on a Saturday afternoon. But the money now must go to the white uniformed derrick stewardesses not for trips over Louisville and farm land and the wide Ohio River but instead over the exotic landscape of an oriental carpet one of us, the conqueror, brought home in 1945. She commutes daily over that tree of life from bed to chair and back again, a collapsing dirigible, swinging over the tree of life, moored there by television set and urine bottle. She's mortally certain she has her fare. It must be one of the reasons she lives. We can't be completely to blame.

"I was out of my mind there for a while," she says to each of us who comes to call, searching over her glasses for something more than acceptance, something less than forgiveness. Then to her gentle, noncommital sons she talks a great deal about the lost civilizations of South America, the early days in Alaska, real estate in New York until they will agree with her and with each other later that she certainly is not out of her mind now.

Before her eldest daughter she sometimes cries for need of morphine and for the shame of it. No one wants to deprive her, but she would like to deprive herself. She, who has never been able to diet, budget, or curb her tongue, has always set her will against the impossible. She walked for thirty-five years after she was told she could not. She spent money all through the ruin of the depression until she had it again. She would not accept the reported losses during the war, and her children all came home. But even her will does not seem strong enough to defy addiction. The drug is not really at issue. She is addicted to life.

She speaks now with growing reverence about her husband who never saw the inside of a hospital. One day, while she waited for him in the car, he went into the bank and died. His best gestures had always been spontaneous. "Gifted" she calls him, with less irony than when he was alive.

And a little out of his mind from the beginning, surely, or he wouldn't have married her. (Don't imagine that's any one of us speaking. We have never been allowed to be on his side, and now there aren't any sides to take, really. Perhaps there never were.) St. Paul and his mother and some reckless gallantry of his own . . . well, she couldn't have been really beautiful, already twenty-six, six feet tall, with a man's stride which she had learned in the Yukon, in Salt Lake City, from the troops her father commanded. She did have curly auburn hair, high coloring, and ambition. So had he. They were second cousins. And she had been sent home to Kentucky to his own mother to be found a suitable husband. The indignity of it used to sharpen the edge of the courtship recounted. He had to be humiliated, too, a youngest son, spoiled, impractical, and, of course, sick with love. But, if she could not allow that he had rescued her from spinsterhood, neither could she force him so low as to be unworthy of her. He was gifted. That much, with his help, she proved to the world. He died in a bank, rich.

Yet now sometimes she says, "I should have learned to play the piano or to sing. It would have given him such pleasure," she who can't stand the sound of music. It makes her nervous. It always has.

The older twin has married a woman who does sing and play the piano. Obviously he is happier than our father was, but not as successful. And the second generation of that family, genetically so threatened, sing much too much of the time, not only in church and at home but in bars and on stages. It makes her nervous. It always has.

And this woman has nerves like an international communications system. Any impulse travels not simply along the inroads of her own body to arrive at gesture or malfunction but along transcontinental highways, over seas, even down dirt roads to find a home in one or more of us. We bite her nails, have her diarrhea, and her fainting spells. How can we then resent her indignation? Any sympathy from her would be self-pity, particularly for the other women of the family.

She is not as strict about females as the Dame of Sark, for instance, who tolerates no bitch but her own on the island. She could not be, having herself produced twice as many females as males. But her preferences, like her nervousness, are better expressed in us than in her. In the second and third generations the ratio of male to female is more than reversed. For this minority she has created special distinctions in language that go far beyond the conventions of English. The women, for instance, have migraine headaches while the men have bilious attacks, the first to be scorned as unreal weakness, the second to be tended with maternal concern. Girls are fussy, boys meticulous; girls are stubborn, boys tenacious; girls are uppity, boys proud; girls are smart, boys intelligent. And it's not just nouns and adjectives but verbs as well. Girls whine, boys protest; girls chatter, boys discuss; girls lie, boys invent. That is, when girls are allowed an active voice, when they are not trapped in the passive: seen not seeing, told not telling, chosen, not choosing, made, not making. But language is not unquestionably magic, and her specialized vocabulary for the women among us has not saved us from either her self-scorn or her power. Nor has it restored supremacy to the men among us. She has raised extraordinarily good husbands, faithful, fatherly, friendless.

NO? Is that a protest vote from the majority opposition? Or is it several individual counterclaims against the editorial we? We are trying to let all flowers bloom, but, of course, prose is not a flower bed, a space, but time, one thin line of it, an Indian file of syllables which can explore the field only moment by moment. Or fence it? The we is the fence, defining our limits. Some of us are climbing it, trying to get out. But point of view is a concentration camp of time, not space, and nobody can go until we are released. Not even she can go, as she has tried to, out of our time, not until we are released. And rebirth is never premature birth, not in this family. Get off that fence, John.

He isn't faithful. *He* isn't fatherly. And he has *lots* of friends, right over there on the other side who could turn we into they in a moment if he could just get there. John's been trying ever since he was a little boy, which wasn't for long, for even at three, when we left him at nursery school, he was mistaken for a first grader with a speech impediment because he couldn't pronounce his own full name properly, having at the end of it, as it did, III. The law could have changed his name but not the fact of being the third; he's by now himself admitted it with a son whose name ends IV. And, if that's sadistic, reality is. John's tried just about everything really. He used to say that Mrs. McGillicutty who lived in the garden arbor, which was really a bathroom where she was always taking a bath when we wanted to meet her, was his mother, and Mavon Dunner, three inches tall and asleep in a humming bird's nest, his twin. Or John wasn't John at all but two bears, never one, always two of something. In the person of these two he could not be nice to little girls, shouted "grunty!" in the nursery school car pool and did it, not behind anyone's chair but on someone's front lawn, an act of real bravery because he was terrified of dogs. Oh, he could tell stories, but he wanted to tell them all backwards, and long after most of us had forgotten how to write, he was still busy writing poems to be read both forwards and backwards. And he wanted to plant a garden, a marvelous garden, from thousands of seeds tossed in a gunny sack, emptied slowly as he carried it, leaving a snail trail of carrot, fir tree, pumpkin, monkey pine, snap dragon, beet, bean, rhubarb and redwood tree, all by slow accident. Finally he wanted to construct a mobile, a huge mobile, to ride on. Perhaps he still does. But John has found out that he is our name carrier. He can call himself typhoid Mary if he wants to. He can say that a name carrier is a name dropper in this family. He can even be right. He often is. But he can't get out.

She wasn't always as indulgent of John as she is now. "Your father could have been like John. He had it in him, but he also had me and God." In reverse order, historically anyway. According to family legend, our grandmother was a saint, a perhaps forgivable exaggeration to balance the other legend of a diabolical grandfather, who so acknowledged the sins of the world that he lost sight of God and was relieved of his church and his calling. Three of his sons gave their lives for his redemption. The fourth, our father, chose Mother and Mammon. Our grandmother, the saint, must have arranged it that way. Someone had to support the family.

Should something be said here about our dead father? He seems as out of place in these pages as he did in life, though none of us would deny the vital importance of his five seminal interruptions of our mother's life. (Could they have done it for fun? It's possible.) He traveled. He bought grapefruit groves and apartment houses. He liked women. The one rumored Lesbian in the family—Arachne isn't really her name, but our lawyer says leave it at that—claims her tastes come from him because he's the only one in the family who did like women as much as she does. But nobody, not even Arachne, wants to admit that he slept with any of them. He did fear God and Mother, and he was so blatant about it that he couldn't have been guilty, bills for women's hats, night clothes, and underwear always sent to the house for Mother to pay, snapshots of secretaries in bathing suits always falling out of family albums. And he wrote such unthreatening, romantic love letters, at one time or another, to all the women in the family, even some of the in-laws, that the source of his pleasure was obviously sentimental and esthetic. He liked giving women away, in church, to other men. It was, perhaps, his only fatherly instinct. But that is not to say that he was not proud of his family. He liked us enormously in photographs, particularly group photographs on important occasions, the twins' birthday, the christening of a child or a ship, the wedding of the youngest of us, the funeral of his mother, a victory at the Olympics. We hung on his office walls long before we were hung about her in her single, old age. He was also a giver of gifts. He once sent a letter to each member of the family: "If you had one wish in the world. . . ." But the replies must have disappointed him because it was our mother who then compiled a Christmas list which included writing paper with the family crest, roller skates, pipes, home permanents. That year he sent only one gift himself, a check to Arachne who had not answered his letter. She bought a cross for the altar of a church she didn't belong to, being a giver of gifts herself particularly to people she is suspicious of, like the Virgin Mary. Perhaps he knew that's what she'd do because he was always more generous to his brothers than to his children, installing a toilet in their house, a milking machine in the barn, a church on the back quarter. For lack of water, they flushed the toilet only once a week, a Sunday ceremonial after each one had used it. The milking machine was even less practical because the cows at the Kentucky farm were all neurotically hard milkers who responded to no one but the gentle, eldest brother singing Presbyterian hymns. The church was a Godsend, of course, and the brothers were ingenious at collecting and keeping a congregation. Once they spent a very wet day in the Ohio River reclaiming about a dozen who had been convinced by a traveling Baptist that total immersion was the only way to salvation. Our father was proud of his brothers' broadmindedness.

Our mother had another word for it. But, if she never suffered her brothers-in-law in silence, she tolerated their long visits with some devotion, teaching us, too, to be careful, contemptuous and kind. Mark, the second brother, the one who never married, lived with us for some time. All buck teeth and feet, he had a sluggish violence about him. He had a job for a while, reading meters on the Bowery, but every derelict he brought home to be saved made off with silver, an upstairs maid, or a piece of farm machinery, and finally, just when even our father was persuaded that Mark's job was an extravagance the family couldn't afford, he was fired for preaching temperance to his customers. He took singing lessons for a while, but Connecticut made him short of breath, he said. He went home to Kentucky.

So did we, singly and in groups, all generations of us until the last. Sometimes it was a disciplinary measure, sometimes a restorative, sometimes a treat. It was a place for children, perhaps because there weren't any there for a very long time until Luke, the third brother and the only ordained minister, in a sudden, unfastidious moment, impregnated his aging wife, who bore him a daughter as beautiful as any traveling salesman has ever described. She grew up between our first and second generations, a dirty joke, a crime, a myth, a secret, our only cousin, for whom our mother cannot feel sorry, with whom our father was obviously in love. She looks more like him than any of us do.

Which is to say that our father was beautiful? He had been, a fact somewhat embarrassing to those of us who have more traces of his vanity than his good looks. A beautiful father is, anyway, something of a bewilderment in this culture. Because of his beauty, we have to suspect our mother, for it is her weakness, not his. As a young woman, she must have looked not into the mirror but into his face for reassurance. Later, when we knew him, he moved about the house with averted eyes; yes, that's the phrase because it does call up archaic modesty along with guilt. He was a shy man, for all his enthusiasms, and he must sometimes have been filled with awe at his own audacity for having mounted the virgin goddess and ridden her into such matronly domesticity. Put it another way: his mother had hoisted him onto the biggest rocking horse of them all, and he couldn't get off; he didn't know how. But why belittle him? He did stand taller than she; he was more beautiful. He was gifted as mortal men are gifted. He is our trace of humanity, which is the attractiveness we have, and we all have it, even those of us who take the mole hill of our Olympus most seriously. While some make whispered claims to be children of the gods, we are relieved to have proof of a mortal father, John I, the beloved, farm boy tycoon, obsessed with grapefruit groves and toilets (apartment buildings are the palaces of democracy, housing the thrones of private men), women and churches. Did we say he was bald? He was. He had even more androgen than our mother.

Yet with all that hormonal magnificence, between them they produced twice as many females as males, until the second and third generations. The reversal of ratio has not corrected the original error, for the two sons of the first generation produced only one son apiece in the second, and of those two only John III has a son. He won't have any more, not legitimate ones anyway. And his cousin is our literary critic whose celibacy is a greater disgrace than John III's promiscuity. Simply, our women bear sons, our men conceive daughters; therefore, out of six in the first generation, only two carry our father's name; out of eighteen in the second generation, still only two carry our father's name; and in the third generation, which stands at twenty-six, only one carries our father's name, John IV. Our father is dead. His name is dying.

Six plus eighteen plus twenty-six equals fifty. It takes something approaching black magic to reduce a name to one hope out of fifty. Our mother will not be shamed by this fact. "You are all mine," she says, for it isn't her name that is dying. It committed suicide on the day she was married, and she survived it. She still survives it, in herself and in us. She is no one's property; she is the country of our birth.

All stand to pledge allegiance to the united states of our mother, numen of a continent, whom we cannot escape from sea to shining sea or even overseas to lands she will not let us live in, to wars she will not let us die in. We are not nameless. We are America, from the mountains to the valleys to the oceans white (mark white) with foam, god bless our mother, land, our HOME SWEET HOME where we see through the night that our bombs are still there.

All bow heads in prayer: our mother, who art on earth, hallowed be any name in this kingdom of thy will.

All clap hands.

All fall down.

No one stands alone.

That's the trouble. For together we are bound to confuse religious and political rituals, and all our voices make it difficult to determine whether we are in church or officers' club, in town meeting or sanitorium, in crib or king-sized bed. Any general statement of our issue is obviously so much counterfeit currency, but it's all we have to spend. No one stands alone, not in this cold war corps of begotten fidelity. We were born to carry on.

And in precisely that confusion of military and sexual terminology we do, from generation to generation. Orestes and Arachne, who are also twins, have theories about both themselves and the original twins, their father (the younger) and their uncle (John II), whom we all call the Captain and the Colonel, retiring ranks for retiring men. Male twins are supposed to be culture heroes, claiming one mortal and one immortal parent, whose gifts include unusual intelligence, second sight, success in love and in war.

"But they lose their power," Orestes reads carefully, "if they eat food prepared by a menstruating woman."

Our mother either observed the taboo or triumphed over it to provide America with one ruler over the land and one ruler over the sea. She offered her twin sons to West Point and Annapolis before they were full grown, a tradition that has been observed in all generations of the family to avoid the danger of disqualification. She offered her four daughters, as we have all offered ours in turn, to her sons' classmates so that America might also have goddesses of earth and water. By these devices she also created a friendly rivalry between the services, a sport that has, from time to time, rocked both the family and the nation. The struggles between culture heroes always have.

Colonel John II, though a handsome and unhairy man, has always been in danger of selling his birthright to the younger twin, and some of us think it not at all unlikely that one day he will have his head knocked into the lap of our dead father by the youngest and most energetic of us. He has Esau's appetites for pottage and firearms. He did win the war single-handed, having lost the other one and all his men on a strategically insignificant little island in the Pacific, a costly victory only because the Navy shelled instead of covering its own invading forces. The Colonel was given a medical discharge, the Captain a desk job in Washington for a decent period before he was retired.

"If a woman brings forth twins a second time," Orestes reads carefully, "the country will be destroyed."

It is not hard to imagine, but Orestes and Arachne, cognizant of those dangers, limit their own mysterious powers to an influence for evil over other members of the family and to a gift for curing wounds and injuries. As children at the Kentucky farm, they practiced their craft of curing colic by kicking sick animals seven times in the stomach, an experiment which did not win them the blessing of our father's brothers, who, under the influence of a Presbyterian god, did not extend brutality to animals.

"Being a female twin," Arachne discovers, "I will never be successful at cooking tamales or squash."

She has, as a result, never cooked at all. But she has other gifts, our giver of gifts, our maker of the web, frail, perfect net to catch a nourishment of enemies, who, bound in silk, become the episodes which teach the errors of the gods.

"One twin is often born inhuman, a snake or a crab," or a spider?

"Twins are often sacrificed," miscarried?

"The persecution of twins and their mother leads to their being avengers of mother, sister, betrothed, or wife," or, in a matriarchal subculture, avengers of a father?

Not the Captain and the Colonel, certainly. They are our mother's beloved sons, who have struggled in her womb for the privilege of being the first born, who have struggled in the world to be the first blessed by her. It is into her lap each would like his head finally to fall. And we can accept their struggling in womb and world, but we speculate with moral horror at what must have gone on between Orestes and Arachne. And so must they, who did not, after all, choose to be so intimately enclosed for nine months, prenatal swimmers in the same sea. They have really neither challenged nor avenged anybody, but they behave as if they had, and rumors of their impotence, guilt and defiance threaten the whole family with catastrophe. To be related to a male literary critic and a female artist is almost as embarrassing as to have had a beautiful father.

The threat of twins, both the two sets mentioned and the mythical miscarriage of foetal sacrifice, continues. The women of the family are very careful not to eat double almonds, double yolked eggs, or any of the other ritual foods, but there are already two new sets of twins in the third generation. Publicly, of course, we are proud of them, for our mother is proud of them, liking almost everything in quantity. She makes of their forced intimacy a virtue she would have us all practice. With uncertainty, nervousness, and circumspection, we do.

Even John III, who would like to debase or deny our spiritual incest, has been unable to do so, for, while he refuses to love his relatives, his wives do. His first wife became so enamoured of the family that she divorced him at the moment of his most confident rebellion. When he married again, a woman over six feet tall like all his female relatives, he decided to keep the marriage a secret. It was impossible to hide the woman herself, except at a family gathering where she would be inconspicuous; therefore he allowed her to share an apartment with Arachne so that she might attend various reunions as Arachne's friend. She grew so fond of Arachne, however, that his own relationship with her was threatened. We thought his jealousy so distasteful, particularly when he made scenes in front of his first wife who also attended family reunions as mother of John IV, that he had no choice finally but to confess to his second marriage, at which moment his second wife confessed that she was about to divorce him. She continues to move among us inconspicuously as Arachne's friend. John III, our name carrier, attends alone or not at all. He imagines that our incestuous source, parents who were second cousins, explains our mass idiocy and deformity.

There is not an idiot among us. Very few of the women have been given university educations, but they have all been educated by the educated men they married. Not one is unable to balance a check book, drive a car, take advantage of foreign servants, tyrannize over the wives of junior officers and manipulate the wives of senior officers. They all have Irish linen, silver tea services, and oriental carpets. And most of them can say "How much?" and "No" in at least five languages. Their ignorance of politics is not so much a limitation as a fidelity to the traditions of the old Army and real Navy. Their indifference to the arts and social welfare is a mark of discipline rather than laziness. They are the good earth of self-reliant conservatism, breeding bright sons for each new war.

Our men are intelligent. Not one has been killed in action or deprived of a pension. Some of our in-laws have even made money. We are all looked up to.

Height is not a deformity. To be born at least twenty-three inches long and to achieve at least six feet is our proud expectation. Not one of us has failed. And we are secure enough in our superiority to admit the little self-consciousnesses of adolescence. The boys are inclined toward clownishness, chinning themselves on rafters and street signs. The girls are a little aggressive, offering to hold doors and carry luggage for small, male strangers. Each of us during this period has probably suffered a momentary disloyalty to our inheritance, but once we are acclimatized, discovering that the air is not really thinner nor the weather more turbulent, we enjoy our advantage. We take advantage easily, particularly when we are together. By ourselves, we take exception, being exceptional.

It is a privilege to be excluded not from the rank but from the file of men who are foreigners, yankees, niggers, and midgets. But we are neither blind nor unkind. We can see the little people. Each has his little charity, as our mother has her coat hangers. We support such selective institutions as the Home for White, Southern, Unwed, Presbyterian Mothers and the Home for White, Southern, Disabled Officers of West Point and Annapolis. We also contribute to any disaster fund for Florida Fruit Growers and New York Real Estate Owners. We do not contribute to organizations for America First or Moral Rearmament just as we don't put our money in broad investment funds. We make a clear distinction between opinion and fact, knowing that, except for the military, the world is usually run by amateurs. We believe in control, in our own authority, because we have a history of victories.

ALL'S WELL IN WINNEMUCCA, Mother. She likes to know that even now. Whenever any one of us passes through, we stop to send the message: ALL'S WELL IN WINNEMUCCA, Mother. If there has just been a hold-up or a murder, the telegraph clerk may take a skeptical view of our reporting, but she does not understand that our mother wants to be assured of just one thing: that her father did put down the last Indian uprising there. We look for federal troups and redskins. The bare plains and hills are still. Colonel John II, on his way from Washington, D.C., to the south Pacific early in 1942, was almost arrested in Winnemucca, and the message went through censored: ALL'S WELL IN XXXXXXXXXXX, Mother, but she understood. "Each war ends war," she said. When Arachne cabled, early in 1947, ALL'S WELL IN HIROSHIMA, Mother, she nodded with the same vision. Redskins, yellow skins, black skins: each war ends war and extends the dynasty.

The dust, radioactive and otherwise, settles again, but we do not. Does it really matter that we can't go home again? Any of us? Our tradition is transience, in war or peace. Family seats on this continent turn into old people's homes, private schools, power generators and super highways even before our mothers have hysterectomies, our fathers heart attacks, ourselves commissions or children. We move in and out of houses even more rapidly than presidents and first ladies move in and out of the White House. Army posts and navel bases provide the same kind of continuity: one wide, prisoner-tended lawn, one set of uncertain back stairs, one basement toilet is much like another. We learn to be at home without having a home to go to, except our mother. She has wanted it so, offering a security no wider than her own great width, wider than the world. She has taught us to occupy seats on planes, park benches, and chairlifts with the confidence of permanent reservation. There isn't a seat to set a bottom on that isn't as uncomfortable and reassuring as the family pew, which our father set up in Kentucky and our mother sold out from under us the day after we laid him to rest in the one piece of ground that should have been incontestably his. She also sold the Connecticut shingle chateau, but that had already been loaned out as a home for retarded children in the thirties, a club for officers in the forties, our mother's pity and patriotism more eloquent than the motivating financial reversals. (Our father was slow to get into war industry.) We never went home to Connecticut to our own simple memories, the ghostly games of Mongolian idiots threading through our dances and riots, mindless nightmares among our own sweet dreams; and later, in the service, we returned to beds made unheroic by unknown soldiers who had probably, without the proper sense of profession, died. The Kentucky farm had given us a certain softness of speech, rural sexuality, and southern pride which the real landscape only threatened. It was not an estate but a small country slum, bottom land of the Ohio, silt and sewage of river myths we remember better for not having to die there. Perhaps even our father rests in greater peace for having been sold down that river. No one wants to go home again. We pass through, reporting: ALL'S WELL, Mother. ALL'S WELL.

She used to take the tour of inspection herself, stepping from child to child across the continent. Those of us not directly in her path always gathered along the route for whistle stop love and campaign promises. She liked the train, an inverted Mrs. Roosevelt who never failed to make the porters homesick for the north and west they traveled through, herself at home anywhere because of her children or her own childhood, there in Salt Lake City, for instance, where as a girl she had gone through the unconsecrated Temple. This is the place. Every place is the place. We all heard ALL'S WELL IN WINNEMUCCA one winter when she passed through. She did not mention the blizzard which not even she could put down. John III left the crap table at Harold's Club to meet the train in Sparks. "Get off, Mother." But she would not. What Donner had dared she could not fail to do. "It's rumored that they finally ate each other, Mother," but what began as a warning sounded instead like a promise: you old cannibal. The train reached the summit but did not cross it.

"Where do you think you're going?" the troupers asked him at Truckee.

"To dinner with Mother."

On snow shoes with a dog sled, he went in with the rescue crews to find her. She was pleased to see him, who had left not so much as one toe in the snow all that long way up, but she turned down the dog sled, being too heavy and immobile a cargo. He had dinner with her, sandwiches and hot coffee, was interviewed by the press, helped to subdue a drug addict in violent withdrawal, and then discussed chances of survival with the engineers. He would have stayed on the train, but the dogs had to be returned.

"They say the train will get to California, Mother."

"I believe it."

He walked back down the mountain, leaving Paul Bunyan tracks in the snow, and read over morning coffee, under a very flattering picture of himself, the story of the one irresponsible tourist who had arrived on the scene with an empty dog sled, demanding a share of the food brought in for the survivors. Then he took a telephone call from his uncle, the Captain, in Berkeley.

"I see you had dinner with Mother last night."

"Since I was in the neighborhood, it was the least I could do."

"Is she well?"

"Yes, she seems to be fine, but she may be a little late into Berkeley."

"We understand."

"Well, all the best, Captain."

"All the best to you, John."

It was tough competition, but the Captain took up the challenge two nights later when the train finally did arrive in Berkeley, where the storm had slopped that bowl of bay over the shoreside tracks and was firing rain from a tilted, almost perpendicular sky. There was no shelter. There were no wheel chairs. The Captain drove his car right onto the station platform, relieved two exhausted porters of the bulk of our mother and carried her off. She was not ungrateful, but she is used to that kind of attention. What she wanted to recall of that journey was John III, elegant on snow shoes, at Donner Summit in a blizzard, dropping in for dinner and offering her a ride on a dog sled.

"Like the old days in Alaska."

"You certainly have an amazing, marvelous family," her friends all exclaim.

"I didn't reckon on raising any fools."

It is her own reckoning that matters. When she went on to Texas to look into the broken engagement of an uncertain granddaughter, she did not have to listen to any explanations.

"He wasn't your sort of man anyway."

"Grandfather wasn't you sort either," the girl answered in perverse grief.

"Ah, but marrying him made all the difference."

Home is where the heart is, darlin', not necessarily deep in the heart of Texas. Simply choose to brood over any state from marriage to Maine, and that makes all the difference.

We brood, doves and madmen, old hens and soldiers, over the amazing landscape of her authority, without choice. For her 'to be committed' is a pledge, for us a confinement. Her 'conviction' is a belief she holds, ours a judgment we would like to avoid; therefore we restlessly populate the green, unquiet neighborhoods of the vast middle class (whether military or civilian) carefully isolated between the madhouse and the jail. But while others are advised by refugee psychiatrists (whose uncertain command of English is the triumphant cliché) to practice moderation in all things, are warned by politicians against the passions of the lunatic fringe, are prompted by ministers to tolerance and understanding which grow out of group anxiety and group guilt, we will be neither committed to nor convicted of any ideal but our mother. She does not sympathize with either those isolated from the law or those isolated in it. She is the law, which cannot identify with poets in asylums, rapists in jail, any young man in the grave, which cannot feel pity and terror because it does not admit that, in a democracy, anyone who comes within the law can lose his mind, his trial or his life; therefore we are not her victims but her heroes.

Here's a bit of subversive sympathy, siblings: there have been presidents who have lived through their terms of office. There are Negro leaders who have died of old age, still black. There are ministers who have preached in unbombed churches and gone to heaven in their own sweet time. Pound's second asylum was the whole of Italy. Chessman was killed, but the Birdman of Alcatraz died of his own accord, and prisons all over the country are setting up typewriters in death row so that men can earn their own defense with badly written best sellers. (But reprieve is only temporary relief from the law.) Well, avoid signing contracts, joining organizations, contesting anyone's will, dead or alive, and obey our mother, who has done all these things for us and is not afraid. There is, even without choice, one kind of independence: if we must obey out of both habit and necessity, we can also cooperate willfully, unnecessarily. That is called love.

Which damned well will lead us into the madhouse or the jail, finally into the grave! Unless we become her comic rather than her tragic heroes, self-nominated, self-elected, against all tradition in our public schools, committed to a mother we are willing not to die but to live for in ridiculous, culpable power and delight. Comic heroes who live for their mothers ought to set an entirely new fashion, no Oedipal eye for such appetites, nor sick, silver cords, but picaresque morality of gigantic proportions. And if there has to be a little suffering here and there, let it be erotic sadism. The Colonel's hand, for instance, was never anything but a comic device, and, if he finally loses his head as well, he'll still be larger than life. We all will, even the women, who, though they have lately taken birth control pills even more regularly than tranquilizers, are still some sort of symbol of life. We are obviously a traveling comedy, a road show, a side show, that's the whole show, because this is the place. Every place is the place of the unconsecrated temple, into which our priestess mother has taken us, not to pray but to play out our huge, silly, heroic lives in the shadow of all unblessedness. ALL'S WELL IN WINNEMUCCA, Mother, is the tune we have to dance to, the fact we take our stance to, for it is American historical garbage out of which our nursery rhymes and myths must finally come.

Are we ready? One two three, up to and including fifty strong, if we can keep Orestes from taking up residence outside the country so that his citizenship prevents him from being a citizen, if we can keep John III from having anything but babies by that colored maid of his, if we can keep Arachne from enlisting two other fates to spin, wrap, and cut us down to a fly-sized tragedy, we may really learn all the routines of joy.

The trouble is that depression was the natural climate not only of *the* thirties but of *our* thirties, through which the first generation passed in the forties not without lasting consequences, through which the second generation thinks it may never get, sharing premature careers, mortgages, transfers, and Mother. We are all busy, in every generation, foreclosing each other's earlier illusions, which may be a comic routine but takes its toll of even the funniest heroes. The joy ride, the travel grant, the Pacific theatre, become tours of duty with armies of occupation and early retirement for one generation, become the commuter trains of civilian resignation for the next. So shall we say that the war joy has been a kill joy, leaving us all unaccountably alive with more rank than peace has use for, more power than lawn mower, golf club, personal enemy or wife can accommodate? Frame and hang our medals on the wall, like our faces, small suns for small sons to reflect on. If there's not much chance of killing a Russian, if Cuba and Red China are to be intimidated with unmilitary starvation, there are still hopes of a larger peace army, who can set up and overthrow the same government during a lull in sponsored civil war. But where do old soldiers go to die? Is there an elephant graveyard for us, too?

Oh, Elephant Mother, who has taught us not to pray for peace in our time, do you know where you are going, where you will lead us? Is there under the tree or under the carpet itself or up in the sky, beyond your blimp shadow, some place to stop? Must we always, following, pass through in the shadow your murderous life casts on some one else's grave home? Is all really well?

We do believe in our own authority, don't we? We, who have been coupling and competing from the womb, to spring ungrown into a world born by women where men fuck and fight for holy honors, clean language at the dinner table, and a respected old age? We, who are living through that world, expecting to outgrow it into some giant peace of, of course our own authority, which is..?

Our mother. How can we allow her to die, source and measure, our landscape and salvation? Yet there is a rumor that she is dying, not spectacularly now so that we can rally to rally her, but slowly, almost privately. Listen, this woman has been dying for the last fifty-seven years, a dying that began on the day she married our father. It has been so gradual a decline that it might be thought of—and usually is—as her living. But the big, blimp goddess will not live forever. Her heart is a tired sack in the tired sack of her body. Intravenous television cannot feed her mind much longer, nor can the urine bottle contain forever the waste of years. Her tree of life, her grand delusion, is really this forest of family, these tall, shallow-rooted trees, trying to live in a cold place, the place of her dying, threatened ourselves by the rumor of that last high wind. We must go to her one by one, quickly, for judgment, for blessing, for love. March on the beloved. She is mortal.

AUDREY THOMAS

Aquarius

Born in 1935, Audrey Thomas grew up in upper New York State, and came to Canada in 1959. She has written a collection of short stories, Ten Green Bottles *(1967), a novel,* Mrs. Blood *(1970) and two short fictions,* Munchmeyer *and* Prospero on the Island *(1972).*

They had been warned what to expect; yet the explosion—what else could you call it?—and the quantities of water which leapt at them—for as the whale descended the water did, indeed, seem to leap, as though it had almost taken on the shape, or at least the strength, of the great beast which had violated its calm—there was a collective "aaahh" from the little group of spectators, and a band of elementary-school children drew in closer to their teacher and shrieked in fearful delight.

"Brian, Daniel," called out the honeyed, public voice of the teacher, "Settle down now; come away from the side."

The man started, as though he had heard a voice calling to him from a dream. He felt disoriented, his glasses spattered with water—as though he were looking out from the lower portholes of the whale pool, not in and down from outside—and his head still echoing to the sound of the whale's re-entry into the pool. And disoriented in another way as well, for something had happened to him as the whale leapt up towards the sound of the keeper's whistle: like the water, he, too, had felt the shape and thrust of all that energy and had been strangely thrilled by it and strangely envious. Standing there now, still only vaguely aware of the schoolteacher, the children, the other spectators, blinking as he rubbed his glasses clean, terribly conscious of his thin body and his pale, scholar's hands, he felt abandoned, cast down from some unimaginable height of strength and brute beauty and thrust. Wished, for a moment, to be one of the children who could close up, like delicate petals, around the tight bud of their teacher's serenity. He felt his separation from the whale. "O Ile leape up to my God," he remembered, "who pulles me downe?"

As if in answer he heard his wife give a low laugh and murmur something to her neighbour, an American who was worriedly examining the water-splashed lens of his camera and paying no attention to the whale who was now circling the pool, faster and faster, just below the surface of the water. Occasionally a brief island of dark, rubbery back would rise up above the surface and then disappear again, as the whale plunged deeper and deeper into the heaving water. The attendant, perched on his little platform like a circus artist, explained through a hand mike that the whale could reach speeds up to thirty miles an hour. Mentally he went round and round with the rushing whale, faster and faster, five, ten, fifteen, twenty—he riding the slippery back as though it was the easiest thing in the world, waving his hand to Erica as he passed, casually, as one might wave to an old, almost forgotten friend seen suddenly from a taxi window; then up and up with the whale, out away from the blue water of the pool, which burned upwards after them like transparent, ice-blue fire. A triumph against gravity, captivity, everything. "O Ile leape up to my God."

Erica laughed again. Before the performance began she had moved around to the other side of the pool, almost directly under the platform so that she could be in front of the whale as it leapt. He took off his glasses once more, nervously, for he did not need his eyes to see her: long hair tied back artful-carelessly with a bright silk scarf, the top button of her cardigan undone, a mannerism he had observed in her for almost twenty years. He knew the shape of her neck as it rose from the cardigan, and the texture of that neck, with its tiny orange mole, like a rust spot, and the texture of her pale, coarse hair. She would be smiling up at the attendant, of whom she had already asked one or two extremely intelligent questions, amused no doubt by the boy's look of amazement and respect. How could *he* know the way her mind worked, or the extraordinary talent she had for seeming to know more than she really did. He had watched her leaf quickly through the paperback on whales which had been on display in the souvenir shop as they came in. But the boy was not to know this, or to know that years before she had typed for him an article on the reality-factor in *Moby Dick*. She would look up at him, leaning back a little, and ask her questions with an air of polite apology, as though only too aware that *everyone* knew the answer except her; and the attendant (or museum guide or gallery official) would regard her with a kind of wonder—as though he had heard a flower speak. Yet sex was not really her game—not in these casual encounters at any rate; she simply wanted, had to be, always, on the side of the professionals.

And that, he thought, (his mind reflecting, ruminating, while his body still unconsciously swayed slightly in a circle, in time to the rhythm of the whale), was precisely where he had failed her. A serious poet—a new Eliot if not a wild, new, apocalyptic bard—was one thing; a scholar who wrote poetry for a hobby was quite another. What was this fellow's name? Perry or Percy—something like that. The little mini-skirted girl had announced him at the beginning of the show. Something Frenchified and out of keeping with his tee-shirt and sneakers and buckets of raw herring. What had his mother been thinking of when she gave her son that name? Perhaps she hoped he'd grow up to be a poet. His name should have been Harry or Dan or even just "Red".

"Now I'll get Skâna to give me a kiss," the boy said, descending from his perch and standing next to Erica, but in front of the low glass breakwater. He blew his whistle twice.

The whale stopped circling immediately and sped over towards her master, lifting her great, blunt head up towards his inclining cheek. They touched and the spectators "aaahhed" again. Then the young man held up a fish directly over the whale's head, so that her mouth gaped open and her forty-four teeth, blunt and sawdust-coloured ("George Washington must have looked like that when he smiled," he thought irreverently) were exposed. The boy patted her on the head and gave her the herring. She thrust her head up again and the audience duly chuckled. He gave her another fish and another friendly pat.

Again the watching man felt a strange thrill of identification and envy. There was nothing patronizing in the boy's attitude: he and the whale were a team—they complemented one another. The boy explained that the teeth were used only for holding and grasping. The man felt his tongue move almost involuntarily in his mouth, trying to imagine the tactile sensation of a mouth full of those quaint, wooden-looking molars, trying to imagine the stress of those molars against something they had chosen to grasp and hold. And suddenly he remembered the feel of Erica's teeth that first time, and how something within him had willed him, just for a moment, to set his teeth against her determined seeking, a something that had been almost immediately forgotten in the great conflagration of his desire.

Tipping the rest of the bucket into the water, the attendant thanked them all for coming, switched off the mike and prepared to walk away. The older man, on the other side of the pool, watched his wife touch the boy lightly on the arm (just one more intelligent question for the road). The man moved back towards the door where he stood idly, used to waiting, rubbing his index finger against his thumb and still feeling that terrible sense of loss. He decided he would have to come again, without her, and try to define more explicitly what it was he really wanted from the whale. For he wanted something, that much he was sure of: maybe a new poem; maybe only reassurance; maybe something more. As his wife turned he noticed that her sweater and the front of her slacks were wet. He was annoyed—not because she would insist upon going home, but rather because she would stay, moving unconcernedly and triumphantly amongst the curious. And she would have a story to tell the children or her friends.

"My dears, I was nearly *swallowed up,* like a female Jonah or Pinocchio or someone!" and still later he would watch her bury her face in the wrinkled clothes, inhaling the faint aroma of her triumphal morning, before she tossed them in the hamper. Suddenly he was thoroughly disgusted and decided to ignore her smile and wave (was he mistaken, or was the red-headed young man beginning to look just a trifle bored?), moved out with the last of the stragglers, back into the aquarium proper. Now just Erica and the boy were out there by the pool. Erica and the boy, and somewhere below them, Skâna, the killer-whale. The children, pulled along by their teacher's authority, as though by an earnest tug, had long since disappeared to look at other things.

Had Erica experienced a genuine thrill when the whale leapt? She might have, once. And the creature was powerful and female, sleek and strangely beautiful—like the woman herself. He had always associated her, too, with the sea—because of her name and her pale blonde hair and cold blue eyes. When he first loved her he even saw himself as something Scandinavian, a Siegfried, and exulted in her restrained, voluptuous power and her ice-blue eyes. ("Except for that one moment," he thought, "when I set my teeth against her thrusting tongue. Strange I had forgotten that.") Later, because the Siegfried role was not his true self-idealization, he allowed himself to be mothered by her. She had been lonely when he met her and he sensed she needed to be needed. She had taught him all he ever knew of sex (he never asked her where she got her knowledge), and cooked for him thick homemade soups in a huge copper kettle she had discovered at the Salvation Army shop. And she it was, too, who willed him to be a poet, encouraged him, made do with bare floors and tipsy, mismatched chairs. She was afraid of nothing, neither accidents nor poverty nor death. "I am terrified only of the mediocre," she told him once, and he had thrilled to hear her say it, wrapped in his old dressing gown, drying her long, pale hair by firelight. It had all been heaven then: the thick soups, the crazy chairs, the bottles of cheap wine, the crusty bread, the basement flat which—with her incredible luck—had contained a fireplace and a priceless, abandoned, Hudson Bay "button blanket" on the wall.

She had seemed the ultimate in womanhood, the very essence of female with her full, Northern figure and her incredible self-assurance and practicality, so different from the flat-bosomed, delicate foolishness of his own well-bred female relatives. And what excited him most, although he would never have admitted it, and indeed felt actually ashamed, at first, even to himself, was a certain sluttishness about her—the top button of her inevitable cardigan always left undone or missing, her legs crossed thigh over thigh, quite casually—his mother and sisters had always crossed only at the ankles. Her strange desire to make love when she had her period.

But even more than this, the things she said. Once, in the very early days, she had run her hands along his thin flanks and kissed him there and laughed with delight at his thinness.

"I will fatten you with kisses," she had cried. And indeed, he could feel his body firmer, fuller, where she had traced her fingers and her lips. Then suddenly she had grabbed his head between her hands, kneading his scalp in her beautiful capable fingers and licking his face with her warm tongue—as though he were her kitten. He had already grown a beard, even then, and she had whispered, rubbing her cheek against him, "Your beard is all soft and springy—like pubic hair." So that his face flamed up at her bold words and for days he found it difficult to go outside, to expose his face to others, so deep was his sensual delight, so wanton his happiness.

He walked slowly along the illuminated displays and admired the care that had been taken with the lighting and accessories of each exhibit. Shells, sand, gravel, anenomes and kelp: like with like or near-like. Everything conspired to give the illusion of a real beach or cove or lake or ocean home. It was spacious, tasteful, and most effective. Yet he felt cold and claustrophobic in the aquarium, as though it were he who was shut in, not the fish and other specimens. An iguana observed him wipe his forehead with a cynical, pre-historic eye; the octopus flattened his disgusting suckers against the harsh reality of glass; the alligators slept with tourists' pennies clinging to their heads and backs. The wolf-eel, however, looked as though a mere quarter-inch of glass would not stop *him*. "Fishermen will sometimes cut the line," he read, "rather than handle this fish." He believed it. The thick, sensuous lips, the small eyes, the conical front teeth convinced one that here was evil incarnate, a creature who would not hesitate to attack. Erica, he thought, would have laughed loudly and squatted down with her nose against the glass, grinning, daring the eel to pit his aggression against hers.

He read that they had been captured up to a length of eight feet. Taller than a man. Imagine finding *that* on the end of your line! Where was Erica?

Had it all been a trick, her violent lovemaking which somehow was in keeping with her Nordic looks—a love like waterfalls and mountain torrents, a love which suggested terrible deeds to be done for love or hate or kinship, quite in contrast to his own, soft, dreamlike attitude. But in those early days she could rouse him up until he forgot that he was thin and lank and weak of vision; and he would take into himself her passion and her fury until the little flat rang with their cries, like the harsh, triumphant cries of eagles or giant sea-birds, and he thought his heart would burst from excitement and exertion. He was transformed, transfigured, under her incredible shaping hands. He entered her as Siegfried leaping through a wall of fire. He lived.

But she had never been able to rouse him to the heights of poetry. All his best work was done before he met her. He felt, now, that this was as much a failure in her as it was in him. Vampire-like she had renewed herself with his passion; and then, having won him and worn him out, she had begun to cast him off as worthless—to shed him as a snake might shed its winter skin. On the strength of the acceptance of his first book they had married. When his second group of poems had been repeatedly rejected she initiated her first affair. Her children, tall and blonde like her, came to take the place of the poems she had urged him to create, just as her anonymous lovers (sometimes he could even smell them on her skin—what a bitch she was!) had taken his place in her body. It was as though, after the first wild, dreamlike years when he made poetry all day and love all night (she blonde and buxom, like a 17th Century genre painting then in her spotless kitchenette, with the first child, round and rosy-cheeked, hugging the backs of her knees; and at night a rich dim honey-coloured nude), it was as though she had peered down into a well, assessed the amount of liquid remaining there, and then, with a practical shrug of her shoulders, had shut up the cover and gone elsewhere for her water.

And the water in the well became stagnant, scum-covered, undrinkable. Noises from outside filtered down, as distant as summer thunder —and as deceptive. When he tried to write about his anguish he found that he was no longer interested in the old pre-occupations with beauty and order and truth. He could only dryly mock himself, forsaken merman, and mocking, failed again. The money from his mother's estate, the small advance from his first book: these vanished even more quickly than his dreams. He had always taught part-time, to guarantee they wouldn't starve. Now Erica suggested coldly that he apply for a full-time job; and he, with a sinking heart, accepted his defeat. He began to see himself as a man walking slowly towards the exact centre of a low-walled bridge. He had not yet reached the centre but it would draw him on and on and someday—over. He taught reasonably well, but he was always tired; and the mountains just beyond the city, mountains which had always thrilled him, began to oppress and even frighten him. They seemed to be growing larger, hemming him in against the sea. A worrisome phrase kept running through his mind: "with one stride came the dark." Often, lately, he had had to leave his class for a few minutes and light a ciga- rette in order not to weep. Sometimes he wished that Erica were dead.

"Open water fishes," he read, "are darker above than below." To fool the enemy. And somewhere he had read that even fish grow pale with fear. Not the wolf-eel though. But is an eel a fish? And where was Erica?

But the paleness might be camouflage, not a symptom. Like Erica's pale hair and honeyed skin. "The good heroines of the Western world are always blonde and fair," he thought, "like Erica." But the Vikings were blonde too, or red-haired and fair. The 'Rus'. And destructive. Ravenous in appetite if not appearance. "The fish's pallor is a mask," he said to no one in particular. Where was Erica? Not making love to the young attendant, even if he had turned out to be a novice marine biologist. Oh, no. Her taste ran now to higher things: historians, art critics, young writers (especially poets) on fellowships. A boy in a tee-shirt, whose hands smelled of herring, would no longer physically excite her. And he remembered again, "The only thing I'm afraid of is the mediocre."

He hesitated in front of the Mozambique Mouth-Breeder, at- tracted by its name. Were the young fry snug or struggling, which, behind the closed gate of their mother's teeth, coming awake in the slimy warmth of their mother's mouth? How did she eat without swallowing them? How catch her food? Or did she not eat at all while she carefully manoeuvred the African waters, aware of her incredible mouthful. He had always felt the aloneness of his own infant children, had carried the first strapped to his back in a harness of his own devising—his unique example of mechanical inventiveness. He had told her it was to save money—for he had been slightly afraid of her, even then—and she had been very proud of him. They had been, he reflected now, naïvely picturesque as they padded along the busy streets on Friday mornings. Friday had always been a day of re-organization for them, of doing the week- ly shopping and changing the bed and answering any letters. Later she would wash her long blonde hair while he worked on the latest poem, the child asleep on his lap. They were poetic about their poverty too, acting out the romantic role of the artist and his barefoot wife, for she had given up shoes (at least indoors) long before it was fashionable to do so. And had named their first child Darius. It was all so transient: money and fame were not be- neath them but just ahead of them; and they accepted their poverty with style and good grace because they knew it was only temporary, accepted it the way the wise accept the bitter winter, knowing of the spring.

But it was not to be. Wherever he sent his work it came back rejected: first (on the strength of his book) accompanied by a kind and sometimes helpful letter, later by the now-familiar oblong of paper or card, clipped to the upper left-hand corner. Thank you for your submission. Thank you for giving us the opportunity to read . . . Thank you but no thank you. He couldn't believe it. Eventually he had to. Once he had received his manuscript back with a letter attached, quite a long one, only to discover it was from a fellow-struggler who had received the two manuscripts clipped together under a single message of dismissal. The writer of the letter was ironic and amused; but he was furious, and felt publicly exposed in front of this stranger from Brickchurch, New Jersey, U.S.A., who had also offered inadequate libations to the gods. He even thought of writing to the editors. Surely there was an ethical principle involved? But in the end he didn't—it was too humiliating.

And so, in the end, she took a lover and he a full-time job. That night he had shaved off his beard in a fury of bitterness—a mask for the wrong dance. Why had he ever let it grow again?

He looked at his watch. Where the hell was she? Surely she couldn't be *still* talking to that boy. And he was bored with all these strange, slippery creatures that surrounded him, lost in their own dream-like, antiseptic coffins. The vague bubbling noise and shifting light had given him a headache. And it was nearly lunchtime. She would want to go to Chinatown and have a meal, knowing he hated the kind of restaurant she always chose—the dirtiest, tackiest one she had not yet tried, with peeling, musty oilcloth-covered tables and slimed menus, where the lukewarm soup was served in heavy, cracked white bowls and the smells from the kitchen made him gag. "Ahhh," she would exclaim, giving him a wicked smile, "Now this isn't one of your bloody tourist traps, my darling; this is the real thing!" She would enjoy watching his discomfort, would eat quickly and with great show of appetite, scooping the liquid up towards her bent, blonde head, almost lapping it up like a cat, in her haste to get on to the next course (which was usually a revolting and expensive something which was not on the regular menu), afterwards licking the film of grease from her upper lip with one sweep of her tongue. He couldn't bear it, not today. He'd have to find some excuse.

She always laughed when he told her such places disgusted him —"You weren't always so disciminating!" And it was so. He felt a physical revulsion now for anything that smacked of foreignness or dirt or unclean, hidden things. Three nights before she had unexpectedly thrown her heavy, blue-veined thigh over his as she was getting into bed, and had cried out in triumph, "Look how thin you are getting! I could crush you!" And his sudden leap of desire had been quenched by a smudge of lipstick on her teeth. He couldn't bear it if someone forgot to flush the toilet.

He was beginning to feel a little giddy, and turned back towards the fish, as though seeking some answer or relief. Perhaps she had simply gone home without him? She liked to mock him, now, in front of their nearly-grown children, and she had to work out the story of her wet clothes. "Darlings, I was nearly drowned! This morning—at the aquarium—you nearly lost me!" She was afraid of nothing and she despised him. The Pacific prawns, delicate as Venetian glass or transparent drinking straws, moved gently just ahead of him. How beautiful. He wondered at their strange reversal of sex and envied them their beauty and, for a long moment, their eternally ordered environment. He and Erica had had a reversal too—but ugly, unnatural. She had dominated him always, more and more, had emasculated his body and his soul and having done so, cast him aside, an empty shell. Even this trip to the aquarium was her suggestion. He had wanted to cross the bridge and drive out to Horseshoe Bay, have a quiet lunch beside the water. It appeared to him now that even the exhibits he had seemed to choose at random had been chosen first by her, as living illustrations of her strength and his incredible, female, weakness.

He remembered how she had told him, captive, everything about her labour during the birth of their third child. Had described it in such detail he had sickened and begged her to desist—this in the semi-private room at the hospital, while the woman in the other bed remained an implied smile behind the plastic curtains. She had raped him—truly—as the Vikings raped their conquered women. And she had desecrated him and everything he dreamed of. That night, while he sat wretchedly with his head between his knees, she talked of herself and the young doctor who assisted her as though they had been lovers who created the child between them. And he had visualized the gloved hands of the doctor reaching forward between her bloody thighs to draw out the thing that was *his*, and had fallen from the chair and onto the coolness of the hospital floor. That story was one of her best ones.

He decided to go home. Let her walk or take the bus. Let her disappear forever. Let her get knocked down by a taxi-cab or knocked up by the chairman of the Symphony Committee: it was a matter of indifference to him. But out in the corridor he saw the door to the pool was standing open and felt irresistably drawn to the dark shadow of the whale, floating down there somewhere below the surface of the water. No one was about. A bucket of fish and the big pink plastic ball stood ready beneath the empty platform. The red-haired boy was nowhere to be seen. He was vaguely aware, through the glass, of the back of Erica's cardigan and her bright scarf near the counter where they sold the shells.

At the water's edge he hesitated, peering down uncertainly, then stuck his fingers in his mouth and whistled twice, a high, thin, sound that came back to him out of his childhood, a sound that would reach down and pierce the heavy blanket of the water and draw the big whale up to him. He inclined his cheek, waiting. "Skâna," he whispered, "Skâna." But the surface of the pool remained a calm, indifferent blue. The whale did not hear or did not choose to answer.

He got up, slowly, awkwardly, and went to join his wife.

ETHEL WILSON

Haply The Soul Of My Grandmother

Ethel Wilson was born in 1890 in South Africa, and came to Canada at the age of eight. She was educated in England and taught school in Vancouver until 1920. She has written five novels, including The Innocent Traveller *(1949), and* Swamp Angel *(1954). A collection of her stories has been published under the title* Mrs. Golightly and Other Stories *(1961).*

CLOWN What is the opinion of Pythagoras concerning wild fowl?
MALVOLIO That the soul of our grandam might haply inhabit a bird.

—Twelfth Night, IV, ii.

'It is airless,' said Mrs. Forrester.

'Yes there is no air,' said the woman half beside her half in front of her. The mouth of the tomb was no longer visible behind them, but there was light. They stepped carefully downwards. Mrs. Forrester looked behind her at her husband. She was inexcusably nervous and wanted a look or a gleam of reassurance from his face. But he did not appear to see her. He scrutinized the yellow walls which looked as if they were compounded of sandstone and clay. Marcus seemed to be looking for something, but there was nothing on the yellowish walls not even the marks of pick and shovel.

Mrs. Forrester had to watch her steps on the stairs of smoothed and worn pounded sandstone or clay, so she turned again, looking downwards. It did not matter whether she held her head up or down, there was no air. She breathed, of course, but what she breathed was not air but some kind of ancient vacuum. She supposed that this absence of air must affect the noses and mouths and lungs of Marcus and of the woman from Cincinnati and the guide and the soldier and that she need not consider herself to be special. So, although she suffered from the airlessness and a kind of blind something, very old, dead, she knew that she must not give way to her impulse to complain again, saying, 'I can't breathe! There is no air!' and certainly she must not turn and stumble up the steps into the blazing heat as she wished to do; neither must she faint. She had never experienced panic before, but she recognized all this for near panic. She stiffened, controlled herself (she thought),

176

then relaxed, breathed the vacuum as naturally as possible, and continued her way down into the earth from small light to light. They reached the first chamber which was partly boarded up.

Looking through the chinks of the planking they seemed to see a long and deep depression which because of its shape indicated that, once, a body had lain there, probably in a vast and ornate coffin constructed so as to magnify the size and great importance of its occupant. The empty depression spoke of a removal of some long object which, Mrs. Forrester knew, had lain there for thousands of years, hidden, sealed, alone, yet existing in spite of the fact that generations of living men, know-alls, philosphers, scientists, slaves, ordinary people, kings, knew nothing about it. And then it had been suspected, and then discovered, and then taken away somewhere, and now there was only the depression which they saw. All that was mortal of a man or woman who had been all-powerful had lain there, accompanied by treasure hidden and sealed away by a generation from other generations (men do not trust their successors, and rightly), till only this great baked dried yellowish aridity of hills and valleys remained, which was called the Valley of the Kings. And somewhere in the valley were dead kings.

Peering between the boards and moving this way and that so as to obtain a better view, they saw that a frieze of figures ran round the walls above the level of the depression. The figures were all in profile, and although they were only two-dimensional, they had a look of intention and vigour which gave them life and great dignity. There was no corpulence; all were slim, wide of shoulder, narrow of hip. Mostly, Mrs. Forrester thought, they walked very erect. They did not seem to stand, or, if they stood, they stood as if springing already into motion. She thought, peering, that they seemed to walk, all in profile and procession, towards some seated Being, it might be a man, or it might be sexless, or it might be a cat, or even a large bird, no doubt an ibis. The moving figures proceeded either with hieratic gesture or bearing objects. The colours, in which an ochreous sepia predominated, were faintly clear. The airlessness of the chamber nearly overwhelmed her again and she put out her hand to touch her husband's arm. There was not much to see, was there? between these planks, so they proceeded on downwards. The guide, who was unintelligible, went first. The soldier followed them.

If ever I get out of this, thought Mrs. Forrester. The airlessness was only part of an ancientness, a strong persistence of the past into the now and beyond the now which terrified her. It was not the death of the place that so invaded her, although there was death; it was the long persistent life in which her bones and flesh and all the complex joys of her life and her machine-woven clothes and her lipstick that was so important to her were less than the bright armour of a beetle on which she could put her foot. Since all three of the visitors were silent in the tomb, it was impossible to know what the others felt. And anyway, one could not explain; and why explain (all this talk about 'feelings'!).

The farther down the steps they went the more the air seemed to expire, until at the foot of the steps it really died. Here was the great chamber of the great king, and a sarcophagus had been left there, instructively, perhaps, so that the public, who came either for pleasure or instruction, should be able to see the sort of sight which the almost intoxicated excavators had seen as they removed the earth and allowed in the desecrating air—or what passed for air.

Since Mrs. Forrester was now occupied in avoiding falling down and thereby creating a small scene beside the sarcophagus which would annoy her and her husband very much indeed and would not help the lady from Cincinnati who had grown pale, none of the guide's talk was heard and no image of the sarcophagus or of the friezes or of the tomb itself remained in her mind. It was as a saved soul that she was aware of the general turning up towards the stairs, up towards the light, and she was not ashamed, now, to lay her hand upon her husband's arm, really for support, in going up the stairs.

They emerged into the sunlight which blinded them and the heat that beat up at them and bore down on them, and all but the two Egyptians fumbled for their dark glasses. The soldier rejoined his comrade at the mouth of the tomb, and the guide seemed to vanish round some cliff or crag. The two soldiers were unsoldierly in appearance although no doubt they would enjoy fighting anyone if it was necessary.

Marcus and Mrs. Forrester and the lady from Cincinnati whose name was Sampson or Samson looked around for a bit of shade. The lion-coloured crags on their left did of course cast a shade, but it was the kind of shade which did not seem to be of much use to them, for they would have to climb onto farther low crags to avail themselves of it, and the sun was so cruel in the Valley of the Kings that no European or North American could make shift to move one step unless it was necessary.

'Where's that guide?' said Marcus irritably, of no one, because no one knew. The guide had gone, probably to wave on the motor car which should have been waiting to pick them up. Mrs. Forrester could picture him walking, running, gesticulating, garments flowing, making all kinds of gratuitous movements in the heat. We're differently made, she thought, it's all those centuries.

'I think,' said Mrs. Sampson timidly, 'that this s-seems to be the best p-place.'

'Yes,' said Mrs. Forrester, who was feeling better though still too hot and starved for air, 'that's the best place. There's enough shade there for us all,' and they moved to sit down on some yellow rocks which were too hot for comfort. Nobody talked of the tomb which was far below the ground on their right.

Mrs. Forrester spoke to her husband who did not answer. He looked morose. His dark brows were concentrated in a frown and it was obvious that he did not want to talk to her or to anybody else. Oh dear, she thought. It's the tomb—he's never like that unless it's really something. They sat in silence, waiting for whatever should turn up. The two soldiers smoked at some distance.

This is very uncomfortable, this heat, thought Mrs. Forrester, and the tomb has affected us unpleasantly. She reflected on Lord Carnarvon who had sought with diligence, worked ardently, superintended excavation, urged on discovery, was bitten by an insect—or so they said—and had died. She thought of a co-worker of his who lay ill with some fever in the small clay-built house past which they had driven that morning. Why do they do those things, these men? Why do they do it? They do it because they have to; they come here to be uncomfortable and unlucky and for the greatest fulfilment of their lives; just as men climb mountains; just as Arctic and Antarctic explorers go to the polar regions to be uncomfortable and unlucky and for the greatest fulfilment of their lives. They have to. The thought of the Arctic gave her a pleasant feeling and she determined to lift the pressure that seemed to have settled on all three of them which was partly tomb, no doubt, but chiefly the airlessness to which their lungs were not accustomed, and, of course, this heat.

She said with a sort of imbecile cheerfulness, 'How about an ice-cream cone?'

Mrs. Sampson looked up at her with a pale smile and Marcus did not answer. No, she was not funny, and she subsided. Out of the rocks flew two great burnished-winged insects and attacked them like bombers. All three ducked and threw up their arms to protect their faces.

'Oh . . .' and 'oh . . .' cried the women and forgot about the heat while the two vicious bright-winged insects charged them, one here, one there, with a clattering hiss. Mrs. Forrester did not know whether one of the insects had hit and bitten Marcus or Mrs. Sampson. She had driven them away, she thought, and as she looked around and her companions looked up and around, she saw that the insects, which had swiftly retired, now dived down upon them again.

The car came round a corner and stopped beside them. There was only the driver. The guide had departed and would no doubt greet them at the hotel with accusations and expostulations. They climbed into the car, the two women at the back and Marcus—still morose—in front with the driver. The car started. The visit to the tomb had not been a success, but at all events the two insects did not accompany them any farther.

They jolted along very fast in the dust which covered them and left a rolling column behind. At intervals the driver honked the horn because he liked doing it. In the empty desert he honked for pleasure. They had not yet reached the trail in the wide sown green belt that bordered the Nile.

The driver gave a last honk and drew up. As the dust settled, they saw, on their right, set back in the dead hills, a row of arches, not a colonnade but a row of similar arches separated laterally a little from each other and leading, evidently, into the hills. They must be tombs, or caves. These arches were black against the dusty yellow of the rock. Mrs. Forrester was forced to admit to herself that the row of arches into the hills was beautiful. There seemed to be about twenty or thirty arches, she estimated when she thought about it later.

There they sat.

'Well, what are we waiting for?' Marcus asked the driver.

The driver became voluble and then he turned to the woman behind, as Marcus, who was impatient to get on, did not seem to co-operate.

'I think he has to w-wait a few minutes for someone who m-may be there. He has to pick someone up unless they've already gone,' said Mrs. Sampson. 'He has to w-wait.'

The driver then signified that if they wished they could go up to the tombs within the arches. Without consultation together they all immediately said no. They sat back and waited. Can Marcus be ill? Mrs. Forrester wondered. He is too quiet.

Someone stood at the side of the car, at Mrs. Forrester's elbow. This was an aged bearded man clothed in a long ragged garment and a head-furnishing which was neither skull-cap nor tarboosh. His face was mendicant but not crafty. He was too remote in being, Mrs. Forrester thought, but he was too close in space.

'Lady,' he said, 'I show you something,' ('Go away,' said Mrs. Forrester) and he produced a small object from the folds of his garment. He held it up, between finger and thumb, about a foot from Mrs. Forrester's face.

The object on which the two women looked was a small human hand, cut off below the wrist. The little hand was wrapped in grave-clothes, and the small fingers emerged from the wrapping, neat, grey, precise. The fingers were close together, with what appeared to be nails or the places for nails upon them. A tatter of grave-clothes curled and fluttered down from the chopped-off wrist.

'Nice hand. Buy a little hand, lady. Very good very old very cheap. Nice mummy hand.'

'Oh g-go away!" cried Mrs. Sampson, and both women averted their faces because they did not like looking at the small mummy's hand.

The aged man gave up, and moving on with the persistence of the East he held the little hand in front of Marcus.

'Buy a mummy hand, gentleman sir. Very old very nice very cheap, sir. Buy a little hand.'

Marcus did not even look at him.

'NIMSHI!' he roared. Marcus had been in Egypt in the last war.

He roared so loud that the mendicant started back. He rearranged his features into an expression of terror. He shambled clumsily away with a gait which was neither running nor walking, but both. Before him he held in the air the neat little hand, the little raped hand, with the tatter of grave-clothes fluttering behind it. The driver, for whom the incident held no interest, honked his horn, threw his hands about to indicate that he would wait no longer, and then drove on.

When they had taken their places in the boat with large sails which carried them across the Nile to the Luxor side, Mrs. Forrester, completely aware of her husband's malaise but asking no questions, saw that this river and these banks and these tombs and temples and these strange agile people to whom she was alien and who were alien to her had not—at four o'clock in the afternoon—the charm that had surprised her in the lily green and pearly cool scene at six o'clock that morning. The sun was high and hot, the men were noisy, the Nile was just water, and she wished to get Marcus back to the hotel.

When they reached the hotel Marcus took off his outer clothes and lay on the bed.

'What is it, Marc?'

'Got a headache.'

PS
8310
.S7
1972

25.816

CAMROSE LUTHERAN COLLEGE
Library

It was plain to see, now, that he was ill. Mrs. Forrester rang for cold bottled water for Marcus to drink and for ice for compresses. She rummaged in her toilet case and found that she had put in a thermometer as a sort of charm against disease. That was in Vancouver, and how brash, kind, happy, and desirable Vancouver seemed now. Marcus had a temperature of 104°.

There were windows on each side wall of the room. They were well screened and no flies could, one thought, get in; so by having the windows open, the ghost of the breeze that blew off the Nile River entered and passed out of the room but did not touch Marcus. There was, however, one fly in the room, nearly as dangerous as a snake. Mrs. Forrester took the elegant little ivory-handled fly switch that she had used in Cairo and, sitting beside her husband, flicked gently when the fly buzzed near him.

'Don't.'

'All right, dear,' she said with the maddening indulgence of the well to the sick. She went downstairs.

'Is that compartment still available on the Cairo train tonight?' she asked.

'Si, madame.'

'We will take it. My husband is not well.'

'Not well! That is unfortunate, madame,' said the official at the desk languidly. 'I will arrange at once.'

It was clear that the management did not sympathize with illness and would prefer to get rid of sick travellers immediately.

Mrs. Forrester went upstairs and changed the compress. She then went and sat by the window overlooking the Nile. She reflected again that this country, where insects carried curses in their wings, made her uneasy. It was too old and strange. She had said as much to Marcus who felt nothing of the kind. He liked the country. But then, she thought, I am far too susceptible to the power of Place, and Marcus is more sensible; these things do not affect him in this way, and, anyway, he knows Egypt. However high the trees and mountains of her native British Columbia, they were native to her. However wide the prairies, she was part of them. However fey the moors of Devon, however ancient Glastonbury or London, they were part of her. Greece was young and she was at home there. The Parthenon in ruins of glory was fresh and fair. And Socrates, drinking the hemlock among his friends as the evening sun smote Hymettus . . . was that last week . . . was he indeed dead? But now . . . let us go away from here.

Below the windows, between a low wall and the river, knots of men stood, chattering loudly—Egyptians, Arabs, Abyssinians, and an old man with two donkeys. The air was full of shouting. They never ceased. They shouted, they laughed, they slapped their thighs, they quarrelled. No one could sleep. The sickest man could not sleep in that bright hot loud afternoon. This was their pleasure, cheaper than eating, drinking, or lust. But she could do nothing. The uproar went on. She changed the compress, bending over her husband's dark face and closed eyes and withdrawn look.

It's odd (and she returned to the thought of this country which in spite of its brightness and darkness and vigour was fearful to her) that I am

Canadian and am fair, and have my roots in that part of England which was ravaged and settled by blond Norsemen; and Marcus is Canadian and is dark, and before generations of being Canadian he was Irish, and before generations of being Irish—did the dark Phoenicians come?—and he finds no strangeness here and I do.

In the late evening Marcus walked weakly onto the Cairo train. The compartment was close, small, and grimy. The compressed heat of the evening was intense. They breathed dust. Mrs. Forrester gently helped her husband onto the berth. He looked round.

'I can't sleep down here!' he said. 'You mustn't go up above in all this heat!' But he could do no other.

'I shan't go up,' she said consolingly. 'See!' and she took bedclothes from the upper berth and laid them on the floor beside his berth. 'I shall be cooler down here.' There she lay all night long, breathing a little stale air and grit which entered by a small grid at the bottom of the door. 'Oh . . . you sleeping on the floor . . .!' groaned Marcus.

And outside in the dark, she thought, as the train moved north, is that same country that in the early dawning looks so lovely. In the faint pearl of morning, peasants issue from huts far apart. The family—the father, the ox, the brother, the sons, the children, the women in trailing black, the dog, the asses—file to their work between the lines of pale green crops. There again is something hieratic, ageless, in their movements as they file singly one behind the other between the green crops, as the figures on the frieze had filed, one behind the other. Here and there in the morning stand the white ibis, sacred, unmolested, among the delicate green. How beguiling was the unawareness, and the innocency. Then, in that morning hour, and only then, had she felt no fear of Egypt. This scene was universal and unutterably lovely. She . . .

'*A little hand,*' said her husband loudly in the dark, and spoke strange words, and then was silent.

Yes, buy a little hand, sir, nice, cheap, very old. Buy a little hand. Whose hand?

When morning came Marcus woke and looked down in surprise. 'Whatever are you doing down there?' he asked in his ordinary voice.

'It was cooler,' said his wife. 'Did you sleep well?' and she scrambled up.

'Me? Sleep? Oh yes, I think I slept. But there was something . . . a hand . . . I seemed to dream about a hand . . . . What hand? . . . Oh yes, that hand . . . I don't quite remember . . . in the tomb . . . you didn't seem to notice the lack of air in that tomb, did you . . . I felt something brushing us in there . . . brushing us all day . . . . That was a heck of a day . . . . Where's my tie?'

He stood up weakly. Without speaking, Mrs. Forrester handed her husband his tie.

Marcus, whose was that little hand, she thought and would think . . . whose was it? . . . Did it ever know you . . . did you ever know that hand? . . . Whose hand was it, Marcus? . . . oh let us go away from here!